S

The Wild Cards Universe

JOKER MOON

A WILD CARDS MOSAIC NOVEL

Edited by
Melinda M. Snodgrass

Assisted by
George R.R. Martin

And written by

Christopher Rowe | Michael Cassutt | Leo Kenden
Steve Perrin | David D. Levine | Victor Milán
John Jos. Miller | Mary Anne Mohanraj | Walton Simons
Melinda M. Snodgrass | Caroline Spector

HARPER
Voyager

First published in Great Britain by HarperVoyager 2021

This paperback edition 2022

1

Copyright © George R.R. Martin and the Wild Cards Trust 2021

George R.R. Martin and the Wild Cards Trust assert the moral right to be identified as the authors of this work

A catalogue record for this book is available from the British Library

ISBN: 978-0-00-823972-5

MIX
Paper from
responsible sources
FSC **FSC® C007454**

This book is produced from independently certified FSC™ paper to ensure
responsible forest management.

For more information visit: www.harpercollins.co.uk/green

Copyright Acknowledgments

This one is for
Mark Meadows, Mordecai Jones, Candace Sessou,
J. Bob Belew, Dr. Henrik Adrianus Pretorius,
Charles Santiago Herriman, Ice Blue Sibyl,
Ángel Jesús "Jesse" Rodríguez Márquez,
and the father of them all,
Victor Milán

The Moon Maid

by Mary Anne Mohanraj

PART I

1948

AARTI DUCKED INTO THE Bird and Babe, hoping that she wasn't too late to snag her favorite corner for lunch. Thankfully, it was free—the Inklings hadn't descended on it yet with their smeared manuscripts and typical high spirits. They'd probably be in soon—it was Tuesday, after all—but if she were firmly ensconced, then perhaps they would let her keep it and find somewhere else for their literary endeavors.

She slid onto the bench beside the fireplace, thankful for the heat. After three years in Oxford, she still hadn't adapted to the dampness of English winters. A nasty February drizzle fell on the cobbled streets outside, and she shrugged off her soggy coat with relief. The dark, panelled walls added to the coziness of the room, and for a moment, she could forget England, forget Oxford, maybe even forget that her heart was breaking.

The server came over to wipe down the table. "It's good to see you, Miss Aarti. How's the painting going?" He'd seen her in here with paint-smeared fingers often enough.

"Fine, John, fine. Just had a show, actually." Her first gallery show, which should have been a triumph. Aarti was studying astronomy because that's what her father expected of her, what her scholarship was for, the scholarship that had brought an Indian woman all the way to England, where she could be a prodigy, a curiosity. A woman at Oxford was rare enough, though more common since the War had taken so many brave young men. A brown woman at Oxford was unheard of. She loved astronomy—the first time one of her teachers had let her look through a telescope at the Moon, she had gasped in wonder. But Aarti had a second passion: She loved to paint. Her family hadn't taken it seriously, but in this town, at least a few people thought she had real talent. Did she have to pick between the glory of the stars and the glory of paint on canvas? Couldn't she have both?

"Where's your young man?" John didn't mean to be cruel—he was just used to seeing her come in with Raj. Aarti had never actually been in a pub by herself, and Appa would be furious if he saw—but she was twenty years old now, and her father was in Bombay. She didn't really care what he would think.

"He's gone, John. Gone for good this time." Raj had never found it easy, putting up with Aarti's sharp tongue, but their families had been pushing the match hard, and there weren't that many reasonable prospects for a boy like him in Oxford. Even fewer for her, of course. And they'd had art in common, at least—attended lectures together, painted dozens of dour English landscapes side by side. But eventually, she abandoned the English landscapes, and started painting her work instead. Galaxies and constellations bloomed across the canvas. The rings of Saturn, the moons of Jupiter.

And the Moon—oh, Aarti loved to paint the Moon in all Her phases, the craters and mountains. Mare Imbrium, Mare Serenitatis, Mare Tranquilitatis. Mare Crisium, also called the Sea of Crises. Mons Pico, Mons Argaeus. And the craters: Aristarchus, Boussingault, Copernicus—she memorized a host of them, from *a* to zed. Zagut.

Copernicus, Tycho, and Kepler's bright rays were a pleasure to paint, and she couldn't resist the Alpine Valley, Bay of Rainbows, and the Straight Wall. But Aarti had her personal favorites, too—Mons Argaeus sat between Serenitatis and Tranquilitatis, on their eastern border. She painted it over and over again, drawn to it for reasons she could not name, and with each repetition the work improved. Another layer of paint, or perhaps a scraping away, highlighting the curve of a dark sea, the play of light and shadow on mountain rise.

At first Aarti painted the images as if from a ship, circling the Moon, gazing upon Her. But over time the perspective shifted, until at last it was as if you walked the surface yourself, and the mountain rose before you in edged chiaroscuro.

As it turned out, other people loved her Moon paintings, too. As time went on, Aarti's work started getting more recognition, and Raj's didn't. He couldn't stand it. Their last fight had been an ugly one, on the steps of the gallery, in full earshot of dozens of people.

Everything is about you, isn't it? Aarti Aarti Aarti.

Not everything. Just this! Why can't you just be happy for me?

Why can't you be like other women, and support your man? Is this what it's going to be like when we're married?

I can't help it if I'm better than you!

Raj turned and walked away, leaving Aarti standing there in the rain, knowing it was over. She shouldn't have said that last. Her mother always said her tongue would get her into trouble. But was she expected to bridle it for the entire length of her marriage? Amma would undoubtedly say yes.

Aarti met John's eyes and said quietly, "Raj and I are over."

John clucked his tongue in sympathy. "Sorry to hear that, lass. Chin up—you're pretty enough to find yourself another man soon. Plenty of fish in the sea."

Did people really say that? Apparently, but she wouldn't complain as long as John fetched her drink. He brought it quickly enough, but his hand brushed against hers on the table as he set it down. She pulled back, setting her spine against the corner of the fireplace; John wandered away without saying anything else.

Maybe she *shouldn't* be in here on her own. John was handsome, but the last thing she needed was to start something with a white man. If her father got word of it, he'd never let her stay at Oxford, and if Aarti couldn't have Raj, she could at least have her degree. With it, she could go home and get a teaching job, finally get some independence from her family. It'd probably be basic mathematics taught to schoolgirls instead of serious astronomy, which would break her heart. But it was better than being forced into a loveless marriage. Just one more year . . . Aarti's fingers curved around the stemmed glass, tightening. She would survive this.

Loud voices from the hall—the Inklings had arrived, inevitably. Aarti braced to repulse their invasion.

"Lewis, do you regret agreeing to the debate with that woman? She demolished your arguments regarding naturalism and the possibility of human reason rather handily, I'm afraid."

"Let's not discuss it, please. I have some new chapters of my Aslan story that I'd like you to look at—Miss? Miss, are you not feeling well?"

"I'm fine," Aarti wanted to snap, wanted to demand that they simply leave her alone with the sherry she hoped to drown her sorrows in. She would have said that, but the room was spinning strangely. Aarti tried to stand up, but that was a mistake. The room tilted and fell away, and she fell with it, into the arms of one of them—Lewis, Tolkien? The pale face blurred and darkness descended.

The ceiling fan spun lazily overhead, above the tent of white mosquito netting enclosing the large four-poster bed. A lizard skittered across the ceiling, and for a moment, Aarti wanted nothing more than to lie there, watching it go.

She had been lying in this bed for too long. The day had slipped away, like so many other days, and the Moon would be rising outside the window. Aarti pushed herself up, wincing at the pain in her arms, the pain that throbbed across her body. Every inch of skin ached. Her arms, her legs, her entire body was swathed in bandages, everything but her face; she was sure her family would insist on covering that, too, if they could get away with it. Aarti wore a length of fabric wrapped over her head, like a hood, although it did little to disguise her condition. Her parents had been appalled when the English boat brought their daughter home, whimpering and twisting in the grip of the alien virus. It had almost killed her, but not quite. Aarti couldn't help thinking that it would have been easier for them if she had died—after all, her father had bluntly said so.

A dead daughter was easier to explain to the neighbors than one whose skin turned a sickly gray, erupting in strange protuberances, sunken craters. Her hair fell out entirely, and her head swelled to almost twice its size, grown round and bulbous, like no human on this Earth. A few of the craters painfully oozed fluids that would surely contaminate anyone who came into contact with her. That was what her father believed, her mother, the temple priests brought in to consult, the astrologer who cast her horoscope again, with every prediction gone dark. Her brother cast a last look at Aarti as they quickly shuffled him out of the room—all the gods forbid that the little prince should be put at any risk!

You cannot be near Kish, her mother said. No parting kiss on Aarti's forehead from the woman who had borne her, raised her. Aarti's sharp tongue had won her no fondness, no kindness that might soften the goodbyes. *Pray—pray that the gods will forgive you for what you have done, for the bitterness in your heart that has laid you open to this.* Her mother's prayers, her father's curses—the last words

Aarti heard as they fled, leaving her alone with two servants to see to her needs in this big, lonely house.

Manju would be in soon to change Aarti's bandages and slather a homemade turmeric poultice over the open sores, as if it would help. But for now, Aarti hobbled over to the window, each step a misery. She pushed the shutters open, letting moonlight and the scent of jasmine flood into the room. She had never been much of one for praying, but in the weeks since her parents' departure, she had tried praying to every god she knew of. Vishnu, Shiva, Brahma, Saraswati, Lakshmi, Ganesha—a long litany of them. She'd tried praying to the Christian god, too, just in case, but no luck there, either.

She had also tried to work, but the pain made it hard to think, to run through even the simplest calculations. No chance now of finishing her degree—but at least no one would be trying to force her into a marriage. The virus had saved her that, at least! But it had also driven away any chance of friendship, of love, of family. Only servants were left to her, paid handsomely to endure her gross and repugnant form.

The only consolation Aarti found now was in moments like this, when she could gaze at the Moon, so bright, so far away, could dream herself gone, away from here. From this place where she must wear mask and hood to dare walk to market, flanked by a phalanx of watchful servants to guard her from abuse. Or to guard the residents of Bombay from her contagion. Who could say? Even her servants—Manju, Yajnadar—watched her with pitying eyes. They patiently tolerated her bitter outbursts, and she Could. Not. Stand. It.

Aarti closed her eyes against the brightness, flung her arms wide, heedless of the pain that cracked through her. She wished desperately to be gone, to be anywhere but here, to be there, on the Moon, finally alone. . . .

She opened her eyes. Rocks and nothing else, as far as the eye could see. Her room was gone, her bed, the garden with its bougainvillea and hibiscus. Colors bleached away, all whites and grays—except there, overhead, a gibbous blue glory hanging in the sky. The Earth, four times bigger in appearance than the Moon appeared from Earth, and so much brighter and sharper than Aarti would have expected, with swirls of white clouds, distinct to her eye. But the greater miracle than all of that—there was no pain. For the first time in months, her body felt no pain. Nothing else mattered.

Aarti danced, joyfully and spectacularly, bounding higher than she ever could have under the rules of her home world's gravity. She danced under the earth-light, the Moon's landscape bathed in a dim bluish-white twilight. Brighter than the light of a full moon, but still night-like. Aarti didn't understand how she could be here, on what was clearly the Moon, in the shadow of her beloved Mons Argaeus, how she could breathe—though did she *actually* breathe? Aarti felt no breath leaving her body or entering it again.

Yet that didn't seem to matter. Her body was her own again. Aarti's skin was still gray and cratered, her head still swollen. But the pain was gone, and in its place, a strange new awareness. It was almost as if her body, her skin, carried a map of the Moon on it. She could feel the impact of tiny meteorites on the

Moon's surface, like monsoon rains hitting parched land. If Aarti closed her eyes and stretched out her arms, she could feel the dust of the Moon collected on the tiny hairs of her skin, warning her of the tiniest disturbance.

Much of what she experienced was what she might have expected if she had ever dared to dream of actually visiting the Moon. But there were surprises, too—from her telescope, the Moon had looked rough and jagged, but here on the surface, the Moon revealed Herself to be soft and round and welcoming. Another surprise was a buffeting of wind from the sun that varied in its force, but was quite palpable. Did this solar wind visit the Earth as well? Did Earth's atmosphere shield it? Aarti didn't know, but she gloried a little in knowing something about the Moon that the Earth's most respected astronomers couldn't dream of. Her discovery, and hers alone! She could feel the sun's light, too—sunlight bathed the light side of the Moon, with the added glow of reflected earthshine. It surrounded her now, inviting her to ecstatic communion.

That would have been enough—more than enough! But it got better. When Aarti spun barefoot in the gray dust, her sari skirts flying and her arms flung wide, color streamed from her fingertips. They had gone long and strange, thinned to filaments—brushes, the finest brushes she could imagine. All Aarti had to do was think it, and the color changed—azure, ultramarine, indigo. Verdigris and malachite, orpiment and vermilion. No clogging of the brush, no weary soaking in turpentine, just a pure rush of color, translating the images in her mind directly onto the air. And then fading again—oh, that was a sadness, seeing her creations disappear into the lunar haze. Cats and castles, mountains and monkeys, here one moment and gone the next.

Still, when she'd been granted such gifts, it seemed churlish to complain. Aarti danced and painted for hours on end; she felt no hunger in her belly. It was like a dream, yet it felt more real than any moment of her life thus far. This was her true life; she would stay here forever.

If only she had a chair, comfortable, to sit in, to gaze at the Earth hanging overhead. Painting was a little tiring, as if it drew from her inner self; a chair would be nice to rest in. Aarti painted it, a sturdy English chair, cushioned and wing-backed, upholstered in buttoned-down brown leather—oh, how scandalized she'd been, the first time she'd sat down in a leather chair! Not that she'd ever been a *good* Hindu, but still. She painted the chair with fierce concentration, every ounce of longing she had rising up and flowing out through her fingertips. When she finished, she took a step back, admiring its smooth and gracious lines, waiting for it to fade.

It didn't fade. It sat there, a little squat, quite solid. Aarti stared at it, waiting—but it stayed, as solid as her own hand. Until finally, she couldn't bear it anymore, and flung her body into the chair, and oh, oh—it felt so *good*, the soft leather pressing against her pocked skin, like a lover might.

Not that she and Raj had ever gone that far; even she had not been so daring. But they had kissed, under the gray arches of Oxford, and his hands had moved, urgent, on her waist, her hips. *We will be married soon,* he'd said. Aarti hadn't quite trusted his promises, though; she had been right to be suspicious. But the chair—oh, the chair did love her. It had stayed for her, but why? Because she had wanted it so? Perhaps. She would have to explore her powers further—

—but then the Moon fell away, and Aarti found herself back in her room. The sun was rising outside her window; pain pulsed through her once more. Aarti fell to her knees and wailed her fury to the uncaring world, tears streaming down cratered gray skin. Amma would have told her to behave better, but why shouldn't Aarti make a spectacle of herself?

There was no one here who would care.

The Moon Maid

PART II

1958

HER SECOND NIGHT ON the Moon, Aarti wept with relief. Soundless sobs fell to briefly dampen the silvery dust, then quickly disappeared. Aarti spent that day in tortured misery, called Manju an idiot and Yaj a fool, driven almost mad in her terror that the previous night's visit to the Moon had been only the briefest of dreams. Aarti hadn't been able to sleep that night, and had finally knocked back three shots of whiskey; those hit her like a hammer, sending her to sleep at last. To awaken, thank all the gods, in her beautiful black-and-white world.

Since then, night after night, month after month, Aarti went to the Moon. She couldn't go every night—the Moon rose and set on its own cycle of twenty-four hours and forty-nine minutes, so there were terrible weeks when it was up only during the day. As long as the sun shone in the sky, Aarti seemed tied to the Earth, and all her Moon-gazing and wishing did nothing to lift her to the skies. Eventually the Moon cycled around again to rise at night, and then she was gone, like a shot, to her starlit haven.

Aarti lived through her days in a daze, prompted by the servants to wash and dress and feed her pain-wracked body. They kept trying to get her to go out and about, at least to walk in the garden.

Aarti snapped at Manju: "Don't you understand—I'm tired! I have to rest, you stupid woman."

"Yes, Aartibai. But the doctor said—"

"I don't give a damn what the doctor said. Get out of here, and shut the damned door. Leave the bottle. Let me sleep!"

Manju was old enough to be her mother, and deserved more respect. In the old days, Aarti would have been appalled by anyone who treated a servant so poorly, but the constant pain had worn away at her patience, turning her into a darker, more bitter version of herself. Her father would be shocked by how her language had degraded, which gave Aarti a certain sour pleasure.

Her parents had come to visit, a few days after they'd moved out. When Aarti's father didn't embrace her, didn't kiss both cheeks as he normally would, Aarti felt the rejection like blows to her face. He kept his eyes down, as if he couldn't bear the sight of his daughter now, and muttered, "Cover up! Why aren't you properly covered?" Aarti pulled the dopatta more carefully over her bald scalp, as if the thin chiffon could somehow disguise her head's massive size.

Her mother didn't even come into the room, too terrified of contagion. She spoke to Aarti from the veranda, through the wood latticework window, and had nothing but lectures for her. "You must go to temple and pray. Minita Aunty says that she knows a girl who was cured of this affliction after spreading turmeric paste on her stomach for a full year and bathing in the waters of the Ganges. Of course, now the rules are stricter, and they wouldn't let you bathe there, but I think the turmeric was the real thing. Maybe if you mixed it with ginger, and drank some, too—very healthy, you know!"

It was torture, listening to them. What was worse was when they stopped coming. The last thing they told her was that her little brother, Kish, was married now, to a girl Aarti had gone to school with. Niru had a cow-face, Aarti had always thought, which went along nicely with her cowlike placidity. Kish must love Niru's dull and tranquil nature, though it undoubtedly also pricked his pride that his wife was barely passable to look at.

Aarti had been more beautiful than Niru. Was more beautiful still, on the Moon, when she wanted to be. It had taken time, to learn how to change her own form. At first, Aarti had had to fight for it. She'd started with a mirror, tall and freestanding—she couldn't paint what she couldn't see. Then she worked, standing in front of it, painting new features on her face over and over again with an effort that exhausted her, dropped her to her shaking knees. It took hours to make the smallest of changes—to adjust the curve of cheek, or shape of lip. Worse, when she left the Moon and then returned, it all had to be done over again. Her body seemed more resistant to conscious change than anything she painted in the air. It took months, in fact. But eventually, Aarti fought through, learned how to change her Moon body to suit her desire. She had no shortage of time, after all.

Aarti reshaped herself to a face and form that would have stopped Raj in the street. Voluptuous as the heroine of one of the films from the cinema halls; Yaj brought back posters and plastered them up in the kitchen with Manju's approval. Her mother had always said Aarti didn't have enough backside to wear a sari properly, that the fabric looked like it was about to fall off. Well, not anymore. Aarti boasted kohl-darkened eyes, a symmetrical face, glowing brown skin, diaphanous clothes that clung to heavily rounded breasts and hips—hips that swung with every barefoot step. Aarti had no need for sandals on her Moon; her steps glided through the dust, never turning on a stone or stumbling on a pebble. The Moon would never hurt her.

Her second year on the Moon, Aarti lived in that Raj-envied form, exploring her glorious isolation as a goddess of the Moon. She crisscrossed the landscape, exploring every feature she had heard of, and so many that she hadn't. Mostly she walked, though eventually Aarti learned that if she focused her attention on a part of the geography she knew well, she would soon find herself there. Her sense of body would dissolve around her, and the Moon's body, which was already always superimposed on her own, took its place. Then her body re-formed in the new location, as if it had always been there, as if no time had passed at all. Not that Aarti could tell for certain—no watch she wore ever worked on the Moon.

The third year, Aarti turned to other faces, other figures. She let her skin go pale and white, lightened her hair to a sunny blonde, and reshaped her figure to that of a tall, Nordic Amazon. Amusing enough, but light skin would win her no privilege on the Moon, and soon enough, Aarti abandoned it. She went darker instead, a glorious dark brown that would have set her mother screeching, demanding to know why Aarti had dared to leave the house without her protective parasol. Back when her mother had cared what happened to her.

Once, Aarti tried walking the Moon as a man, but that felt so foreign, so wrong, so *offensive*, that she abandoned it almost immediately. She could, perhaps, have been a man on Earth. An astronomer, a professor at Oxford, a famous artist—the world would have opened up to her. But the Moon was female, a woman's domain—it always had been, in all the old stories, its tides defining a woman's flow. Aarti felt sure that she would never have been allowed to visit as a man—men were simply not welcome on the Moon. So Aarti went back to a woman's form, to her own form, more or less. A better version of her former self.

Over time, some of the details slipped away. There was no Raj here to taunt with her unavailable beauty, no men at all to perform for. It had grown easy now, to reshape her face and body, but why bother? There were much more interesting things to do on the Moon. A decade slid by, almost without notice.

Sometimes Aarti couldn't believe that ten years had passed; the time had disappeared in the blink of an eye. Earth was growing ever more cruel to jokers. At times, Yaj did manage to chivvy her into going outside. Aarti wrapped herself thoroughly in the robes the Indian government required, affixed jangling bells to her ankles proclaiming "plague carrier." They walked, slowly, through the streets surrounding her home; Yaj ignored her hobbling steps, yet was always ready with an arm to brace her, should she stumble. He wanted to take her to the city gardens, the market. Yaj wanted her to join the crowds celebrating Holi in the streets, throwing vast clouds of colored powder before retiring to nap, minds thick and heavy with intoxicants. *Are you mad, Yajnadar? To be surrounded by so many people—what if something happens? I refuse, I utterly refuse!* Even thinking about it made the breath tight in Aarti's chest; she had grown accustomed to her solitude.

Then Yaj developed a passion for the new cinema halls—one would soon open that was even air-conditioned, a "grade-A establishment," the glorious Liberty Cinema! He was always talking about the latest movies—there was a vast array now. South Indian cinema at Matunga-Chembur, Marathi cinema in Dadar-Parel, Gujarati cinema at the sea near Juhu–Vile Parle. Though apparently, Yaj primarily went to lower-rent halls along Falkland Road, the sort of place "not suitable for a lady like you, not suitable at all." If Manju overheard him talking about those, she'd snatch his ear for going to such a place, muttering something about prostitutes.

Still, Yaj was indefatigable. "You must see *Madhumati,* Aartibai. I've seen it seven times; it is so romantic! A love through time, reincarnated generation after generation . . ."

"What is romance to me?" Aarti barked in response, and Yaj fell silent, abashed.

But the man was relentless; eventually she gave in to his prodding and agreed to go.

"One movie—that's it. Then you have to shut up." In truth, her heart beat a little faster at the thought.

He smiled broadly, and the little lines at the corners of his eyes creased in that charming way she found hard to say no to. "Yes, Aartibai. You won't be sorry."

Yaj drove the car as far as he could, but the last few blocks were impassably crowded; they had to walk. Past street vendors selling cinema memorabilia: booklets of songs, posters of matinée idols. Past fashion accessories, photo studios with cutouts of the stars, tea and street food stalls. Past mothers who drew their children aside with whispered curses. She had bought out the entire hall for this showing, so that she might watch the movie in peace. If Aarti tried to simply enter the cinema hall and sit among the unafflicted, she didn't know what would happen. Should her arm brush against another's, might they turn to her with violence? There had been more than a few jokers attacked in the streets of Bombay—one poor soul had been beaten to death, and another, soaked in petrol and lit on fire. As if the virus weren't curse enough.

Right outside the cinema doors, it happened—pain flared, a current running from her heels to her spine, sending her back into spasm. Aarti stumbled, and though Yaj was there to brace her, her sudden stop blocked the flow of human traffic in the busy street. A rock thrown into a steady stream. A bicycling man cursed at Aarti, swerving to avoid her, narrowly missing a street vendor hawking pav bhaji and coconut water. *Tichayla disat nahi ka?* She wanted to swear back at him, but dared not raise her voice. In her head, though, she was shouting furiously.

A gaggle of poor children laughed and ran around her, their bare feet slapping the dirt, their hands reaching out to grab at her robes—had they dared one another to touch her? More cursing now—a child's mother, furious that Aarti had allowed it, though how could she have prevented it? The noise of the street was rising, the tone growing ugly. *Go home, cursed one! Stay away from decent people.*

In the old days, Aarti would have screamed right back at them. She wanted to fight! But it was just her and Yaj in a street full of hundreds of angry faces, and now a child had grabbed a clot of mud and dared to throw it at her, staining her pristine white robes. They were almost to the cinema doors; she could duck inside to safety, to lose herself for a few hours in cool bliss and a big-screen black-and-white romance—but no. A bucket of dirty water was dumped on her from a balcony above, drenching her clothes. The smell of shit surrounded her, and Aarti knew herself defeated.

"Take me home, Yaj."

Silently, he complied.

Aarti did worry—was she only dreaming? Sometimes she told Yaj what she had done the night before, couching it as a dream—it was too difficult to keep the wonders of the Moon entirely to herself. But it felt so real, more real sometimes than this battered body of hers, this prison of a house.

Aarti was thirty-two when the Russians first attempted to send a man into space. His name was Konstantin Feoktistov, and they called him a "cosmonaut," but his rocket exploded as it left its launchpad. Feoktistov parachuted to safety, lucky to escape with his life. She had Yajnadar bring her English-language newspapers; she listened to the shortwave, trying to pick up British broadcasts that might mention it. She was glad the Russians had failed. If their cosmonauts had achieved orbit, they might have tried to send one to her Moon. Aarti's heart sat in her throat at the very thought. How impossible, that her Moon might be despoiled by men like these. They would not care for Her, they would only want what they could steal away. They would rape and loot Her, leaving only Her carcass behind.

And then the Americans started in. Those smug white men, undoubtedly just as arrogant as her Oxford professors. Probably worse. If she could, Aarti would have reached down from the Moon and smashed their little ships into a thousand pieces. She would hurl asteroids from the sky down onto their heads. She prayed for their missions to fail . . . and for once, her prayers were answered. The spaceship the Americans called the X-11A blew up, killing two ace astronauts.

But now she had to know—was she really there, up on the Moon, every night? There was only one way she could think of to tell—she had to mark the Moon somehow, so that they might see it. A giant X dragged through Tycho Crater—how the world would shriek in wonderment! But Aarti would not mar her beloved so. No, instead of digging into the surface, she would build up. Construct a structure tall enough to be visible from the Earth.

It went up fast. The Moon was watched all the time—humans loved to gaze at Her face. Aarti stood, hands outspread, color flowing from them in a steady stream. She chose red, the color of blood, a uniquely female color. Aarti started with vermilion, but changed to carmine for a deeper, darker shade. It would be simplest to build a solid block, a huge rectangular projectile pointing at the sky. That's what a man would do, she suspected; they couldn't seem to help reproducing phallic symbols wherever they went. And she did want it to be visible, of course—but couldn't it be beautiful, too?

Aarti poured carmine out of her brush-tip fingers, and it coalesced into a fantasy of bends and twists, girders that rose from the Moon's surface, crossing against one another. She realized early on that she would also need to be high if she was to build the structure tall enough to be seen, so Aarti stood in the center as she worked. As her masterpiece grew, she shifted her body ever upward, finding purchase on flat surfaces. She sent the beams swooping and curling around her, above her head. She was as high as a cinema hall, as high as a Christian cathedral, as high as the Taj Mahal. Now she was higher than any building she had ever seen, high enough to grow dizzy if she looked down. Her structure was so beautiful—as striking as any building on Earth, more graceful and lovely than any of her paintings.

When the structure was finally over a quarter-mile high, when she knew she'd be able to see the long shadow of it from the telescope Yajnadar had installed on the roof of her home—a six-inch Unitron refractor—Aarti allowed herself to stop. She had never worked so hard in her life. Aarti was trembling with exhaustion, drenched; she could feel the sweat dripping down her spine. It was almost dawn in Bombay, but elsewhere in the world, astronomers were watching the night sky. Aarti waited for the world to notice.

The next morning, Bombay newspaper headlines blazoned the news: NEW FEA-TURE ON THE MOON! Some were more sensational: MOON MEN REALLY EXIST! WE ARE NOT ALONE! Many were frightened: MOON INVASION IMMINENT! WILL THE ACES BE ABLE TO SAVE US??? Aarti exulted to know finally, for certain, that her time on the Moon was no virus-driven fever dream. It was entirely real.

She could only imagine how frenzied the conversations must be in astronomy departments the world over, how the Russians and Americans must be franti-cally scrambling in the wake of their failed launches. She was briefly, wickedly gleeful, imagining the panic of all those supposedly brilliant men. And then, her heart breaking a little, Aarti pulled her masterpiece down.

It was the best work she had ever made, but she couldn't let the structure stay up forever—it could spur a space race, send the countries of the world scrambling to reach her beloved Moon. Aarti was briefly bewildered as to exactly how to get rid of it. She hadn't thought about that. She had no corrosive that would eat away at its bones, no wrecking ball big enough to knock it down. Finally, Aarti painted a crevice in the Moon's surface, grieving for even the brief wound; she let her beautiful structure tumble down into the depths, and then closed it up again.

The humans would forget—it would be a seven-days' wonder. They'd assume it was just a glitch in the tech and nothing more, a transient lunar phenomenon; that's what they'd be telling themselves, all those so-clever men. The Moon was Aarti's now, finally and forever.

The Moon Maid

PART III
1970

GRACEFUL CURVES ARCED OVER the dusty lunar surface, silvery towers around a central dome. Aarti had painted herself a mini Taj Mahal, just one story tall, holding a single large room. She'd painted the image over and over, each time it had started to fade, until eventually it had achieved permanence. Would it outlast her death? Aarti had no idea, but it hardly seemed to matter here on the Moon, where she was the sole inhabitant. Aarti had built it in the Tsiolkovsky Crater, on the far side of the Moon, as far from Earth view as possible; even the Moon's librations would not reveal it. The Russians had sent a probe in 1959, had even published an atlas detailing a host of small craters on the far side, but their maps were woefully inadequate, and her little palace was safely hidden. Aarti didn't need protection from the elements, per se—her Moon body required none. But spending several hours a night there, she'd discovered that she sometimes wanted the comfort of a home, an enclosed space in which to rest, relax, and, eventually, work.

Aarti painted the fundamentals first—a drafting table and easel, canvases and walls to hang them on. Mostly she worked standing up, but sometimes she perched on a stool. She painted great glowing lights, so she might better see her work. Eventually, Aarti even painted herself a sofa and a bed, that she might lie there gazing at her paintings, considering their next iteration, or simply gazing out a window at the Earth.

Her paintings had started out realistic enough—moonscapes and spinning Earths. Over time they morphed as she began populating her solitary landscape. Small, strange creatures filled the rocky craters, slithery things and furry hopping beasts. Winged beings, as tall as coconut palms, stalking across the landscapes.

Aarti wondered, if she wanted it badly enough, if her creatures might come to life, keep her company. But so far, they never had—they stayed firmly on the canvas. Which probably meant that she was happier having the Moon entirely to herself.

♣

Yaj pulled the curtains open, sending afternoon sunlight streaming into the room. "Time to wake up, Aartibai."

Aarti groaned. The servants had gotten used to the fact that their mistress slept until midafternoon, but they didn't know that she was awake all night, and by around three o'clock, they inevitably became impatient.

"Yaj, please. You make me feel old—we're the same age! I told you to call me Aarti. I have told you a thousand times. After twenty years trapped together in this house, can we not dispense with the formalities?"

"No, Aartibai. It wouldn't be proper. If we did, I might forget my place." He smiled, and the sun caught the lock of hair falling across his forehead, the strands shining. No gray in it yet; Aarti would have taken gray hair for herself, if that were the price for actually having hair. It was hard to feel like a woman without it. She had no wrinkles yet, but what use was such vanity when the joker marks still stretched across her skin, when she had to watch her swollen head when crossing a doorway? At least she had gotten used to the pain, had learned how to manage it after so much time.

Manju's salves had grown more effective with experimentation, though Aarti hesitated to ask what the old woman put in them. Manju had given up body-servant duties to Yaj a few months ago, when Aarti had refused to get in a new girl to help. Manju had been scandalized, but she knew better than to argue with her stubborn mistress. And really, Aarti could mostly manage her dressings on her own these days, after long practice—she only needed help reaching the ones on her back. Yaj had a gentle touch, and she found herself looking forward to the moments when his fingers brushed against her spine. Not that she imagined he desired her; she wasn't such a fool.

"See that you don't," she said. Joking, joking. That was how they had learned to get through their days. Let us pretend that everything is fine, that we are ordinary middle-aged people living an ordinary life.

"It isn't easy," he said, in a tone that hovered on the edge of seriousness—no, it couldn't be. That look in his eyes. Turn away, turn away. Aarti busied herself with rinsing the sleep from her eyes in the washbasin, ignoring the pain as she lifted her arms to rub sandalwood oil across her bare scalp. For a time after she'd discovered the Moon, she had ignored her body's needs, let it lie in the bed, festering, but the servants grew too distressed. It seemed cruel to make them suffer, so she dragged her body from its bed, cleaned and cared for it as they insisted she do. Over time, the routine grew automatic so that Aarti could move her body and let her mind drift, planning what she would do when night finally fell and she could return to her true home.

"Will you be painting today?" Yaj kept the room she had laid out as a studio spotless—rows of brushes in their metal tins, an indulgent assortment of pigments.

"Maybe a little. We'll see."

She ought to paint, though it was frustratingly difficult, compared to working on the Moon. She could at least sketch out some ideas, develop them. Yaj and Manju loved her drawings—kept trying to get her to send them to a gallery, maybe even sell them. It felt pointless to her, though—they were so inadequate, compared to what she could paint up there.

Still, it was good to work a little here, too. The day went faster when Aarti went through the motions—cleaning herself and dressing, cloaking and masking enough to go to market, or walk on the beach, inhaling the reek of the fish vendors, their nets spread wide, their catch glistening in the Bombay sunshine. And there was breakfast, lunch, and dinner—her body still needed sustenance, and eating made time pass. She even took pleasure these days in the fresh mangoes Yaj cut for her, in Manju's delicate akuri, mixed with green chilies and fresh coriander. There were small pleasures in this world—but none to match the Moon.

Not even a dream of Yaj's dark eyes could keep Aarti from that moment, pressed against the bars of her window, waiting for the Moon to rise once more.

She watched them come in their ugly spaceship. Hating them even before they landed, and so much more when they stumbled out in their clumsy suits. Aarti built herself binoculars, so that she might lurk in the distance yet track their every move. She couldn't hear what they said, but she could watch as the hatch slid open, as a man stepped onto the surface. Polluting the sanctity of the gray dust with his filthy feet. He started walking, on a path that would bring him past her, eventually, and Aarti watched, wondering what she would do if he discovered her.

What would an earthman think of her? These days Aarti mostly dispensed with clothes and walked stark naked across the lunar craters, letting her hair swirl around her. She walked in the body she once had, one that looked as young as when she had stepped onto the boat for Oxford. In her mind, she appeared to be forever eighteen. A pardonable vanity. If the earthman saw her, he would surely think himself mad.

The man was getting closer. Aarti couldn't be sure it was a man in that suit, but who else would they send? It must be a white man, full of arrogance and swagger, come to lay claim to yet another land they had no right to.

Get out! Get out! She wanted to scream the words at him, but there was no air on the Moon, nothing to carry sound. Any screaming she did would be only in her own mind. *Your greed has no place here on my beautiful Moon. You want to build ugly buildings here, bring machines to mine whatever you can find, strip Her of everything of value She possesses, leave Her raped and bruised and broken behind you.*

Aarti leaned forward, her pulse racing as he came closer. *Look at the legacy you left behind in my homeland, the millions dead. What of Amritsar, atrocity committed under your very rule? You swore that you would raise us up, to reach the heights that only the white man could command. And instead, you drag us down with you, into the filth and the muck, stinking of your shit.*

Her Appa would be appalled at her language, but perhaps also a little proud to see his daughter finally stand up to the white man. Although she couldn't be sure—was he even British? It was more likely that it was an American or a Russian in that suit, but oh, did it matter? They were all the same. They had pillaged their way across much of the Earth, and now they had come for the Moon. *Her* Moon. Aarti's fists clenched at her sides, soft brush-tips hardening into edged claws with the force of her fury. If he came a few steps closer . . .

He turned. Headed back to the ship, where the hatch had opened again and another figure emerged, sliding down the side of the ship, falling to his knees in the beautiful gray dust. Good. Let him stay there, on his knees, where he belonged.

But no. That one clumsily climbed to his feet, and now the two of them were working together, gazing at something on the ship—she narrowed her vision, sharpening it. Ah, a gash that ran across the bottom. Enough to keep them here, to die here in the dust when their air and water ran out? A fitting end, but she didn't want them here for even that long. How could Aarti force them to leave?

They were assembling a machine. It took at least an hour, under the glare of the naked sun. And then they went back to their ship, one man pausing to draw something in the dust as they went. And then they were inside, the hatch closing. *Oh, leave, leave—risk it and go!* Aarti was shaking with the force of her longing, her wish that they might simply depart.

The engine started up—then died. She started walking, then running toward the ship. Aarti couldn't let them climb out again—if she had to, she would figure out a way to somehow *hurl* them off the lunar surface. Her fingertips had gone to brush tips again, and she reached forward, eager to paint something that would send them away, away—but then, in an impossible leap, the ship surged into the sky. No engine noise, no burst of rocket flames—they were simply up and gone, inexplicably, but Aarti didn't care. She spun around in triumph, raising a dust storm to swirl with her.

When the dust finally settled, she was alone again. The mechanism they'd built remained. She smashed it to pieces, lifting it and pounding it back down into the Moon's rocky surface with her own two hands. Whatever it was, Aarti wanted no part of it. They would undoubtedly assume it had simply failed; the Moon was too harsh for human tech. *They did not belong here!* Whatever the man had written had now been completely erased, and Aarti took pleasure in that small victory.

Aarti waited for the sun to set, for the Moon to rise. It would be hours yet, and who knew what was happening on her beloved Moon? She had imagined herself utterly inviolate there, but now strange men had come, and Aarti felt soiled by their presence.

She sat on the veranda, her feet tucked up beneath her in the cane chair, grateful for the extra cushioning they'd added to it so as to not add pressure to the sores. Aarti bandaged them less these days—a combination of Manju's salve applied while she slept and fresh air when she was up and about seemed to minimize her discomfort most effectively. There were no children to be frightened here; she had no need to hide away. "Yaj, what would you do, if an intruder came here?"

He paused in his sweeping of the veranda, and Aarti was struck by how rarely she saw him this way, still.

Yajnadar had been constantly in motion for the last twenty years—whenever she saw him, he was tending to the house, the garden, the car they had purchased a few years ago. His hands were long and slim, and she liked to watch them, surreptitiously, at their tasks—tying up bougainvillea branches, stirring a pot of jackfruit curry, smoothing down the sheets on her bed.

Manju had asked permission to retire; she had a niece who would take her in, and the old woman was tired. Aarti had agreed, of course, and so now it was just the two of them in the house, two ghosts circling around each other, waiting for—she wasn't sure what. Death? Not yet, not yet—Aarti was not even forty years old, and her great-grandmothers had all lived past a hundred. There were days when she thought she couldn't bear the pain of the sores a day longer—but Aarti had never seriously considered ending her life. She wasn't ready to give up on this body yet, for all the ways it had failed her. But if she lost the Moon . . .

Yaj frowned. "Aartibai, have you heard something? At night? I have told you, you must hire more servants. A young man who can defend the house if needed, a young woman to tend to your needs . . ."

"No, no—please, no strangers in this house." The thought made her heart beat faster. She and Yaj were comfortable together—she had long ago stopped bothering to cover her face around him. He didn't seem to mind her bulbous head, or the craters and protuberances that spread across her cheeks, her neck, her upper chest, her arms. If she could see herself with his eyes, maybe she wouldn't notice them, either. But if there were new people here, they would surely be shocked, repulsed, or, worst of all, pitying.

Yaj said, "They wouldn't be strangers for long."

"Are you tired?" Had she been thoughtless, a cruel mistress? Aarti was stricken by the lines on his face—Yaj didn't look old, but he didn't look young, either. What would she do if she lost him? Maybe she should hire more servants to ease the load. "Do I ask too much of you?"

"Never," he said firmly. Yaj smiled, and with that smile, the years dropped away, and he looked young again, as she was when she walked the Moon. "You know me, Aartibai—I wouldn't know what to do with myself without the work."

Still, she felt obscurely guilty. "You should go to school, Yaj, do more than tend to the needs of an old woman for all your life—my family has not done well by you, I'm afraid."

He shook his head. "I am content where I am, and you are far from old. But if you have heard something, we should make a plan, hire someone—"

Aarti had to head him off, though for a moment, she wished she could tell Yaj what she was really worrying about. If only she could take him with her—"No, no. It was just a thought. *If* someone were to bother us, what would we do?"

"Whatever we had to, Aartibai." His voice was low, and his gaze direct. "Whatever is needed to survive." Yaj frowned. "What's wrong? Is the pain bad today?"

She shook her head. "No, no. It's nothing, Yaj." Nothing he could help her with. He asked, "Do you want to go for a drive?"

Since buying the car, that had been one of Aarti's few earthly pleasures—to fight their way through traffic until they were out of Bombay, and then drive and drive on country roads, with the windows down and the wind streaming across her scalp. Aarti could forget everything then, losing herself in the pleasure of sun and wind against skin. She liked to sit beside Yaj in the front, rather than letting him chauffeur; she could see the road better that way, and he tolerated her demands, as always.

Sometimes Yaj would sing to her, old folk songs or Tamil film standards. He would sing of love undying, passions that could withstand family betrayal, societal disapproval, and she would be painfully aware of how close his thigh was to her own, inches away. He should have married. Married and had children and even grandchildren by now. It might have been nice, having children running around the big, empty house. Why hadn't Yaj married? Aarti had never had the nerve to ask, afraid of what his answer might be.

"No drive today, thank you. If you could bring me a cup of tea?" Her mother had used to say that tea cured all ills. Manju had taught Yaj the way of it, boiled in milk on the gas range, heavily sweetened. With enough tea, you could face down an army.

"Of course, Aartibai. It'll be just a moment." He ducked back into the house, leaving her alone on the veranda.

Making the tea and drinking it would consume twenty minutes. Twenty minutes, with an eternity to follow until night.

After the men came, Aarti realized that she had been far too blasé in her ownership of the Moon. Men had come—would they come again? Had they come before? Might there be men on the other side of the Moon right now? She sensed no other humans there, but how much could she trust her senses?

Aarti began systematically quartering the Moon's surface, mapping its peaks and crevasses. She painted herself a literal map, a golden globe that hung in her miniature Taj Mahal, marking each section that she explored. She was three-quarters finished before she found anything unexpected—but what she found shook her to her core.

It was nothing human—she was sure of that. She'd almost missed it at first—a cave entrance led to a subterranean cavern in the Ocean of Storms. The passageway down was narrow; she'd had to re-form into a thinner version of herself to squeeze through its twists. But it opened into a vast space, curving domed walls made of a strange, crystalline substance. Rooms filled with strange, metal objects, complex machines that sat on the floor, on tables, propped up against the walls. There had been no attempt to make the space airtight, as far as Aarti could see. Who could possibly have lived here, without needing to breathe? Nothing human. Yet someone had lived here, and for some time. The crystal floor of the cavern was scraped and worn, as if large objects had been dragged against it. A thick layer of moondust had drifted in, coating the machines. Aarti poked at them for a long time, but if they were meant to be powered, she had no idea how to turn them on. There was no way for Aarti to tell who had been here at all, or how long ago. Five years, fifty, five thousand? Might they return tomorrow?

Aarti's hands clenched uselessly at her sides.

"Aartibai—what's wrong?" Yajnadar had brought her tea as he did every day, but she wasn't sitting at her desk waiting for him. She was under the covers still, pulled tightly into herself, arms clasped around knees pulled to her chest. Aarti's refuge had been stolen from her. There was no peace for her there, no safety. But she couldn't hide here, either—was she to live her life out in this bed? Aarti took a deep, shuddering breath. Released it and pushed the covers back, sitting up.

"I'm sorry. I didn't mean to worry you." There must have been something in her face, something that told him this morning was not like the others, because Yaj came closer, and actually sat on the edge of the bed. Not touching her, of course—he was too proper a servant for that. But he waited there, patient expectation in his face. If only she could talk to him, could pour out her troubles and her worries; he would surely know what to say to make her feel better. He was right there, just inches away. If he wanted to, Yaj could lean forward and kiss her.

Instead, she kissed him. It was an impulse; if Aarti had stopped to think about it, she would never have done it. But she had been so lonely for so long. She had told herself that she liked the solitude, but Aarti was human, and a woman, and she remembered, faintly, what it had been like to kiss a man. This was different, though.

It was the briefest brush of lips to lips, and then she remembered where she was, what her body and face looked like on this Earth. She was no young moon maiden—a forty-year-old woman in a joker form, her head alone twice as large as his. Yaj must be disgusted, repulsed; Aarti jerked away, appalled at what she'd done. Worst of all, he was a servant; she had put him in an impossible position. "Yaj, I'm so sor—"

He was kissing her. Before Aarti could even get the words out, he had leaned forward and pressed his lips to hers. He didn't seem to care that her lips were gray, that her skin was pocked and cratered, that despite all of Manju's salves, there were still a few open sores. Yaj slid his right arm around her back, pulling her closer; his left came up, that hand cradling her cheek as he kissed her with a combination of tenderness and desire that left her breathless. Heat rushed through her, from tingling lips to a suddenly pounding heart.

Gods—this was madness! But every time Aarti tried to talk, to protest, he just kissed her harder. And somehow, her hands were tangled in his hair, and she was leaning back against the pillows, and Yaj was moving above her, his long body sliding under the covers, his hands—oh god!—his hands pushing up the cotton salwar she wore for sleeping, sliding under the fabric to cup her breasts. And Aarti finally let go, let herself relax into pleasure that made the pain—not disappear, exactly, but not matter. If there was still pain, here and there, it was subsumed in the electricity that Yaj's fingers and mouth brought, the soft and urgent heat of his lips and tongue, grounding her in this bed, this Earth.

Right now, there was nowhere else she'd rather be.

Everything changed. Now, when she returned from the Moon, Yaj was waiting for her. He pressed fevered kisses on her gray skin, without fear or hesitation. There were days when Aarti mourned the wasted years, but he reminded her, smiling, that they were lucky to have what they had. Month after month together, and it wasn't as if there hadn't been a relationship before that. They were almost an old married couple even before they fell into bed together, though bed definitely added something significant to the equation.

A little scandalous, the relationship between mistress and servant, but they were old enough now that no one really cared, not even the neighbors who might suspect their situation. Aarti and Yaj walked through the city together side by side—they went to see movies, browse bookstores, even shop for clothes. Yaj liked choosing saris for her, filmy creations, blues and greens and silvers that complemented her gray skin. *I am too old for such nonsense, Yaj.* He only smiled and added another sari to the pile on the counter. He was spending her money, of course, but that didn't matter.

Even better, there were children in the house. Yaj had a nephew, Suresh, and Suresh had a wife, Saila, and four children. Yaj persuaded Suresh to come live with them and take over the bulk of the gardening and housework, which had become difficult for him to manage. Saila cooked for them all, and the children ran wild through the halls of the house. It pleased Aarti immensely to think that this house might eventually be inherited by four lower-caste little ones whom her parents would scorn. A fitting return for their bigoted ways.

Her only sorrow was that Yaj couldn't go with her to the Moon. Aarti tried to take him with her—night after night, she wished herself there, her body curved around his in the wide four-poster bed, only to awake there, entirely alone. Her power had its limits, and this was one of them—it was for her alone. So she hadn't told him of her power. In any case, it would surely be impossible for him to believe. As the months passed, she found herself sometimes staying home at night. Aarti was tired when she spent her nights on the Moon, and she wanted to squeeze as much pleasure out of her days with Yaj as possible.

Aarti heard the riot on the news—the crash of broken windows, shouts and screams. All India Radio covered it—in Delhi, there would even be TV footage, but that didn't reach to Bombay yet. Massive anti-joker riots had broken out in Jyotiba Phule Market, though no one seemed certain what had started it. When she went to the kitchen, Suresh and Saila were discussing the violence in hushed tones. The children were still in school, thankfully.

"Hundreds dead!" Suresh said as he chopped onions, tears streaming down his face, as they always did.

"Thousands," Saila said. She pounded the massive pestle into the wide mortar, grinding chilies for the week's meals. "It started when one of *them* tried to go to temple, interrupted a wedding." She wouldn't use the word "joker," thought it wasn't respectful, living in Aarti's house. Aarti couldn't give a damn, and had said so, but Saila didn't believe her.

Suresh frowned. "I thought it was a funeral."

"No, a wedding. Some big muckety-muck in Parliament, and his father—"

"Saila, I'm sure it was a woman, maybe his mother—"

She sighed. "Oh, hush, husband. You don't know anything."

They fell silent when they realized Aarti was there, listening in the doorway. Then Saila offered quietly, "Don't worry, mistress. No trouble will come here."

"If it does," Suresh added stoutly, "the gates are very strong, and I will beat the goondas with a stick!"

"Where is Yajnadar?" Aarti asked. She was trying to breathe steadily, to seem unafraid. Mustn't scare the servants. "Shouldn't he be home by now?"

Saila and Suresh exchanged frowning looks. "He went shopping, but you don't think—"

Aarti snapped, "Call me when he arrives. As *soon* as he arrives." Who did she think she was fooling? She went back to her cold bed to wait. Hours passed, until at last a policeman came to the door to confirm what they all already knew.

The body was delivered that night. Saila set it up in the back garden, washed and dressed in clean clothes, surrounded by flowers. Aarti knelt beside it, night and day, for almost a week. She wanted to weep, but since her card had turned, she'd been unable to; Aarti's eyes were burning and dry. Finally, she succumbed to Saila and Suresh's pleas that she allow them to take the remains away for cremation. What remained? Nothing, really—Yajnadar was long gone.

Had Yaj been killed by a joker who assumed he was anti-joker? Or murdered by a nat who thought Yaj had been protecting jokers? Aarti could imagine both scenarios; in fact, she imagined them in great detail, picturing every moment of those interactions. She went to the Moon at night and painted the scenes, acting them out, though in her versions she was there, intervening at the right moment to save him. Aarti should have been with him—he'd asked her to go with him that morning, invited her as he always did.

"Come with me, love. I want you by my side." Yaj had bent down, dropped a row of tender kisses across her forehead.

"Do you have to go?" Aarti hated when he left her, counted the minutes until he returned.

He chuckled. "I'm afraid I do, if we don't want conflict in the household. If Saila didn't insist on meat and fish for the children, I could live on rice and lentils forever. Rice and lentils and kisses." Yaj kissed her lips then, first gently, then with a passionate heat that sent her arching up to meet him, her fingers clenching in the white sheets. Then he released her, smiling an invitation.

Aarti didn't want to face the crowds. She shifted instead so the sheet slid down a little, baring her breasts. "I'll be here when you get back. Naked in this bed. Hungry."

"Witch. I'll hurry," Yaj said, and kissed her once more, and left.

No more of his kisses, ever.

Aarti couldn't find the ones who murdered him. No way to know whether they'd been killed themselves, or swept up by the police, or simply disappeared in the streets, headed back to their homes. She had no power of perception here, no network of dust and instinct to tell her what had happened, what had gone so terribly wrong. All of her power was up there, on the Moon.

The only way she could hurt them would be from up high. Oh, Aarti had thought of it. The night they took the body away to be burned, she fled to the sanctuary of her Moon. Fell to her knees in the thick dust, dragged her perfect brush-tip fingers through it, wishing that she could do more, feel more. Aarti wanted to breathe, wanted to sob her misery into the night, drown the Moon in a flood of grief.

Aarti could crack the Moon in half, hurl pieces down, killing all of the humans, and herself with them. No way to fine-tune her aim, but surely she could take out Bombay, at least, be certain of getting every last rioter. Maybe most of Mother India. While she was at it, why not throw the whole Moon down, cause a global extinction event? Humans could slaughter an innocent, good man in the marketplace out of fear and hatred and sheer idiocy. Humans were too flawed to be worth saving; time to wipe the board clean, start over with fresh chalk.

She was not so far gone. Not quite.

But Aarti would reclaim the Moon, drive the vermin from it. If any other human came to her Moon, she would not hide between some veil of assumed morality. Yaj was beyond judging her now; she needed not worry about his good opinion. The Moon belonged to *her,* and if any dared to trespass upon it, Aarti would gladly see them burn. She would light the torch herself, with steady hands.

Flat Man

by Steve Perrin

ALMAZ

1979

AS COSMONAUT PILOT LEONID Sumaroyov kills the last burst of the retro-rockets, Yuri Serkov flips off the straps holding him to the cosmonaut cradle modified to hold his virus-altered body. Yuri stretches his folded body out of the cradle, leaving him floating in midair between cradles and viewing ports.

"*Soyuz 22* has achieved assigned 350 km orbit." Leonid reports back to Baikonur control, at the same time pushing Yuri away so he can look out to see if the other capsules are in place. They're already on the radar screen, but Leonid only really trusts his eyes. "Please do not spread your fat ass all over the ports, Flat Man," Leonid adds, this time with the mic off. The nat cosmonaut grimaces at his Soyuz-mate through his already flourishing mustache. Yuri ripples the offending body part in Leonid's face and rotates himself away from the port. He's entirely too used to the mocking nickname and intolerant snarl. The Takisian virus—or Star Gift as the official Soviet line has it—makes his body shape twice as wide but only a third as deep as his fellow cosmonauts'. Some of his colleagues compare his hairless body form to Gumby, an American animated character, but Yuri refuses to see the cartoons. Despite his misshapen physique, he has a full set of organs and can maneuver weightlessly with the best of them, and he has some other advantages in weightless conditions.

Spinning his body like a Catherine wheel and pushing off of the capsule's overhead, Yuri brings his head to where he can join Leonid at eyeballing the rest of the capsules sharing their orbit.

Three of the Almaz modules—numbered 3 through 5 because two previous individual stations had climbed to orbit, been used for a couple of years, then dived back into a fiery funeral—are already in orbit. Demerov and Olderov in *Soyuz 21* had already tested 3 and 4 and reported the systems in good shape.

"As long as we're in the neighborhood"—Yuri folds himself into his custom space suit—"we might as well check out *Almaz 5*." The smell of the relatively unused space suit is a temporary relief from the already ripe interior of the Soyuz capsule. Sumaroyov reports their intent to Baikonur and *Soyuz 21* and wiggles his Pingvin-clad body into his suit, and then the two check each other's systems.

Sucking the air out of the capsule into the air tanks, then opening their hatch, Yuri latches his line to the anchor point on the capsule and launches himself toward the nearest capsule, emblazoned with the number 5. "Good setup, Leon," he radios back to the pilot who put them so close to the capsule.

"Just my duty to the Soviet state," responds Leonid in a not-quite-mocking tone. Whatever the Ukrainian's real attitude toward the Soviet Union, Leonid took pride in his piloting.

Almaz 5 holds the communications gear and the photography platform. Entering through the posterior lock, the two cosmonauts make sure all the pieces are in place, breaking out tables and shelves that had been folded for the launch. Yuri unpacks a camera and takes a few pictures of the assembled capsules and the camera seems to be in good shape. There's no power to the capsule—the nuclear reactor intended to power the station is coming with the fourth and final unit.

The two spacewalk back to their *Soyuz 22* capsule, refill it with the already used air, and settle down to rest for the next day's activities. It will take at least two days for the Baikonur spaceport crews to prepare the last two parts of their project, and that is working at incredible speed. The whole Soviet space station project has been delayed years while they worked out just how to launch so many payloads in such a short time.

Leonid is cordial but uncommunicative. He combs his beard, reviews the next day's instructions without his usual sotto voce comments that generally invite listeners to pitch in, reports their status to Baikonur, and puts on his sleep mask. Yuri doesn't expect anything more. As the engineer, he is responsible for the connections that would turn the space station segments into the mighty Almaz Space Defense Station. The connection is his innovation and justifies his inclusion onto the team, but the other cosmonauts still have much of the usual nat prejudice against Star Gifts—even though he has been working with them for more than five years. He sighs and looks over his procedures for the central "tent" he devised. Soon his unique whistling snores join those of Leonid.

Two mornings later, a combination of cosmonaut muscle and judicious use of the station's maneuvering rockets arrange the three modules in a splayed fan arc with posteriors to the bottom of the arc and the anteriors pointing out like a fan.

Yuri watches from his capsule as the station's modules pass by. After all the effort to get them ready to be connected, the arc rotates right next to his capsule. Also, as it happens, the 20 mm guns affixed to each module seem to keep pointing in his direction when the fan rotation takes them there. Leonid Sumaroyov mutters under his breath in Ukrainian every time he sees one of the barrels go by.

"They are not really aimed at us," Yuri says with a smile.

Sumaroyov looks at him with a sardonic grin. "What do you mean 'us,' Flat Man?"

Yuri has long since become resigned that his fellow cosmonauts are often jealous of his adaptations to a space environment. And they don't know the extent of it. Some aspects of his condition he is even attempting to hide from his Star City masters, though he can never be sure they don't know everything and are just hiding it from him. Yuri prefers to think of it as a game.

The cosmonauts cannot take up residence in the station because the modules are working on battery power that has to be conserved. The on-station cosmonauts wait for the fourth and final Almaz that is bringing up the largely experimental Kosmos-952 nuclear reactor. That and the third and final Soyuz with two more crewmen, including Mission Commander Andrian Grigoryevich "Iron Man" Nikolayev, are due the next day as the crews in Baikonur work steadily on the fastest turnarounds for a space mission ever so far.

Yuri worries about the timing. Arranging multiton station segments, even in weightlessness, is tiring work in a space suit. Even resting, the cosmonauts use a lot of oxygen. Yuri's oxygen dependency is less than normal cosmonauts', but the capsules carry only so much oxygen and the module supply should not be tapped until the station activates. If a winter blizzard shut down Baikonur they might have to scrub the mission for lack of oxygen.

But so far the schedule has only slipped by five hours because of some weather back in Kazakhstan, where the rockets launch. Yuri has heard rumors that the Soviet Union has a weather-controlling Star Gift called Father Winter working on keeping launch days free. Perhaps it is true.

Olderov in *Soyuz 21* reports. "Orbit adjustment flares seen south 275. I think it's the last Almaz module."

Sumaroyov touches the adjustment jets and the capsule swings so he can look in the right direction. Yuri looks over the pilot's shoulder. "Yes, it's adjusting per the program. Two more blasts and it should be right up with us."

"Unless it decides to ram us," Yuri responds. The Salyut program had been plagued with misfiring rendezvous programming.

"If it does, the chief designer will rip the programmers a new programming port." Yuri grins at Sumaroyov's witticism. The chief designer had died in 1966 and only then had the cosmonauts learned his real name, Sergei Karolev. He had been notorious for his responses to nonfunctioning hardware and software. He wasn't very forgiving of malfunctioning cosmonauts and support crew, either. Now the cosmonaut corps invoke his old title as the ultimate punisher of errors in the program.

The final module follows the program as best it can. Yuri has to spacewalk to it to attach a line and winch it into proper formation with the other modules, maneuvering the four modules into a roughly cruciform formation. By the time he is finished the *Soyuz 23* has also arrived, carrying Mission Commander Andrian Grigoryevich Nikolayev, the third man in space and the cosmonaut who lasted longest in the infamous isolation chamber—which got him his Iron Man nickname. (Yuri had been pulled from the chamber after five days and got a pat on the shoulder. As far as anyone was concerned, he was still Flat Man.) With him is cosmonaut Georgy Grechko, who pioneered use of the Orlan space suit they are all using—though Yuri's is highly modified. Nikolayev pronounces the preliminaries as properly completed and the team rests for four hours before starting the next, and hopefully final, steps of attaching the modules to one another and starting up the reactor to power the station.

The second man in Olderov's *Soyuz 21* is Yuri Demerov, a nuclear engineer. He and Yuri have the job of setting up the Kosmos nuclear reactor that will power the station. Previous stations used solar power, but some military genius rightly pointed out that the solar sails made easy targets for an invader who wanted to cripple the station but leave the contents available for later use. Yuri is not convinced making it necessary to target the station itself improves the survivability of anyone in the station, but no one asked him.

The two Yuris trained together for six months, but now they make the usual comments about men named Yuri being attracted to the space program for the benefit of the other team members. Yuri Gagarin has a lot to answer for.

First all of the cosmonauts maneuver the modules into the cruciform layout for the station, all posterior locks pointed toward the crux of the cross shape. Then the two Yuris enter the new station module, *Almaz 6*, and begin to unpack the small reactor. Yuri was surprised at the small size when they began training on the assembly, back at Star City. The cooling hardware and the shielding carry more mass than the reactor itself, largely due to the need for the special cooling fluid that the system has to recycle. All the parts are brand new and very polished and carefully labeled. Assembly goes quickly, even in space suits. Yuri notes apprehensively how many parts have "experimental" code numbers.

"No problem," Demerov responds. "It just means the parts worked so well that they didn't bother to make production parts, they are just using the pieces meant for testing the models they didn't have to fabricate after all." Yuri is a spaceship maintenance engineer, not a nuclear physicist, but he has the distinct feeling that his fellow Yuri quotes the Party line.

Soon enough, Demerov declares that Yuri has done everything he can toward helping get the reactor ready for the job; Demerov only needs to make some connections and throw a switch. "Don't you have something else to do?" he finishes. As it happens Yuri devised the simple "tent" of fabric and cable that will connect the posterior docking ports of all four modules, turning them into a cruciform unit with their anterior docking ports extending out to receive future crew replacements, Progress resupply capsules, and any other space-going vehicles with the right docking mechanism. Naturally, the fixed 20 mm cannons guard each of the four anterior ports.

Yuri exits the posterior port of *Almaz 6* and finds the other four cosmonauts have been busy. First they attached their spacecraft to the anterior docking ports of three of the station segments, 3, 5, and 6, fastening their umbilicals to the station connections, ready to recharge batteries and get scrubbed oxygen from the working station when the reactor goes live.

Then they donned their space suits and began fastening the space tent together, cabling the struts that would keep the metallic fabric stiff to resist any aberrations that could collapse the tent. There is only a small gap in one flap of the tent that lets Yuri join them outside the station to manage the final tent raising.

Everyone feels the exhaustion that accompanies any work in a space suit, including ducking into the station's shadow every time it faces the Sun. The working chatter comprises about half the complexities of the task and half anticipation of going in through *Almaz 4*'s extra personnel lock, built to allow spacewalkers in and out, and cracking open the cognac bottles Nikolayev brought as his "personal cargo" for just that purpose. Despite their guarded language, Baikonur has already warned them to keep their attention on the job.

"You guys go ahead," Yuri tells them. "Georgy and I will make sure everything's tight. Demerov says he will be activating the reactor any minute." Grechko good-naturedly accepts his inevitable fate as the man with the most space-suit experience and willingly goes over what has been done for Yuri's approval. Yuri finds a couple of iffy seals and a cable not tightened to spec. He notes that they are all in the section Olderov worked on, and makes a mental note for his report even as he and Georgy make temporary corrections that will have to be reinforced and protected later. Olderov and Demerov are slated to be the first crew of the station. Hopefully the pilot will learn to keep his own safety secure while in residence.

As Yuri and Georgy climb hand over hand to the spacewalkers' lock, they hear Demerov say, "The reactor's running. All systems are operational." Some outside work lights come on now that they don't need them. Typical efficiency. They grin at each other and finish their journey, helping each other through the lock and stripping off helmets and oxygen gear. Yuri instinctively looks for the air hose installations that can be hooked to a suit at a moment's notice, and points them out to Georgy. "I had the lectures, Flat Man, and I like to breathe," the other returns, but he grins instead of grimacing, so maybe one fellow cosmonaut is willing to look past shape to comradeship.

Nikolayev's voice comes from the next compartment. "Leave off the lectures, Flat Man. Get in here before the cognac is all gone."

Having everyone in the compartment strains its capacity—it is normally meant for three, not six. Most of the others, including Demerov, have stripped off their suits and are in their Pingvin ship suits. Yuri accepts a bulb containing about 2 ml of the brown liquid. Everyone has a bulb, and no one has taken a drink. Nikolayev raises his bulb, holding on to a chunk of cabinet to keep from spinning away, and calls a toast. "To the two Yuris, whose technical expertise made the Almaz battle station possible."

Demerov toasts Yuri, who responds, and both sip from their bulbs, immediately joined by the others. The cognac is superb, though several hours of hard work in a space suit probably has something to do with their appreciation.

They are on the second bottle when Georgy looks at Olderov's chest and asks, "Is your dosimeter malfunctioning, Vladimir?" He pulls out the front of his space suit and twists his head to look at his own radiation meter. Its normal low glow intensifies as he looks at it. "Oh, Kristos!" he says.

No one in this group of putative atheists seems shocked at his invocation of the Christian religion. They are too busy looking at one another's detectors and yelling at Demerov. "What the fuck did you do, Yuri? Your reactor is killing us!"

Demerov clambers toward the posterior air lock, too busy to respond. Serkov follows him immediately, yelling at the others to get back to their capsules, now attached to the non-spacewalk docks. Olderov and Demerov's capsule docked at Almaz 6, the reactor module. The others are also in the modules connected via the tent. Yuri can feel the other crewmen scrambling to the Almaz 4's spacewalk reception area to get their helmets and oxygen gear.

Demerov and Yuri slam through the lock first, looking with horror at the radiation detector over the air lock to Almaz 6. "Crap, I forgot to engage the alarm system," Demerov snarls. He fed power to the life-support system and maneuver jets and outside lights, but no one hooked up the alert system yet.

Pushing off from the Almaz 4 lock to the reactor module opposite them, they collide at the lock and as they sort themselves out and start opening the lock, Olderov smashes into them, too panicked to control his free-fall flying. A hairball of the other three cosmonauts sorts itself out in the center of the tent, barely two meters away. Pilots Nikolayev and Sumaroyov struggle toward their capsules. Georgy stops to watch Yuri and the other two, shrugs ruefully when he realizes he would just be in the way, and follows after the mission commander to their capsule.

As Yuri fends the pilot off, Demerov wrenches open the lock and pushes off toward the reactor. Yuri follows on his heels, Olderov behind him. As Yuri catches a stanchion to stop himself, the pilot flashes past him, his flight under better control now, and ducks through the doorway to the anterior compartment, where all the life support and auxiliary power controls reside.

Demerov desperately swarms over the reactor, looking to Yuri like a snake trying to find some place to bite into a particularly large victim. "Nothing," Demerov snarls. "Everything is to spec. The damn shielding just isn't good enough."

"Can you shut it down?"

"It will take a while to shut itself down once I flip the switch. The whole station will be a radioactive hot spot for centuries."

"Smash it?"

"Radioactives everywhere. Same problem."

"Then flip the switch and let's get out of here. Let the chief designer figure it out."

Demerov shrugs. "All right." He pushes the red button. "Look at your dosimeter. It's almost blinding." Demerov already seems to be feeling the effects of the radiation slashing through his body and his dosimeter is a beacon.

"I'm fine," Yuri says, and realizes it's the truth. "Get yourself into your capsule. I have to get to mine."

Demerov looks like he can barely move. Yuri sees his fellow engineer will never make it on his own, scoops him up, and pushes off for the anterior module. He flashes through the compartment and twists to take the impact as they slam into the lock. Olderov, inside the lock, enters the capsule.

"That was quite a hit," Demerov groans. "Are you okay?"

"You call me Flat Man. The girls in Star City call me Mattress Man." Yuri grins as he stuffs Demerov into the lock and Olderov grabs him. No one is bothering about air-lock protocol.

Yuri pushes off again, agilely snaking through the compartments, past the slowly humming reactor, and into the tent. All the air locks hang open, which makes his trip up to where he had left his helmet and oxygen gear in *Almaz 4* easy. Demerov's and Olderov's are still on their pegs. Hopefully they would not have an air breach on the way home.

Yuri's comm crackles with radiation. "Nikolayev here. We are detached from the station. Status?"

"Detaching now," comes Olderov's weakened voice. The trip through the reactor room has done him no good.

"Don't wait for me," Yuri says. "I can take this longer than you round people." As he says it he knows that Leonid does not have his resilience.

"I am on station," comes Leonid's status report. "About two kilometers off Almaz."

Putting on his gear as he goes, Yuri swoops back to the tent, then through the posterior lock to *Almaz 5,* which Sumaroyov had obligingly left open. The communication room is in this module, and Yuri can see the radio lights on. No doubt the engineers in Star City and Baikonur had detected the radiation expression and consequent decompression of the station and want a report. The air loss has already made any sounds coming from the radio too attenuated to be heard. No time for that, now.

But when he gets to the just-closed anterior lock, there is no capsule. Right, Leonid said he was two kilometers away.

Finishing donning his helmet and oxygen pack, he cycles the lock and works his way out of the module. There is *Soyuz 22,* on station two kilometers away. Leonid did not want to get close to the radiation that was already filling space around the station, but Yuri is appreciative that he doesn't want to leave Yuri behind. Even at that distance Leonid has to be watching the radiation meters inside the capsule climb their deadly ascent.

There are no kilometers of line handy, and Yuri's suit doesn't have a propulsion unit. How is he going to reach *Soyuz 22*?

His radio, hitherto filled with radiation-produced static, suddenly allows a voice to punch through. Or is he hearing something else? "Captain Serkov, Captain Serkov, are you receiving?" It's Baikonur.

"Serkov," he responds.

"Captain, our suit telemetry shows that you have received a more-than-fatal dose of radiation. Can you still operate?"

"I feel fine." Not exactly the truth. He feels no pain or nausea, but has a particular lightness of head. Also, he is seeing auras around warm objects like he might if he was wearing infrared goggles. Moreover, he feels like he is in a warm bath. One in which the water is moving *through* him—cleansing but still penetrating. What is going on?

Yuri swings his arm toward his chest to read his dosimeter, but his suit arm is not moving, just an image of his naked arm, glowing with warmth and fuzzily outlined with a heat aura. Moreover, it certainly feels like it is his actual arm out there. He yanks it back into his suit—for whatever safety that gives.

"Captain Serkov?" Yuri realizes the radio voice is not coming from the suit's speakers. He is receiving directly to his ears. He thinks about switching the voice off, and it fades away. *Wish I could do that to anyone trying to give me orders,* Yuri thinks. *Now what the hell is going on here?*

Yuri starts a breathing exercise he calls "zen breathing." He stops. "I'm not breathing at all," he mutters. The mutter comes over the radio like an echo. His physical ears, if he still has physical ears, catch nothing. Taking a deep breath, which does nothing physically but makes him feel better, he steps out of his space suit, as if stepping out of a localized mist. There is a faint tugging, and then he is free of the suit. He turns around to look inside the tinted faceplate, half expecting to see his radiation-desiccated body. No body. Apparently he is still alive, whatever alive is in this condition.

Yuri has heard of experiments in creating three-dimensional visual images. In the West they call them holograms. As far as he can tell, he is a living hologram. A naked hologram. Even stranger, his dimensions are those of a normal man, rather than the flat body he has lived with since his Gift manifested when he was a thirteen-year-old Young Pioneer. He still doesn't have any body hair, but he notices that he is missing dead fingernails, too.

Well, I guess Comrade Einstein was right, all of my matter has turned into energy. He leaves the question of why he doesn't just explode hanging. Just another manifestation of the psionic effects of the Takisian virus.

As he stands in the air lock, he sees *Soyuz 23* ignite its retro-rockets and start the reentry back to Mother Russia. The station shakes as Olderov and Demerov's Soyuz disconnects from the station. Angling his head, he can see the flare that has to be Nikolayev and Grechko's capsule. They must have assumed the radiation had killed him and decided to get out of the radiation zone.

And why isn't he dead? His suit dosimeter glows a bright red. At the least, he should be puking his guts out. Not to mention blowing up with explosive decompression since he's outside his suit and at least one of his fellow cosmonauts apparently didn't close any air locks before abandoning the station.

Yuri turns to reenter the station and finds it like swimming upstream. Something is pushing his immaterial body away. Thinking about it, he realizes it's the escaping radiation from the overcharged reactor pushing against the resistance of his still-visible body. If only he can change his energy signature to something that the escaping radiation does not affect. He can feel his body shift and flow, maintaining its outside structure but altering itself on a molecular level. Suddenly there is no more pressure. He's light-headed and a bit nauseous, but the radiation no longer has an effect on him. His body has converted itself to pure visual spectrum energy—the radiation is passing through him as if he isn't there. Just how much control over this energy form does he have?

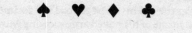

Within That
House Secure

by Christopher Rowe

I

THE GRID-LINED PAPER BROWNED along one edge and began curling over neat lines of script and formulae. The little girl leaning over the notebook, pen in hand, drew in a sharp breath and forced calm on herself. The page did not burst into flame. This time.

Mathilde set down the pen and pushed the notebook away. A clumsy jumble of English and French curse words sounded in the quiet room, her piping eleven-year-old voice in no way matching her crude language. Malachi, had he been present to hear, would have chided her, probably reciting some obscure line of poetry about keeping one's temper in check. Not that she hadn't heard him losing his own temper more than once through the thick oak door to his library, usually while talking to someone on the phone.

Malachi, though, was not present. Mathilde was alone in her room in his house—in her father's house, though she had never called him that in French or English—with only the housekeeper somewhere on the premises. Her last tutor for the day had left an hour before, following a few hours' work on history and literature and art. Malachi felt that afternoons were a more civilized time to study the humanities.

Mathilde didn't mind the afternoons, but she liked the mornings better. Mathematics and the catch all hours spent on "the sciences" kept her attention in a way that battles and poems never did, even if rhyme schemes were at least passably interesting.

A soft knock at the door meant that the housekeeper, Ms. Lott, had come to tell her it was time to get dressed. Mathilde had, as usual, carefully recorded her day's schedule in her notebook just before turning out the light the night before, and needed no reminder. Ms. Lott knew that, too, but answered to Malachi, not Mathilde.

"Come in," Mathilde called. "I know it is time to pick a dress."

Ms. Lott, it turned out, was holding a dress already, one Mathilde had not seen before. "Delivered just after lunch," she said, hanging it from a hook next to Mathilde's dressing table. "From that same woman up in New York who made your Easter dress."

All of Mathilde's clothes were custom made. When she was still living in France, before her mother had died, that had meant rugged, functional jumpers made by Mathilde and Maman herself. Maman had been a transportation engineer, and probably could have afforded to find someone in La Rochelle to accommodate Mathilde's needs, but had taken to the problem of providing her daughter's clothing the same way she took to problems involving high-speed passenger trains. She had taught herself—and Mathilde—to measure and cut and sew and mend.

A few of those jumpers, all too small now, were carefully folded and stored in boxes in Mathilde's ridiculously oversized closet. So many things in America were ridiculously oversized.

Malachi did not make Mathilde's clothes. Instead, the two of them flew to New York twice a year and visited various specialized ateliers staffed by courteous people who were happy to provide every kind of clothing imaginable, cut specially for Mathilde's squarish, broad-shouldered frame.

This dress was a brilliant green. Malachi often chose green shades for Mathilde because, he said, they set nicely against the coppery red of her skin and eyes. Mathilde thought the frocks the colors of emeralds or the forest or the sea made her look like a Christmas decoration, but had resigned herself to Malachi's taste in this instance.

"What's she done about my neck?" Mathilde asked, hopping down from her desk chair and marching over to the dressing table.

Ms. Lott, who had lasted the longest in the string of caregivers Malachi had hired in the two years since Mathilde had come to South Carolina, winced, but only said, "It zips up the back, dear, nothing to worry about there."

Mathilde had asked because she didn't really have much of a neck at all. Her head and face were more or less normal, for all her crimson skin and hairless pate, and her delicate features were, according to Maman, "elfin," but her head set squarely between her shoulders with nothing in the way of a neck at all. This was of little consequence when it came to jumpers, but the makers of haute couture, even joker haute couture, found it challenging.

Mathilde spared the dress a moment's study. "I can put it on myself," she said.

Ms. Lott started to object, but then thought better of it. "Mr. Schwartz will be home in half an hour and said the two of you will be leaving for the Witherspoons, immediately," she said. She paused at the door on her way out and added, "I'll be downstairs if you need anything."

This was something Ms. Lott said often. Mathilde knew it didn't mean everything it promised—Ms. Lott couldn't answer all her questions, assuage all her doubts, satisfy all her curiosities. Nobody, not Ms. Lott, not even Malachi, could give Mathilde everything she needed.

For that to ever happen, Mathilde would have to know what she needed herself.

Malachi was not given to affectations, but his employers were. The car he and Mathilde rode in to the party at the Witherspoon estate had been a gift from Mr. Witherspoon, a reward for some bit of financial wizardry Malachi had performed—savings on taxes, expanded revenue, Mathilde didn't really pay much attention to those things. They involved numbers, true, but Mathilde liked numbers that measured things like distance and mass and energy, not money.

The car was called a Duesenberg. It was very old and, Mathilde had to admit, very fancy. That was probably why the Witherspoons had picked it out. Their enormous house was old and fancy and full of fancy old things. Even Theodorus's room, for all the boy's fascination with spaceships and technology, was crowded with antique furniture that he and Mathilde were constantly having to shove to the side to make room for their elaborate games.

"The dress looks nice," said Malachi, from behind the *Wall Street Journal*.

"Thank you," said Mathilde. She was looking out the window. Malachi's house was in an older part of Charleston, near the city center, but the Witherspoon estate was miles outside the city, on the grounds of an old indigo plantation. They had just turned off the state highway and the driver was stopping at the wrought iron gates. A pair of uniformed guards, one holding a clipboard, stood outside a small gatehouse.

"They want your invitation, Mr. Schwartz," the driver said over his shoulder.

Malachi dug through some of the papers in his bulging briefcase, muttering to himself. Then he checked the pockets of his suit jacket. A joker like his daughter, Malachi also wore specially tailored clothing, his tastes tending to conservative business wear that did little to disguise the shape of his nearly spherical body.

"Send them back here," he said after a moment, rolling down the window.

The guard with the clipboard leaned in and smiled. "Mr. Schwartz," he said. "You know Mrs. Witherspoon and her security protocols."

"I don't have an invitation," Malachi said. "I'm not sure I was even given an invitation."

The guard—Mathilde didn't have to read his name badge to know he was called Carl, because this ritual of always being stopped for paperwork Malachi had always misplaced was a familiar one—checked his clipboard. "You're listed here, sir."

"Then let us in, please," said Malachi. "We're a pair of jokers in a bright orange sixty-year-old limousine and we've been here dozens of times. You know who we are."

Carl looked embarrassed. "No offense, sir, but didn't you yourself once tell me that there are jokers and aces and so on who can change their shapes?"

Malachi sighed. "Yes, Carl. I did tell you that."

"Let them through, Carl," came a new voice, a boy's voice on the young side of puberty. "I'll vouch for them."

"Theodorus!" Mathilde said, opening the door and forcing the guard to step back. "Did you ride down here on your bike?"

The slightly rotund blond boy grinned, one cheek dimpling deeply. "Sidecar attached! Let's go!"

"Hold on—" said Malachi and Carl simultaneously, but the children were already scrambling through the gate and onto—and into, in Mathilde's case—a scaled-down motorcycle with a bullet-shaped sidecar. The bike was painted metallic red, with fanciful gouts of flame stenciled on the fuel tank. Blue streamers hung from the ends of the handlebars.

Theodorus, somewhat clumsily, operated the kick-starter, and the bike more purred than roared to life. "We'll see you up at the house, Malachi!" he called, and Mathilde waved at her father as they sped away.

"Does your mother still think you're in danger of being kidnapped?" Mathilde asked, half shouting.

"I wouldn't mind being kidnapped," Theodorus replied distractedly, intent on operating the bike. "If it was by pirates, maybe. Or Takisians. Anyway, I don't know. Mother's just overprotective, like always."

Mrs. Witherspoon, like most adults and most "natural" people, presented Mathilde with challenges. The cheerful woman insisted that Mathilde call her "Alice" even while Malachi, in turn, insisted that Mathilde address all adults besides himself with honorifics, which meant her world was full of people she called Mrs. This or Mr. That or Dr. The Other. So Mrs. Witherspoon, Alice, had entered into a conspiracy with Mathilde that required her to carefully check to see if Malachi was in earshot every time she spoke to the woman. Like most things concerning adults, it was exhausting.

Seeing Theodorus, though, even at a party that promised to be populated with nobody but misses and misters and doctors, with the odd professor and colonel thrown in, made up for it. The only time Theodorus ever went by an honorific was when he was Captain Theodorus Witherspoon, kid pilot, youngest ever recruit to the U.S. Space Command, and the two of them were lying on the floor with their legs straight up against some expensive piece of furniture, prepared to blast into orbit and do battle with aliens or Russians.

In these instances, Mathilde was Lieutenant Maréchal, with responsibilities including navigation, weapons control, and watching for Mrs. Witherspoon when Theodorus made one of his frequent raids on the kitchen for extra snacks.

Which was something they did now.

Theodorus brought the bike to a halt outside the exterior door to the kitchen and Mathilde clambered out of the sidecar. The two of them made for the door at a dead run, but stopped short when the way was blocked by a Black man wearing a tuxedo. It was James, the butler and chief of the Witherspoons' domestic staff. He was carrying a jacket and a tie.

"Let's see the pants legs," he said, not trying too hard to hide a smile.

"I was careful," said Theodorus, turning around and putting his legs in and out like he was doing the Hokey Pokey. "No grease, see?"

"I see," said James. "Do you need me to tie this? You remember the half-Windsor knot?"

"I remember," said Theodorus, taking the tie and jacket. "I'll put this stuff on when they call us down."

Then on into the rambling kitchen, where the cook, a Black woman named Dorothy, was casting a critical eye over the nervous gaggle of catering staff who'd been brought in for the event. Mathilde waved to get Dorothy's attention and raised her eyebrows, enquiring.

"On the butcher's block, Miss Mathilde," said Dorothy.

The two of them scrambled to the far end of the kitchen and found a tray of mille-feuilles topped with toasted almonds and a dusting of confectioner's sugar. Dorothy had learned to make the complicated pastry shortly after Mathilde began visiting the estate.

"Hurry," said Theodorus. "We want to get a good start on our mission before they make us come downstairs and do boring stuff."

Malachi had recently asked Mathilde if she thought Theodorus, who would shortly turn fourteen, wasn't getting a little old for pretending. She hadn't answered him, but she'd spent a fair amount of time thinking about the answer. She'd decided that while it was possible that Theodorus behaved the way he did—Mrs. Witherspoon would have said "carried on" the way he did—either to humor her or because of some kind of lack of maturity on his own part, it was unlikely.

She remembered the first time she had ever seen him, perhaps a week after her bewildering and grief-stricken move from France to South Carolina. Her father, whom she had met in person just once before her mother's death, had told her that he was going to introduce her to other children, but that turned out to mean just a single other child, and she had seen at a glance that he was older than her, a nat, and yes, a boy. Which might have been, as the Americans said, three strikes, but Theodorus had looked up from the elaborate model train set he was working on and greeted her in clear, grammatically perfect French that somehow managed to retain his cultured Low Country drawl.

And so, the friendship and partnership that constituted Mathilde's only peer relationship began. They were both educated far beyond their years, both voracious readers, both dreamers of big, colorful, somewhat incoherent dreams having to do with their individual futures. Theodorus, of course, would somehow manage to be both a space pilot and a spy. Mathilde would be an engineer, of spaceships perhaps, sure, why not? And also possibly a spy.

They would stay friends their whole lives, despite everything; this had been solemnly sworn. It seemed impossible that anything could stop them.

Until this day, the day of a boring adult party at the Witherspoon estate in July of 1979. The day they escaped the guards at the gate and sneaked through the kitchen and up the back staircase with armloads of sandwiches and sugary drinks, bound for Mars.

The day Theodorus got sick.

The day his card turned.

Eleven years old is a very young age to tease out the difference between knowing something "intellectually" and knowing something down at the bottom of your heart.

"So you see, Mathilde," finished the man; this was a Dr. Something brought in by the Witherspoons from a northern clinic to treat Theodorus, recruited in turn by Malachi to talk to her, "the wild card simply isn't contagious in the way you're thinking. There's absolutely no way you could have infected your friend. The virus had almost certainly been present in Theodorus's genome for years, maybe even from birth—we're still running tests."

"Neither of his parents are jokers," Mathilde said quietly.

The doctor shook his head. "That doesn't really figure in, dear. The fact that both you and your father are jokers is actually somewhat unusual." He looked uncomfortable with this line of thought, and abruptly stood.

They were in the dining room of Malachi's house, and the doctor placed his hand on some papers he'd left on the table. "Your father tells me that you're a very bright little girl, so maybe this material will help you see things more clearly. They're educational pamphlets from the Van Renssaeler Clinic in New York, where Dr. Tachyon works."

Mathilde nodded, not looking at the man or at the papers, not getting up from her chair. The man awkwardly patted her on the shoulder, stood still for a moment, then left the room. A moment later, Mathilde heard the low sounds of conversation in the foyer. Malachi and the doctor, no doubt talking about her.

She considered going to the door to see if she could hear what they were saying more clearly, but when she climbed down from her chair, she found her gaze drawn to the pamphlets on the table. The one on the top showed a black-and-white photograph of the famous Dr. Tachyon, the alien from the planet Takis who had spent the last three decades trying to combat the wild card virus developed by his kinsmen. He had long hair and was wearing a hat out of a Dumas novel. He was looking out of the picture seriously, deep concern in his eyes. Printed below the picture, in large type, was a headline. SO YOU'RE A JOKER. NOW WHAT?

Mathilde brushed the pamphlet with her fingers.

It burst into flame.

"He doesn't want to see me!" Mathilde said, yet again.

Malachi looked at her from across the car's passenger area. His features were not capable of fine expressions, but she had now known him long enough to see that he was not his usual distracted, more-or-less friendly self. *Is he sad?* Mathilde wondered.

Malachi cleared his throat. "You are right. He doesn't want to see anyone. Not you, not me, not even his parents. It's been a month since the party, he's been home from the hospital in Charleston for two weeks—though why they kept him that long is a mystery, for all the good they were doing. And all that time he's insisted on being left alone, hiding away in the rooms they've set up for him off the kitchens."

Mathilde asked, "Why isn't he in his bedroom?"

Malachi looked away from her. "Do you remember Mr. Taylor, the architect who designs the buildings for Witherspoon Holdings?"

Mathilde shrugged. She was sure she'd met the man at some function or another, but didn't remember him specifically among all Malachi's colleagues.

"Mr. Taylor was at the party and saw them take Theodorus out when he was still . . . transforming. The Witherspoons took him into their confidence when they realized they were going to have to make changes to their house. He told them that he isn't sure that the second floor will support Theodorus's weight."

Malachi had been vague about the final details of Theodorus's card turning. Mathilde had been there at the beginning, of course, when the boy suddenly lurched over and cried out in pain, and began sweating profusely. She had run downstairs to find her father or Mrs. Witherspoon, anyone really, and in the ensuing commotion hadn't been allowed back in Theodorus's presence.

"What is the dark wood from Thailand?" she asked.

Malachi looked at her sharply, but not in confusion. No matter what anyone ever said or did in his presence, Mathilde had never seen Malachi react in confusion about anything. "What are you asking me?"

"The statue of the elephant in the hall outside of Theodorus's room," she answered. "He told me once that when his parents brought it back from Thailand they had to have part of the roof removed and hire a crane to lower it into the house. He told me it weighs over a thousand pounds. So the second floor will support that much weight, won't it?"

They reached the familiar iron gates. Carl was standing beside the gatehouse, clipboard in hand.

"Teak," said Malachi. Then, as Carl waved them through without stopping the car, "The dark wood from Thailand is teak."

Mathilde had never been in the warren of rooms behind the main kitchen of the Witherspoon house. They constituted their own wing, and Mathilde thought she may have overheard once that some of the people who worked for Theodorus's parents actually lived in them. Or had, she supposed, because now, it was clear nobody lived there. Nobody "natural," at least.

The parts of the ground floor of the Witherspoon house Mathilde knew were all high ceilings and hardwood floors, where it wasn't even higher ceilings and tiled or even marble floors. Once, when an elaborate plan of Theodorus's involving a slingshot and a model airplane had caused a bit of damage, Mathilde had been lectured alongside her friend about the differences between plaster and wood crown molding, and how the first required the services of a master craftsman to repair. Mathilde had been genuinely sorry for her part in the incident, but happy to learn about hand-built molds. She liked the phrase *master craftsman*.

She realized, looking where the walls of the rooms where Theodorus now lived met the low ceilings, thinking about how there was no crown molding of either plaster or wood there, that she had been standing in the doorway for quite some time. She took a deep breath.

"Theodorus?" she called.

There was no answer. She looked back into the kitchen, where Malachi was talking to the Witherspoons. Malachi saw her watching them, but no encouraging expression came across his face. He didn't gesture for her to go on. After the briefest glance, he looked away.

She walked through the room, which had been stripped down to the floorboards. There was no furniture, no curtains hung across the single window, even the carpet had been taken up. An open door, draped in a heavy sheet of plastic, led deeper into the rooms.

She pushed through the plastic and found herself in a hallway where more of the sheeting hung from every wall and lay stretched across the floor. The doors off the hallway had all been removed. Plastic sheeting, everywhere. And something else, pools and trails of some glistening substance that Mathilde carefully stepped around and over as she walked down the hall.

"Theodorus?"

Something moved behind the door farthest down the hall. Something massive.

"Go away."

Mathilde did not recognize the voice. It was deep and gurgling, liquid somehow.

"It's me," she said. *C'est moi,* she thought.

"I know it's you. But I'm not me. Not anymore. Go away. Please."

Mathilde remembered the pamphlet burning on the table in Malachi's dining room. She wondered now if she should have read it. "I am a joker, too, Theodorus. I don't care what you look like."

"You're barely a joker at all. Your skin is red, that's it. You have legs. You're normal-sized."

Mathilde thought for a moment, then said, "I am very small. Is it a bad thing to be large?"

She would never know whether he pulled the sheeting away just then, or if it gave way by happenstance, some cruel coincidence, the way that most coincidences in the lives of jokers were cruel. But it did give way, in a tumult of noise, the plastic folding down, the tacks that had held it to the ceiling and the doorframe pinging as they flew free. One of the tacks landed at her feet, coming to rest atop one of the pools of glistening not-quite-liquid.

It rolled around for a moment, then came to a stop with its sharpened point down, piercing the jellied substance. The point broke the surface, and the pool opened and swallowed the pin into its milky interior.

She looked up, and saw what her friend had become.

"He is a tremendous snail," said Mathilde, her voice still ragged from crying.

Malachi, unusually, had seated himself next to her in the back of the limousine instead of across from her, so they both rode with their backs to the driver as they returned to the city. "He is," he answered her. "And he is also a little boy."

Mathilde bristled at that. "He is almost fourteen. He is not little. I mean, not even in the way you mean."

Malachi nodded. "Yes, I suppose you are right. But if I am wrong to say he is a little boy, then you must see that you are wrong to say that he is a snail. He has arms and a face. And of course he has the same mind he always did."

"He's like a centaur," said Mathilde. "Except that where a centaur has a horse's body he has that giant whirling shell. And that . . ." She broke off, English and French both failing her.

"Foot. The bottom part of a snail's body is called a foot. And yes, a centaur is an apt metaphor. They were great scholars and warriors, you know. Fierce in their devotion to the gods."

"Do you think Theodorus is fierce?" asked Mathilde.

"I think he could be," said Malachi.

Mathilde did not see Theodorus face-to-face again for weeks and weeks after that. But it was only a few days later that Malachi brought home the first of many notes.

"What is this written with?" she asked, holding the flexible sheet covered in large, scrawled letters. "What is it written on?"

"Nothing so elegant as your little orange notebooks from Voekler Papeterie Exclusive back in La Rochelle, eh?" replied Malachi. "I think he's using some sort of outsized felt markers his mother ordered in from an art supply store. As for his stationery, I'm fairly sure that's one of the plastic place mats from the cafeteria in my office building."

She could read it plainly enough.

*I am sorry I was rude. I shouldn't have sent you away. My parents say that Doctor Tachyon himself is coming to consult on my case and I hope you can come meet him.—*T

Doctor Tachyon! The psychic alien prince! Theodorus must have been beside himself with excitement. Or at least, the old Theodorus would have been.

"When is this happening?" she asked, sure that Malachi had read the note before he gave it to her.

He looked over his newspaper, not pretending he hadn't. "Tachyon? In a few weeks. That's taken some doing. That's taken some money. That's taken some phone calls to some of the Witherspoons' most powerful friends."

Since she had come to America, Mathilde had lived in a strange world of adults who had more money and power than she'd ever imagined in France. A few tangents of thought came together—her mother taking her to see the submarine pens by the water in La Rochelle, a snatch of conversation at one particular boring party at the Witherspoon estate, money and power.

"Wasn't Mr. Witherspoon on a submarine in the Navy with the man who is president of the United States?" she asked.

Malachi looked back down at his paper. "That would be a powerful friend, now, wouldn't it?"

"*Ils me disent que vous êtes français,*" said the man from the pamphlet. He really did look like an illustration from an old adventure novel. His broad-brimmed hat, which he had swept off in the same dance-like set of motions that saw him bow to her and take one of her hands up to his lips, was light purple. It clashed violently with his yellow frock coat and green pants. His boots, at least, were black leather, polished to such a high sheen that Mathilde could see herself in their pointy toes.

"*Oui,*" she said shyly. "But I am also American."

"A woman of the world," Tachyon replied. "Destined for great things, I am sure. My dear, your skin is simply lovely." Her skin was very close to the same shade of red as his long curly hair.

They were in the kitchen, waiting for Theodorus's parents to return from talking to their son back in his new rooms. Malachi had gone into the library to make phone calls, saying something about how the Witherspoon fortunes wouldn't maintain themselves even during family crises.

Mathilde had already been told that Theodorus had not responded to any of Dr. Tachyon's treatments, at least not physically. He would remain as he was for as long as he lived. She didn't really know why the alien was still there at all, if it had taken so much to coax him down from New York.

In an effort at polite, adult-style conversation, she said, "Did you take the train here, or did you fly?"

A completely unexpected expression transformed the man's face at that. He looked delighted. He looked joyous. "Oh, child, I flew." He laughed, and said again, "I flew!"

Just then Theodorus thrust his glistening gray head and torso into the kitchen. The door was too narrow and too short for him to move his great shell through, though he must have been trying, because the wooden frame creaked and swelled. From behind, Mathilde vaguely heard his parents telling him to calm down.

"Mathilde!" he said, and for all its rumbling depth and its strange liquid vowels, Mathilde could hear joy in his voice, too. What was going on?

"Mathilde!" Theodorus shouted. "He's brought his spaceship! We're going for a ride in a spaceship!"

The architect, Mr. Taylor, had been busy at the back of the house. A ramp extended from a wide new door in the wing where Theodorus now spent his days and nights down into Mr. Witherspoon's beloved gardens. Theodorus was gliding down this as Mathilde and Doctor Tachyon rounded from the front, so they were all together when they saw . . . what they saw.

"Is it . . . a rock?" asked Mathilde, genuinely confused.

Sitting squarely in the middle of the formal English rose garden that occupied this part of the grounds was an enormous something that seemed to be made of stone, or perhaps coral. Except that it was all swirls and swooping lines, and colorful lights danced across its surface, highlighting its strangeness.

"Far from it!" said Doctor Tachyon, seeming somewhat offended. "This, children, is my personal spacecraft, and my oldest friend."

Malachi had just stepped into the doorway where Theodorus had exited. If he was concerned about what the trail Theodorus left behind him was doing to his expensive shoes, he didn't show it. The only thing he showed was a narrowing of the eyes when the alien spoke.

"It's alive?" asked Theodorus. "My father told me that was one of the theories about . . . it? Should we call it it?"

"The ship's name is Baby," said Tachyon. "And now let us aboard!"

A glowing rectangle of lines appeared on the side of the ship, and this folded down into a much stranger ramp than the one the Witherspoons' architect had built for Theodorus. Mathilde walked over and peered inside.

"It doesn't look like the inside of a spaceship," she said.

Tachyon urged her up the ramp. "But my dear, when have you ever been aboard a craft capable of interstellar flight?"

It had been at least a couple of months, if lying on Theodorus's floor with her legs propped up against the wall counted.

Theodorus made his way inside, and the three of them found themselves in an ornate chamber. The ship was as unexpected on the inside as it had been on the outside.

"It looks like a bedroom," said Theodorus, and Mathilde was learning enough about his new intonations to recognize disappointment. "Where is the command chair? Where are the navigation and piloting controls and the science station? Where is the viewport?"

Almost, almost, thought Mathilde, Doctor Tachyon almost said something dismissive. But he was still in that joyous mood that had come upon him in the kitchen. He nodded.

"Do you know, Theodorus, that this will be only the second flight I've taken since Baby was returned to me by your government? From where she was held to your home, and now this . . . this demonstration. So I am, of course, out of practice at piloting."

As he spoke the various furnishings and wall decorations that had made it look so like a bedroom began to shrink, as if they were melting into the walls and floor.

"But it sounds like you, young man, know a great deal about the subject," Tachyon said, and now things were growing out of the floor and walls and ceiling. A large screen manifested on one side and on it they could see the Witherspoons and Malachi looking up at the ship. A number of smaller screens showing planets and the sun were at either side. Toward the front, a panel crowded with a great number of buttons and levers and dials grew up to just about the height of Mathilde's waist.

"That's your station," Tachyon whispered.

Mathilde studied the controls. They were mystifying.

"And you, of course, will be here in the center." Tachyon beckoned Theodorus to a circular platform that had risen from the floor. On the edge nearest the large view screen, another panel grew, this one featuring a pair of pistol-like grips and a large red dial that was labeled VELOCITY.

Theodorus took the grips into his hands. He said, "Are we secure for takeoff, Doctor?"

Tachyon had retired to a comfortable-looking couch near Mathilde. "Aye, Captain, secure for takeoff."

"Lieutenant Maréchal," Theodorus said, "initiate main engine sequence, if you will."

Mathilde looked at her friend. She looked at the senseless jumble of controls before her.

Then, inside her head, she heard Doctor Tachyon speak quite clearly, though she knew that he had not said anything aloud at all. *Just push a button.*

So she did.

There was barely any sense of movement, but the screen showed the Witherspoon house shrinking below them. They were flying.

"We're flying," said Mathilde.

In a spaceship.

"In a spaceship," said Mathilde.

"How long do we have?" asked Theodorus. He sounded pensive, suddenly.

Tachyon shrugged. "Where do you want to go?"

"I want to go to the Moon," Theodorus said firmly.

"Ah, well, that would be quite a trip. And take too long, alas. Perhaps you will be satisfied with an orbit or two around the Earth. The planet is quite lovely, and we'll see spectacular views of the Moon as well."

Theodorus bobbed his head slowly up and down. He was nodding, Mathilde thought. She could not yet read his expressions, and she wondered if he was disappointed.

"Perhaps you'll get there someday," said Doctor Tachyon, trying to sound cheerful.

"Perhaps," said Theodorus.

They had risen so high that the curvature of the earth became apparent. It glowed blue and green. In the distance, the Moon hung like an ornament. It was all so beautiful.

"Not perhaps," Mathilde said softly, looking around at her friend, watching him watch the worlds. "Not perhaps," she said louder, and the two of them looked at her. "Definitely."

Ghost of a Chance

by Steve Perrin

ALMAZ

1980

THE LIVING HOLOGRAM THAT is Captain Yuri Serkov has been alone on the station for six months. It isn't the same as the sensory deprivation tank. There are sensors and equipment that still work even flooded with radiation. After all, they had been built to withstand the normal radiation environment of orbital space; the extra radiation will probably degrade them faster than spec, but the gear is still good for a few years.

The telemetry is still feeding back to Star City. This includes some television cameras. Yuri stays in the infrared spectrum when passing in front of the pickups, except once he moved slightly into the visual spectrum. Someone who didn't shield his mic yelled and someone else said something about ghosts. He's tempted to appear again, but so far has resisted the impulse.

He does keep the station's radar in operation. Already two American Hornet spaceplanes have made close approaches, but both turned away when they got close-range readings on the radiation emanations.

Now the approach radar shows that a Soyuz capsule is definitely on an interception course with the radioactive Almaz station. It is reaching visual range. Yuri shrugs and moves his body toward the *Almaz 4* section, with the spacewalking air lock. If someone is coming to inspect, they will probably be sent over on a line, rather than bring the Soyuz into the center of the spilling radiation.

The station rocks slightly and he realizes the Soyuz is actually docking at *Almaz 4*. Surprising. The radiation should have screwed up the automatic docking program by now. Obviously the shielding is more efficient or the programming more robust than he has assumed.

Not at all sure of his reception in his current form, Yuri tries a trick he came up with after a few weeks of experimentation. Looking at himself in the lounge's mirror, he sees himself fade from sight. Finally all he can see is the infrared signature rebounding from the mirror surface. As far as he knows, he now only exists as an infrared hologram. Of course, all he can detect now is infrared, so he can be sitting out in plain sight in all his naked glory but only be able to see in infrared.

The port cycles open and a woman in a space suit enters. Yuri hears her radio statement: "The station is in vacuum." She flips a switch near the port and some objects floating free in the station section start moving away from the air vents. Yuri keeps still and listens. The radio reception is full of radiation static, but the voice seems familiar.

"There is still atmosphere in the system," she reports and moves farther into the section, obviously not seeing Yuri. As she passes him, enough heat emanates from her suit to give him some idea of her identity, but Yuri can't quite place the memory.

The next entry through the port is a figure in a bulked-up space suit with reinforcement in the joints and boots. The figure manages to float ponderously. His voice is as heavy as his form. "I, Major Constantin Radianskyev, take command of the Almaz Space Defense Station."

Major Constantin Radianskyev, code name Lead Man (Vedushchiy). Yuri recalls him, a Star Gifted who is theoretically not affected by radiation because his bones and other organs are like lead. Radianskyev is a common soldier picked for the cosmonaut program purely because he survived handily when an entire regiment died of various kinds of radiation poisoning when they volunteered to be subjects of a bomb test.

Volunteers? Right, thinks Yuri as he remembers Radianskyev. The man is large and sullen. His current rank was brevetted onto him when he joined the cosmonaut corps. Before the revelation of his Star Gift he had been an Army corporal. As an Army officer, he resents all the Air Force officers and even the civilians in the program. As a newly minted major he tends to push his weight around, and since he is made of lead, he has a lot of weight to push.

Rumor in Star City has it that the psychers portrayed Constantin as a reluctant cosmonaut and not terribly bright. However, he proved a natural at maneuvering spacecraft.

As the station fills with air, the female cosmonaut removes her helmet. Yuri sees that she has two noses and two toes on her face and head. Now Yuri knows who she is.

Major Anya Vetsenyenk, code name Many Toes (*Mnogo pal'tsev nogi*), has the Star Gift of a body that resists mutation by turning cancer cells into new internal and external organs that function. She was already a cosmonaut trainee when she got her code name; the first manifestation was toes that grew all over her body when she was exposed to radiation while working on a ground-side satellite. Yuri smiles at the memory. Many Toes was an active bedmate before he was assigned to the satellite project. The extra parts are often sensitive in exotic ways and Anya readily explores all the ramifications.

Since then other organs grew on inappropriate parts of her anatomy, turning a reasonably pretty girl into the start of a monstrous freak—though still enthusiastic, as Yuri knows. Yet nothing grows where it can cause ill effects to her body's functioning, and working weightless probably takes away many of the possible difficulties her situation can provide.

Yuri watches as the two move into the body of the station. Obviously, Star City had decided that the station is still needed, so these radiation-resistant cosmonauts have been sent. Yuri decides he doesn't want to expose his existence just yet.

Yuri left his space suit in the last section of *Almaz 5,* where he stepped out of it. He thought about moving it to some other part of the station, but to move it he would have to get back inside and become solid, and he is not ready to risk the effects of radiation on his material form.

Anya finds the suit as she explores *Almaz 5* and dogs shut the inner door of the port, which Yuri had never bothered to close. Yuri follows her and picks up her radio message to Constantin. "I have found Yuri's space suit. There is nothing inside!"

"He probably got out of it and jumped off into space when he realized he was as good as dead. His body is probably pacing the station somewhere out there." Constantin sounds just as happy not to have to deal with a body.

"But it is still intact! It hasn't been opened." Anya is starting to sound a bit hysterical.

"Are you sure it is Serkov's suit?"

"How can it be anyone else's? And it has his name on it."

Yuri wonders, *Am I actually a ghost, then? No, then my body would be in the suit. It's the Star Gift—I just never knew the extent of it.*

As Anya and Constantin continue to shout at each other over the radio, Yuri drifts away. He has already figured out that he isn't actually moving as a material person does. He is essentially projecting his image, and he has already mastered the very slow-drifting projection that looks like a cosmonaut in a weightless environment, assuming anyone can see him.

The two Star Gifted cosmonauts settle into a routine. Yuri is amused and gratified that Constantin seems to have no interest in Anya sexually, or for that matter in any other way. The lead in his bones seems to make him even more surly and solitary than Yuri remembers him back in Star City. He spends most of his time initially making the adjustments to the reactor that Star City mandated to lower the level of radiation, though it cannot be reduced to a livable level for normal people, what the Americans call "nats."

After that is done to their masters' satisfaction, he spends his time studying the maneuver controls and creating targets to send out a port and shoot at with the 20 mm cannons. The station periodically shakes with the recoil of the guns. After a month of this, the cannon on *Almaz 3* breaks some of its brackets, giving Constantin the job of spacewalking to reweld them. After that cosmonaut control tells him to restrict his practice to once a week. They can't forbid it, since that is one of the reasons the station exists, after all.

On the other hand, Anya apparently likes her assignment despite the hostility of her station mate. They do not fight. She maintains life support and communications, having discovered several tricks to deal with the ongoing radiation's effects on the station's delicate electronics.

For three weeks, Yuri ghosts around the station, maintaining his body in infrared status so he is not noticed. He is slowly getting weaker. He does not feel hungry in this state, but maintaining the condition wearies him. How can he restore his energy? The only way he can think of is to return to corporeality and eat something, but the crew has no real eating schedule. The only established pattern is to not be in the same place at the same time. He needs one of the crewmen to realize he is sharing the station with them. The crew person best suited is obvious.

Yuri finds Anya floating in front of the proximity radar monitor. She spends a lot of time there, looking for threatening space junk. Checking that Constantin is wrapped up in his sleeping cocoon, Yuri moves to a spot behind Anya and assumes visibility. Still immaterial, he makes no immediate impression, until Anya notices his faint reflection in the monitor screen.

She gives a disgusted snort and spins around. "Constantin, I told you—" She then stops, confronted by a vaguely familiar stranger more ghost than man. "Who? How?"

Yuri replies over the earphones she is wearing. He moves his lips in sync with the image. "*Das Vedanya,* little Many Toes. It is your Mattress Man, Yuri."

"No, impossible. Yuri is dead. I was just looking for his body." She takes a breath, then asks, "Are you a ghost?" She swings her arm out, intersecting his image in the close space, bracing herself on the Earth camera with a practiced move to keep from spinning. She squeals when her arm passes through the image without stopping. "You don't look like Yuri."

He doesn't, of course. For some reason his body image in energy form looks like what Yuri might look like if he had not received the Star Gift. He is still essentially hairless—but many cosmonauts remove most of their body hair. Yuri thinks for a moment. After all, the energy form is an image, and images can be manipulated. Anya watches in wonder as the image before her widens out, turns in place to show a diminished cross section, and comes back to a flattened image with an all-too-familiar smile. "Do you recognize Mattress Man now, little caterpillar?"

It is probably the use of an endearment known only to the two of them, rather than Yuri's attempt to simulate his material body in light image, that convinces her. "But Yuri, we found your space suit. . . ."

"Without me in it, yes? And if you have been looking for my drifting body outside the station, you have not had any success, yes?" As she nods, he continues, "Apparently my Star Gift was not fully realized on Earth. Here, I find that I can be matter, or energy, as I wish."

"So you can be your old self?" she asks winsomely.

"I've done so, briefly. Unlike you and Constantin, I am not immune to the deadly effects of the radiation filling the station." He pauses, then decides he might as well go for his primary goal. "Besides the chance to be with you again, my dear, I have a problem that you can solve for me." She cocks her head, and he can see that she has added an additional ear behind the one she had been born with. "Whatever energy form or material I assume, I cannot help but emit energy. I must replenish myself. But I do not think that Constantin should know of my presence. The only way I know I can replenish my energy is by eating in my material form. I must eat, but his meal schedule is mostly notable for being irregular. I don't want to be caught with my head in the food locker."

"And what do I get for my trouble playing lookout, and perhaps interceptor, while you raid our delicious food tubes?"

"Is there still no evidence of anyone having sex in space?" Yuri asks with a sly grin that Anya recognizes from times in Star City.

"As far as I know. Unless some Star Gift had an independent experiment."

"Well, then, we owe it to science."

"I live to serve Soviet science."

Yuri's best ally in keeping his presence from Constantin is Constantin himself. Rampant speculation back at Star City is that he had a lot of lead in his system already from tainted water in the collective he had been raised in, so the Star Gift had just followed the line of least resistance to turn him into Lead Man. There were a number of other, less flattering, code names the man had earned during the time Yuri and he had both been in Star City. Yuri had not been part of the name-creation process, but has used the fruits of the process on many occasions.

In the station, Constantin does as little as possible. He knows he is virtually irreplaceable—Star Gifted who can ignore radiation are few and far between. He spends most of his spare time practicing with the 20 mm cannon, mostly dry firing with the laser sight against trash he evacuates from the air locks. Occasionally he manages to persuade someone on the ground to put more ammunition in the Progress resupply capsules.

"Take that, Imperialist star pigs," he shouts when he succeeds in hitting the targets, while the station shudders with the recoil.

Avoiding Constantin is fairly simple, especially with Anya standing lookout to warn if the massive ex-soldier is suddenly feeling peckish. And when Constantin wraps himself in his sleep cocoon to take one of his frequent naps, she has other plans for Yuri.

As far as anyone knows, sex in space has not yet been attempted. Cosmonauts and astronauts alike sleep in cocoons that resemble the venerable "mummy bag" familiar to outdoorsy folks all over the world. These are hung from secure points and bind the occupant tightly to make sure a flailing limb doesn't suddenly evacuate all the air out of the station.

Telemetry on the cocoons lets ground control know that the sleeping bag has been occupied and sealed. Because Anya's Star Gift can mean she needs a new bag at unscheduled moments, her bag is a bit larger than normal, and she is under strict instructions to keep the bag away from easily jostled equipment. Once sealed the bag telemetry turns off until the bag is unsealed again.

Smiling slyly, Anya seals the cocoon. Altering his form to infrared, Yuri insinuates himself into the bag. Initially all Anya feels is warmth, then a strange itching sensation as the warmth turns into a warm living creature. The bag is large, but Yuri's Flat Man form bows it out. Careful placement puts his hands in the right places as they materialize, made easier because Anya's erogenous zones increase with her extra organs and protrusions.

"Oh, Yuri, it has been so long."

"For you? At least you had some company."

"The Lead Head? I can barely get a word out of him, much less a friendly regard." She giggles. "They used to say everything on him turned to lead except his pencil, and I think there is more truth than humor in that."

"I remember similar speculation in Star City when I arrived," says Yuri. "There was a pool about whether my 'pencil' was too two-dimensional to do the job."

   "I think we proved them wrong," Anya says as she confirms that Yuri's pencil is ready. Yuri smiles and kisses her and licks behind both left ears. No sense re-marking that Anya is not the only lady of Star City who discovered the rumors were wrong.

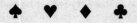

Have Spaceship, Will Travel

by Michael Cassutt

IT WASN'T MUCH OF a fair, as fairs go.

Maybe it was the time of year—mid-May, too early for summer fun even in the South—or the weather, which was rainy, or the crowd, which was dispirited, but Morehead, Kentucky, was an unpleasant event.

And after the past eight years of appearances at such events up, down, and all across this great land of ours, I have become an expert on the subject.

The big state fairs are predictably worthwhile, but I've also appeared at the Houston Livestock Show and Rodeo, which is not to be missed even if you don't know a steer from a cow, and the Big Duchess in New York, the Florida Strawberry Festival, and the York Fair in Pennsylvania.

What makes a good fair? You want food, of course, music, thrilling rides, amusing feats of skill and strength, intriguing sideshows, and girls girls girls of both nat and sexy joker blend.

Also unique and theoretically informative presentations. Some deal with the wild card, of course, others with various aspects of human behavior and accomplishment.

Which is where I came in: Cash Mitchell, with the one and only, can't-be-seen-anywhere-else, check-out-my-posters-proclaiming:

THIS WAY TO THE MOON SPACESHIP!
FIRST FLIGHT TO THE MOON!

I was winding up my spiel. "So there we were, stuck on the Moon in this very vehicle." I pointed at the big teardrop-shaped craft looming behind me.

The hoochie dancers were clicking their heels on the stage not far away and some god-awful music was playing as I told the story of our daring liftoff and clandestine return to Earth, all in December 1968, over a dozen years ago.

There was some applause, but people were drifting away before I got the spaceship *Quicksilver,* my two fellow travelers, Eva-Lynne Roderick and Mike Sampson, and me halfway back to Earth.

My associate Ridley Hough walked over from the milk-bottle break. He was ten years older than me, past fifty, though given his weathered look—think a chunk of beef jerky in human form, and no, not a joker—it was hard to tell. At the moment he was carrying a stuffed Takisian.

"Seriously? How many times have I told you, we're here to make money, not spend it."

You'd think I slapped him. "It only cost a dollar."

"Did you tell them you used to pitch semipro?"

"They didn't ask."

Well, why would they? "Time to close down the operation." Ridley nodded and headed into the darkness toward our truck and RV.

Even though it had rained most of the weekend, the clouds had just begun to part, leaving Morehead with a lovely evening in late spring. With the end of the awful fair music, you could hear birds and some kind of cricket chirping.

There was also a full moon on the rise.

I'm a sucker for a full moon.

Which may be why I lingered in the midway as late fairgoers headed for their vehicles, making myself a big fat target.

I had no warning, just found myself with a light in my face. All I could make out was one squat individual who cast a toad-like shadow. And spoke, "Cash Mitchell! How can you claim to have flown to the Moon?"

I shaded my eyes so that I could see that this toad held a camera with a microphone. "Say what?" Okay, I'm not reflexively witty.

"You've been making money off this claim for a dozen years. How do you justify it?"

"The truth is my best defense. I did indeed fly to the Moon in 1968."

"But there's no proof."

"Are you intelligent? No proof of that, either." This was not the first time my story had been challenged.

I put my hand on the camera and shoved it aside. So yes, officer, I did that much. And then this squat creature shoved me. Yes, hand on my chest.

So I balled up a fist and swung at him, connecting somewhere near his right ear, I think. It was about chest high for me. I felt the usual glancing contact, heard a slappy kind of thud, and had the satisfaction of seeing the creature recoil, performing a cute little stagger, grubby hand to his face as he screamed, "You attacked me! Now I've got it on film!"

I kept walking, but this pest followed me with his camera, saying, "You saw it all, ladies and gentlemen—when confronted with the truth, Cash Mitchell, who has been traveling the country for years claiming he was first on the Moon—"

I stopped. "Not true. One of the first. There were three of us. You could look it up, if you had any sense."

This joker, four foot five, squat, green where I could tell, and wearing some kind of goddamn coverall as if he should be changing oil at a filling station, kept hopping up and down. "There's no proof! Space Command has never confirmed it!"

"Because they're embarrassed. We borrowed one of their vehicles and made it do things they hadn't thought of."

"You never bothered to take pictures, collect samples—"

"No time. We were lucky to get back alive."

"How convenient."

"There are a few lunar dust samples floating around. But you're not interested in the truth."

"Oh, I am. And you've been selling lies."

"You'd think I'd be better at it. I'm working county fairs and living in an RV. Does that look like some master con man?"

I kept walking, but the troll dogged me. "What's your name, anyway?" I said.

"Bertram Neal."

"And you work for . . ."

"I'm freelance."

"So no better off than me."

"A lot better off when I sell the footage of your attack on me."

Now I had to face him. And I couldn't help smiling. "Oh, you silly shit. No one cared about humans going to the Moon in 1968. The planet had been attacked by space aliens twenty-two years earlier!

"And no one cares now. Every time I show people the ship and start telling my story, it might as well be some Wild West story about fighting Indians."

I could see my RV fifty yards off. Safety.

Neal seemed to be considering his situation. He surely thought he could get me on an assault charge, but he wasn't the first doubter who had confronted me—or I'd punched—in ten years of fairs and school events. I could prove aggravation and justification . . . if he used his film as evidence it might actually work against him.

I thought I was free when behind me, he said, "Whatever happened to Eva-Lynne?"

I tried to get away, but this made me turn back. "She is none of your business."

"Word is she's a junkie whore in California. If she'd really gone to the Moon, would she be blowing truck drivers—"

He never finished the question because I grabbed him by the throat. My deuce ability, aka heavy lifting, works by contact and pressure; I was restrained enough to simply lift Neal high and fast and, okay, a bit roughly—then let him fly.

Momentum carried him into a magnolia tree, where he was embraced by branches and leaves with a satisfying crunching rustle. I left him hanging there and put many yards between us as fast as I could.

I had barely started up the RV when a flatbed roared up, its headlights blinding me. As the big beast idled roughly, making me think it was overdue for service, Ridley dropped out of the cab. "We're supposed to be halfway to Memphis by now," I said. Which was an exaggeration, but Ridley was definitely supposed to be well out of Morehead.

"One of the guys said a reporter was after you. Thought you might need help."

"Well, the reporter did."

Ridley turned to follow my eyeline toward the magnolia tree across the parking lot, where Neal's form cast a shadow against the evening sky. "We better make tracks."

"I think Memphis is the wrong way to go."

"I'll follow you east," he said. He had made two steps toward the flatbed when he turned back. "What do we do about the date in Memphis?"

"I'll call and postpone when we get across the state line."

I'm a deuce. I've always believed I should use my ability for good, or rather practical reasons. Especially when it might get me into legal trouble.

But launching that squat little fucker into the distance was worth it.

You see, I had this spaceship.

You may know the story if you have any interest in what steps humans took in space independent of the Takisians. How for one week in December 1968, all of America was united in pride and wonder as three of its citizens rode a modified *Quicksilver* orbital space fighter to the surface of the Ocean of Storms, and then back again.

Well, it didn't happen like that. The *Quicksilver* flight by Major Mike Sampson, Eva-Lynne Roderick, and me did take place—we did indeed reach the Moon. Two of us even walked on it.

But we returned to silence. Several members of our ground crew knew, of course, but they operated under harsh if informal nondisclosure agreements. (The whole *Quicksilver* endeavor had its origins in the shady activities of a former associate of mine, a Mr. Tuominbang, who sadly died under mysterious circumstances right around the time of our flight. How that happened is a tale I have written up; you might be able to find a paperback in some used bookstore.)

But if you take the not-invented-here aspect of our mission, the fact that a deuce (me) was involved, and throw in those ties to Asian criminal jokers—well, the important parties were happy to see the Moon story remain undiscussed.

And let *Quicksilver* turn brown in the harsh Mojave sunlight in its final resting place in the Tomlin salvage yard.

The Air Force museum in Ohio sure didn't want it.

It was my fault. Up to the *Quicksilver* flight I had been employed by a Mr. Warren Skalko of Lancaster/Los Angeles/Las Vegas, best known as the Mojave Mob Boss. I can say this now: Mr. Skalko was indeed at the heart of several nefarious enterprises, from narcotics, gambling, and protection down to automobile thefts (with chop shops). I had been involved in the latter. With the fame—short-lived and sad as it was—that came my way, however, Mr. Skalko gently terminated our association. I may have been the first person to have left his employ alive, in fact.

Sampson transferred to the Pentagon in 1973, but before he did, he hit on this notion: "You can make *Quicksilver* fly."

"Sure," I said, "I have and could again. But no one wants me to."

"Kids might. Schools do all kinds of show-and-tell programs."

What he had in mind was for me to take *Quicksilver* on the road, setting up in various locations and telling my tale.

And by God, Sampson delivered, arranging for me to "lease" the *Quicksilver* vehicle for one dollar per year indefinitely. He even got me a grant large enough to buy an RV and a flatbed to haul the spaceship.

It was my purchase of the flatbed that led to a partnership with Ridley Hough. I had known of him prior to *Quicksilver* as one of Mr. Skalko's wheelmen, drivers, loaders. His story, and you never heard it from him, was that he had a joker family he was supporting back in Wisconsin.

I do know that Ridley was tight with money and sent a portion of his income elsewhere.

For the last eight years, then, Ridley and I have traveled this great land of ours, forty weeks or more each year, showing yokel audiences, largely children, more at county fairs than at schools.

It was a tough life in most ways. Never much money, and long hours of open road. On the other hand, there were the occasional joys of seeing young people and even some middle-aged and elderly people, nats, aces, and jokers, brighten to the tale of this happy moment in their history. I doubt that any of them ever again looked at a full moon the same way. . . .

Sampson arranged for me to wear a nifty blue Air Force Space Command jumpsuit, too, complete with mission patches, and a unique *Quicksilver* patch that a student in Amarillo designed for me in 1978.

Eva-Lynne is not part of the story. So far.

We were across the Big Sandy and into West Virginia within an hour, too fast for local law enforcement to really act on Neal's complaint, assuming they did. There is deuce-on-deuce violence that, in my vast experience, your basic cop or sheriff tends to discount.

If they wanted to run me down for assault, there was a chance they'd call ahead to law near the border with West Virginia, but they would probably look west first—or into Ohio, where Ridley and I had just been.

Years of travel on a budget had given Ridley and me a good idea of where to lay low, that being our usual mode of travel. There was a north-south road just past the Big Sandy, and I took that rather than continue on to the metropolis of Huntington a few miles farther down the highway. We turned south and found a trailer park just outside of Neal.

Parking my RV was no big deal, but stashing the big rig with *Quicksilver* was a greater challenge. Leaving it at a truck stop was stupid; even just leaving it on some little-traveled roadside would guarantee questions, eventually.

Thanks to a conversation with Mrs. Bonnie Keithley of the Neal RV park, we found a hiding place in a barn owned by her cousin, or so the tale went. In memory of my working methods from the Skalko days, I offered Mrs. Keithley a bit of cash; it worked the way it always does.

We had *Quicksilver* hidden before ten that night and had grabbed some takeout from the one crossroads diner.

Feeling relatively safe, if a bit unsure about how to continue the tour, we bunked down for the night.

From the beginnings of my tenure with Mr. Skalko in 1966 as a lad of twenty-four, I have had trouble sleeping. Wise moralists will nod and say, of course, you were a petty criminal. In fact, I had already done a bit of not-so-petty criminalizing since dropping out of college, and slept just fine then. I blame age.

So it was no surprise that I awoke well before dawn and smelled bacon frying—Ridley making his amazingly hearty (given his thinness) breakfast.

And a voice on the radio, some local news guy talking about a "police manhunt in four states."

I could see the look on Ridley's face—never especially happy, this morning it was unusually grim. "That can't be about us," I said.

Ridley was always reluctant to contradict anyone directly. Except now. "They mentioned you by name. Said you were probably driving an RV."

"Nothing about you?"

He sighed. "Oh, I was mentioned. Ridley Hough, last known residence Palmdale, California." He actually seemed flattered. "And our other truck."

"God, they make us sound like felons or fugitives."

"And because you stood up for decency and fairness." Ridley was not, as a rule, sarcastic, so I took this as offered. I was aware that if one investigated, one might find a record of my California offenses—no convictions, I am proud to note, but a number of charges under the general heading of theft. And a couple of assaults.

"I didn't kill the guy. He had to have survived in order to identify me."

"Well, another station says this guy's father is lieutenant governor."

That clarified matters. Here was the joker prince phenomenon, where a nat parent goes overboard to protect and coddle a joker son.

At that moment I heard a siren and even saw flashing lights—a law enforcement vehicle racing down the highway toward "downtown" Neal.

It passed by, and as soon as it vanished, Ridley said, unnecessarily, "They'll be back."

"And we ought to be gone. West Virginia's full of hills and hollows and people who don't like law enforcement." I was also thinking the smart play might be to double back into Kentucky. You will note that turning myself in was not a consideration.

Before either of us could take the next step, there was a knock on the trailer door.

At that moment my eagerness for fight or flight disappeared. Ridley and I were unarmed in an RV; we weren't going to get into a shoot-out. "Well," I said, "so much for that scheme."

I opened the door expecting to see two state troopers in Smokey hats. What I saw instead was a fat, hunchbacked joker in a suit that probably cost more than I make in six months. His skin was gray, his eyes, lips, and nasal slits black. He had no nose. "Mr. Cash Mitchell?" he said. "My name is Malachi Schwartz. I believe I can offer some help with your current situation, if we can get out of here with some dispatch."

Then he spotted my uneaten breakfast: "May I?"

Even though he ate like a man discovering cooked food, Schwartz managed to share a considerable amount of information. "Your Mr. Neal is in a coma."

"That's impossible," I said. "I launched him into a tree. He was hanging there in the branches and moving."

"Apparently he hit his head when he fell." He was examining *Quicksilver,* the flatbed truck, and the RV, and shaking his head at the hobo nature of things.

"And no one blamed the people trying to get him out of the tree."

"That would surely be explored in a trial, but that's a long way off. And one would hope . . . never to happen."

"Why are you here?"

He dabbed at his mouth with a napkin. "I am offering you a, well, a private engagement. To display your vehicle and demonstrate its abilities, as you have been doing for years. And possibly to perform some . . . related educational duties."

"Educational for whom and how long?"

"The whom we can discuss, but I assure you there is nothing illegal or especially challenging about the engagement."

"Fine, how much?"

"An amount equal to three weeks of your current rate . . . shall we say $1,500?"

Fruits of my association with Mr. Skalko: Never take the first offer, even if they have a gun to your head. "Three," I said. "And ten percent up front, as in now."

Schwartz actually looked a bit nervous. "I believe time is of the essence here, Mr. Mitchell."

"There's always time for a back-and-forth between gentlemen."

Schwartz reached for his wallet and opened it, allowing me to see an impressive number of bills. He removed half a dozen fifties. Which left twice that many. He handed the money to me, and I handed four of the bills to Ridley. "Is Mr. Hough your treasurer?"

"I don't like to carry money, since I can't seem to hold on to it." Hence the ironic origin of my name. (I am not going to reveal my birth name, since I loathe it.)

"Are we done?" he said. I nodded. Schwartz rubbed his hands together. "Now to create some magic."

Within minutes we had the tarp off *Quicksilver.* Even though we were largely in shadows inside the barn, the big old teardrop definitely showed its age . . . rough patches on its formerly shiny skin like liver spots on an eighty-year-old.

But it was still unique—one of three originally built, the other two long gone—and impressive. Its successors, Space Command Hornets, were zipping to and from Earth orbit every week, but *Quicksilver* reeked of real accomplishment, history, and human history, too. (It also reeked of oil, mildew, and rust.)

Or so it seemed to me whenever I saw her. Of course, this might have been the result of proclaiming that story for the better part of a decade. I have reached the age where the legend has been repeated so often that it has become my history.

And that would include my time with Eva-Lynne.

"What sort of information do you need in order to lift this vehicle to a location near Charleston, South Carolina?"

"Well, I managed to find the Moon—"

"Be serious, Mitchell." He was losing patience. So I told him that most of my lifts were short distances—literally from one point to another I could see. "Cross-country is trickier, but I can take us to a thousand feet and use visual flight rules to avoid planes."

Schwartz closed his eyes for a moment and actually appeared to be talking to himself. Then he said, "I can guide you."

"You're coming along?"

"Yes, and Mr. Hough, too."

"What about our vehicles?"

"They can be retrieved later, and so can my auto. If confiscated, you will be compensated. How much time do you need before takeoff?" He seemed agitated.

"Ten minutes," I said.

"Eight of them trying to remember what button to push," Ridley said, one of his automatic and blessedly rare jokes. Inaccurate, too: the only buttons deal with interior lights. I, Cash Mitchell, am the power.

"You'd better get aboard then," Schwartz said.

Ever practical, Ridley said, "I'll grab our gear." And ran into the RV.

It was a quick climb up the ladder to the truck bed. The *Quicksilver* hatch had not been designed to lock—you wouldn't expect car thieves in Earth orbit or on the Moon. However, this fine nation of ours is rife with such persons, so Ridley had welded a padlock to the hatch. Unlocking it was the operation that consumed several minutes. Then I was inside, finding the light switch and working my way forward to the cockpit and its three cramped seats.

To my momentary consternation, Schwartz took the copilot seat, leaving Ridley to crowd into the jump seat, two small duffels in his arms.

I grabbed the lift tiller—specially installed for me back in December 1968, to improve my vital contact with the object to be lifted.

And out and up we went, the pocket of farmland, the local roads, and soon the whole collection of wooded hollows dropping away.

Only then did it strike me that this launch might be observed.

Just as there were finite limits on how much I could lift, I could not go supersonic with *Quicksilver,* or anything close to that, and had to poke along at something between a hundred and two hundred miles an hour.

The trip required almost constant lifting, too. I could release my grip and let the vehicle drop a bit, but by and large I was in for a workout. It was especially tricky going over the Appalachians . . . in a rainstorm.

I had no memory of the highest peak in that range, nor its location, but realized that I had to be much higher than 1,000 feet to avoid danger. With a considerable amount of sweating and cursing I nudged *Quicksilver* up to 7,500 feet and above the clouds, even as Schwartz peered out the forward window in something close to terror. And Ridley dozed.

Eventually, after what seemed like several hours though likely was not more than twenty minutes, the skies cleared and I judged that I was now over northern North Carolina, which Schwartz confirmed.

He wisely realized that I had no mental space or energy for chat, so left me to my own musings on missteps I had made in my life and career. Those that took place prior to the age of thirty would consume a notable amount of brain time, but I chose to concentrate on the last dozen years—the sad end of my marriage to Eva-Lynne, the multiple business failures, and have I mentioned the drinking?

I haven't had a drink since I started on the road with Ridley. (We met in A.A. He's my sponsor.)

I also spent a few moments fretting about Ridley and Schwartz. My partner was uncomfortable around jokers, and Malachi Schwartz, with his gray skin and hunched back, would be a test of his tolerance just on appearance alone. The fact that he was an arrogant bean counter would only make things worse.

An hour in I realized that this was now the second-longest *Quicksilver* flight in its history—since returning from the Moon in December 1968. I had moved the vehicle frequently, off and back onto the truck at every stop, but none of those hops lasted longer than ten minutes.

"We are on approach, Mr. Mitchell. Well done. In a few moments I will ask you to turn to the west."

The terrain had changed from fields and woods to tidal plains. It was getting on toward late afternoon, and the clouds had rolled in as I flew over old plantations and new suburbs. The city center was spread before me, a twisty collection of peninsulas and docksides. I could even see the old Fort Sumter out in the harbor.

"Anytime," I said to Schwartz. I was feeling seriously weak, too, and not sure I could hold *Quicksilver* aloft for much longer. And that was if my bladder held.

"Now. You will be crossing the Ashley River there."

We bore west, crossing said river into genuine plantation land. We were still well off the ground, so I wasn't able to appreciate the ancient magnolias, fine old gates, mansions, and whatnot. Not that my mood allowed for that.

Schwartz guided me to a lower route that took us up a private lane, right through an impressive open gate that featured a wrought iron *W*.

"What's the *W* for?"

"Witherspoon. The family that will be hosting you."

"Does this place have a name?"

"It was known for a century as Dayton Place, Dayton being Mrs. Witherspoon's maiden name."

"So she had a bit of family money."

From the look on Schwartz's face, you'd think I commented on the Witherspoons' sex life. "To descend into the vulgar, and frankly none of your business, zone, both of the Witherspoons come from families with long, fruitful histories here in Charleston."

"My apologies."

We flew over a flagstone parkway of sorts in front of an honest-to-god three-story mansion straight out of *Gone with the Wind*.

Beyond that, surrounding another parkway, were several outlying buildings—a garage on one side and a two-story guesthouse on the other. At Schwartz's direction, I landed *Quicksilver* in front of the garage, next to a huge flower bed.

We popped the hatch and, with considerable grunting and groaning, exited into a flood of fragrance. Whatever might be said of the Witherspoon estate—and I would have issues with it—it smelled pleasant.

Schwartz gestured. "You will sleep in the guest quarters. You can take your meals in the kitchen there." He pointed to an entrance at the rear of the main house. "Tomorrow we will begin at eight."

"Do that," I said, reaching for the door to the RV. "I'll be there at nine."

My dramatic exit was spoiled by Ridley. "Hey, what's that up there?"

He pointed to the roof, where a strange silhouette stood out against the setting sun. The being was reaching for some kind of cylinder mounted on a tripod, itself on some strange-looking platform.

"That," Schwartz announced, "is Master Theodorus."

The guesthouse was large, but most rooms seemed to be occupied. An African American man of about fifty, James by name and clearly one of the senior Witherspoon staff, directed Ridley and me to a small upstairs room.

The first thing I noticed was a shelf of books, someone's cherished Civil War collection—Catton, Freeman, Foote. And even what appeared to be a first edition, in two volumes, of the *Personal Memoirs of U. S. Grant*. I've done a lot of reading during my road years, and the Civil War is a frequent subject, often because Ridley and I found ourselves near battlefields and monuments. At that moment, however, the collection only reminded me that this guesthouse had probably housed slaves. And that the Witherspoon fortune had almost certainly depended on slave labor.

There were also bunk beds. Ridley threw his duffel on the top, but I grabbed it. "My turn," I said. Bad enough that he had been caught up in my current mess. "You heard what Schwartz said about that Neal guy?"

"Yeah."

"You're involved, too."

He shrugged, as if this happened every week. I said, "I have to lie low, but you could get Schwartz or someone to drop you in town. I'll give you the rest of my money and you could vanish."

"Nah," he said. "I'm still working for you."

"Even though this isn't our usual job, and you might wind up in jail."

He grinned, this time in resignation mode. "Still better than what I've got back home."

I can't speak for Ridley, who in sleep could be taken for dead, but I had a good night for a fugitive from justice in a top bunk. The Witherspoon estate was blessedly quiet, a nice change from the freeway noise or trash pickups that normally cursed my evenings.

As Ridley and I staggered out of our quarters the next day, it was clear that my threat to appear late wasn't something I could hold to: I was hungry.

We emerged into a cloudy, muggy morning. Daylight allowed us to appreciate the extensive renovations performed on the Witherspoon mansion: the roof had been modified to create an actual platform—the one that the so-far-mysterious Theodorus had used last night—and there was a two-story addition ten feet across that I quickly judged to be an elevator shaft.

"Lotta work here," Ridley said. He seemed to approve.

An open garage revealed an old car in the middle of a remodeling. "What is that, Ridley?" If he didn't know a car, it wasn't worth asking about.

"Used to be a Duesenberg, I think, 1937–38. Not sure what it is now."

We presented ourselves at the kitchen door, knocking.

No answer. Repeated the knocking. Nothing.

So I opened the door, into a pantry. Ridley followed me through to the biggest kitchen I've ever seen, dominated by a huge central workspace or island.

And occupied by a short, somewhat stout African American woman in her fifties, I judged. She was scrambling eggs, though she turned enough to look us over as if we were selections in the meat section of a grocery. "You must be Mitchell and Hough," she said. "I'm Dorothy and I am the cook. We make breakfast, lunch, and dinner here. I will assume you are here for all three, unless you tell me otherwise. I do appreciate at least an hour's notice of any absence. I hate to waste food."

She stirred the eggs into a bowl. "Toast? Bacon? Coffee is over there, and we operate on the help-yourself system."

Ridley and I both nodded eagerly and accepted full plates. We were headed to the dining room when she said, "Hold on."

We froze. "You're the help, like me. You eat in there." She nodded to a small dining area, table for four. Nice windows.

"Really?"

"Count your blessings, young man."

I didn't really resent being shunted to the servants' area, since I had a good sense of my place in the Witherspoon ménage.

I really wanted to see a newspaper, however. Wasn't sure how I would arrange that.

We had just sat down and eaten perhaps two bites each when Malachi Schwartz materialized. He was wearing a fresh suit several shades lighter than yesterday's. It occurred to me that the weather in Charleston might be uncomfortable, not that I had many clothing options. "Good, you've had your meal," he said, prematurely. "Come with me."

With Schwartz as our escort, Ridley and I were allowed into the rest of the house.

Which consisted of a spectacular dining room just beyond the kitchen, an enormous foyer and staircase, and what appeared to be a living room the size of a small village. The ground floor clearly contained other rooms, too, and I could only imagine what the upper floors were like.

Notably, it appeared that every entrance had been modified—widened. There was a pungent odor in the house, too, a mixture of turpentine and something unidentifiable.

As we toured, Schwartz insisted on telling us all about the paint and furniture and wallpaper and history of these rooms. I don't remember much of it, but the terms Queen Anne and antebellum were mentioned frequently.

He did not discuss the improvements.

I had other priorities, saying, as quietly as possible, "Any news about us?"

"Oh, a considerable amount," Schwartz said, then damned if he didn't resume his travelogue.

I may have stepped in front of him at that moment. "I need to know."

He raised his head. "Let's just say that you are sought . . . but not in this area."

"Neal's still in a coma."

"At latest reports."

"I'm facing felony assault charges, and I'm more than a little worried about what happens if he dies. I can't just disappear, and I can't stay here forever, either!" This nugget of worry translated to this: I needed to meet Master Theodorus and get to whatever it was I was supposed to be getting to.

"I have just commenced my legal efforts on your behalf, Mr. Mitchell. All part of the Witherspoon service. You are, however temporarily, family. And as for your departure date—"

He didn't finish that sentence. Never did, in fact, because we all heard—

"Malachi, is that Mr. Mitchell?"

Our attention turned to the staircase, another example of recent renovation, with the left half rebuilt into a series of steps more suitable to a giant—there were probably six as opposed to a couple of dozen on the classic, dare I say nat, side.

And down the stairs came a tallish woman of about forty, with flowing dark hair, green eyes, and a manner I instantly judged to be regal in spite of her mundane clothing—a short-sleeved white blouse and tight pants that my mother called pedal pushers, displaying a trim, even athletic figure. "I'm Alice Witherspoon," she said, extending her hand and walking toward me in sneakers. Her voice was throaty, relaxed, with a hint of the South.

Schwartz made a half-hearted attempt to interpose himself between us, but Alice glided past him like Ginger Rogers. I choked out my name; Ridley, his eyes gone saucerlike, did the same, with even less savoir faire.

"Let me just thank you both for taking time out of your busy schedules to help out with Theodorus. He is such a fan of all this space-flying, and to have you two here in the house—"

"I didn't fly," Ridley said, rediscovering his voice.

Alice simply laughed and touched Ridley on the shoulder; I could feel the jolt of sensual electricity from two feet away. "Let's not be burdened by technicalities." She turned to me. "Let's say hello to Theodorus. Just give me one moment. . . ."

She turned and seemed to glide up the nat side of the stairs. I had to ask: "Does she know about our situation?"

"It has been my experience, in all the years I've worked for her, that Mrs. Witherspoon knows everything."

"She must be very tolerant."

"She loves her son." And here Schwartz acknowledged the situation. "The house, as you might have noticed, has been . . . modified to accommodate the needs of Master Theodorus."

"I noticed."

"He is a pleasant young man, but personal interactions may require . . . forbearance."

"I have grown up in the wild card world, Mr. Schwartz. And my presentations have exposed me to humans of all shapes, sizes, and abilities."

"I do hope so."

"Where is Mr. Witherspoon? I look forward to thanking him."

"In Washington at present."

"And where do you lurk, Mr. Schwartz? Do you have an office somewhere, a practice?"

I had pricked a nerve. "I have an office in the city proper, though I make use of Mr. Witherspoon's office here, in his absence."

Aha, I thought. Mr. Malachi Schwartz was both unsure of his status with the Witherspoons and maneuvering frantically to solidify it.

He went ahead of us up the stairs. As we followed, I glanced at Ridley, who looked unusually nervous.

I was distracted by another presence—a young girl from the billowy dress and slim figure, though crimson-colored and bald. Her manner was elfin, if polite, since she stopped in her tracks and literally bowed to us. She had a notebook of some kind pressed to her chest.

"Her name is Mathilde," Schwartz said. And he offered nothing else.

Alice Witherspoon was waiting for us at the top. "We had to remodel everything up here, and some of it is still new, so apologies!"

She escorted us toward the room at the end of the hallway, stopping in an open doorway twice as wide and at least two feet higher than one might expect.

As we got there, I noted the odor again. I should note that I am quite sensitive to smells—and this was pre–wild card. It wasn't unpleasant, more musty and moist, like a swamp, but distinctive.

"Theodorus, may I present Cash Mitchell and Ridley Hough."

A teenaged male voice said, from inside, "Hey, cool!"

Then, like a TV variety show hostess, Alice stepped aside, allowing us to enter.

I would like to say that the first thing I noted were the models hanging from the ceilings, so much like my own room back in Solvang twenty-five years in the past. Instead of JB-1s or Mustangs or Nazi Focke-Wulfs, however, there was a Hornet, a Takisian Baby, and, surprise, a Soviet Sever from the late 1950s, and to my even greater surprise, the linked X-11A and its mother ship from the awful accident in 1958.

Maybe I did register those before turning to Theodorus himself. Though he was impossible to miss—in fact, his sheer physical presence may have overwhelmed me.

I don't believe that Malachi Schwartz's description of Theodorus Witherspoon as a "snaillike centaur" was sufficient. Technically, yes: the boy's body had the shape and appearance of a snail perhaps a hundred times larger than it ought to be. In a poor light, or let's just say in a severely cropped image, the young man might have presented as nat-ish human . . . head, two arms, and upper torso, that is.

From sternum south and rearward, it was a different story: he was pretty much a giant snail who, it was obviously apparent, moved as a snail might, propelled by a foot. Taller than me by more than two feet, and even a foot taller than Ridley, who stands six feet four when he doesn't slouch. I put his weight at half a ton.

There was no bed in a normal sense, but rather some kind of rack with a hammock. He would have filled a normal bedroom to bursting.

"My lord." That was from Ridley, in a voice so soft that only I could hear it. I hoped.

Theodorus was wearing a custom jersey of some size emblazoned with the logo of a team—baseball, football, I couldn't have told you—called the Pilots.

And he held out a hand. I shook, feeling a near-crushing grab, which was understandable, given Theodorus's mass. I must not have hidden a reflexive grimace, though, because he said, "Sorry." I thought I saw him blush in shame, a wildly unlikely reaction.

I kept telling myself, *He's fifteen*.

"Theo has been so looking forward to having you here, Mr. Mitchell."

Talking to Alice Witherspoon was the easiest thing I have ever done. "We're glad to be here, and please, everyone call me 'Cash.'" I turned to Theodorus. "You."

"Okay."

I gestured toward the spaceship models. "You really are a fan. I don't think I've ever seen models of a couple of these."

Alice Witherspoon beamed and touched Theodorus's shoulder. It's possible I was the first person to ever compliment the collection.

Then there was an awkward moment when none of us knew what to do or say next. I could almost feel Ridley vibrating next to me. Finally I said, "So, Theodorus, do you want to see *Quicksilver*?"

The kid had a great smile.

For Theodorus, even the simplest journey out of his room was a major operation. But Alice Witherspoon demonstrated leadership and familiarity with the maneuvers. "I'll take Theodorus to the elevator while you gentlemen go to your spaceship."

What was clear, from her tone, was that she did not want us offering assistance. Which made sense, both for Theodorus's pride and for the simple reason that we weren't going to be part of such extractions for more than a few days.

As Ridley, Schwartz, and I headed toward *Quicksilver*, the money man addressed my partner. "And what is your role?"

"I, uh, move things around."

"In that case, we will summon you when such assistance is required. Though your help in removing the tarp would be welcome."

Ridley blinked at Schwartz, then looked at me, and shrugged. "Fine." He did help pull off the tarp, not that it required two people.

Once Ridley and I had it stowed, and we grew aware of Theodorus and Alice's approach, Ridley said, "Mind if I go into town?"

"Sure. I guess you're not needed at the moment." Ever practical, I then said, "Do you need a ride?"

"Nah, I'll walk. Or hitch."

Then I knew he was steamed: Ridley hated to walk. But he was so eager to be elsewhere that he jogged around the east side of the house. Which left me to turn on Schwartz. "Why did you do that?"

"It's obvious to me, and therefore obvious to Mrs. Witherspoon and Theodorus, that Mr. Hough shares the prejudices of most Americans when it comes to jokers."

"He never acts like it."

"My dear Mr. Mitchell, he acted like nothing but." He raised his hand to prevent further protests, an unnecessary gesture since Theodorus and Alice had arrived.

"Wow," Theodorus said. I had had the foolish notion that he might be able to go inside *Quicksilver,* but his sheer bulk made it unlikely that he would even be able to peer far inside.

But he gave it a good walk around, and was tall enough to touch the skin—only after an inquisitive look and affirmation from me.

"It looks a lot like Baby," he said.

"It should; it's a knockoff in a lot of ways. Less alive."

"Smaller."

"Is it? I've never actually been close to Baby."

"I got a ride in her a couple of years ago. Dr. Tachyon brought her here for an afternoon."

My mouth must have fallen open. I somehow closed it and said, "Sorry to be such a low-rent following act."

"He was pretty weird. I already like you better."

I was amused at the notion of a giant centaur-snail describing the humanoid (if eccentrically styled) Takisian as "pretty weird"—ah, teenagers. "Thank you. Uh, too bad we can't grow spaceships like her."

"Someday, maybe."

Alice stood back, arms crossed, indulgent and, let's face it, a bit skeptical as I ran through my well-worn spiel about *Quicksilver's* origins, features, and my own modest abilities.

Even as I talked, I began to realize that I might have been hasty in signing up for the Witherspoon gig. I didn't have three weeks' worth of material. I didn't have more than maybe two hours. And there was the fresh challenge of being more interesting than a Takisian.

Just then Theodorus completed his orbit. "Can I ask you something, Cash?"

"Sure."

"Tell me how you managed to fake that landing on the Moon."

I opened my mouth to utter my usual snappy reply, but didn't, perhaps because I saw Alice step forward, her face flushing with anger. "Henry Theodorus Witherspoon! You apologize right this instant!"

No apology required. I saw the look on Theodorus's face:

He really was a joker.

And so it began.

We, that is, all the players, agreed that I would spend two hours with Theodorus in the mornings and two in the afternoons, leaving him free for medical tests (still ongoing) and for other visiting instructors. (I learned that I was the latest in a series, which made sense, since Theodorus was incapable of attending school.)

That first morning we spent talking about *Quicksilver* and, yes, the Moon flight. (Once Alice saw that Theodorus and I had genuine interests in common, she departed, taking a reluctant Schwartz with her.)

After ninety minutes, the rain commenced and we were driven inside. No retainers emerged from the house to offer assistance or take me elsewhere, so I simply followed Theodorus to his elevator.

"Whatever happened to Eva-Lynne?" he asked, almost shyly.

"Well, we got married not long after the flight."

The trip to the second story took an unusually long time. I would later learn that the elevator was a custom model because it required twice the standard weight limit.

"Are you still married?"

"We split up ten years ago." In fact, the marriage ended as swiftly as it began, but he didn't need the gory details.

"Do you ever see her?"

"Not for years." And there I was, talking about Eva-Lynne with a fifteen-year-old. "Why do you want to know?"

By now we were back in his room and he was, in his clumsy, massive fashion, turning toward two chests of drawers that had been stacked one on the other. From the top of the lower one he pulled out an autograph book. "Most of these are Pilots," he said. "Our Triple-A baseball team." Which explained the jersey. He flipped to the middle. "But here I have space pilots. My parents got me General Sampson. He works for one of our companies."

By golly he did—"BGen Michael R. Sampson" in the general's copybook hand, under the inscription, "Ad Astra!"

Theodorus produced a pen. "Would you sign this for me?"

Neal would probably not believe this, but I have given a number of autographs over the years, though usually to children who had been urged forward by enlightened parents.

This felt different. Before I could even make my fingers write my name, I wanted to create something memorable. What struck me was this: "Looking forward to YOUR Moon trip!"

The moment I handed the book to Theodorus I wanted it back. Idiot. This poor kid could barely go out the front door of his own home—he may have flown in a Takisian spaceship, but how many of those would he have access to? He couldn't fit in an airplane.

And the look that passed across his face said it, too.

"What I mean is—"

Then he smiled as he put the book away. "You mean, don't stop dreaming, no matter what, right?"

"I think that's better."

"Now all I need is Eva-Lynne for completion." I may have let my ignorance show. He added, "It's what autograph collectors say when you have the whole team."

"Ah. You would not only be complete, you would be unique. I don't think Eva-Lynne ever signed anything."

That afternoon I took Theodorus through the whole history of human efforts in space, from the largely fruitless attempts in the late 1940s and early 1950s to reengineer Takisian technology—which was only, what, five hundred years more advanced?

Then to the first human attempts to go beyond the atmosphere by the Soviets and the United States, largely piggybacking on missile development programs. I was able to share wicked stories about the colorful pilot Al Dearborn, survivor of the disastrous X-11A incident. Theodorus loved that.

I skipped the whole tawdry business of the Rosenbergs, the traitors who gave the Soviets what little we had learned about Baby. Nor did I touch on borderline events like the U-2 spy plane, since it was on a mission triggered by the whole Rosenberg affair. Besides, I needed to leave some stories for Day Two.

I went into great detail on the Hornet spaceplane flights of the 1960s and 1970s—because Theodorus knew enough to drag details out of me. And those vehicles were descendants of *Quicksilver*. The last few years had seen tremendous strides in human space exploration, but they presented difficulties, since half of the activity was in the Soviet Union and not well publicized. And the half that was American was frequently outright classified.

Now, I had spent some free time collecting all the information I could on the Soviet efforts—even learned to read Cyrillic and puzzle out space-related documents. I couldn't speak Russian beyond a phrase or two.

But simple diligence had allowed me to be familiar with the spacecraft and their capabilities, to recognize the program managers and pilots, and to have some awareness of what was launched when, and what happened.

Here I will admit that Theodorus was my equal, if not superior. After all, he had a model of the Soviet Almaz hanging from his ceiling. It was too high for me to really judge. "Is there any way I could hold that?"

I clocked his hesitation, and understood it. I used to build airplane models. "You don't have to—"

"Oh, God, Mr. Mitchell, you're the only person in the world who would actually recognize it."

"Outside of Russia."

"Well, yeah." He giggled. "Can you reach it?"

I tried but, not being the tallest person in any room, just couldn't touch it.

Theodorus looked around his room. There was no furniture beyond a desk that was clearly nailed down and not movable, and not within reach of the model, plus the giant rack of a custom "bed" and a hemispherical frame that served as a chair.

I tried to use the chair frame, but it was almost too heavy to move, and when I stood on it, it rocked and tilted.

"Nope," Theodorus said. He took another look around his room, a slow, ponderous process that made me feel sorry for him again. Theodorus sounded young, but he moved like an old elephant. I think he was still adjusting to his newfound bulk. "Why don't I just—?"

He positioned himself under the model and reached for it.

Crushing it with his human-looking but joker-powered hand. "Oh god!" he said.

Pieces of the Almaz scattered on the floor.

I almost slammed into Theodorus trying to pick them up. I did rescue the larger pieces, and there were only half a dozen. "Look," I said, "a little glue and good as new."

I was lying, however: no amount of glue was going to un-crush the Almaz pieces.

Theodorus just sat there sobbing. "I'm so . . ." He wanted to utter a curse word but was too well brought up to do that in front of me.

"Fucking clumsy?" I said.

He laughed as he wiped his tears. "I haven't gotten used to this. I mean, I know how to eat and get around, but sometimes . . . the little things."

"When did it start?"

"I was almost fourteen," he said.

"Two years ago."

That big head slowly bobbed up and down.

I understood. I was the same age, thirteen rising fourteen (and for years I have wondered if puberty was a wild card trigger) and living a nat life with my parents in the Santa Ynez Valley, just north and inland from Santa Barbara. It was ranch country, one of the most beautiful landscapes in California or anywhere (something I could not appreciate until years later). My mother taught junior high in Solvang; my dad managed a hotel. My mom was a native, having grown up in Los Olivos; my dad was from Iowa and came to the area just prior to WWII, searching for a life that had nothing to do with dairy farms.

I was an only child, smarter than most, based on my grades (and my mother's embrace of education), athletic enough to fit in with the other boys in the neighborhood—but also obsessed with toy soldiers as well as ship and airplane models. Yes, I had Jetboy's JB-1, but rarely used it, preferring the North American P-51 Mustang, as any sane human would. (The P-51 was victorious.)

Early in the summer of 1955, not long after school ended, I came down with a fever after a camping trip. In another time, my parents might have suspected a bugbite, but not since Wild Card Day. They had me at the clinic within hours, ran a T-test, and heard the news that my card was turning.

The usual protocol was a hospital stay in the wild card unit, but the Solvang Hospital was too small. And my parents wanted me home. The doctor warned them that I might turn into something "challenging," the 1955 code for monster joker, but they insisted.

Then . . . home to wait.

I knew none of this at the time—I was simply told I had the flu, though I had my suspicions: everyone in my eighth grade class knew of a girl in Buellton who had been stricken in the past year, turning into a kind of butterfly (according to one account) or a dragonfly (most others).

When I awoke from the fever, I found only my father in the house. My mother had been stricken with that season's flu, and it had killed her in two days. You can imagine my grief and, for years thereafter, sense of blame.

Another thing—while I knew I had been infected with the wild card virus, I didn't know what the hell it meant or how it manifested. For the first few weeks, I kept hoping for some kind of mental power, the ability to peer into other minds, for example.

I only learned the truth when my father, emerging to some extent from his mourning, finally decided to discard my mother's clothing and other possessions. Including a chest of drawers that he, with considerable strain, moved alone from the bedroom to the front door. "Give me a hand," he said, and I did just that, literally. I barely touched the chest and it rose to eye level.

And then thumped down with a bang. "What was that?" my father said.

In the next few moments I demonstrated to myself, and my father, what the wild card had given me—the basic ability to overcome mass with a touch. I could lift almost anything indefinitely, it seemed, though heavy objects and great distances tired me out. In the right circumstances, I could launch an object, too—all I needed was to hold on to it, or as we've seen, him, long enough to create some momentum.

My father was as relieved as I was to know that this was the worst of it, or so we believed. (The joker side effects turned out to be clinical depression and alcoholism, but it would be hard years before I realized that.)

Through my teens and into my college years I was able to make use of my power to lift—hiring myself out to various construction firms in the Santa Ynez Valley.

I paid for college that way, but eventually found the work boring and nowhere as lucrative as illegal activities.

Looking at Theodorus, I floundered for a safe subject to raise. "Is there something you can do?" With his physical state, I meant.

"You mean, other than break things?"

"That could happen to anyone."

"All I know is . . . I used to be normal, now I'm this."

That was the saddest thing I'd heard in a long time.

I had dinner alone in the servants' kitchen and was back in the guesthouse top bunk pondering my next lessons when I heard scuffling in the gravel outside.

I found Ridley climbing up on *Quicksilver*. "Nice walk?" I said.

Never one to return sarcasm for sarcasm, Ridley said, "Caught a lift outside the front gate."

"What did you do?"

"Saw the sights. Fort Sumter."

"Good?"

He shrugged as he kept running his hands over the pitted, discolored skin of *Quicksilver*. "Seen a few forts by now." That was true: bored and stuck in Baltimore over a weekend last autumn, Ridley and I had actually toured Fort McHenry.

"How's your money holding out?" I was battering him a little, but that's what one does with Ridley. And I felt like shit because he'd been banished.

"Still good." He was staring up at *Quicksilver*.

"You have a plan."

He nodded. "She needs fixing."

"That's been true since you started working with me."

"You weren't flying her 'til now."

"That was a onetime thing," I said. "I hope."

"Never know. But there's at least one leak on the top side. If water gets in, air gets out."

"Come on, even if I have to fly out of here, I'm not going to ten thousand feet, much less into space."

"She ought to be flightworthy and looking good." He nodded toward the house. "For the kid, if nothing else."

"Fixing the skin will cost money." It wasn't an especially exotic metal, and, heck, you could certainly patch from the inside with almost anything. "Not to mention batteries and anything else the systems need."

"I've got some stashed here and there."

"You're not spending your money on repairs. We've got extra on this gig, so we'll use that. And it's not like I have other plans for it."

That seemed satisfactory. "I'll take the cab into town and see what I can scare up. Then come back with a bid and my hand out."

Thus occupied for the next week or three, Ridley grinned. "I bet I missed dinner."

"There's probably something in the kitchen fridge."

He grinned some more and ran inside, leaving me to return to that lingering issue of . . . other plans.

During many a long drive, I had asked myself where Ridley and I were headed, separately or as a team. Ridley's money nests suggested a plan for some kind of retirement, though dribs in savings accounts was no strategy for wealth creation.

At that, he was ahead of me. I had gone on the road in 1973 and a simple extrapolation of my life, health, and prospects would see me dead in a trailer camp around the year 2000.

Or, given recent events, in jail.

Either way, broke, and lonely.

The next afternoon, after another amusing session with Theodorus that had to be cut short by the arrival of other tutors, I chanced to see the strange girl again.

I was passing through the kitchen in search of a fortifying afternoon snack when, glancing out the window, I chanced to see the crimson elfin girl walking toward the house with Malachi Schwartz in pursuit.

He caught up with her, grabbed her arm, and spun her to face him—

"Something I can help you with, Mr. Mitchell?"

Then she saw what I saw out the window.

"Who is she?"

"I don't believe I have any information for you." And then it struck me that Dorothy thought I was fantasizing about the girl. This has happened to me often enough that I know protests are futile, and only make matters worse. I thanked Dorothy and made my exit.

It was our fourth afternoon, three days after Ridley drove out with the cab and did not return, nor make contact. This wasn't unprecedented, and in fact I was relieved, since I didn't have to feel guilty about his third-class treatment.

As I was walking toward Theodorus's room I heard several new voices, younger, and upon entering found three teens present. Two were boys, one large and either shy or sullen, the other short, lively, and socialized. "You must be Mr. Mitchell," he said, offering a hand. "I'm Tom, that's Eric—" The big lump in the corner.

"And I'm Mathilde," said the third, the crimson elfin girl I had seen twice already. She had a lovely French accent.

I realized that they were talking about going to the local ballpark for a Pilots game, clearly their first group outing in a long while. I tried to be innocuous as they discussed transit challenges and the like, realizing that Theodorus's wild card had deprived him of friends his age.

Midway through this conversation—a painful one to listen to, with three of the four individuals using the word *like* as an all-purpose adjective, adverb, or interjection—I sensed a change in the mansion environment.

You know this: Once you're in a house or apartment for even a few days, there is a certain level and type of sound that says all is as it should be. There is often, and there definitely was in the Witherspoon mansion, a sort of electronic hum that had grown familiar.

But now I heard hurried footsteps.

A door opening and closing.

I heard voices, not words.

Eric did, too. "What's going on?"

I slid past the teens toward the windows, but they looked over the rear of the house.

Then there was a knock at Theodorus's door. In spite of his bulk, he reached it before I did. It was James saying, "It's the police."

The three visiting teens looked at each other with alarm, the usual teen fear that, whether you know it or not, you did something wrong. Theodorus, however, lit up like a Halloween pumpkin. "Where from? How many?"

James had no idea about where the lawmen came from, but was sound on the number. "Two."

"Nat and J, or two of a kind?" Theodorus asked. It took me a moment to realize that this was police slang for the nat/joker teams frequently found in your bigger cities. He explained, "My favorite TV show is *J-Street Blues*."

"They appear to be nats." Which made things slightly worse for me.

And now both of them looked at me. Well, I would have, too. "Time to face the music," I said, and meant it. "Nice meeting you all. Sorry for the circumstances."

"Cash," Theodorus said, "you can still escape!"

That made me feel quite affectionate toward Theodorus: he could still dream for others if not for himself.

James held the door, however. I believe he was eager to see me dealt with. "If I don't see you again, Theodorus, it's been fun! Keep dreaming!"

Out I went, feeling unusually fearful and even embarrassed that these three teens were present. And hoping that Ridley was far away and safe. I had yet to reach the top of the stairs when Alice intercepted me, taking me by the arm and guiding me into a bedroom. "This way."

I was happy for the interception for two reasons, the lesser of them being any delay in my arrest and removal to the grimmer parts of Kentucky.

I was about to speak, but Alice actually placed a finger on my lips. I could have remained in that awkward but delicious state for some time, but within seconds we could hear raised voices from outside—the windows were open.

Standing nose to nose a foot apart, we waited. I was, shall we say, acutely aware by now that I was attracted to Alice Witherspoon—sufficiently so that had she leaned closer I would have eagerly kissed her, even knowing it was oh so wrong, not to mention impolite.

It may have been the moment, but I had the feeling that she shared the impulse.

Whatever might have happened didn't—we were distracted by the commotion outside, which was soon punctuated by slamming car doors and the sound of a vehicle driving away.

"That sounds promising," I said.

Alice instantly ran to the window. "They've gone."

I heard footfalls that I already recognized as belonging to Schwartz. He pushed the door completely open. "They have departed without incident," he said. "You are free to emerge."

He clearly meant, to me, get the hell out of here.

Alice said, "Malachi, what happened?"

As we exited the room, then hurried downstairs, we found Theodorus in the driveway, all half-ton of him in his baseball jersey, which was soaked with sweat. Wide-eyed with curiosity and, I think, admiration, Tom, Eric, and Mathilde were behind him. Theodorus was jubilant. "Cash, did you see?" He had put the run to a pair of South Carolina state troopers.

"I heard," I said, exaggerating only slightly.

It turned out that two state troopers had knocked on the door, announced that they were looking for Cash Mitchell and Ridley Hough in connection with, etc.

One of them had stepped away from the door and started to walk around the house, where he surely would have seen the *Quicksilver* truck and RV.

Schwartz had been summoned by the retainer, but before the joker could work his magic, Theodorus had come roaring around the north side of the house, direct from his elevator.

For the two troopers, it must have been like facing an elephant charge.

In fact: "One of them reached for his revolver!"

That alarmed all of us.

"I don't believe he actually unholstered his weapon," Schwartz insisted.

"Did you say anything?" I said.

"I just roared."

"What in God's name did you hope to accomplish?" Alice said.

"To get them to run away." He smiled. "And they did!"

We all exchanged glances. Theodorus had won a small victory, but only by exploiting the automatic fear of strange jokers. I felt sorry for any joker unlucky enough to get pulled over by those two cops.

Alice nodded toward Theodorus's elevator. "I think you've had enough excitement for one day, young man. Time to get cleaned up for dinner."

"And we should be going," Tom said.

"Wicked work." Eric uttered his first actual words.

"See you guys later, then," Theodorus said. The boys climbed into a beat-up Ford.

"Mathilde," Schwartz said, "inside."

"*Oui*, Papa." And she ran into the house. I realized then that she was not only happily at home when visiting the estate, living at the estate, she was Schwartz's daughter. Theodorus shuffled off, clearly proud and happy. I hope he didn't see the pity on my face or on his mother's.

Oblivious to the teenage hormonal drama, Schwartz was about his business. "This won't stop them for long. They'll be back with warrants and reinforcements."

"I think not," Alice said. "I'm calling Bryce. And Cash . . . please join us for dinner."

She ran into the house and Schwartz said, "To save you the obvious question, Bryce is Mrs. Witherspoon's brother. He is chief of the Charleston Police Department."

"I see."

"He is a man of strict adherence to the law, except where family is concerned—and especially where outside elements intrude."

"I have another obvious question—"

He let it hang.

"Mathilde is your daughter."

"One might assume I already knew that."

"What is she doing here?"

"Mathilde is a valued member of our household. She will be joining you at dinner." He clearly planned to say no more.

As we entered the house, I said, "How do I dress for dinner here?"

"This is not the 1920s, Mr. Mitchell. A simple sport coat will do." He took extreme relish in relating that. His manner suggested that he violently disapproved, that he rarely dined with the family.

Fortunately I have a sport coat. One.

"Oh, by the way . . . Mr. Witherspoon will be home."

I returned to the RV to clean up and to wonder where in God's name Ridley was. If roaming Charleston and environs, he was subject to arrest, and he wouldn't have Malachi Schwartz or Theodorus Witherspoon to save him.

Henry Witherspoon was not what I expected.

Having met Alice I had naturally made assumptions about what manner of mate she would have, and was prepared for a handsome scion of the South: tall, Aryan, all of that. Perhaps with a mustache, possibly drunk.

Instead I shook hands with a pudgy gent several inches shorter than me, with a receded hairline and glasses. I wondered how on Earth he had managed to land Alice Dayton, whom I pictured as a rich debutante with a penchant for stealing Daddy's cars and flirting with the most eligible and non-eligible men of all ages.

Not with this . . . well, accountant in front of me.

Perhaps I had let my fantasies run away with me.

"Hello, Cash," he said, in a voice with no notable accent. "Alice and Malachi tell me you're being vastly helpful to Theodorus."

"I hope so."

"Can't tell you how pleased we are to have such a celebrity here."

"I doubt that I rank high on the celebrity scale, but it's a pleasure nonetheless."

Theodorus was already sliding into his place at the foot of the table, which had been widened and reshaped, with a giant snail-shaped piece cut out to allow the young joker to reach his plate. He had "dressed," too, in a blazer perhaps altered by Omar the Tentmaker.

Dressed in a pretty little summer dress, Mathilde took a place at the table, too, favoring me with a perfectly appropriate nod of hello, as if we had been introduced.

No one did so; perhaps the Witherspoons just assumed we were acquainted. In any case, she was seated far enough from me that conversation was impossible, and she did not seem to engage with anyone but Theodorus.

The meal itself was . . . unexpected: a stew of greens, onions, and what I took to be dandelions. Alice saw my surprise if not outright shock, and said, "We have adjusted our dining habits to honor Theodorus's condition."

"Yeah, I'm a vegetarian now," he said. "A hamburger would probably kill me."

Henry was at the head of the table, with Alice across from me. The staff swirled around like attendants out of some BBC drama about lords in a country manor.

I dealt with the soup, and made some inroads on the entrée, which was largely tasteless in spite of a healthy amount of seasoning.

There was a bit of small family talk—given the Witherspoons' interests, make that business—with Alice and Henry doing their best to engage Theodorus.

Politics. The Witherspoons were quite liberal for that time and station, big not only on joker rights (logically enough with Theodorus, though I wondered when they had crossed over) but on the Negro question.

This seemed tricky, given that everyone on the staff was Black. At one point, however, Henry turned to James, the primary retainer/butler, and asked his opinion about some pending legislation in Washington. "I would like to see it pass, but I doubt it will change many minds around here."

It struck me that James was "James" and not, say, "Mr. Smith."

There was some business talk, too, about the family holdings in various aviation and missile firms, and also in new computer processing organizations.

Theodorus took an active part in the aviation and missile discussion—so, to my surprise, did Alice. The most urgent matter, apparently, was the need for the United States to field a new intercontinental ballistic missile and the family's hope that Dayton Enterprises (the first time I actually made the connection) would win the prime contract.

Theodorus urged his parents to get out of the missile business—"space platforms and computers will make them obsolete"—and I was charmed by the way they engaged him on it.

I followed the chat, chiming in where I could, but largely began to fade into silence.

I had made a serious mistake.

A wineglass had been set for me, and one of the staff poured a red. Now, I have had problems in the past, basically from age twenty to thirty-three, when the collapse of my marriage (to be euphemistic: it swirled down a drain) and the opportunity of a life on the road convinced me that I needed to give up alcohol.

There had been relapses, but none for long and without real damage, so perhaps I had lulled myself into believing I had control . . . but I grabbed that wine without a thought, as if I had a glass every evening at dinner.

Maybe it was the environment.

Surely it was the company. Whatever the reason, I drank.

As Alice said, closing the conversational door on business, "You have a colorful past, Mr. Mitchell."

"That's one way to describe it. The honest word is *criminal*—"

"—isn't that a contradiction in terms?" Alice said. "Honest, criminal?"

"Without admitting to any specific malfeasance, I would compare my past to political operatives working in the 'honest graft' system." I told them my stock story of the classic Pendergast political machine in Kansas City in the 1920s, where a group of nonelected but powerful individuals controlled city jobs and contracts, but operated on this principle: my brother-in-law may get the city contract to put a roof on the orphanage, but it will be a good roof!

Alice and Henry laughed. Theodorus smiled, if that was the expression on his face. "'Honest graft,'" Henry said. "I wish more of our business partners practiced that."

"Oh, darling," Alice said, "they aren't all criminals."

"A good percentage. I have never understood the need to cut corners and cheat people. Surely once one has accumulated a certain amount of wealth and security—as we have—what is the point of adding to it? Especially some tiny amount of money."

"It's all about power, isn't it?" Alice said. "Who is on top, who is biggest?"

Theodorus snickered—that sound was unmistakable. Alice sailed on, as if she had made no racy reference, though I believe I saw a faint blush to her neck.

And I said, "There is a lot of power right here, isn't there?" The wine had been given voice.

"How so?" Henry said, his eyes narrowing a bit, as if waiting for me to say something challenging.

"You Witherspoons are not only able to pluck me out of nowhere and move me here, but you are also able to protect me from the long hairy arms of Kentucky law."

A bit relieved, Henry smiled. "I could fall back on the old argument, one that any of my neighbors would make, that I don't hold with out-of-state law coming to my door to make life difficult for my guests." The last two-thirds of that were issued in a Southern drawl worthy of a Civil War movie. "In truth, I'm just a contrarian."

"We also believe in your innocence," Alice said, and now I suspected I was the object of some sport.

Henry said, "And if not that, Malachi is convinced this whole matter will dry up and float away—"

"With his able assistance," I said.

"I have to confess, Cash," Henry said. "While I find you to be perfectly pleasant company, and a superior citizen, it's hard for me to believe that that object in our driveway actually flew to the Moon."

"And back," I said, falling back on my old routine. "That was actually the most important part."

"God, Dad," Theodorus said. "You're as bad as that idiot in Kentucky!"

"Oh, he's not poking a camera in Cash's face." I do believe Alice also had drunk a bit more wine than was wise.

"Both of you," Theodorus said, his words very clear now. "The *Quicksilver* flight was tracked by the Space Command!" He then launched into a point-by-tedious-point refutation of all claims that our flight was some kind of hoax.

Not only couldn't I have done it better, I couldn't have done it as well, since Theodorus cited several supporting facts I had forgotten, including the dusting of moondust on *Quicksilver*'s skin. I applauded; smiling, Henry and Alice joined in. "I appear to be overwhelmed and convinced," Henry said. "Not that I truly doubted."

I raised my wineglass in acknowledgment. My unsteady grip should have been a warning.

"You've been on the road for, is it seven years?" Alice said.

"Eight." The number was right; the word was slurred.

"But you do have a home."

"A house I see about sixty days a year."

"Don't you miss it?"

"Frankly, no." I had never asked myself the question, so by default, that was the truth.

Henry said, "Do you miss anything? Or are you a man who only lives for this moment and the next?"

And here I just blurted: "I miss Eva-Lynne."

Her name was out of my mouth before I knew it. The only gratifying moment—if that's the word—was seeing Alice Witherspoon blush.

"Excuse me." I stood up and quickly regretted it.

Okay, (a) I hadn't been drinking in years, and (b) I had hardly eaten. The wine hit me like a couple of shots of pure vodka. I swayed and, taking a step, staggered.

I would have paid good money to have the earth open up under me at that moment, because I knew I was making a fool of myself in front of, in ascending order of value, Henry, Theodorus, and Alice.

James arrived with dessert, creating a blessed distraction, allowing me to slide out of the dining room without further incident. Somehow Schwartz, who never seemed to leave the Witherspoon mansion, had located Ridley, and my buddy was waiting as I staggered out the kitchen door.

"Hey there, hey there," he said, like a cowboy with an injured pony.

"I relapsed," I said. Just forming that word was an accomplishment, given my condition.

"Happens," he said.

He essentially put me to bed, where there was no sleep to be had.

I spent hours pondering my failures with Eva-Lynne.

I had lusted after and longed for her in the months and weeks before that trip to the Moon, and suffered the agonies of her affair with Al Dearborn before the universe chose, in a weak moment, perhaps, to stop shitting on me.

Upon our return, she moved in to my tiny shack above the Pearblossom Highway. We found low-rent jobs—she temping at Tomlin, me doing odd but legit construction work.

We were blissfully happy for months. By late spring I was dying to make her Mrs. Mitchell, and she was happy to wear my ring.

The newly promoted Lieutenant Colonel Michael Sampson was my best man. Eva-Lynne had the improbably named Honey Burke, one of her coworkers from Haugen's Bakery, as her maid of honor.

It was my second marriage. As to how to count Eva-Lynne's prior engagements, well, that was trickier: she had grown up in a polygamist compound in the Arizona Strip and had been officially married to an older man whose name she would never reveal and, when he died, at least one other, though that had yet to be consecrated before her escape.

So I was Husband 2.5. We never spoke of her sad phase as a hooker in that awful period between escaping polygamy and landing in a bakery in Palmdale.

So we played house. Husband and wife. The loving couple who brightened each evening with a bottle of wine or three when they weren't closing down Pablo's, our local saloon.

Eva-Lynne had never finished high school, much less college, so we talked about enrolling her at Lancaster High in the fall of 1969—we even visited the school to talk about the GED and what tests she could take to shorten the road to graduation.

I thought about going back to college myself, having left Cal Poly San Luis Obispo, and majoring in business, at the very least. I flirted with the notion of engineering, possibly this new computer science stuff.

And thought about having a family.

This was tricky.

I had known about her polygamist life, but not her motherhood.

This conversation took place moments before we made love one night, as Eva-Lynne detoured to the bathroom for her birth control pill. "Why bother with that?" I said. "We're married, right?"

"We haven't talked about kids at all," she said, sliding back into bed, naked and impressively erotic.

"I just assumed."

"Since when do you make all these assumptions about us?"

"Sorry. Is it my wild card?"

She shook her pretty head, her blond hair cascading in ways that made me forget my uncertainty.

We talked rather than making love—this was in our bottle-of-wine-per-night phase—and she revealed that she had already given birth to two children, the first when she was fifteen. That night ended in weeping, as much from me as from her, and one of us on the couch.

That night, in fact, ended our marriage, though that wasn't obvious for months. I announced that I was deferring all talk or thought of children. We resumed passionate love- and homemaking as if nothing had happened. Eva-Lynne took to visiting Pablo's every day beginning at noon. Her companion for much of this was Honey Burke, her pal from the bakery—and who was free that time of day.

I had actually commenced a series of classes over the mountains at San Fernando Valley College, a trip that took me out of the house at eight four days a week, returning at dinnertime or later. Until the day I had a flat near Agua Dulce and was so hot, tired, and filthy that I gave up on class and returned home at 3 p.m.

And found a man I did not know leaving my house with a just-fucked look on his face.

I was hot, tired, dirty, not at my best. There was shouting and screaming—I had been a faithful husband to her, didn't deserve this, etc. Her counterargument was that I didn't deserve her, that I was a loser, a boozer, and a crook.

The aftermath might have gone differently—there might have been some steps toward forgiveness—had I not already seen her cheat on me, with Al Dearborn. (Now, Eva-Lynne and I were not in a relationship at that time, but she knew of my interest. And knew that sleeping with the ace pilot would hurt me . . . because she told me so.)

And had she not taken cruel glee in enumerating the number and type of her extramarital encounters. "I hope you were using birth control," I snapped at one point. (Again, alcohol was a factor, both in her actions and in our nasty arguments.)

Taking her share of what was left of the *Enquirer* money, Eva-Lynne moved out and then in with Honey Burke, though she did not take up her old job at the bakery, no sir.

I quit going to Valley and did a lot of drinking and moping around until Sampson showed up on my doorstep with his offer.

I would get reports of Eva-Lynne and Honey as the party girls of the Antelope Valley, "dating" nats, aces (especially those horny flyboys from Tomlin), and jokers, too. It was said—and in my pained hearing—that Eva-Lynne had a thing for jokers.

And before too long, it was also said that money was changing hands, and that Eva-Lynne and Honey were not only boozing but dealing and using other substances.

One Sunday morning in December 1970—it was the thirteenth and you could look it up—almost two years after Eva-Lynne, Mike Sampson, and I had touched the surface of the fucking Moon—I was passing Haugen's Bakery. Out of some misguided surge of nostalgia, alcohol-fueled (it was shortly after dawn, after a late night with former Skalko associates), struck by the sight of the full moon high in the western sky, I pulled into the lot.

There were a few customers, of course: the local gentry needed their pastries.

Through the plate glass window I could see Honey Burke filling orders. At the wedding, eighteen months earlier, she had been zaftig, red-haired, bright, and jolly.

This morning she was only one of those things. Still red-haired, she had lost a notable amount of weight and looked sad and grim.

Eva-Lynne flitted past, so thin that her bakery uniform looked like a shroud.

I got out of there.

I went on the road some months later, and though the Pearblossom house was then and still is my base, it was only really home during the two most brutally hot months of summer.

Let's just say that Eva-Lynne and I lost touch.

The latest word, perhaps six months back, was that she was ill—with what I didn't know. By now the trail had gone cold . . . I had no mailing address and no phone number for her.

I like to think she believed she had failed me and was, as more than one person has told me, acting out.

I know it was the other way around.

Eventually I did collapse into something resembling sleep, waking not long after my usual 7 a.m. I was spared the classic hangover I remember oh so well, the sharp blade of pain between the eyes, the dryness. After all, it was only a couple of glasses of wine.

But the psychic hangover was worse. All I wanted to do was hide out in the guesthouse for the day, possibly forever. That option vanished when Ridley returned, indecently perky, toting a glass of tomato juice. "Try this."

"I hate tomato juice."

"Tough shit."

I choked it down, and feared that it was going to come right back up. But that moment passed, and I suspected that I would live, if in infamy. "Can I still get breakfast?"

"Dorothy's still in the kitchen."

As we left the house I said, "Any fallout?"

"Not that I've heard, not that I would here." He smirked. "You think you're the first person to have one drink more than you should in a joint like this?"

No doubt this was true, but it didn't make me feel any better.

By the time I met up with Theodorus, I had regained a bit of my usual vigor and was even less embarrassed about my lapse. (Ah, human resiliency and expediency.)

It helped that Theodorus was filled with questions about Moon hoaxers. "I just don't get how they can't believe facts."

"There are still people in the United States, quite a few, I think, who don't believe the Takisians unleashed the wild card. Some think the whole Takisian attack was a total hoax."

"By who?"

"The Nazis, the Russians, our own government. I've heard all three."

"That's stupid."

"You're going to learn, if you haven't already, that many people are quite stupid. And here's some advice: You can't change their minds by telling them the truth, or facts. All you can do is avoid them."

"And hope they don't reproduce."

I laughed. Theodorus had a sharp mind and was beginning to display some wit.

"Oh, I have something for you." He handed me a manila folder stuffed with a quarter inch of paper.

"What's all this?"

"The life and times of Bertram Neal."

I opened the folder and took out half a dozen newspaper clippings, a typed "bio," and a few odd flyers for Neal movies and speaking engagements.

I read the bio first, learning that Neal was thirty, a Kentucky native who was prominent in joker rights—at least to the extent that he'd been arrested—and had no education beyond high school.

His conspiracy-skepticism wasn't just limited to my flight to the Moon, but included the exploits of the Four Aces ("hyped nonsense"). As for what he did when he wasn't harassing me—"He's a *chimney sweep?*"

"He has a business where he repairs roofs and things like that. Does that make a difference?"

"It shouldn't." I had to ask myself, what background did I expect of a conspiracy theorist? It wasn't likely such a man would be a scientist or engineer.

I did expect him to be a rich nutcase, but the notes confirmed what Schwartz had told me—that Neal came from money, a family that clearly downplayed their connections, or why else would the son be a roof troll?

Then there were clippings, most of them from the *Lexington Herald-Leader,* chronicling the adventures of their "local lunar conspiracy theorist" and his trips to California to picket the main gate of Tomlin Air Force Base. There was even a picture of him outside our shabby little hangar at Tehachapi-Kern Regional Airport, where he was quoted as saying, "Does this look like the launchpad for a flight to the Moon?" With the helpful subhead, BERTRAM NEAL: NEW MOON FLIGHT STORY A FANTASY.

Well, we had kept it secret—all of us, Sampson for his military career, Eva-Lynne because she didn't think it was all that important, and me because of Warren Skalko.

Skalko died in November 1971. (Given the skill and completeness of the research accomplished by Theodorus's tutors, I half expected to see clippings on my former mob boss.)

The last clipping was dated eleven days ago and reported that Neal had been "badly injured in a scuffle at a county fair," that he remained in a coma in the joker wing of Baptist Health.

"How did you collect all of this so quickly?" I didn't need to add that he couldn't have spent much time at the local library, assuming even that they would possess most of these items.

He smiled. "My parents have hired all these other tutors."

"I know. Sometimes I feel I should take a number."

"I gave one of them an assignment."

"Well, please thank this mystery tutor and researcher," I said, handing the file back to Theodorus.

"Oh, no, keep them."

I didn't actually want them. The less I thought about or heard of Bertram Neal the happier I would be.

And here, wanting to change the subject and undoubtedly triggered by the unique odor, I said, "You should get some plants in here."

"What kind?"

"Flowers. Maybe some vines."

"It's that bad?" He must have realized that the room had an odor.

"I'm thinking decoration, color, and just general . . . inspiration."

He pondered this, nodding his head and, for that moment, looking human. Then he grinned. "What if I get hungry and eat them?"

"Win-win."

"Plants are the last thing I expect you to bring up." Fair point. Had I been a contestant on *The $100,000 Question* with plants as a category, I'd have failed so badly I would not only have been shown the door, I'd have been mocked by people in the streets.

Maybe it was thinking about Eva-Lynne again. She had brought no pictures, no family mementoes (God, I could only imagine what they'd have been if she had) to our married life.

But she had turned my little rat shack into a greenhouse, with daisies and camellias and roses—the latter from several rosebushes she nurtured at the side of the house.

If nothing else, it smelled better. No one who knows me believes this, but I kept those plants alive long after Eva-Lynne left. "I'm more than I appear to be, or at least I hope so." I was joking, but I must have revealed something of my lack of direction.

"Cash, what are you going to do? When you leave here?" He didn't add, though probably assumed, *if you're not in jail.*

"Set up my schedule for fall, when schools are back in session. And I have a few carnivals this summer."

"Is that it?"

"Is it that bad?"

"Oh, it sounds fun for a while. Better than being a giant snail in a mansion. But . . ."

"It's not very ambitious." Which is what everyone from Warren Skalko to Mike Sampson to Eva-Lynne Roderick had said to me at one time. I would have to plead guilty to never having settled on an actual career—forget heavy lifting and what that might have led me to—or finished school. Christ, I didn't even have hobbies, other than my former drinking.

I used to fret about this, but from about age seventeen to thirty-four was able to suppress any real worries by, well, drinking. Since then I had told myself I had a career and a direction—I was an "educator."

"How old are you?"

"Thirty-nine." Then I laughed, and not happily. "You know, I haven't actually said that out loud more than once."

"Shy?"

"My birthday was only six weeks ago, April fourth. And it does sound old."

"Wait 'til the next one."

"Don't be mean, Theodorus."

"You just told me my room stinks."

He had me there.

The next week was a blur. I found myself spending only mornings with Theodorus, as other "tutors" began to take up his afternoons.

Ridley drove in and out, bringing pieces of aluminum, rented welding gear, then various cylindrical tanks. "I'm not a rocket scientist," I told him after a particularly unique collection of equipment showed up, "but it looks to me as though you're getting *Quicksilver* ready to go into space."

He actually blushed. "Who told you?"

Sometimes Ridley is a bit dense. "No one, and I'd just like to know why."

"It just seemed the right thing to do. I hated seeing it take off with holes in its side."

"I appreciate that and approve. But tell me how, or who's paying, because there's no way you're buying all this with a couple hundred—"

Not only is Ridley sometimes dense, he is frequently stubbornly silent or deflective. He got a familiar faraway look in his eye and I was afraid I was going to have to battle for answers. Then he said, "Ask him."

"Who?"

Ridley pointed past me, so I turned.

Striding toward me was a red-going-gray-haired man in his mid-forties dressed in khaki trousers and a short-sleeved blue shirt.

None other than Michael Sampson, Major General, USAF (Retired).

He had returned from our 1968 excursion determined to keep it quiet—not only was our flight funded by criminals, off the books, but it was an unauthorized activity forbidden to an active-duty officer.

Some of the troops at Tomlin knew immediately, of course. They tracked air traffic and saw us coming and going. They told NORAD, of course—I think those boys were happy to be tracking something human headed for the Moon, not some alien piece of crap headed this way.

I heard later that they also got Mount Wilson, Jodrell Bank, and some radio telescope in Australia to track us, too. And they intercepted our air-to-ground with Tuominbang.

Ah, yes, Tuominbang the visionary ahead of his time, hoping to place a relay unit on the Moon that would allow him to make "wire" transactions that were untraceable and untaxable.

Fortunately, Sampson reported to a wing commander who liked him and liked audacity, and got him promoted to colonel quickly, "because he figured that the first Air Force pilot to go to the Moon had earned it."

Then the general select commanding the Hornet spaceplane development died suddenly, and Sampson was given his job, which got him to brigadier general two years later. "I became a fast burner." Actually, he was being modest: with test pilot and combat experience, and a degree from Caltech, he was already being groomed for leadership in the Air Force even without the flight to the Moon.

But it shortened his path to major general by four years. Then the whole story came out, and there was a bit of a bobble, since the Air Force leadership was heavy on joker-haters, and even the hint of associations with such types as, well, Cash Mitchell, was enough to stall Sampson's rise. Fortunately, in a Pentagon assignment he was able to work enough secret magic to help establish me in my new career as a carnival barker.

He languished at the Pentagon, hoping for another promotion and a final major command. "I had gotten the Hornets to fly and I wanted to run the ops." But no. He was forced to retire and, as often happens with high-ranking ex-military types, made a smooth transition to corporate boards and consulting, including . . . Dayton Enterprises.

We shook hands. Then, shockingly, he hugged me. I barely suppressed a comment about the new homoerotic Air Force, settling for a basic hello, leading to, "What have you and Ridley been doing?"

"Henry and Malachi told me about your, uh, teaching job."

"So you really are a friend of the family."

Sampson gave me his basic crinkly-eyed, indulgent smile. "Just took advantage of the, uh, confluence of events to see *Quicksilver* again."

"And help restore it."

"It needed some help."

"I'm not objecting."

He laughed. "How is it that we seem to disagree, but actually don't?"

"Different styles, I guess." Sampson was five years older than me, but we had enough shared experiences that I could describe him as "my good twin." He was smarter than me, clearly more moral, more even-tempered, and generally just a more productive citizen.

If he had a flaw it was that he tended to trust in people's honesty. Of course, I knew him best circa 1970—I'm guessing a few years as an Air Force general, Pentagon staffer, and now corporate leader might have enlightened him.

I turned to Ridley, who had been standing to one side, mute. "You two obviously have met. What do you have planned?"

"Fuel her up," Ridley said.

"And take a short hop," said Sampson.

"I don't think I'd be comfortable lifting her here." I had been able to set *Quicksilver* down here, but lifting, with the overhanging trees and nearby windows, was another matter.

"We don't need you for the hop," Sampson said. "We're going to use the jets." *Quicksilver* had small but powerful hybrid motors that were originally designed to get it off the runway and, after in-flight refueling, into low Earth orbit. For our Moon mission, they had served to get us clear of a commercial airport—and to ease our landing on the Ocean of Storms.

"Those motors will blow this place apart."

"Oh, heck, we're going up to the road," Sampson said. "There's a small base called Goose Creek. The director of ops used to work for me and is going to let us play a bit."

I was always struck by the web of connections within the military, where everyone seemed to have served with or under someone else who might be useful. "What else haven't you told me?"

And here Sampson looked at Ridley, who just looked away.

"I'm not your only visitor."

I had no idea what he meant.

"Cash?" Alice Witherspoon was at the back door. "Would you come with me, please?"

Feeling that I might be facing arrest, but curious nonetheless, I followed Alice and Sampson into the house.

"What's going on?" I asked as we headed for the front door.

"Call it a surprise," Sampson said.

And so I found myself standing in the majestic doorway, recently widened for Theodorus, with General Sampson and Alice Witherspoon and, naturally, Malachi Schwartz. It must have looked like the receiving line at a poorly planned wedding.

A car, one of the Witherspoon sedans, had already pulled up to the front door. James and another retainer were there to assist the arrival. And behind me I heard the thumps and slithers of Theodorus's arrival. He was never going to be able to sneak up on anyone.

A slim blonde woman I judged to be fifty emerged from the back seat.

Eva-Lynne Roderick Mitchell, my lost love, my ex-wife.

I could not have been more surprised if Dr. Tachyon himself, or the Easter Bunny, had emerged.

My first thought was that she looked and moved like death, or at best one step removed. But when she smiled and said, "Hi, Cashie," the apparent years slipped away.

We hugged and while I found her thinner, she fit in my arms as she once did. Something was off, though I wasn't sure what. "Where were you?" I said, realizing as I said it that it sounded judgmental.

"Las Vegas."

"Why don't we let her get settled?" Alice said, slipping into gracious hostess mode.

"Thank you for having me," Eva-Lynne told her. She raised her head. "This might be the biggest house I've ever been in."

"I'll give you the tour." Alice let Eva-Lynne slip past her into the foyer, all the while shooting me a look that said *back off, be kind.*

The retainers carried Eva-Lynne's luggage inside, and I was left with Theodorus and Sampson. Before I could utter the obvious question, harshly, Theodorus said, "It was my idea."

"But I agreed," Sampson said.

"I'm happy to see her, but . . . why? Old times' sake?"

Theodorus and Sampson exchanged glances, and I had the unpleasant feeling that I had been the subject of considerable discussion. "That would cover it," Sampson said.

Of course, I didn't believe that.

The surprise was that straight arrow Michael Sampson had, in middle age, learned to shade the truth.

Eva-Lynne and Sampson were guests at dinner that night—another vegetarian dish, though more successful—with Alice and Theodorus and me. No Mathilde. Henry was in D.C. but expected in a day or so.

"Do you see Henry often?" I asked Sampson.

"The first year," he said. "Not so much . . . lately." He had been about to say "the last two," I believe, and his embarrassed blush confirmed it.

Theodorus spoke up. "I wish Dad and the Air Force would listen to you, General." It turned out Sampson was famous in the space underground for his promotion of robot battle stations in Earth orbit, and at least one if not two bases on the Moon. "We need that Farside Base," Theodorus said. "What if somebody attacks us again?"

Alice laughed nervously. "Theodorus, that is highly unlikely."

"Not as unlikely as the Takisian event," Sampson said, his drive for honesty overwhelming his sense of dinner decorum. "Until 1946 we could have believed we were alone in the universe, for all practical purposes.

"But being invaded once by a race that possesses star travel and is perhaps only two centuries more advanced than we are—it only proves that there are dangers everywhere. We are not only defenseless, we are largely blind. The Air Force has developed useful surveillance systems aimed at the Soviet Union and China, but they look down, not up. We are unprepared."

"Well," Alice said, summoning every bit of her considerable charm, "we can only hope that you and Henry are able to change that situation and make better use of the Moon."

All through this, and most of dinner, Eva-Lynne was quiet, her usual mode in gatherings with strangers even a dozen years ago. I did note that she frowned when Theodorus and Sampson began talking about the Moon. Well, she was one of three people who had been there: perhaps she felt proprietary.

No wine was served, whether in deference to my weakness or to Sampson or Eva-Lynne's preferences, I don't know. All in all, it was still my best experience at a sit-down dinner in the main room, but, then, the bar was pretty low.

As we rose to separate, Theodorus attached himself, metaphorically speaking (though only barely), to Sampson, and they went off to plan the future exploration of cislunar space.

I was left with Alice and Eva-Lynne. Alice said, "I am going to see to the cleanup. You two surely have matters to discuss." Before either of us could object, she was gone.

Eva-Lynne glided into the vast living room, going to the window to gently touch the lace curtains.

"How did you settle on Las Vegas?"

"Close to where I grew up," she said. "And not that far down the road from Palmdale."

"Only two hundred miles across the nastiest desert in the U.S."

She smiled. "Well, I guess I needed a barrier."

"Between you and me?"

She didn't say no, but instead, "Between me and that life."

"I would have thought you wanted to keep the barrier between you and your Mormon life."

She turned toward me, and she took my hand. At that point I realized that there were two things about Eva-Lynne that were different.

One was that she had a different fragrance. I have said that I'm unusually sensitive to smells—I can detect a cigarette smoker at fifty paces—and each person has their own. Eva-Lynne's had changed, and not due to booze or cigarettes, either. It was the touch of her hand that gave me the larger surprise—she had always worked and her hands, while never rough, were those of a working woman. Now her hands felt like smooth leather, and when I looked at them I saw new lines, squiggly filigree, not grids.

I must have reacted. We were both older, but not that much older. "Yes," she said, "my card turned."

I was surprised; she came from a community that, due to isolation, had the lowest percentage of wild cards in the whole United States. "How does it manifest?"

"My doctor isn't entirely sure. He calls it a slow burn." She laughed.

"So you don't know the endgame."

She shook her head. "But Cash, please, all that . . . foolishness?" Not the word I would have used to describe her drinking and sleeping around. "It made me feel better for a while, more human. Not much of an excuse or an apology."

"Good either way," I said.

"It was also one of the reasons I didn't want children."

That made sense. But I took the hint. "There were other reasons?"

"Two of them."

She walked back to the dining room and retrieved her purse, taking out two snapshots.

Both showed jokers, one a kind of lizard that resembled a human-sized javelina, the other even more grotesque, looking like a squarish thing made out of rock, with deep, vacant eyeholes. "Amos and Orson. My sons."

I'm a joker; I've been around seriously "diverged" (from human form) jokers since I was a child. Amos and Orson were about as bad as I've seen. "I thought you'd lost touch with them."

"Yes, after I had to run away. Nat boys are usually kicked out of fundamentalist communities, but they keep the jokers because . . ."

She didn't say it, but I did. "Because they aren't a threat to the patriarch's pleasures."

She barely nodded and, in fact, began to cry softly. "I thought they'd be safe, that they were safe and cared for. Then, once it started to happen to me—" She had written to one of her former sister wives, and learned that Amos and Orson had been cast out and were living raw and homeless somewhere in the Arizona Strip. "I had to go."

I put my arms around her. She was trembling and sniffling, but determined to tell me all.

She'd found a small place in Las Vegas, and a job at a casino (I didn't ask but suspect it was not dealer or waitress), then performed a search and rescue on the boys, bringing them there and finding a halfway house that would take Orson. "He's going to be twenty-one and can't support himself, though he's smart, so smart."

"What about Amos?"

"He's twenty-three and actually had some schooling. I don't think he's as smart as Orson, but in Vegas he can fit in. He's a janitor at the casino." I didn't know what to say, and it was obvious. She was less teary now, and a bit more resentful. "You want to know what I've been doing, that's it. Supporting two damaged boys."

"Where are they now?" I tried to sound neutral even as Eva-Lynne stiffened in my arms.

"Both at Orson's house. Amos likes to be with his brother, says he's the only one who likes him. And it's so nice to see you finally taking an interest."

I have poor impulse control when challenged. "How could I take any interest when I didn't know about them, and then you left me?"

She slid out of my arms. "You didn't make an effort, not to find out about them or what I was going through."

"I'm sorry about that," I said, even though I didn't agree with her description. "And I can see why you wouldn't have anything to do with me . . . so why are you here?"

She just shook her head. "Good night, Cash."

She grabbed her purse, wiped the back of her hand across her eyes in a gesture that was more suitable to a girl of five, then headed for the stairs.

As I stomped through the quiet main house back to the guest quarters, I found Alice Witherspoon in the kitchen, alone except for a bottle of red wine and a half-full glass.

The bottle was on the counter, the glass was in her hand, and she was drinking from it.

Southern charm and composure: She did not react like a person caught in the act, completing her sip and gently setting the glass aside. "How was the tender reunion?"

"Surprising and enlightening," I said.

"Reunions can be like that." She reached for the glass again. "I'm prepared to offer you a drink, but won't be offended—"

"Thanks, no. But please . . ."

She inclined her head and took another sip. "By the way, I am aware that this is likely to become a problem for me, if I'm not careful."

"Has it been in the past?"

"No more so than for any young woman of my position. Thank God I learned to avoid the amber liquids."

"So wise."

Another sip. "You only have another week with us."

"I miss the place already."

She could not have missed the sarcasm. "Has it been so bad?"

"In all honesty, working with Theodorus has been fascinating. Meeting you has been—gratifying. The sense of being the unknowing subject of some intrigue, unappealing."

"Welcome to my world, Cash."

"I imagine that growing up in a . . . powerful family"—I almost said rich—"would be a serious challenge. Then having your son . . ." I realized that I should just shut up.

Because Alice was crying. "It's been horrible."

"But he seems—"

"Oh, Theodorus has been a marvel, trying to cope, make a new life for himself. He gets that from his father, believe me. I'd have curled into a ball and died."

And there was a moment. An offer of comfort, a hug, was clearly acceptable, possibly even mandatory. Alice's posture demanded it.

But I was paralyzed. Hell, this was twice in the last twenty minutes that a woman had collapsed in tears while talking to me. "You're strong," I said, weakly.

She shook her head several times, as if trying to convince herself. Then she uttered a ragged, "Yeah," forced a smile, and walked out.

Leaving the bottle, half-full, and the glass.

I stared at them for far too long. But ultimately left them untouched.

I awoke the next morning feeling better than I should have. It might have been pride in my restraint on sexual or alcohol-related fronts—or just knowing what had been going on with Eva-Lynne. I had obviously slept soundly, since Ridley was gone, and so was *Quicksilver*. I would have bet a lot of money that no one could have gotten my ship away without waking me.

After breakfast in the servants' dining room, an event I was beginning to enjoy (who doesn't enjoy having breakfast prepared?), I headed up to Theodorus's room, a bit apprehensive should I meet (a) Sampson, (b) Eva-Lynne, or (c-z) Alice.

I saw none of them, realizing that Sampson was probably off with Ridley and *Quicksilver,* and that Eva-Lynne and Alice were likely off together . . . elsewhere, surely with some discussion of my failures as a human being.

Oh well.

Theodorus was still bubbling over General Sampson's presence in the household, wanting to talk about the Moon and nothing but the Moon. As one of three humans to have been there, one could rightly expect me to be the source of some information, but Theodorus surely knew by now that all I had to offer was a set of twelve-year-old personal impressions . . . the desert landscape under that frightening black sky, the fear, the confinement in *Quicksilver,* the hour I spent scuffling on the lunar surface while wearing a stiff, ill-fitting pressure suit.

Aside from my intimate moment with Eva-Lynne, and the undeniable feeling that, at age twenty-six, I had finally done something worth doing, I had no insights to share. Fortunately, Theodorus was in a manic mode, spinning his own fantasies of lunar fortresses scanning the skies for alien invaders, dispatching defense drones and cruisers as needed.

It was fun, if exhausting.

After lunch, Malachi Schwartz intercepted me on my way back to the RV. "Bertram Neal woke up."

I scurried to keep up with Schwartz. "That's good, right? If he'd died, I'd be facing murder or manslaughter charges."

Schwartz stopped and faced me. His expression suggested that he might be explaining basic arithmetic to a three-year-old. "You might have been better off if he'd died, since he is a joker and authorities in Kentucky aren't noted for their eagerness to pursue such matters."

"Even if the joker is well connected."

"Especially then. Well-connected families are prone to downplay the presence of jokers in their lineage." Yes, he said that with no apparent awareness of our current situation. I had concluded that Schwartz was not all-seeing, all-knowing.

Perhaps his unconcealed glee at my predicament affected his judgment. "Now he's awake and telling what he knows. We were able to . . . forestall an investigation by those troopers. But now there will be warrants."

"Let me turn myself in."

"Tempting, Mr. Mitchell, but I fear it would sadden Theodorus to see you in jail, even on an assault charge. And Mr. Witherspoon is very old-school about external threats to those to whom he has granted hospitality."

"Then we should just leave—Ridley and I can run, saving everyone a lot of grief."

"How far do you think you'd get with your two very distinctive vehicles? I would give it twenty miles, and now you would have a fugitive charge added to your impressive list."

"What do you suggest, then?"

"Go about your duties here. Though I would encourage Mr. Hough to complete whatever project he has been working on." He smiled that mean little smile again. "The term of your employment here has little more than a week to run."

Then he skittered off with what was definitely a lighter tread. Some jokers just enjoy trouble—for others.

When I stumbled outside I saw that where my pumpkin-seed spaceship usually sat there was a large shipping crate perhaps six feet on a side, strapped down and covered with warning labels saying FRAGILE and RUSH.

Ridley was emerging from the guesthouse with a plate of food, last night's leftovers from the looks of it. "It's too late for my birthday," I said.

"It's not a present," he said between bites, and unnecessarily.

"What is that, and where's *Quicksilver*?"

"Ship's over at Goose Creek with the general." He used a last hunk of bread to swipe up sauce on the plate, then set it on the truck bed and climbed up. "He's testing the jets and configuring guidance and communications."

"I'm guessing this crate is part of whatever he's doing."

Ridley slapped the side of the unit. "It's your space suits."

In 1968, *Quicksilver* had carried two primitive space suits, essentially high-altitude pressure suits that the late Mr. Tuominbang's team had modified with extra layers of protection in order to allow the wearer to survive in total vacuum, which is to say, on the lunar surface.

"Where were they?"

"Some warehouse in California. Tomlin, somewhere."

"That's the Air Force base." I am frequently surprised by how little Ridley knows.

It turned out that Sampson had made a request to have the suits shipped here even before arriving in person. "He says there's a guy at Goose Creek who can shine these things up or whatever."

"Well, they were only worn once."

I brought him up to date on related matters, notably Neal's awakening. For a man who frets easily, Ridley took the news well. He said, "You should look at this."

He handed me the newspaper, the *Charleston Post and Courier*. Finally.

In a box on the upper left was this headline:

MOON FLIGHT TRUTHER AWAKENS
BETS ON THEORY

And it was a story about Bertram Neal recovering from his coma and then instituting an honest-to-God prize for the first proven flight to the Moon. So now there was a quarter of a million dollars waiting to be claimed . . . "If the participants in this mythical 1968 'mission' have proof, such as lunar samples or pictures, time to produce them."

Neal had apparently assembled a damned tribunal that included a professor of geology named Gold from Cornell, whose name I recognized, and a bunch of strangers.

"He didn't do this himself," I said. "He's been in a goddamn coma."

Ridley nodded to the paper. "Says that he was working on it all along. Probably why he ambushed you in the first place."

I didn't like the notion that Ridley knew more than I did, especially on this subject, so I flipped to the continuation. "Wonder where the money came from?"

"All I know about money is how not to get it." That made me laugh. It appeared that Neal had concocted some clever little insurance scheme with Lloyd's of London, putting up a few thousand dollars and betting that no proof of our landing would be revealed by June 30, 1981. This Neal may have been a troll, but he was a clever troll. "That's less than ten weeks from now."

"Yep."

"Are you taking these suits over to this base?" Ridley nodded. "Let's go."

♠

Goose Creek Air Force Base was only ten miles down the highway. A small operation compared to Tomlin, it was largely hidden by trees, much like the Witherspoon estate. Only when you reached its main gate did you really see admin buildings, barracks, hangars, a control tower, and several distant radomes scattered around the runway. The aircraft were largely transports, and a few helicopters.

It struck me, as the gate guard waved us through, that I had not been off Witherspoon property in two weeks. We drove to an old, clearly unused hangar at the far end of the base. Inside we found *Quicksilver* on jacks and looking shinier than the first time I'd seen her a dozen years ago. Several men and women in coveralls were at work, a couple of them in the open hatch, others on the exterior or underneath.

It was all being overseen by General Sampson. "What do you think of our girl?" he said, beaming.

"Ready for the prom," I said. "Or a long-distance flight, say, back to the Moon."

"That has come up."

"Just out of curiosity, when? And when was anyone going to tell me? Since I would have to be part of it. Unless you've figured out some magic beans space drive."

Sampson looked embarrassed. "I've wanted to go again for years. You had to face skeptics and I'm sure that was annoying, but my career got killed."

"You wound up with two stars."

"Should have been three or even four."

I have just never understood true ambition and arrogance on that scale. "Flying to the Moon again and back won't make you a super galactic general now, so what's the point?"

"Pride in a real accomplishment."

"Or getting killed. Have you forgotten that we almost died?"

He literally shrugged. "There's a risk every time you take off, or walk down the street."

"Not quite as high."

He pointed to *Quicksilver*. "We've swapped out the old comm and nav for new systems. She's safer now than she ever was."

"Safer without ever really being safe."

"A new flight would give inspiration to a country that really needs it right now. And to young people."

"Theodorus Witherspoon doesn't need more inspiration."

"Not just him. And now there's a financial issue."

Sampson gave me a look that made me want to punch him. "I could use the money, but I don't need the money."

"I wasn't thinking about you."

It took me maybe four seconds to understand who he meant: Eva-Lynne.

"Assuming I say yes to this, what's the goal? Take a flag we can plant?"

"Did you read the prize rules?"

"There are rules?"

He waved that away. "We bring back photographs of our steps, lunar soil samples, and, if possible, a piece of the relay station."

"Did that ever work?"

"For a while, though it never did what Tuominbang wanted."

No, because he got dead.

"Space Command would bounce signals off it every few weeks for several years, but nothing ever came back. It was proof that we landed."

"Are we sure some Takisian didn't steal it?"

He smiled. "More likely the solar panels got dusty and the batteries died."

"So we would have to go back to the same spot."

"The new nav makes that easier."

"You keep forgetting that it's me doing the heavy lifting."

"You seem to be in good shape. Your buddy Ridley and Malachi Schwartz said you hauled *Quicksilver* from West Virginia."

"Nowhere near as far as the Moon."

He slapped me on the back, all hail-fellow. "But going to the Moon is just a couple of big lifts, not several hours straight."

"Easy for you to say."

"You're fighting this, Cash, and you really don't want to."

In fact, here's where, somewhat in the manner of a wild card turning, a new Cash Mitchell emerged. I had been adrift all my adult life, rarely committing to anything, never making a decision. Even my first trip to the Moon was just something that happened.

No longer. "I'm not fighting," I told Sampson, and shook his hand. "I'm in."

Sampson made me try on my space suit, which still fit even though it smelled like machine oil and something worse. The techs then took it away to make sure it was airtight and to test connections with a small oxygen pack.

Then *Quicksilver* was hauled out to a taxiway where Sampson burped each rocket, the three mains and a dozen smaller steering jets, in turn. I had to join him in the cockpit for this boring nonsense, and then demonstrate my heavy lifting for the team, popping our ship up to a hundred feet with only my pinkie finger on the tiller.

Sampson had had a TV camera installed in the cockpit, so the support team had an inside view of the moment when, at our peak altitude, Sampson fired one of the side steering jets.

And it blew.

Viewers below saw Sampson and me flung to one side, then Sampson performing some quick magic with the primary control stick. For me it was like being in a nearby earthquake, a sudden but notable jolt.

Before I had time to panic, Sampson had stabilized us and set us down safely.

My heart rate was elevated and my mouth was dry. But Sampson was merely shaking his head and flipping switches on the control panel. I guess he was used to such moments. Without a word, we clambered out to find the team already swarming *Quicksilver,* examining the damage. Ridley was waiting for me. Bless him, he looked worried. "How are you doing?"

I held out my hand, which was still trembling. "Same as ever."

Then I turned to Sampson, who was peering at the blackened hole in *Quick-*

silver's skin where a steering rocket used to be. "Back to the old drawing board, huh?"

"We can replace and patch this in a week."

"No doubt. But it failed. Don't we want to know why?" I may have signed on, but I didn't want to be foolhardy.

Sampson smiled, and for once it made me want to punch him. "There are usually only two or three reasons a rocket like that fails, and they're easily repaired."

"Until next time."

And now he became an Air Force general, all steel. "I am confident that this vehicle will be ready and safe for launch by the end of next week."

"What's the rush? The prize deadline isn't until June 30." You'll laugh, but I was actually thinking about my ongoing commitment to Theodorus—and the final payment.

"Positions of Earth and Moon. Don't you look at the sky? We're just past new moon; it's night on the Ocean of Storms. We'd like to arrive at lunar dawn. But," he said, and left that word hanging.

"But?"

"There's a reason we're on a military base."

"Beyond your personal connections and the location?"

"Security, Cash. There are people who don't want us to prove we can go to the Moon."

"Well, there's Bertram Neal—"

"—or a dozen other people in business, or in other countries. And never forget the Takisians and whoever they have running around."

I had to remind myself that Sampson, for all his virtues, was still a military man—a professional paranoiac. "So, just to be clear, one of the three reasons our jet failed might be . . . sabotage?"

"Don't be an ass."

And so my partner in one and possibly two flights to the Moon was done talking to me.

On the drive back to the Witherspoons', I said to Ridley, "Hey, you wanna fly to the Moon?"

"With you and the general in that little thing? No thanks."

"It's only for a few days. Come on, you'll be famous!"

"Like you?"

"Better than me."

"I'm happy right here."

He went silent at that point, allowing me to ponder the question of the third member of the *Quicksilver* crew. Sampson was a given and I was mandatory. The subject had simply not come up, no doubt due to the ridiculous haste surrounding the whole idea. Was there some scientist lurking in the background? Someone associated with this prize?

For a crazy few seconds I wondered if Theodorus might be the best choice. But (a) he was a kid and (b) he simply wouldn't fit in the cabin.

We didn't reach the Witherspoons' until the house was as dark as it ever got. Too late for dinner, though we had leftovers in the RV. After a sad meal,

Ridley grabbed the first shower, and I was sitting with my feet up when Malachi Schwartz knocked.

"We have a change in plans."

At 5:13 a.m. (the precise time was noted) on a humid Friday, May 22, 1981, a whole team of law enforcers, federal and state (both Kentucky and South Carolina), nat and joker, appeared at the gates of the Witherspoon estate with warrants.

Well, only four appeared at the front gates. Having grown wise to Witherspoon ways, other teams took up position at the other three exits.

Malachi Schwartz met them in his robe and graciously invited them to present their papers and demands, which were to produce Mr. Cash Mitchell and Ridley Hough to face charges of felony assault and flight from justice, and to search as they might.

The sheer scope of the Witherspoon household with its three buildings made such a search an hours-long event.

Naturally they did not find us.

I only heard these details from Theodorus and Alice. We had been tipped off and at 5:13 that morning my RV and the *Quicksilver* truck were already hidden inside a hangar at Goose Creek Air Force Base about ten miles to the northwest.

Where, get this, we were preparing to launch the human race's second flight to the Moon. With something like eight hours' notice.

With a crew of Major General Michael Sampson, USAF (Retired) as commander and pilot, Cash Mitchell as whatever the hell I am, propulsion specialist and cargo—and the third?

That news had been announced to me as I was climbing behind the wheel of my RV, about to follow Ridley and the truck. Alice climbed in with me. "Drive, please."

"Shouldn't you be riding with the grown-ups?" A sedan had pulled up out front, ready to take Eva-Lynne and others out of harm's way. Theodorus's special van was standing by, too.

"Don't you like me, Cash?" I got just a burst of Alice Dayton on full flirt, enough to make me her creature.

An answer was not required. I merely fired up the RV and headed out.

"You're taking Eva-Lynne on the flight."

An answer, or protest, did not seem required here, either. Nevertheless: "Why?"

"She was on the first."

"And now she's sick, possibly dying."

"That's why. She needs the prize money."

Which shut me up.

The Witherspoons, to use a phrase my father uttered frequently, quite possibly translating from the Babylonian, had more money than God (or probably "the gods"). Surely they could have offered to support Eva-Lynne and her boys for the rest of their lives.

One thing I had learned about people with lots of money—they like to hold on to it, and if they do let it go, it's when they want. And . . . it was quite likely to the point of certainty that Eva-Lynne did not want charity.

So there we had it: Eva-Lynne Roderick Mitchell was our third crewmember.

I was too tired to be as angry as I should have been—at Sampson, Schwartz, the Witherspoons (Henry met us at Goose Creek), at everyone who was behind this scheme—and was largely acting like a sleepwalker.

Sampson and Ridley were supervising the refueling of *Quicksilver*'s rockets. The failed steering jet had not been replaced, but simply patched. As I pointed to it, about to ask the obvious question, one of the techs said, "We didn't have time to replace it, so we just disabled its twin on the other side."

"So neither of those is really necessary."

Noting my verbal assault on the tech, Sampson strode toward me. "You've got a big lift ahead of you, Cash. Shouldn't you be eating a hearty breakfast?"

"You remember what triggered my biggest lift, don't you? Off the Moon?"

The damage *Quicksilver* had suffered on our first landing had caused a fuel leak; we did not actually have sufficient rocket fuel to rise off the lunar surface to where my lifting would take over. What gave me the equivalent of an adrenaline boost was making love to Eva-Lynne right there in the *Quicksilver* air lock.

It took Sampson several moments to remember the event—less a case of poor recall; he was just a prude and had surely repressed the notion along with any ecstatic sounds and fleshy sights. "Well," he said, "I can't help you there."

Henry worked his political magic on the base commander, who turned out to be a frat brother. (Another reminder that I somehow failed to enter so many different and beneficial worlds.) Alice tended to Eva-Lynne.

During the first moments after we arrived at the hangar, my ex seemed energized. I even saw her smile and heard her laugh as she and Alice crawled in and out of the *Quicksilver* cabin. This annoyed Ridley. "What are they doing?"

"Personalizing the cabin," I said.

"What, putting up curtains?"

"Close. Putting a few plants there." I didn't need to add that Eva-Lynne had also taped pictures of Amos and Orson to the wall near her couch.

When I found a private moment with her, however, I saw that she was trembling, on the brink of a breakdown. "Why are you doing this?"

"Alice told you."

"Let Sampson and me do the flight. We'll give you the money!"

"I left those boys, Cash. I owe them."

"Maybe you owe them support now, but who cares about the past?"

"You don't understand." Not the first time she had used those words with me. "It's the only thing I can do for them."

And then she walked away from me.

Maybe it was the way she paused to look up at the sky, quite a pretty one now that the clouds were clearing. Or the oddly intimate moment where she just spread her arms and took a break, as if embracing all of Earth and life—

I knew then: she did not expect to survive this trip.

I might have said something—to her, to the Witherspoons, to Sampson. But I already suspected that all of them knew, and were complicit.

And, really, what future did she face? A transformation into a joker high on the hideous scale? Or death in some grim hospice—?

Better on the Moon.

Having arrived in his custom van, driven by James, Theodorus Witherspoon lumbered to a spot well away from the tech teams swarming *Quicksilver*. As I was still debating my options regarding Eva-Lynne, I saw him and approached.

"Sorry about the rest of the lessons," I told him.

"You've got the perfect excuse. I wouldn't accept anything less than going to the Moon, though."

I realized that I not only liked Theodorus but felt that he would do all right in life. Then he said, "Shouldn't you have some kind of cool uniform?"

I was wearing my usual clothing, slacks and a polo shirt. I realized that Sampson was in a smart blue Air Force flight suit. Eva-Lynne had dressed for the occasion, too, in a dark blue pullover, matching slacks, and white sneakers. She complemented Sampson; I looked like a janitor. "Too late now," I said. "And this is pretty much what I wore the first time, and it worked then." I offered my hand, and Theodorus took it, almost crushing it.

And I heavy lifted him right off the ground.

There he was, this massive human-snail-whatever, long tail flapping helplessly. I hastened to let him down. "Sorry!" I was about to add, "nerves," but surely that was obvious.

He was laughing. "You're just warming up."

Nearby, in the hangar, a phone jangled. Henry Witherspoon went to answer it.

I told Theodorus, "Oh, don't forget: if you get Eva-Lynne's autograph, you'll have the world's only complete set of *Quicksilver* space flyers."

"Really?" You'd think I offered him a dragon's horde, or maybe a return to nathood.

He grabbed a clipboard and a pen from one of the techs, then slid over to Eva-Lynne, who seemed to be quite gracious about the request.

Meanwhile, Henry Witherspoon literally ran past us.

"Cash!" Standing in front of *Quicksilver*, General Sampson beckoned to me. The dozen or so members of the tech team were standing around, impatiently. "Do you want to go to the Moon or not?"

"Do I have a choice?" I said.

It all seemed quite casual, until Sampson said, "You can wait for the police. They'll be here soon."

"I think I'll go with you instead."

Before I could reach my crewmates and *Quicksilver*, I had to run a gauntlet. First Henry Witherspoon stopped to shake my hand. "Good luck, Cash. And thank you."

Then Alice gave me a hug and actually kissed me on the cheek. "Come back safely," she whispered. Finally, Ridley waited.

"You aren't going to kiss me, are you?"

Then he punched me in the shoulder. "Hurry back," he said. "We've got a schedule to keep."

Sampson was first into the vehicle, sliding into the left-hand seat. I was next, sliding into the right. Eva-Lynne was last, wedging herself into the third seat, which was slightly off-center, behind Sampson's. I turned to help her with the straps, but she waved me away. "I remember."

"Hey, you two, showtime. That phone call was from Schwartz: the cops are here so we go now or never."

"Well, hell," I said. "Let's go to the Moon again."

The tech team and spectators had cleared the area. With no special preliminary, Sampson fired the main engines and we rose, *Quicksilver* vibrating in a way I did not remember.

As we hovered, I could see half a dozen police cars clustered at the main gate.

"Go for lift number one," Sampson said. And I grabbed the tiller.

I could have sworn I saw the shadow of *Quicksilver* flashing over the trollish form of Bertram Neal, looking up as we disappeared into the sky.

The external events of this mission have been recounted in several publications over the last couple of years. I even published my own sanitized version in *Joker Life*.

Between that, and my earlier account of 1968, I have little to add: a flight from the Earth to the Moon takes three days each way. *Quicksilver's* life-support systems would only support three people for a total of eight days, so time on the surface was limited to two days—one being a smarter choice.

Let's be honest: In 1946 a spaceship from another world arrived and made war on the human race. We have lived with alien beings for thirty-five years.

By comparison, the details of a 500,000-mile round trip, however plucky, are of no real importance.

I had to perform six big lifts.

Number one was launching us from Goose Creek to an altitude of 130 miles and a speed of 17,500 miles an hour.

This was a wrenching experience and left me useless for two hours, time enough to allow Sampson to communicate with "flight control" at Goose Creek about the timing and aim of lift number two. (I had some control over the direction of a lift, and using the special tiller added vital precision: it was like setting off a big bomb under *Quicksilver* and shooting it toward a specific spot in space. You wanted that spot to be somewhere above the Moon's surface, not splat in the lunar dust—or in the wrong direction entirely.)

Lifts number three and number four were actually reverses—number three being a major braking on approach to the Moon, allowing us to fall toward our target on the Ocean of Storms. Sampson would use the rockets to do the final tweaks and I would perform a minor number-four lift to slow us for a gentle landing.

Number five would blast us back to Earth after Sampson used the main rockets to give us altitude.

Number six was designed to be the primary reverse lift, slowing us for entry into the atmosphere, but could actually be broken into three steps—tweaking our path, performing the slowdown, and then a final reverse lift before landing.

Sampson and I spent hours talking about these, writing down the likely times (after consultation with our ground team).

The rest of the voyage, other than eating, trying to stay tidy, and sleeping, was spent looking out the window. There were three forward windows in the cockpit, and a circular one in the main hatch/air lock. Eva-Lynne essentially claimed that for herself. For our first two loops around Earth, she floated there, rapt, and who could blame her? In spite of my jaded attitude—the Moon, been there, done that—I could still be moved by the sight of a blue/brown/green orb rolling by beneath us.

When I wasn't feeling sick. (This happened to me on the first flight, too, a sensation a lot like seasickness, obviously due to being without weight.) Sampson appeared to be immune; Eva-Lynne didn't say and we didn't ask.

As Earth receded behind us (we were looking toward the Moon, or rather, deep, dark space), she was in the air lock with the door closed. Halfway to our destination, during an especially quiet time, when Sampson was asleep in his chair, his arms floating like a sleepwalker's, I tapped on the air lock door. "How are you doing?" I said. "Need food or water?"

The door peeped open, not enough for me to see inside beyond noting that the interior light was off and illumination was coming from the circular hatch.

I held out a sandwich in a bag, and a bottle of water.

An appendage more like a claw than a hand carefully took both items. I heard a croak from inside the chamber that might have been a "thank you"—or a warning.

Then the hatch was pulled shut again.

I was worried about Eva-Lynne, but unable to do anything. And my relationship with her, and everything I had learned about her life prior to that and afterward, made it clear that she would make her own choices about her life, even its end.

We're all of us humans helpless against the wild card.

When Sampson awoke on our landing day, he asked me, with some concern, "What's going on with her?"

"I think she's changing and fading."

He pondered this. "Will it affect our ops?"

"Only if we have to climb over her to get out."

He nodded. God bless the pilot mentality; all he was capable of thinking about was his ability to fly *Quicksilver*. Not that I was unhappy about that.

In the last four hours before landing I rapped on the air lock door again.

No answer.

I pushed it open and was immediately aware of a smell—not decay or death, but Eva-Lynne's new smell, stronger.

What I found was not Eva-Lynne, not as I knew her, loved her, had made love to her.

She had become a smaller being—slimy piles of flesh or other matter had been sloughed off her—wiry, leathery, still bilaterally symmetrical in that "she" had two arms, two legs, and a head. Her clothing was five sizes too big.

I was shocked, yet . . . I was only four when the wild card struck. I'd seen or heard of many transformations like this in the thirty-five years since. This one hurt, though. It was as if I were losing Eva-Lynne a second time.

Sampson called from the pilot seat, "Whatever it is, it can wait. You've got a lift to do."

I pulled the air lock door shut and pulled myself back to my station.

It was strange yet familiar to see the gray pockmarked face of the Moon growing fatter and fatter, even if half to two-thirds was in black, impenetrable shadow.

"Try and stick the landing this time."

We did. You know that. Eleven hours on the surface of the Moon, less than five hundred meters from our 1968 landing site.

The only tricky moment was the prep for our suited walk on the surface. We had three tasks: take photographs, collect samples, and, if possible, remove a piece of the relay station to take back with us.

We had just two suits. Our plan had been for me and Sampson to don them, entering the air lock and leaving Eva-Lynne safely inside the cabin. But she was unconscious. It almost felt cruel to move her, much less leave her. "It's got to be done," Sampson said. "For her as well as us." So in my suit, with helmet off, I picked up the new version of Eva-Lynne and placed her in my chair. The movement woke her. At first she seemed frightened, certainly startled.

"Are we there?" she asked, her voice a bare, croaking whisper.

"Yes, we made it." I reached for a bottle to give her some water.

"They get the money."

"Yes. You, too, you know." I gave her a drink and saw what might have been a smile.

"It's for them." She sounded, and looked, like someone who had given up.

"We'll be back home in three days. We can get you to Doctor Tachyon."

"Whatever you say, Cash." She squirmed, as if getting comfortable in the chair. "You were always straight with me."

If I hadn't already feared that she was dying, that statement would have convinced me. I turned to Sampson with my best pleading look.

"Cash, it's a three-day trip back. Adding two hours isn't going to make a difference. And we need to have proof."

Eva-Lynne's clawlike hand grasped mine. "Go! I have a nice view here. I'm good." I could barely hear her.

Sampson and I sealed the air lock and went outside. As we hopped and slid away from *Quicksilver,* I had tears in my eyes. They don't flow fast in lunar gravity, so my view of the landscape was obscured.

Sampson took pictures. We both dug samples and poured them into cans that we sealed with taped lids, taking pictures of the before and after. I was the one who pried a solar panel off the relay station and brought it back to *Quicksilver.*

Sampson was the first to emerge from the air lock into the cabin. "Cash," he said.

He didn't need to add more. Eva-Lynne was curled up in my chair, cold and dead.

I sat down and simply sobbed for a while. I wasn't weeping for our time together, but for Eva-Lynne and her horrible childhood, her struggles. I may have uttered a word or two, I can't frankly remember. But Sampson patted me on the shoulder. "You were good for her, and she for you." And, being the man he was, he offered a prayer.

Then we suited up again and carried her out to the surface of the Ocean of Storms.

There, on a rise roughly halfway between the relay station and landing site, we buried her, marking the grave with a shipping tag that Sampson pinned in place with a knife.

On the shipping tag were these words: *She walks in beauty, like the night.* The only poem I could remember at that moment, two lines scribbled in pencil.

Then we took off. I found that sadness worked as well as sexual passion as a trigger for a lift.

We touched down just before dawn at Goose Creek, settling onto a concrete pad normally used by helicopters.

There must have been a hundred people waiting for us, a vast improvement over 1968, when Eva-Lynne, Sampson, and I slunk back to our sad little airstrip at Tehachapi. You could see the cars lined up—some of them shining lights onto the pad.

"This is more like it," Sampson said. "I could get used to this flying to the Moon. How about you?"

"Twice is enough," I said.

"I think this time things are gonna work out better for you."

"For some kids, at least."

But it did turn out to be good for all of us, in some ways. Sampson seemed satisfied to have had his lunar flight confirmed. I got booked for actual lectures at decent fees, not just junior high school or carnival exhibitions.

A good thing, since *Quicksilver* was going to a museum. (Which said it would buy the craft from me for an especially decent fee that I planned to split with Ridley.)

As for Ridley, he volunteered to help with my "transition" to public speaker, but allowed as though it might be time for him to return to Minnesota and settle down there.

We did return to the Witherspoons' to say our goodbyes and collect whatever we'd left. Henry and Alice had been present at the landing, of course. Henry beamed and said appropriately congratulatory things, then went off with Sampson. I had one private moment with Alice, who was tearfully apologetic and sympathetic. "Poor girl." She meant Eva-Lynne, I think.

"She was turning," I said. "At least she found a new home where she won't be a freak. And her boys will be taken care of." I had privately decided that my first trip would be to Las Vegas to meet Amos and Orson.

"Cash, that sounds like one of those comforting fictions we tell each other." Before I could get angry, she pointed to herself. "I'm just as guilty. It's all I've been saying since I met her."

I had already suspected that the Neal "prize" was actually a Witherspoon gambit. What I learned from Alice was that the family had also taken out some huge life insurance policy on Eva-Lynne, payable not on her death (though that was the reason we originally told everyone she had died on the trip) but on her failure to return to Earth.

"We all play the cards we're dealt." The motto of the wild card era.

I left thinking that, for all her beauty and power and charm, Alice Witherspoon was more tragic than Eva-Lynne.

I delivered a gift Moon rock to my "student," which he accepted with unfeigned enthusiasm and even some tears.

Theodorus's room had changed in the time I'd been gone: he had filled it with plants, far more than I had suggested. (I had thought three might be a suitable number. He had obtained ten times that number.) "I guess anything worth doing is worth overdoing," I said.

We shook hands, promising to catch up again soon, especially if my new lecture circuit brought me back through Charleston. (As it turned out, it was many years before I saw Theodorus Witherspoon again.)

If you can fucking believe this, Malachi Schwartz refused to pay me for my last five days as Theodorus's sponsor! "But I was working for you!"

"You weren't living up to the terms of our agreement."

I think, now, that he would have given in eventually—he was just one of those individuals who wants a fight. But I didn't care. There was more money to be made.

There was one coda.

A week after we landed, *Quicksilver* was transferred from its hangar to a big transport that would carry it to the Air Force museum in Ohio.

Several scientists and folks from D.C. were there to collect our samples, too.

A crowd gathered to see the little bird, and to meet Sampson and yours truly.

Who should show up but Bertram Neal. He had a camera operator and sound guy with him, and had both of them aiming their devices at me.

"Nice to see you conscious," I said.

"No thanks to you."

"Don't ambush a twitchy joker."

"A liar."

I smiled. "I hope all of that is on film and tape, in case I sue you for libel and slander and anything else that seems appropriate."

"You could have faked all of it." He scuttled around so that he could see *Quicksilver*. "Who could believe that that piece of junk could fly to the Moon?"

"Twice," I said, though I would have to admit—on the surface—that both flights did seem unlikely. Nevertheless, I kept wondering what motivated a troll like Neal, what kept him arguing against what was now overwhelming evidence.

Assuming he actually believed what he said.

"Come here and see some actual lunar soil."

I opened the can and scooped out a bit of moondust.

"That could just be your honey's ashes," Neal said.

Okay, too soon, too far, too stupid. My impulse control had not improved. I threw it in his face.

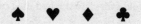

The Moon Maid

PART IV

1981

FOR MORE THAN A decade, no one disturbed Aarti. One might think that time would ease her pain, her grief. India was growing more tolerant of jokers—clothing restrictions lifted after mass protests, jokers coming into prominent positions as heads of corporations, elected officials. None of that mattered to Aarti; for her, the damage was done. Yaj's sweet face stolen from the world, the crinkles at the corners of his eyes gone forever. Year after year, there was no one to touch her; she would not have permitted it if they'd tried. Suresh and Saila's children learned to keep a respectful distance from the mistress of the house on the rare occasions when she left her room. She painted furiously, ferociously, on Earth—her lover's face, the brutal, murderous crowd. The paintings grew darker, year by year.

Then visitors came to the Moon once more. She went to bed in her room and woke up in her moon-palace, only to feel them immediately. Two humans, intruding on her Moon, and a jagged streak of fury raced through her. Aarti let the feel of them call to her, let her form dissolve to moondust and re-form near them. Oh, this ship she recognized, she remembered. How long had it been here, while she'd been wasting time in Bombay, waiting for the cruel sun to release its hold on her?

The men in their suits looked like they'd been working for hours, their arms heavy with recording equipment. They were headed back toward the ship, and Aarti took a quick, deep breath—she would destroy them. Her arms were already raised, fingertips thinned to brush. But before she could paint their utter dissolution, the door of the ship opened again, and the men reemerged, carrying what appeared to be a body. A joker, Aarti saw. She thought it might have been a woman—there was a definitively female sense to her.

Aarti crept closer, close enough that if the men turned, they would surely see her. She watched as the men dug a hole and buried the dead joker. *Did they kill her?* she wondered. They had brought violence and death to her Moon, just as she had feared, leaving a corpse behind to mark where they had been, to pollute the lunar soil. The strangeness of that stopped Aarti in her tracks, which meant that the men had plenty of time to climb into their ship and let the door close behind them. She raised a hand, half-heartedly, ready to paint their obliteration—but how to do it? She hadn't thought this through. Aarti had never deliberately hurt anyone in her life. In the mad fury after Yajnadar's murder, she'd been willing to slaughter anyone and everyone, but she'd never made an actual plan.

Before Aarti could decide, the ship took off, leaving her alone again.

She walks in beauty, like the night, read the words on the shipping tag that the intruders had left behind to mark the joker woman's grave. Aarti stood above the marker long after the spaceship had left, wondering. *Who were you?* she asked the dead woman, silently. *Were you human once? What were you to them? A pet, a child, a friend? Why did they leave you here? Do they mean to make my Moon a graveyard?*

Aarti could feel the tug of Earth upon her again—it was almost dawn in Bombay. But she was resolved—if the human ship came back, Aarti would destroy it. The joker woman might be the first corpse beneath the lunar soil, but she would not be the last. No humans on the Moon! They had the entire Earth to pollute and destroy; they would not wreak their horrors here.

Within That
House Secure

II

MATHILDE HADN'T KNOWN THERE were so many Witherspoons.

Hundreds of people in dark, expensively tailored dresses and suits crowded the church. Those dozens taking up the front pews, many of them, shared other features in common as well. Widow's peak hairlines on the men, watery blue eyes and patrician noses on both men and women.

These were Mr. Witherspoon's cousins and aunts and other relations. A rare only child in a usually fecund clan, Mr. Witherspoon had married another only child. Mrs. Witherspoon—Alice, Mathilde would honor their bargain in memory now, at least—Alice hadn't had so many familial representatives at their shared funeral.

Their only child, Theodorus, was not present. As he had done most things in the three years since his card turned, Theodorus chose to do his mourning in private.

The service was long. At one point, when yet another minister stood to eulogize the couple, Malachi leaned over and whispered, "A three-preacher funeral. These Southerners."

Mathilde didn't say anything in return. She tried to pay attention to what the men who spoke—they were all men—were saying, but her mind kept wandering to Theodorus. He was not alone at the estate, of course, not technically. He would be surrounded by his late parents' employees, all those guards and secretaries and cooks and gardeners, excepting only James and Dorothy, the longest serving of them, whom Mathilde spotted on one of the back rows. But then, being surrounded by people didn't mean you weren't alone. At fourteen, Mathilde knew that very well.

Organ music swelled and people began filing out of the church, one pew at a time, front to back. This meant that the many Witherspoons walked slowly past her and Malachi as they left. None of them glanced their way.

◆

It had been a plane crash.

According to what she had read in the newspaper, Henry and Alice Witherspoon had been in their private jet with a crew of three, bound from Charleston to Washington, D.C. It had been a rainy day, but not a stormy day, so the light-ning bolt that struck the plane shortly after takeoff was described as "rogue."

The pilot and another crewmember had been in the cockpit. The Witherspoons were in the passenger cabin with the third crewmember—a joker woman, as it happened. All five of them had been killed instantly on impact twenty-four miles north of the city. The crash site was closer to the Witherspoon estate than it was to the airport.

The route from the church back to the estate did not go near there, but Mathilde stared out the car window in that direction the whole time. It had been hours since the service, hours taken up with watching the caskets loaded into long black carriages drawn by teams of black horses, then the slow drive to the cemetery, then the graveside service, where all three ministers spoke again, if a bit more briefly.

Now many of the people who had attended were descending upon Theodorus's house for food and conversation.

"No," Malachi had answered her, "they don't call it a wake. That smacks of Catholicism, and they wouldn't want that."

Whatever it was, Mathilde now stood in one of the larger first-floor rooms. It was big enough to hold a dance in, and there was, in fact, a stately grand pi-ano next to the fireplace. In her years of visits here, Mathilde had never heard a single note played on it, but she was sure it was kept scrupulously in tune. Alice would have seen to that. Mathilde wondered if it would ever be tuned again.

Conversation in the room was low, except for a boisterous man who kept be-ing hushed by his Witherspoon wife. Every time he spoke too loudly or let out a braying laugh, she whispered to him and he looked embarrassed and took a drink from the glass in his hand. Circulating servants kept that drink, and the drinks of everyone else present, full.

Malachi walked over from where he'd been talking to an older man. The man followed Malachi's progress to Mathilde's side with those watery blue Wither-spoon eyes. He didn't look very happy.

"Do you think Theodorus will come out?" Malachi asked.

"I don't know," said Mathilde. "This is a lot of people."

"Relatives, though. Mostly. By marriage if not by blood. By money if not by law."

Years in to being an American now, and there were still things Mathilde didn't understand about her adopted country. "You can be related to someone by money?"

Malachi took a careful sip from the tumbler a passing waiter had just handed him, winced, and set it down on the windowsill. "Sometimes I think that's the tightest kinship of all," he said. "Why do you think we're here?"

Mathilde said, "I'm here because my best friend's parents have been killed, and I'm sure he's hurting. Weren't the Witherspoons your friends?"

Malachi's shoulders were practically nonexistent, but he made the motion Mathilde knew was shrugging. "Yes, after a fashion. But they were always my em-ployers first. And Henry in particular had his little ways of reminding me of that, always."

"Are we related to any of these people, then? In your way of seeing things?"

"My way of seeing things . . ." Malachi repeated. The phrase obviously amused him for some reason unclear to Mathilde.

The loud man who must have been related to the Witherspoons by one of the other bonds of kinship besides blood was suddenly standing before them.

"Schwartz, right?" he asked. "Old Hank's bagman. The man who knows the secrets. The man who knows where all the money is."

The woman Mathilde assumed was the boor's wife was beside him, but she did not shush him this time.

"I'm Malachi Schwartz, yes. I'm the CFO of Witherspoon Holdings if that satisfies your description." He shifted his gaze from the man to the cool and silent woman next to him. "And of course, Mrs. Gaspar, I was a . . . confidant . . . of your late cousin."

"Why are you talking to her? I was the one who asked you who you are," said the man.

"I'm terribly sorry," said Malachi. "I'm used to dealing directly with decision makers. A privilege of my position."

The man reddened, but the woman, Mrs. Gaspar, put her hand on his arm and he settled. "And what exactly is your position, Mr. Schwartz?" she asked.

"As I've just said, I'm the CFO of Witherspoon Holdings. Since you and your siblings hold twenty-two percent of the stock in that firm, I'm sure you're well aware of that."

The woman flashed a thin smile. Everything about her was thin. Mathilde imagined even her blood was thin. "I wasn't being clear. What is your position on the matter at hand?"

Now what does that mean? wondered Mathilde, but if Malachi planned to answer—not at all a sure thing—the falling away of all the room's conversations and ambient noises to silence robbed him of his moment. Theodorus had just entered the room.

Mathilde had made several visits to the library and leafed through books trying to determine exactly what kind of snail Theodorus resembled, but of course there were no snails in all the world with whorled shells nearly seven feet in diameter. Theodorus, from the trailing tip of his glistening foot to the point where his human-appearing torso stretched out from his shell, was nearly twelve feet long. Without her having asked him, during the renovations of the house that allowed him the run of the second floor, he had volunteered the information that he weighed something on the order of one thousand pounds.

Over the past three years, he had learned to school the motile features of his face with a great deal of control. If she looked him straight in the eye and ignored everything else, Mathilde could easily imagine what seventeen-year-old Theodorus would have looked like if he'd never been transformed by the alien virus.

She couldn't ignore everything else, of course. Nobody could.

All of his flesh was a greenish-gray color—no watery blue eyes for him, even. His body and foot constantly wept a substance Theodorus himself called Witherslime, but whether he called it that cheerfully or bitterly, Mathilde had never been able to determine.

Some days he withdrew his entire body inside the shell and let a thick crust of the stuff dry over the entryway, sealing him off from the world. Other days,

days when Alice had been proud to say that he was "making an effort," he manipulated his features so that he even had the appearance of hair on his head. He wore specially made clothes that wicked away the fluids his body produced on those days, and gloves, so that he could shake a visitor's hand without them worrying overmuch about cleaning up afterward.

Today was a day that Theodorus had made an effort.

He wore a black jacket and gray shirt, complete with a neatly knotted tie. Cream-colored gloves adorned his hands, and he dipped his head up and down as he glided to the center of the room, greeting his relatives, Mathilde supposed. He did not, however, break the silence.

So she did.

He did not see her approaching from the side, as he was keeping his head positioned more or less as a nat would—not that he didn't have the option of twisting it nearly all the way around if he wanted. Mathilde walked up beside him and knocked on his shell.

The people closest to her seemed shocked. One man looked like he was about to faint.

Theodorus turned his whole torso around. Mathilde hadn't grown much in the last few years; she was still short, still petite. He loomed over her.

"It's okay that you haven't sent any notes," she said. "But I hope you've been getting mine."

He looked so sad. But he reached into the pocket of his elegant jacket and brought out a squared-off package of papers bound in twine. They were printed with a gridline, and the jagged edges showed where she had ripped them from her orange notebooks.

"I was just rereading them," he said.

"So you know how sorry I am," she said.

He bobbed his head. Really, his nods were more convincing than her own attempts, or Malachi's. They were all three robbed of fluidity in the gesture by their physiologies.

"This is all very charming." The cold, thin woman, Mrs. Gaspar, was standing by Mathilde. "But now's time for family business."

The crowd murmured its agreement.

"What do you mean, cousin?" asked Theodorus.

"I mean that Mr. Schwartz and his daughter should find their way home, because the rest of us have things to talk about. About your responsibilities."

"My responsibilities," said Theodorus. There was an unusual note in his voice. Not sadness, but something equally deep and rich. "To the family? To you?"

"Theodorus, no one here is under any illusions about what the wills are going to show. Henry and Alice never made any secret of their plans to leave you everything. But the wills hadn't been changed to reflect . . . to reflect . . ."

"To reflect this," said Theodorus, gesturing back, the sweep of his hand taking in his shell.

To her credit, Mathilde supposed, the woman colored slightly. "No, to reflect the fact that you are a minor, and that the courts will of course not allow you to run your own affairs, much less those of the companies."

Ah, thought Mathilde. *She is related by money.*

"I'm seventeen," said Theodorus. "I'll have more rights this time next year. I'll be fully empowered by the trusts to do whatever I want when I'm twenty-one."

"He's read them," said Mrs. Gaspar's boorish husband. "He's already read the damned wills."

"You'll find that your dearly departed relatives kept no secrets from their son," Malachi said from his place by the window. "You're right, of course, Suzanne. They left him everything. If you'd like to take an early look at the papers, I've arranged for quite a few copies to be stacked on the billiards table in the front room."

Mrs. Gaspar—Suzanne, Mathilde supposed—gave Malachi a narrow-eyed look that matched the one he was giving her. "What game are you playing at, Schwartz?"

Malachi didn't answer though, because Theodorus suddenly roared.

"Game? Game? My parents are dead and here you all are, circling while their bodies cool, and you want to talk about games?"

Mathilde reached out and put her hand on Theodorus's shell. Everyone else in the room shrank back, leaving the two of them in a widening circle of parquet floor defined by frightened rich people.

Not all jokers had ace powers. Perhaps only a minority did. If Malachi had one, for instance, he'd never hinted at such. Mathilde was frightened enough of her own that she rarely thought about it, never experimented with it. Did Theodorus have one?

As with Malachi, Theodorus had never said. As with Malachi, Mathilde had never asked.

Which left open a possibility. A possibility that everyone in that room was considering. Could he freeze their blood—however thin it might be—with a glance? Could he rob them of their youth, their looks, their vitality? Could he, in some way, in any way, harm them? Could he?

Mathilde didn't know.

Maybe Theodorus didn't know.

A moment passed. Nobody collapsed. Nobody, thank God, caught fire.

"I have had a very interesting conversation with my good friend Malachi and some of his associates," Theodorus suddenly said. "I have been learning about something called juvenile emancipation. Do you know what that is, cousin? Do any of you?"

Mathilde was willing to bet that there were at least a dozen lawyers in the room. Probably the dozen of them who were suddenly whispering to the people around them.

"Even if you're emancipated, you can't run the companies," Mrs. Gaspar protested. She was probably a lawyer herself.

"That's true," Theodorus said, stretching up and out to look down at the woman. "But there are no 'ifs' about this, cousin, the emancipation is—what's the French, Mathilde?"

"A fait accompli," said Mathilde. She hadn't known anything about any of this, but she could tell which way the wind was blowing.

"As for the companies, well, until I turn twenty-one, you'll all just have to work with the court-appointed trustee."

The murmuring grew into a babbling, but then Mrs. Gaspar hissed her kin to silence.

"Who?" she asked, simply.

Theodorus turned and looked toward the window.

Malachi was frowning at another drink. "Have you people ever even considered not putting sugar in your tea?" he asked.

Star Ghost

by Steve Perrin

ALMAZ

1981–1985

FOR MORE THAN A year, things keep to the status quo. Yuri starts feeling the walls closing in on him. As pleasant as his dalliances with Anya are, every minute he spends in material form makes it more likely he will be caught by the erratically scheduled Constantin and, more important, more likely that the steadily leaking reactor might adversely affect him.

Once, as Constantin is filling the station with his snores, he looks over Anya's shoulder as she observes the approach of a large object in a slightly lower orbit. "I wonder . . ." he whispers into Anya's earphones.

"What?" she asks with a pensive lilt. Yuri usually says something like that before attempting to stretch the sleeping cocoon in a direction it is not meant to stretch.

"I bet I can step over to that satellite and back."

"How?"

"In energy form I am always maintaining my form as a standing wave, with very little movement compared to what my energies are capable of."

"Can you stop yourself? At the speed of light, you would be at the satellite in nanoseconds. You could overshoot into . . ." She checks their current orbital position. ". . . into the Indian Ocean."

"My reflexes speed up to match my speed. Or at least it seems so when I move around the station." He makes an exhalation sound in her earphones. "Only one way to find out."

Yuri directs himself away before she can make any more protests. In no appreciable time he is outside the station, controlling his movement to stop when outside the station. There is a slight problem; the station continues to move, leaving him behind.

"Damn physics," Yuri mutters over the radio wavelength.

"Are you all right, lover?" whispers back Anya. "You don't register on the radar."

"Not a problem," Yuri reassures Anya, and himself. Using his own radar energies, he locates the speeding satellite and moves to its vicinity. As he appears next to the satellite, it moves on past him, but he can read the lettering on its side. Another Russian bird. He has no idea what it is.

Yuri looks up with his radar. He attempts to use optical energies but space, even in the vicinity of Earth, is too big. The station is already kilometers farther along in its orbit. Using radar, he identifies its radar cross section and moves in its direction. He arrives and watches it move away from him. He speeds to the spot on the orbit just ahead of the station and it moves over and absorbs him. He stops himself once inside and realizes he is, in fact, constantly moving so as to stay with the station. "Damn physics," he repeats.

Anya chuckles over the comm-link.

After that, Yuri gets more and more daring. An attempt to visit a geostationary communications satellite almost kills him. He returns to the station missing almost a third of his mass. Anya calls him "Blanket Man" as he huddles in her cocoon with her, imbibing several tubes of protein. "The Van Allen belts are murderous," he explains when he can gather his thoughts and stop shaking. "I think I can get through them, but I have to be careful just what energy form I am using. It's a good thing my reaction time speeds up with the speed I am traveling, or I would have been cut to shreds."

But within a few months, Yuri figures out what energies to switch to and is freely darting all over near Earth orbit. One trip to the Moon is exciting, but he has a hard time finding the station when he returns, so he only attempts one lunar trip.

When he comes back from his Moon trip he is unusually closemouthed about it. Anya finds that he occasionally stares out at the Moon from one of the few portholes on the station with a puzzled expression on his face. All he says is, "The Moon has its own secrets."

Unlike the common practice for space crews, Constantin and Anya are just left in the station. Very few Star Gifted have the gift of being able to live with intense radiation. Besides the automated Progress capsules, an occasional Soyuz docks with the station. Mostly the crews are there to take care of some maintenance that telemetry showed is needed and neither Constantin nor Anya are checked on. On these occasions, Yuri keeps in the infrared spectrum, but he cannot resist the occasional sudden appearance and disappearance. The station soon gets a reputation of being haunted. Constantin grows more nervous as he hears the rumors, though Yuri avoids him adroitly after all of his practice. In 1983, Constantin insists that one of the visitors take Yuri's space suit back to Earth.

By this time, Premier Brezhnev dies after a long illness and a new face comes to the General Secretaryship, Yuri Andropov—former head of the KGB. The first speech Andropov gives extolls hard work and commitment to socialist goals. Constantin sneers and goes back to sleep, after drinking a bottle of vodka smuggled to him by a visiting cosmonaut.

Fifteen months later, Constantin toasts Andropov's death. The new leader, Chernenko, reverts back to Brezhnev's policy of ignoring problems. Constantin gets drunk on the entire vodka ration for the station. But a year later, in 1985, Chernenko is as dead as Brezhnev and Andropov, and this new young leader Gorbachev is talking reform.

And as Constantin sneers at Mikhail Gorbachev's concepts of glasnost and perestroika, suddenly Earth's sky is full of Swarmling fungi.

"At last!" exults Constantin. He stays up for three whole days, sitting at the 20 mm cannon control console, looking for targets. He looks, and he looks, and looks again. Some drifting fungal scraps get within range, and are savaged by the 20 mm shot, but the entire Swarm event pretty much passes the Almaz station by. As far as Yuri can tell, the Swarm isn't even avoiding the station. It just never puts any Swarmlings in the station's orbit.

Yuri, on the other hand, dives into the fight against the Swarm. He rapidly discovers that he can project his energy, but it takes a lot out of him, literally. It is more effective to just penetrate a Swarm warrior and turn his energy to heat. It still takes energy, but much less, and it is no danger since the very physical Swarmers cannot touch him.

Initially he concentrates on the Swarm landing in Siberia, trying to defend three gulags near the landing site. Still in contact with Anya, only her warning gets him out of the area when the nuclear attack on the Swarm annihilates that landing site and the three gulags. Yuri can feel the radiation tearing at his current form and shifts. No telling what being in the actual explosion would do to him, and he is not anxious to find out.

Tapping into the defense radio net, he speeds to the Ukraine, where the Swarm is attacking a much more populated area—unlikely to be the target of a nuclear strike.

Winged Swarmlings are orbiting the area, fighting the aircraft and very few flying Soviet and Warsaw Pact Star Gifted. Charging into the midst of the fray, he keeps to his infrared form and burns several Swarmlings from within. At least one time he and his victim are targeted by a heat-seeking missile, but the physical explosion just shreds his target without affecting his immaterial body. Diving into another Swarmling, he applies his heat energy and suddenly this target disintegrates, and almost so does Yuri. The energy blast that hits him on several energy levels almost scatters his photons forever, but he manages to pull back enough to keep going.

Falling next to him is a tall, brown-haired man in an electric-blue ski suit. Suddenly glowing with light energy, he turns into a laser beam that fries yet another Swarmling. Becoming human again, he looks up, finds a higher target, and turns into a killing laser. Yuri remembers seeing the man in a smuggled copy of *Aces!* magazine. He's an American "ace" called Pulse, who has the ability to turn into a laser. What is he doing in the Ukraine? Oh well, he is certainly blasting Swarmlings.

Forming his visible body, displaying his cosmonaut uniform, Yuri hovers in midair and watches Pulse in action. With his finely attuned ability to perceive all electromagnetic wavelengths, he can see that the ambient light for a couple of kilometers around Pulse gets a bit dimmer every time he turns into a laser. The American is taking his light energy from the photons around him to allow himself to become a laser bolt. *I wish I could do that,* thinks Yuri.

Almost depleted of energy after that friendly fire strike from Pulse, Yuri projects himself to a staging area for the defenders and walks into a mess tent in his visible form, now wearing the formal uniform of a Soviet Air Force captain. Momentarily baffled by the problem of actually picking up a food tray, he uses hand signals to indicate to a server that he should fill up a tray with something from each food tub and bring it to an empty table in the far reaches of the tent. Shooing the server away after his food is placed on the table, he sits and finally reverts to his material form, a much diminished, naked Flat Man. In the shadows of the tent, he eats his meal, assumes light form again, and gestures to the servers to bring more. They do, and leave at his urging. He sits to eat again.

"You are really putting that away," says a voice across the table from him. The words are in English, which Yuri is not fluent in. He looks up from his plates to see Pulse settling into the opposite chair with his own loaded tray. The blue ski suit he is using as a costume leaves an afterimage in Yuri's eyes.

"Do you always fight in the nude?" the man persists.

"No English," responds Yuri. He wonders what the American is doing in the Ukraine, but apparently he can travel at the speed of light and decided to come help out. Nice of him, but Yuri doesn't need the exposure—particularly since he's in his Flat Man form without clothes.

"What's your name?" persists the American.

Good question. He needs something to identify himself and can't use his real name. Oh well, since the station is rumored to be haunted anyway . . . "*Zvezdnyy prizrak*," he responds. At the ace's look of bewilderment, he thinks for a minute and translates: "Star Ghost." He smiles at the American and quickly stuffs the rest of the stew and rolls into his mouth, ignoring Pulse's follow-up questions. Even as he is chewing the last morsels he stands, converts momentarily to his uniformed visible form again, bows to Pulse, then shifts to X-rays and heads back to the sky.

Yuri makes trips back to the station when he can. Constantin is getting more and more frustrated. Yuri notes that the Soyuz that Lead Man and Many Toes came up to the station in is locked to *Almaz 4,* and there are two Progress resupply capsules at *Almaz 5* and *Almaz 6.* One capsule docked is reasonable since it takes time to unload them, but why are there two? Yuri puts it down to Constantin's laziness and Anya's disinclination to do all the work.

The fight against the intelligent Swarmlings is harrowing, but for the most part they still can't touch Yuri. He starts showing up on news videos, in his cosmonaut jumpsuit image. He has to become visible more often as more and more Star Gifted with powers that could affect him are getting into the fight. At one point, Yuri has to chase a Swarmling masquerading as Gorbachev through the Kremlin. Fortunately the heat signature given off by the Swarmling imposter is entirely different from that of a human, and also fortunate that by this time he has enough of a good reputation that the presidential guards believe him.

Finally, the Swarm invasion comes to an end. Yuri is on his way to the Swarm Mother to bring the fight to the origin of the problem when he sees a peculiarly shaped spacecraft leave the shell of the Mother. Checking the radio emissions, he pieces out the message that the Swarm Mother is neutralized. His grasp of English has improved with having to coordinate with the worldwide opposition to the Swarm.

On his way back to the station, he also learns that Gorbachev has authorized Hero of the Soviet Union medals for the station crew and a higher award for the mysterious Captain Star Ghost. Yuri is amused that the name he gave the American ace has gotten common usage.

According to Anya, Constantin thinks the medal is an empty gesture to honor futility. He drinks himself to sleep on the few remaining bottles of vodka.

After the Swarm debacle, Constantin constantly mutters under his breath. Yuri just avoids him and spends more time practicing his travel abilities. He makes several trips to the Swarm Mother, but it seems to definitely be headed out of the system at its much-slower-than-light pace. It will probably be months until it is beyond the orbit of Pluto.

After several trips, Yuri decides to check on the reported resolution of the Swarm Mother menace, and converts to the frequency of deep radar to slip inside the shell.

The inside is roughly the volume of Crimea. He can see many sections where Swarm monsters lie quiet. Dead? Or just waiting for orders? Speeding about the shell, he eventually comes to a chamber. Inside, the apparent brain of the creature seems to half encompass the body of Mai, the ace who is reported to have achieved a symbiosis with the Mother and directed her from her career of devastation.

"Hello?" Yuri ventures as he reverts to his material form. His English is much improved from the experience of the battle against the Swarm. One breath confirms that the atmosphere in this chamber, at least, is breathable. It is filled with intriguing smells.

"I greet you," replies a voice that seems to come from the girl, but has an alien vibration. "Why are you here?"

"I heard of your unique status and thought to offer to provide some human contact."

"You are very kind," replies the symbiotic voice, "but I would not keep you from your fellows."

"No fear of that. I travel at the speed of light and can return to Earth at any time."

Their conversation continues for several hours. Then Yuri takes his leave and heads back for the station, with the invitation to come back at any time.

Very confident in his abilities, Yuri gets a fix on the radar signature of the station, and comes up short. He realizes that the station is fifty kilometers closer to the planet than it should be. He crosses the distance in a short hop.

Standing as still as anyone can in orbit, he sees the station venting its maneuver rockets and falling toward the Earth.

Further, there are two more spacecraft in the station's orbit. One is another Progress capsule, locked to *Almaz 3*. Now all the docking portals are blocked. The other is a winged craft somewhat like the American Hornet spaceplanes. This one has the designation MiG-105 on its fuselage. It seems to have just arrived, as Yuri can see it still using maneuvering jets to establish a parallel course to the station's decaying orbit.

"Yuri, this is Many Toes," Yuri hears over the special band that he and Anya use exclusively. "I am barricaded in *Almaz 5* and most of my communication array has been subverted by Lead Man. This station is in great danger, and so is the Kremlin."

"The Kremlin?"

"Da. Constantin intends to crash the station, or what's left of it after reentry, into the Kremlin."

"No way he can guide this conglomeration into the Kremlin."

"So he dumps a highly radioactive station into the suburbs? How is this an improvement?" returns Many Toes. "I tried to fight him, but he broke three of my noses and smashed my dorsal arm." Yuri wonders why the ground-side medical telemetry hadn't picked up on that, but they notoriously do not track every peculiarity of a Star Gifted's anatomy. And Many Toes has a lot of peculiarities.

Yuri speeds to the spaceplane. Looking in through the cockpit, he can see a pilot and another seat with no one occupying it. He recognizes the pilot from their days in Star City. Cosmonaut Colonel Aviard Fastovets has mostly dealt with suborbital missions and has never been to the station. But he is the best pilot with the experimental MiG-105.

Yuri switches to his visible form, this time in a space suit like the one he had left on the station six years before, and slips into the unoccupied passenger seat.

"Who in hell's name are you?" asks Fastovets, trying to figure out how Yuri has appeared so suddenly.

"You have heard of Star Ghost, certainly?" he replies. "What do you know of this situation?"

"No reports for the last three weeks. No Progress capsules released to burn up in atmosphere for the last three months. Telemetry shows both station keepers alive, and radiation levels rising. And now I had to chase the damned crate all this distance," Fastovets says. "The station's now in a more northerly orbit and at least fifty kilometers closer to Earth than it should be." He looks out at the Progress-festooned station. "Now I can't even knock to let me in. I tried to ap-proach the spacewalk port on *Almaz 4* and he shot at me."

"I think someone doesn't want visitors," Yuri says into the pilot's earphones. He moves his image lips to look like the pilot is hearing it live.

The regular communication channels are full of static due to the radiation.

"Attention spaceplane *Spiral II*, attention spaceplane *Spiral II*. Almaz station to spaceplane *Spiral II*." It is a signal on another band, but Yuri picks it up.

"Switch to station intrapersonnel band," he instructs Aviard. As the pilot does so they can hear the message over their speakers. The words are static-filled and faint, as one would expect from the interior communications of a station still several kilometers away.

It is Anya. "Almaz station to *Spiral II*. Mayday."

"*Spiral II* to Almaz station." Fastovets speaks over the intrastation band. "This is Colonel Aviard Fastovets in MiG-105 to Almaz station. Is anyone re-ceiving?"

"Yes, Colonel," replies Anya. "My station mate Major Constantin Radiansk-yev has gone insane. He intends to crash the Almaz station into the Kremlin!"

"Colonel," says Yuri, "I can enter the station easily, but it would be good if Lead Man is not fully aware of my capabilities. Can you bring this craft up to the cen-ter of the station? It will mean you have to get by the cannon."

"No problem." Aviard initiates the main engine of the MiG-105. "Are you ready?"

"Ready, my friend." In the intervening years, Yuri has learned to manipulate his visible image so that he can look like his Flat Man self clothed in a space suit, though Anya has pointed out several times that parts of the suit, and parts of

Yuri, disappear at random moments as Yuri loses concentration because of a momentary distraction.

Yuri assumes this form. Fastovets sees this transformation out of the corner of his eye and a sudden recognition lights his eyes as he turns his concentration back to piloting.

The MiG shoots toward the station, and one of the 20 mm cannons twists in its cradle to aim at the plane. Fastovets slips the ship aside and the burst of slugs goes by. Then they are past the arc of fire and decelerating rapidly to come stationary to the hub of the connecting tent.

With a thought, Yuri is next to the patch he and Georgy put on the tent six years before. No one had ever fixed it. Now the patch hangs off its moorings, the maneuvering of the station having apparently shaken it loose. No wonder the tent is empty of air. Yuri slips his light image through the gap and into the tent.

"Yuri, is that you?" Anya's face appears on a communication screen in the tent as Yuri enters in his visible light form, complete with space-suit overlay. She is in her space suit, helmet hinged back but ready to be applied if there's a sudden air loss. Yuri can see that *Almaz 5,* where she tends to work, is sealed. There are several eruptions of forming organs on her face. Stress must speed up the process.

"Yes, sweetheart. Be ready to evacuate on a moment's notice."

"Yuuuri!" she screams into the screen. Yuri reorients himself to face Constantin. Lead Man is in his space suit and braced in the air lock to *Almaz 6,* and he has a shotgun. The only guns officially allotted to the Almaz station are the external 20 mms.

"You are supposed to be dead, Flat Man," snarls Constantin. "Apparently the stories of the haunted station are correct." Constantin continues moving the barrel of the shotgun in a little arc that includes Yuri every second. "Are you surprised, Comrade Mattress? I have friends among the pilots, too."

Yuri can name a half-dozen "friends" who could have smuggled a gun to Lead Man for enough money. It's not like Constantin has any place to spend his salary. Constantin's space suit gives him trouble aiming the weapon, apparently a hunting shotgun, but at this range he can hardly miss.

Yuri launches himself at Constantin. The gun goes off. Yuri's perceptions speed up and he can see the single slug coming for him. He lets go of reality as the heavy bullet slams through his image. Light changes around him and he can see the haze of radiation that fills the tent and the station.

Yuri continues his path and passes right through Lead Man into the *Almaz 6* module. Going through Lead Man feels like having to swallow the horse pills he'd received from doctors when he was first Gifted. Constantin spins in the air lock, overcorrects, and catches himself. He stares at Yuri, or is it the ghost of Yuri?

Yuri Serkov drifts in the space next to the reactor. He is proportionally human, what Yuri Serkov would have grown into had the Takisian virus not had its way with him. Every detail of Yuri's disabled potential is on display, because Yuri is naked. The only similarity to Yuri as Constantin had known him is that all of his body hair is missing. The shock of hitting Lead Man's dense body knocked out all thoughts of maintaining the form of Flat Man in a space suit.

Yuri moves his head back and forth. "I know where you are, Constantin. How about giving up this madness?" His voice over the intrastation public address is cold and only phrasing shows it is Yuri's. "You can't hurt me."

"What are you, Flat Man?" Constantin jacks another shell into the shotgun.

Yuri considers the question. He is already shaking because the lunge at Constantin almost took him through the wall of the module and into space. At the speed he is traveling he might have gone too far away to see Earth, much less the station. But his senses speed up whenever he moves like this and his control holds. This time.

Of course, he damps down his reception of most radiation so as to not be affected by all the deadly alpha, beta, and gamma given off by the reactor. Everything is silent, only expected in vacuum, but he isn't breathing. He can hear Anya over the intrastation radio. Mostly she is just breathing hard. Constantin, on the other hand, is approaching him, waving his arm in front of his body.

"If this is you, Captain Flat Man, it is not much of you. I don't think you can do anything to stop me. You can just watch." His waving hand intersects with Yuri's image. There is a slight static along the arc of its movement. "Hah, it seems I might be able to harm you."

Yuri felt that blow. He moves instantaneously to the other side of the reactor from Constantin. Nothing physical has ever affected this form before. Lead Man is so dense that his cellular structure can actually interact with Yuri's energy form.

Concentrating as he has when fighting the Swarm, adding infrared to his visible form, Yuri channels heat energy through his hand onto the cables and conduits leading to the reactor. Some elements of the reactor are missing, though the core is still present, as evident by the outpouring radiation. Something is happening to the element he is heating, but he can't be sure how effective he is being. He speaks through the intercom to distract Constantin. "What do you think to do, Constantin? You can only die by these actions."

"I am dying already, Comrade Light Show. Even my bones cannot keep the radiation from eventually affecting me. And now Comrade Gorbachev says Anya and I must come home and the station be destroyed as an expensive failure. So I am helping that process along."

Yuri has heard the plans to deactivate the station, and worried there might be consequences. *Right again, smart-ass,* he thinks to himself. "Complain to Star City. I am sure they are trying to get that policy changed."

"I will change the policy," Constantin replies. "I will bring this station down around Gorbachev's big ears."

"You'll never hit the Kremlin." Yuri repeats his previous argument to Anya.

"If I hit within one hundred miles of Moscow, the message will be heard."

Yuri agrees with the sentiment. He senses one of the cables holding the reactor together break free, its molten melted end sending hot metal throughout the compartment. Alarms go off, including through the intercom. Apparently, it is also a hose, because some liquid or gas is turning into mist in the vacuum and filling the reactor room. *Good thing I don't breathe,* thinks Yuri.

"What have you done?!" screams Constantin as he rounds the reactor, moving effortlessly in no gravity as only someone who has lived in it for five years can do. Yuri "steps" to the other side of the reactor, again barely stopping from going through the wall of the module. *I have to get more practice with short leaps,* he thinks as he turns to face Constantin. Concentrating slightly, he reassumes his Flat Man shape, then releases one layer of image as blinding light. Another first for him; he had postulated the trick after seeing Pulse in the Ukraine but had never had the opportunity to use it.

Constantin's helmet opaques, but not quick enough. He screams in pain as the light sears his retinas. His swooping dive to smash through Yuri's image also comes up short. It takes Yuri several vital seconds to realize that Constantin's air hose is twisted among the bare framework of the reactor. Another second and he realizes why the reactor is a framework. Constantin has removed all the shielding and recycled fluid tanks. No wonder the radiation levels have skyrocketed. The reactor is running unencumbered. This actually means it is not running as hot, but the radiation from the fuel rods is unblocked.

This has to end quickly. With a resigned sigh, Yuri "touches" Constantin's air hose and applies heat. He can feel the weakness starting to come over him. All of the matter of his body is converted to energy, and he is using his control of the energy to expend energy that is actually the matter of his body. If he keeps this up for much longer there might not be enough left of him to reconstitute his body.

The air hose, already strained, burns through easily. A fire flare accompanies the break as the oxygen hits the heat, but he tamps off the heat immediately. Constantin, just getting his vision back, yells and tries to get to another oxygen hose but the remnant of his old hose still holds him. Yuri watches as Constantin struggles to free himself, but his efforts stop almost immediately. Lead Man's dense body demands a constant flow of oxygen. The floating body jerks twice then continues to float at the end of the nearly severed air hose.

Yuri moves to the patch locker in the tent and he realizes he can't do anything about the hole in the hub tent he entered through. "Anya, I am coming into module five," Yuri orders while regaining the image of the Flat Man form he has lived with so long.

Yuri steps through into *Almaz 5* and nods to Anya, who is ready, her helmet fastened to her suit. "Aviard, are you still with us?" Yuri puts out on the station-to-ship band, without worrying about using comm equipment.

"No problem, Captain Yuri Star Ghost. Do you need pickup?"

"One to pickup, anterior lock five," replies Yuri, and goes to help Anya get ready to abandon the station.

Aviard argues, but the spaceplane really has no room for more than two. It makes Yuri wonder just who the folks in Star City thought would be coming back from this mission. He releases the empty Progress modules from *Almaz 3* and *5*, after taking out any food stores still in them, and sends them to their fiery funeral in Earth's atmosphere, then deposits Anya and what little baggage she had accumulated in six years in space into the *Spiral II*, now locked to *Almaz 5*.

He waves as Aviard disengages, drifts away from the station, wags his wings in response to Yuri's wave, and sets course for Star City. Thanks to the configuration of the spaceplane, Fastovets doesn't have to wait for a special window to make his return and he can land on the Star City airfield runway.

Yuri maintains an almost fully material form long enough to use the station's maneuvering jets to get it back into an orbit that should keep it from hitting atmosphere for at least fifty years. While doing this he feasts on as much of the stores Constantin had been building up as he can—for what he has no idea. Perhaps neither Constantin nor Anya had been hungry after taking in so much radiation. Yuri makes sure his own form is transparent to the usual killers in the radioactive spectrum, just as he had before when he had been close to the nuclear strike. He feels the effects of the food restoring him to the size he had started at.

"Office of Star Gifted Enterprise to Colonel Yuri Serkov." That is interesting; someone must really be pushing a signal to get a message from Earth through the radiation around the station. The office name sounds familiar. Some techs from that office had tested him several times in the lead-up to the original mission. And apparently he has received a promotion.

"Go ahead." No sense in burning bridges.

"Well done, Colonel. We have been monitoring you off and on through the years." Yuri is hardly surprised. In fact, he had been puzzled no one had interfered with him since he joined the cosmonaut corps.

"So now you want to give me a medal?"

"You already have a medal. We want to offer something like that, but you can't display it anywhere." There is a pause. "Are you intending to leave your current location?"

"I think I can do it safely. As the pilots say, it is not the trip, but the landing that's the problem."

"Do you know to the millisecond the distance from your location to the Crimea?"

The Crimea? Not Star City? Interesting. "No."

"In fifteen minutes and thirty seconds it will be eight thousandths of a second at light speed, which we assume you are capable of. It will be forty-seven degrees south and thirty-eight degrees northeast of your position." Yuri understands the initial reference to South actually meant toward the Earth.

"That will get you in the air over the Crimean Naval Base. We trust you can get down from there on your own. Once you are on the ground, find the Coast Guard campus and look for Coast Guard Logistics Command. Go in the eastern door. We will be waiting for you."

Yuri thinks about this, and remembers three gulags burned up in atomic flame when they got in the way of destroying the Siberian Swarm. He thinks about other problems he has seen with the Soviet system. This outfit seems like the GRU, which is not an operation that has a good reputation. "Thank you, sir, but I think I need a change of scenery. I will be gone for a while."

"Where can you go? You can't get away from us on Earth." There was the threat in the proposal he was waiting for. "And there is nowhere else in space you can breathe, and eat."

"Not exactly true, sir. There is a breathable atmosphere where I am going. And it's amazing what nutrition you can get from yeast. And there's someone there who might like a little human companionship."

Yuri finishes off the last piroshky, converts to X-rays, and this time intentionally leaves the confines of the station and sets his course for the Swarm Mother. *This should be fascinating.*

Within That
House Secure

III

AT THE END OF her first semester of college, Mathilde had to be rescued.

Not because she wasn't doing well—she was doing very well—but because the world had gone insane. The world, in fact, had been invaded by alien monsters from the depths of outer space. Just like old times.

The Swarm struck in waves all over the planet in December 1985, and two of those waves were in the eastern United States. The federal government shut down the interstates and the airports and the rail system. Though the closest fighting against the bizarre, mindless creatures was in Kentucky, Mathilde was stuck in Atlanta.

When she'd applied for college a year early, Malachi had dreamed that she would go to MIT, near where he'd grown up. Mathilde had dreamed of crossing the country to Stanford. It turned out that the admissions departments of neither of those institutions had been interested in their dreams. Malachi had muttered darkly about prejudice, but Mathilde was sanguine. Her second choice was Georgia Tech, and Georgia Tech accepted her.

She loved college. She thrived there. She spent every spare moment in the labs and the libraries, sneaking into lectures intended for graduate students, learning everything she could. Her field was aerospace engineering, but that didn't stop her from reading books and designing experiments on everything from poured concrete bridges to microcircuitry. She was diligent about dashing off quick notes to Malachi and Theodorus, but didn't go home even for Thanksgiving.

And then it seemed like she wouldn't go home for Christmas, either, because of the Swarm. She watched the news on television, ate badly, and kept getting busy signals anytime she phoned Charleston. The university, by necessity, made the decision to keep the dorms open over the winter break, so at least she had a place to stay.

The evening after her last final exam, though, there was a knock on her door.

Mathilde didn't have a roommate ("Let me buy you some privacy, at least," Malachi had said), and rarely had visitors.

"Who's there?"

The voice through the hollow-core metal door was muffled, but Mathilde could make out what the man said. "It's me, Crenson. You packed?"

There was neither a peephole nor a chain on the door. The security of the dorm, such as it was, consisted of the locked outer lobby doors and a front desk staffed by an inattentive upperclassman. If she had a visitor from outside the dorm, the desk should have called up—the house phones were working anyway, even if the phone lines to the outside world were all inoperative.

"I think you have the wrong room," she said.

"Are you Mathilda . . . Marechild?" His tone, even through the door, clearly indicated that he was reading her name, not remembering it.

She cracked open the door. A gray-haired man even shorter than her, whip-thin, dressed in an expensive jogging suit, was looking at a crumpled piece of paper in one hand. His other hand wasn't a hand at all. What looked like a miniature samurai sword the color and texture of bone extended from his wrist.

"Oh, hey—" the man said, swinging the sword up casually, and without a thought, Mathilde reached out, rested her fingertips on the back of his normal hand, and pushed.

"What the hell?" The man fell back into the hallway, but Mathilde stepped forward, maintaining contact. His skin was suddenly flushed, as if he had developed a sudden fever. A very high fever.

Another moment, and she might have turned him to ash. If she'd maintained contact, anyway. This proved difficult.

The short man leapt left, whirling through the air in a roundoff that saw his heels grazing the ceiling. He landed with his sword arm extended and his other up in a parrying position. He was red-faced, but since he wasn't breathing hard Mathilde guessed it wasn't from exertion, but from the effects of her power.

She also guessed she was in trouble.

But he wasn't attacking, wasn't even advancing. Instead, he pointed with his chin at the paper that had fallen to the floor outside her doorway. It was, she saw now, pale blue and thick. Stationery. Malachi's stationery.

Keeping a wary eye on him, she leaned down and picked up the paper. In Malachi's casual cursive, she read her name and address, and simple directions from the nearest artery street to the dormitory. She read, even, her schedule of final exams and a note that said, "Make sure she takes all her tests." Clearly, Malachi had sent the man. But he must be having the same difficulty contacting her as she was reaching him, so he hadn't been able to tell her in advance.

The man said, "Did you almost torch me, just then?"

Mathilde read her name again and shook her head. She tossed the paper to the man and turned back into her room, saying over her shoulder, "How do you get 'Marechild' out of 'Maréchal'?"

Without waiting for an invitation, he followed her inside. "Name's got some kind of boomtickie over one of the letters in the middle. How the hell am I supposed to know how to pronounce that?" He stopped, staring at the wall above her desk, whistling low. He extended the sword point, gesturing at the charts and tables she had taped up, the periodic table and the graphs showing thrust values, the calendars showing launch windows. "Shit, this is way past algebra."

❤

Cahier No. 119
17 December 1985
On the Backroads Between Atlanta and Charleston

*Croyd won't let me take a turn at the wheel, and there's no space to stretch out and
sleep. The Jeep is packed tight with my belongings. He insisted on bringing everything
I own from the dorm, not just a suitcase. I told him I have every intention of returning
to Tech for the spring semester. He said I should wait to see if Atlanta was still there
before I registered for classes.*

I've registered already, of course.

*He has a thick stack of county maps that Malachi provided. We're staying clear not
just of the interstates, but any major highway at all. Croyd doesn't seem familiar with
the route—in fact he doesn't seem to be a very experienced driver, which is not surprising considering his New York City accent. We stop frequently to plot our way along
the network of county roads and country lanes we're taking home.*

*He talks a lot. He seems frenetic, manic even. He asks a lot of questions about my
education, about France, about my "secret ace power," about Malachi. He has interesting theories about Malachi, saying that it's unusual that a "straight" business
executive—even a straight joker business executive—would know how to contact him,
how to hire him. "I bet he's hooked up with the rackets," he says. "You said he's from
Connecticut? I've worked with mob types from there before."*

I don't think he expects me to answer him, so I don't.

*We're far from the fighting, but even the people in the Deep South countryside seem
panicked. We've passed abandoned pickup trucks. Once, we had to stop for half an hour
while a herd of black cattle meandered across an intersection, not another human in
sight. Croyd was delighted.*

"This is better than the goddamned zoo," he said, and took another pill.

The wintry South Carolina landscape on the other side of the glass contrasted
sharply with the riot of new growth inside. Mathilde wiped her forehead. The
warmth didn't bother her of course, but the high humidity Theodorus maintained
inside his new greenhouse caused her to sweat.

The greenhouse was a new addition to the Witherspoon house, one of a network of three that were all connected to one another and to the main house by
glassed-in walkways. The doorway from the rooms off the kitchen into the first
one was a complex affair that so closely resembled an air lock that Mathilde had
bent to study the seals. She thought she recognized their manufacturer, but
hadn't thought the company in question sold to anyone but the government.

Theodorus was working at a high potting bench, listening to Croyd Crenson
report to Malachi on his successful "mission" to retrieve Mathilde from Atlanta.

"It was super easy," said Croyd. "I only almost got killed once. That doesn't
even rate hazard pay."

Malachi nodded and wordlessly handed over a thick envelope, which Croyd
pocketed without opening.

"Speaking of hazards, Mr. Crenson," said Theodorus. "Are you going to wait
out the current crisis here? There's an alien invasion force, a squad of rampag-

ing aces, and a sizable percentage of the U.S. Army between you and home. You should be able to find something to divert you here, especially if you've never been to South Carolina."

"Hell, Mr. Witherspoon," said Croyd, "I've never been to any Carolina. But no, I need to get back home in the next couple of days."

"I see. How long have you been up now?" asked Theodorus.

Croyd looked over at Malachi. "Did your homework, didn't you?" Then, directing his attention back to Theodorus, "Long enough that I went through the medicine cabinet in your guest bathroom looking for something to help me stay awake."

Theodorus gestured, and Malachi handed Croyd another thick envelope. This one rattled.

"A gift from our pharmaceuticals division," Theodorus said. "Perhaps that's enough to entice you to hear me out. Instead of going back to New York, maybe you would consider going to Kentucky."

Croyd pursed his lips, thinking. "Seems to me from what I've seen on television that there's an alien invasion and a rampaging ace or two and a big chunk of the U.S. Army there, too, isn't there? Hell, Golden Boy is fighting the Swarm there."

"We don't need you to fight anyone at all," said Malachi. Then he spoke to Mathilde. "Maybe you should go back into the main house and get some rest."

Mathilde looked from her father to her friend to her erstwhile rescuer.

"I think I'll stay," she said. "I am fascinated by these little projects you two have been getting up to over the last couple of years. This one sounds particularly interesting."

Theodorus said, "It's fine. I have no secrets from Mathilde."

She wondered how true that still was.

"You better not have any secrets from me, either, big guy," said Croyd, "at least not concerning this job. What exactly is it you want me to do in Kentucky? I don't bet on the ponies. And I'm more of a Scotch man."

"Malachi?" said Theodorus.

Malachi was still looking at Mathilde, but turned to Croyd. "The Kentucky invasion is centered south of Louisville, which was a bit of luck for our side because that's where Fort Knox is, and Fort Knox is where the 194th Armored Brigade is stationed, along with quite a few other heavy elements."

"I thought it was where they keep the gold. Like in the movie. The guy with the hat." Croyd made a motion with his non sword hand like he was throwing a Frisbee.

"Yes. It's also where they keep the gold, but that's just a coincidence. Not a particularly helpful coincidence for our purposes, but we're not asking you to rob the U.S. bullion reserve."

Croyd nodded. "That's good. I've robbed gold vaults before and that shit is heavy. I'm pretty spry in this body, but my strength is just a little above normal."

This body? Mathilde wondered, but kept quiet.

"Mr. Crenson," said Theodorus, "I'm told that as recently as last year you agreed to break into a secure government facility and retrieve some documents for an acquaintance of Malachi's. I'm told you did so successfully, and that you did so for fifty thousand dollars."

Croyd looked at Malachi, then looked at Mathilde. When he saw that she was looking back, he mouthed, "Rackets." Aloud, he said, "You're a pretty well-informed guy, boss."

"I really am," said Theodorus.

"Could you do something similar for us?" asked Malachi. "Infiltrate a government facility, in this case a laboratory, and bring us something stored there, in this case an item. We'd provide you with a small cooler for transporting it."

"No sweat. Fifty thousand dollars," said Croyd.

"This laboratory is near the center of Fort Knox," said Theodorus, "one of the most secure facilities in the world in peacetime, and currently fighting off an alien invasion with the aid of a man who is possibly the most powerful individual on the planet. The item to be retrieved is a sample of alien Swarm tissue, which has properties at present completely unknown to our science, and which may at any moment grow into a hungry predator that devours everything around it."

Croyd pursed his lips. "A hundred thousand dollars?" he said.

Later, when Malachi had led Croyd into the house to give him more detailed instructions and a package of what was vaguely described as "specialized gear," Mathilde began working at the potting bench with Theodorus.

"You spend a lot of time in these greenhouses now," she said amiably.

He handed her a pair of secateurs and watched her neatly trim back the growth on a potted plant. "I've grown interested in growing things," he said. "I'm learning a lot about biology and ecology. It's just as well. You were always the engineer."

"You've lost your interest in spaceflight?" she asked him.

"Not at all. I'm just . . . exploring alternatives."

"Alternatives that involve sending a mercenary to rob alien tissue from a government laboratory?"

"I'm not sure I'd describe him as a mercenary, exactly," said Theodorus.

She considered letting it stand at that, letting him use that sentence as a deft way of changing the subject. But then she went on. "What are you going to do with it, Theodorus?"

He took up an atomizer filled with some green fluid and said, "I really don't know yet." He spritzed the plant she had pruned. "I'm sure I'll think of something."

The day before she returned to Atlanta for her sophomore year, late in the summer of 1986, Mathilde found herself in the back of the familiar old Duesenberg, alone for once, but, familiarly, bound for the Witherspoon estate. She wondered how many times she had taken this ride, in this car. She wondered how many times she'd done so without Malachi.

"I'll join you out there once I've made sure the journalists are on their way," he had said on the phone from his office. "Joanna will bring me."

Joanna was one of Theodorus's newest employees, a helicopter pilot who seemed to Mathilde to be possessed of a sort of cheerful death wish, which meant that Malachi would be flying out to the birthday party. The birthday party and announcement.

Mathilde no longer knew all of the people Theodorus kept on staff at the house, and not just because she spent so much of the year away at Georgia Tech. It seemed like every week there was a new security guard waving her through when they visited, the trip from the state highway to the main house taking longer each time because of the construction of new outbuildings, new terraced gardens, or the helipad, of course. She tried to see the eyes of her driver in the rearview mirror and wondered if she even knew his name.

"Big day today, Miss," the driver said. He must have seen her watching him. She recognized the voice. "Carl? Are you not working security anymore?"

"Sure am," he replied. "Security's kind of taken over parts of transportation is all."

Mathilde thought about that for a moment.

"Carl, are you my bodyguard?"

The limousine shifted lanes smoothly. He was a good driver. "Just for the day, Miss," he said, somewhat hesitantly.

"Huh. And am I going to have a bodyguard when I get back to my dorm?"

"Not me, anyway, Miss. Don't think I could pass for a coed. Maybe you'd better ask Mr. Witherspoon these questions."

"Oh, I will," she said.

But this proved to be more difficult than she'd thought it would be. Not because she was afraid to broach the subject, but because Theodorus proved impossible to get alone. The front drive at the house was packed tight with vans and rental cars. Mathilde recognized quite a few Witherspoon Holdings employees milling around the lawns, but didn't recognize even more of the dozens of people in evidence.

Carl let her out before the front door, telling her he'd be available to drive her back into Charleston after "the event."

This seems a little elaborate just to be reminding everyone he's turned twenty-one and is taking over the family business, she thought.

Unaccountably, a memory of something from the strange greenhouse meeting at Christmas came back to her. *I have no secrets from Mathilde,* he'd said.

Oh, Theodorus.

She worked her way through the ground floor of the house, stopping in the kitchens to sneak a sample from a vast banana pudding someone had left criminally unguarded. He wasn't in the public rooms. She tried the greenhouses, noticing how much fuller they seemed now, but he wasn't there, either.

He was, of all places, on the tennis court.

A crew was finishing rigging a tent over the court, and Theodorus had ducked into the shade. Direct sunlight caused him difficulties. A tall nat woman—another stranger—was talking to him, making notes on a clipboard and occasionally shouting into a walkie-talkie. Another nat, a man she vaguely recognized, stood listening. He had steel-gray hair and ramrod posture.

Theodorus saw her, finally, and smiled. "Mathilde! Mathilde, come meet Vickie. Vickie is going to be handling press for us from now on."

Us?

"I've done okay handling my own press so far," Mathilde said. The woman had the courtesy to laugh.

"For the companies, of course," said Theodorus. "She's the one who put all this—"

The last word was obliterated by the beating sound of a helicopter swooping in low and fast. Very low. Very fast.

"Where did you find that pilot?" asked the man with the unnaturally perfect posture. "He's a menace!"

Theodorus said, "Joanna? She's one of Malachi's hires. Her personnel file does make for colorful reading."

When he'd spoken, something clicked in Mathilde's memory. "General Sampson," she said, recognizing him. Mike Sampson, a man long in the employ of the Witherspoons. A man who had twice walked on the Moon.

"Miss Maréchal," said the general. "It's good to see you. Quite a day."

A joker, snouted and scaled and wearing Theodorus's household livery, walked up deferentially and handed a slip of paper to Vickie. The tall woman gave it a glance, grimaced, and said, "I have to go handle this, excuse me. It was lovely to meet you, Mathilde."

The messenger started to shuffle off as well, but Mathilde caught him by the shoulder. "Amos!" she said. "Aren't you going to say hello?"

The joker cast a glance from Theodorus to the general. "Hello," he said quietly.

Mathilde knew she should let the man go, but asked, "How is Orson?"

Amos brightened. "He likes it here. Likes working in the library." Then, seeing that Sampson was staring at him closely, he said, "I have to go rake the paths now," and exited.

When he was out of earshot, General Sampson said, "Who was that man? It seems like I should know him."

Mathilde said, "Yes, you should. You buried his mother on the Moon."

The general didn't seem to take that as an insult, and in fact, Mathilde wasn't sure she meant it as one. More of a correction, she thought, and then was gratified when Sampson said, "You've hired on Eva-Lynne's two sons. I think I should go talk to him, if you don't mind."

Theodorus waved him on, and Mathilde found herself alone, for the moment, with her oldest and best friend.

"Happy birthday," she said.

He hummed a note, then said, "Sing it! Sing the song!"

She laughed, but humored him. The people pitching the tent joined in, and then everyone on the yard, and they all cheered at the end, but then the two of them weren't alone anymore, not really.

But she asked him anyway. "What is all this? What has Vickie put together for you? These people didn't all come out here to file stories on you turning twenty-one. And why is Mike Sampson here?"

Theodorus shook his head. "No, sadly, the reporters did not come for my birthday. They came because of our new venture. That's why Mike Sampson is here, too. He's to be our CEO. The public face."

There he was using the plural again. Our, us, we. Who did it mean?

"Why don't I know what this 'venture' is?" she asked.

"Because it's a surprise," he said.

"Clearly," she said.

"No, I mean a surprise particularly for you. It's a present, partly anyway. A present from me to you."

"And I have to wait for the cameras before you'll tell me what it is?"

He smiled again. He reached into the pocket of his elegant jacket and pulled out a laminated badge held by a lanyard. "You won't need this for another few years, really, but by that time, there'll be so much work. So much to do."

She took the badge. She saw that it featured a legitimately flattering headshot of her, next to her name and a line that read EMPLOYEE #1. There was a logo, and a company name.

WITHERSPOON AEROSPACE, it read.

She opened her mouth, but no words came out. She shook her head, felt tears coming to her eyes.

"Don't you like it?" Theodorus asked.

"Of course I like it, you big idiot," she said. "But what does it mean? Are we going to start building rocket ships? Satellites? Orbital observatories? What?"

"Yes," he said. "Yes to all of that." Then he smiled again. "To start."

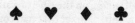

Luna Incognita

by Leo Kenden

"HE SAYS HE SAW a ghost."

Belka's voice was barely a whisper, for which Grigori was grateful. Not that the tiny joker was capable of shouting even in the direst circumstances. But given the early morning, with Grigori barely awake on his hard sleeping mat in a tent on the surface of the Moon, a whisper was welcome.

Grigori shook off the troubling dream he had been having of his wife, Maya, complaining about their flat. He sat up and attempted to stretch, and saw a human less than one meter tall sitting on the edge of a silver equipment box, one of its tiny hands tugging at the thin blanket that had covered Grigori.

"He being Sergei?" Sergei being the joker-cosmonaut who inhabited the support tent, separated from Grigori and Belka by a few millimeters of metal-coated fabric.

Belka nodded. "I heard him stirring around an hour ago. He was talking. Cursing. Screaming, 'Leave me alone! Get out!'" Belka had his own quirks, among them an intolerance for profanity. Grigori wondered how his little joker crewmate had survived an hour, much less a dozen years, in the Communist Party apparat and the Soviet military. "He was also moaning and crying out, like a man having a bad dream."

"What about Terenty and Viktor?" They were the other two nats in Grigori's crew, bunking in the tiny cave beyond the support tent.

"Silence."

Grigori was grateful for that much, though Terenty, in particular, was usually sullen.

"How do you know Sergei wasn't dreaming? It was our sleep time." For the three nats, that is. Sergei slept like a cat, whenever he was not working or eating. Belka required fewer than four hours of sleep and used the quiet hours to perform maintenance, a task he seemed to enjoy—and the wretched state of Soviet manufacturing made mandatory.

"He was moving around. I could hear his feet scraping."

That was a bad sign. Over two months, or to be precise, fifty-eight days, the one sign that Sergei Petrushenko was happy was his willingness to sit silently in a lotus position, disassembling broken equipment that Belka would then repair and reassemble.

"Did he have a session?" Grigori meant a communications session with Control. The Soviet Union had a single deep space communications facility near Sochi in the Crimea. It was only in line of sight with the lunar base for perhaps eight hours out of every twenty-four. A relay satellite in high Earth orbit was supposed to augment Control, but it had failed early in the mission.

Grigori tended to let Sergei and Viktor handle these sessions. With the three-second lag between question and response, with the frequent signal interference from aircraft going into Sochi, the whole experience left him frustrated.

The *Luna* effort was intended to establish a small base on the Moon; it carried water, food, and other supplies sufficient to support the crew for three months, with resupply to follow.

At the two-month point, in spite of careful management, the crew's supplies of oxygen and water and especially food were dangerously low, and the equipment that should have allowed for renewal of those resources kept failing.

Those issues, not to mention the stress of daily command, left Grigori prone to snap at whichever flight director happened to be on duty.

At forty, a Party member and holder of a Hero of the Soviet Union medal due to his victory in a "space battle" with an American Hornet spaceplane, Colonel Grigori Kolesnikov was immune to serious punishments. While Pavlov, the lead mission director, could call him names, Grigori's flat, his pension, his wife's job, his daughter's education, all would be preserved.

Granted, there were great challenges to leading the Soviet Union's first manned lunar landing mission, aka *Luna 87*. Launched from Soviet Central Asia, the "plucky five" (according to TASS) had accomplished a successful three-day climb to the Moon, then landed in the Ocean of Storms.

Grigori could easily imagine the TASS and Radio Moscow presentations, upbeat accounts of "our hero cosmonauts" as they "dug a foothold in the newest frontier!"

The grim reality, however, was three nats, two jokers, all five dirty and hungry and struggling to survive in an environment that threatened to kill them several times a day as they waited for a resupply that might not arrive in time.

They could just board *Luna* and take off again, but Grigori would never allow that. He thought of Arctic and Antarctic explorers of the past, especially Shackleton. He would be a hero, or die trying.

"I spoke with Control," Belka said. "It only lasted ten minutes." As usual, Belka focused on extraneous matters like duration without sharing content, a trait that almost drove Grigori to murder.

"And."

"Oh, it was fine. No criticism. We have been the subject of a story in the *American Life* magazine."

Only Belka would think this important. "Was there any operational news?"

"The next launch has been postponed another two weeks."

Grigori felt ill. "Did they say why?" Even as he voiced this, Grigori realized that the answer didn't matter.

"One of the Carriers isn't assembled." The Carrier was the giant rocket launcher that put elements of the *Luna* into orbit. Grigori and his crew had used three of them during the first phase of their own mission.

The upcoming resupply mission required two launches, one for a cargo vessel that would fly unmanned to a landing, the other for the propulsion and braking stage.

"Did they offer any advice about how we're supposed to survive an extra two weeks?"

"They say their calculations show that we have enough oxygen and water."

"Easy for them to say, sitting there in sunny Crimea."

"I think the calculations were performed in Moscow."

For the second time this morning, Grigori wanted to murder Belka. The tiny joker was oblivious. "What do we do about Sergei's ghost?"

"It will keep for ten minutes," he snapped. Grigori opened a bag of nutrient—it was too crude and organic to be called food. Unfortunately, before Grigori could transfer any of the slurry from bag to mouth, the bag leaked, spilling greenish goo down the front of Grigori's no-longer-white T-shirt. Two months of lunar life had eliminated any interest Grigori might have had in the scientific observation of the slow—to Earth-trained senses—descent of the material down his shirt-front to the fabric floor. He did have time to catch some nutrient and stuff it in his mouth, providing at least a few calories.

He could have simply grabbed his midday nutrient bag, but with the delay in resupply, he preferred to pretend that this meager breakfast would do. But now, with some Sergei ghost nonsense to confront, and the inevitable complaints from Terenty and Viktor, Grigori was going to be in a mood.

To forestall the immediate, knowing that his blood sugar was in flux, Grigori unzipped the curtain to the support tent.

The separation between the tents was barely worthy of the name, yet the environments were different. The hab unit was large enough to hold three sleeping mats, a hot plate, food storage lockers, and containers for clothing.

The only "hab" function housed in the support tent was the toilet, little more than a covered bucket.

All the other equipment crowding it was the oxygen generator, the air scrubber, various pumps and power lines—still connected to the *Luna* lander—and the patch panel for all devices, plus a bed of sad-looking plants. It was noisy, but Grigori had learned that all spacecraft were dangerously noisy.

And here, in the near dark, was Sergei Petrushenko—tall, pale, almost birdlike—crouching at the far end of the tent like a crane in a cage. "Good morning," Grigori said, hoping for normality. A discarded nutrient bag suggested that Sergei had already consumed breakfast. So far so good.

But then the joker launched into his litany of complaints. "The converter is working at thirty percent capacity," he said. "And the seeds are not responding to lunar soil."

Sergei's tone suggested that this was Grigori's fault. "Maybe our leaders should have sent farmers, not engineers and pilots," Grigori said.

Complicating matters—Sergei's joker ability was breathing carbon dioxide, not oxygen. He was an organic air conversion tool. Without him, the *Luna* mission duration would have been six weeks, not months.

Grigori often wondered about Sergei's life prior to his enrollment in the cosmonaut corps. He, Terenty, and Viktor had only been teamed with Belka and Sergei twenty days prior to launch, so they'd had little time to bond as a unit. Two months of confinement in the tents and cave had not resulted in improved personal interactions. The workload was too consuming.

All Grigori knew was that Sergei had had a difficult life in the Kolyma gold mines—part of the Gulag—living at the bottom of a pit where the air was toxic to nats, tolerable only to him. "Belka heard you moaning."

"I'm terrified." A cold statement, no denial.

"We all have strange dreams," Grigori said. "Frightening ones." In this he was telling the truth; Maya's anger was legendary. "Just remember you are one of five humans on the Moon. Nothing can hurt you here—"

"—Except the Moon."

"Is it more dangerous than Kolyma?"

"In Kolyma I knew the bullies," he said.

Grigori knew that he had to be direct. A busy day loomed. "Well, tell me what happened."

"I saw a ghost."

Only a few words, yet they confirmed Grigori's growing sense that Sergei's mental state had been deteriorating since the landing.

Not that his own had survived that hour of horror without cost. The twelve-meter-tall *Luna* vehicle had been designed to land automatically, much as half a dozen unmanned probes had.

But as the retro-rocket fired, with the lunar landscape rising to meet them, and Grigori, Viktor, Terenty, and Sergei strapped in standing positions in the tiny crew cabin—Belka in an alcove behind them—the radar had simply stopped working. "Are we hovering?" Grigori had asked, since the figure for altitude was frozen at a thousand meters. Grigori's pilot eye told him they were lower than that—and continuing to drop toward a cluster of low hills on the edge of the Ocean of Storms. He waited three seconds for Viktor, the systems specialist, to say or do something, then he grabbed the control yoke and flew *Luna* himself.

He did not have the luxury of extra fuel—ten seconds at most. But it was enough to shift the landing point a hundred meters to the lunar north, allowing *Luna* to settle on relatively smooth ground . . . even though there was a tilt, caused by a slight slope in the surface.

A Soviet fighter pilot with eight hundred hours in the air, three hundred in actual combat, he had endured numerous near disasters, but nothing as terrifying as this. As Terenty, Viktor, and Sergei pummeled one another in celebration, and Belka giggled from behind, Grigori urinated into his cosmonaut diaper.

Since then, in spite of the glorious first Soviet steps on the Moon, the deployment of scientific instruments, and the establishment of a crude but working habitat, many things had gone wrong. The most nagging problem wasn't technical: it was Terenty's open contempt for Belka and Sergei. Like most Russian nats, Terenty thought of jokers as subhuman.

Belka and Sergei knew it, but Sergei had taken it hard. As he had learned to do with the tall joker, Grigori resorted to humor. "Where? How close was he?" If he spread his arms, Grigori's fingertips were within half a meter of the tent's y-axis. It was deeper in x, of course, because one side extruded into the cave.

"She," Sergei said.

Terenty emerged at this point, sleepy-eyed, grumbling, "Why so much noise?"

Terenty and Viktor had chosen to bunk in the cave, a fissure perhaps three meters wide and slightly higher when Grigori and the crew first reached it.

They had chopped away at the fissure to widen it. A week of difficult labor convinced them that with a fabric barrier erected at a narrow juncture several meters deep, an air pocket would be created. There were no detectable leaks through the lunar rock.

The crew had set up its mining and processing gear there, and while the equipment generated a constant drone punctuated by hisses and clanks, Terenty had surely heard Grigori's conversation with Sergei.

"Sergei saw a ghost," Grigori said.

"Naturally," Terenty said dismissively, sidling past toward the hab tent. Given the cosmonaut's stocky, blocky frame, this was a tricky maneuver.

Grigori chose to let him go, turning back to Sergei. "The ghost is a she?"

"A beautiful, dark-haired woman."

Now Viktor emerged, grinning. "Does she fuck?" Clearly he had overheard, too.

"She was five meters tall," Sergei said.

"Ask if she's got a shorter friend." Viktor disappeared through the opening to the hab tent.

Grigori turned to Sergei. "Where was she?"

"Out there." He pointed toward the tiny plastic window on the north side of the tent. "Watching."

It was still lunar night and the light from a crescent Earth was too faint for illumination. All Grigori could see was a few square meters of lunar soil, some small rocks, and the footprints and skid marks he and the others had left when transferring equipment from the lander to the tents.

"Nothing, no footprints for a five-meter-tall woman," he said. "Watching or otherwise."

"No, she's gone."

"Then why did you tell me to look?"

"I didn't." Among Sergei's quirks was the desire to argue fine points of conversation.

"Was she doing anything else? Did she just appear?"

"She seemed to be . . . searching. Looking around."

"Why did you think she was a ghost?"

"I could see through her."

"She was naked?"

"No, in some kind of colorful wrap."

"A dress?" Grigori could not believe he was having this conversation.

"A sari, that's the word."

Grigori blinked. "A giant ghostly woman in a sari. Looking, watching . . ."

"She was very close to our pipeline. I think she was tugging at something."

"Tampering with our pipeline?" Grigori's heart rate jumped.

The tented habitat at the mouth of the tiny lunar cave was still connected to the *Luna* lander, dependent on power generated by the lander's solar panels, and still drawing water and some oxygen from tanks. If those failed, Grigori and his crewmates would die. Perhaps Sergei would linger a bit longer as he breathed carbon dioxide exhalations, but only for a few hours.

"I think so."

"It's worth investigating," Grigori said, hoping that he sounded calm and controlled.

He unzipped the passage to hab, and saw Viktor and Terenty finishing their meal. "New task this morning. You two go outside to check the pipeline."

Terenty didn't look up from his food bag. "Searching for Sergei's ghost?"

"Checking for damage."

Viktor collapsed his food bag with unusual force. "He should do it." He being Sergei.

All four full-sized cosmonauts had made excursions—space-suited hikes on the lunar surface—in order to erect the tents and configure the equipment.

But Sergei's suit had developed several troubling issues, from overheating to air loss, during that first intensive week of work. "He would go if he had a suit," Grigori said.

Viktor, as he did so often these days, persisted. "It will cost us a day's air."

"You've wasted more time and money chasing women, so do as you're ordered. Go, survey, report back. An hour at most. And take pictures."

Two hours later, after more grumbling than useful work, Terenty and Viktor, in suits, exited the fabric air lock outside the hab tent.

They were unusually quick with their prep, prompting Belka to complain, "They didn't sit before they left." There was a Russian tradition that before departing on a trip of any kind, one must sit quietly first.

Grigori was surprised that he hadn't noticed, but blamed the lapse on fatigue. "We're engineers, not grandmothers," he said.

Grumbling, Belka went off to the cave to do maintenance on the processing gear. Sergei continued to look after the plants.

Grigori monitored the surface sortie. As commander of the mission, Grigori had information that Terenty and Viktor did not. All Soviet cosmonauts were given preflight intelligence briefings. Earth orbital missions gathered visual and electronic data, so crewmembers had to be briefed on enemy targets in a special access room at the training center.

So Grigori wasn't totally surprised when, a month prior to the *Luna* launch, he was summoned to the Aquarium, the glass-walled headquarters of the Military Intelligence Service in downtown Moscow.

He signed in and was directed to a bare, dark room with a single table and three chairs.

There he sat. And sat.

He waited just long enough to consider departing without the briefing, when finally a pair of agents, one in uniform, one in a baggy suit, entered. The uniformed agent, a major, was tall, pale, blond, and, strangely, wore rubber gloves. "I am Kostin," he said. "This is Polyakov."

Polyakov was solid, bald, perhaps sixty. His civilian clothing suggested that he worked for State Security, not Military Intelligence—two organizations that hated each other more than they hated the Great Enemy U.S.A.

"Cousin Polyakov?" Grigori said. His reward was a tight smile from the civilian.

But rubber-gloved Kostin ignored him as he began to speak. "The Americans returned to the Ocean of Storms six years ago." He meant the second flight of the strange little *Quicksilver* vehicle in 1981.

"I saw the news in *Pravda*." Indeed, Grigori had marveled at the flight of the plucky vehicle, even as he discounted it as a human accomplishment: A joker had made the flight possible.

"Then you know that two of the crew returned—Sampson and Mitchell."

"And the third, the woman Eva-Lynne, died."

"Yes."

"Is there other information?" Briefings at the training center had covered the same subject, since the *Quicksilver* missions were the primary reason *Luna* would be landing in the Ocean of Storms. Oh, the site was level, with suspected caves close by. And visits by unmanned Soviet probes had mapped and surveyed the area more thoroughly than any other on the lunar surface. But the real reason was, if it was good enough for the Americans, it was good enough for the U.S.S.R.

Kostin turned to Polyakov. Grigori sat up, since he knew that State Security had unique sources. The older man cleared his throat and spoke for the first time. His voice was smooth, cultured. "We've studied the lunar surface from orbit. Eleven years ago we spotted a strange structure on the surface of the far side."

"Something built by the Swarm?" Grigori had been recalled to fighter duty in order to fly missions against the alien invaders of 1985.

"Always a possibility. But every analyst who saw the image said the structure resembled the Taj Mahal."

"A secret Indian space effort?" Grigori smiled at his own joke, and Polyakov chuckled. Kostin only examined his rubber fingers.

"At this point, anything is possible. And later attempts to spot the structure failed, with one exception. Whatever built it might have destroyed it."

"Or hidden it." Now Kostin spoke.

"Or relocated it," Polyakov said. "So be alert."

Kostin smirked. "Tell him about the second image, cousin."

Polyakov actually seemed uncomfortable, which Grigori found especially intriguing. "One of the images, inconclusive, seemed to show a human woman we call the Moon Maid, near this Taj Mahal."

"A human female, on the Moon?"

"That was our conclusion."

And that was the end of the briefing. Grigori headed back to the training center confused and amused.

He gave the Moon Maid no more thought. Until today.

There were many challenges for the *Luna* mission, but what frustrated Grigori to despair were those caused by poor design and manufacture. Heading that list were the radios. The Moon-Earth communications system was a joke, constrained first of all by orbital mechanics and basic geography, meaning that the *Luna* crew could only speak with Control for a few hours every day.

During their first two weeks the cosmonauts, notably Viktor, had faithfully transmitted surface images and videos of their work as well as "happy worker cosmonaut" messages, all for public consumption.

But subsequent sessions were limited to operational matters and "psychological support" talks with family members, no doubt disappointing the propaganda ministry.

Surface communications were even worse. The hab and support tents had decent radios, but those in individual sortie suits had short range and questionable direction. Worse, those radios used *Luna* itself as their relay and signal boost, so the suit links tended to work best when the cosmonauts (and the antennae on their backpacks) faced toward *Luna*. When they turned away, or were out of line of sight, the result was static.

So, as Terenty and Viktor followed the line and vanished into the darkness, Grigori and Belka took turns peering out the tiny hab tent window and seeing nothing.

And hearing less. Terenty was not a talker at the best of times, so his relative silence was no surprise. But Viktor was a chatterbox.

Nevertheless, during the first half hour of the excursion, even he limited his communications to odd grunts or brief statements about distance from the tents.

"How are the science experiments?" Viktor's primary accomplishment all during training and operations on the Moon had been the development and deployment of five experiments, essentially metal boxes with antennae that recorded elements of the lunar environment and transmitted data to Earth.

The package was sited near the pipeline and connected to it, since it had its own small but powerful electrical generator. Viktor was unusually slow to respond, and unusually testy. "Fine as far as I know."

Grigori had to ask about damage to the pipeline, and only heard a "stand by," which meant little.

"They're pouting," Belka said. "They didn't want to go out to search for a ghost."

"It wouldn't be the most useless excursion we've made."

"They're tired."

"We're all tired." Grigori reached for the microphone but as he touched it, he heard a blast of static.

". . . something . . ." was the only word he could make out among the crackle. That was Viktor's voice. More static followed, then, ". . . not possible . . . she . . ." Grigori gave the receiver a whack, and heard, ". . . following her . . ."

Then Terenty: "Vika!" A sudden, clear shout, followed by a, "No, no, no." Then a curse and heavy breathing.

Nothing from Viktor.

More static.

And then silence.

◆

Grigori had no choice but to make an excursion of his own. "You have two hours of air," Sergei informed him.

"That should be enough," he said. He would either rescue Terenty and Viktor, or learn their fate.

Space suits had been vital to the success—such as it was—of the mission. But their useful life span was simply unknown. Motors burned out. Fabric and seals hardened in the extreme temperatures. Suits could simply fail, popping like balloons.

That might have happened to Viktor or Terenty, or both.

He entered the air lock, a fabric blister on the exterior of the hab tent barely large enough to hold the three pressure suits, a pump, and an oxygen tank.

Even with full confidence in the suits, Grigori and his team had been careful about making surface excursions. They were inherently dangerous, there was frequently nothing to be learned—and each exit ate up several dozen pounds of precious oxygen.

And while Grigori had performed a dozen lunar excursions by now—a figure he would have thought impossible as recently as last year—he always felt nervous once the backpack was sealed in place. (You entered the suit through its open back, sliding feet and legs inside the legs and boots, then wriggling arms into place as you bent and somehow wrenched your head through the neck ring into the helmet. Then your partner would close the backpack and flip the necessary switches to enable the airflow. You had two hours of air, more or less.)

Grigori had never been able to don a suit in less than half an hour, and that was with full-sized help. But, powered by adrenaline and aided by Belka, who crawled up, down, and around the suit like a monkey, he was wedged into his suit in fifteen minutes. Just before locking down his helmet and sealing himself inside, he called, "Sergei! Have they said anything?"

"No words. Someone is making sounds."

Grigori looked at Belka. "What the hell does that mean?"

"That one of them is still alive. You'd better hurry."

Belka was reaching for the latches on the helmet, but Grigori stopped him. "When Control calls, tell them I want to speak to an official of State Security named Polyakov."

Belka got a quizzical look on his face. "Just do it," Grigori said.

Sergei, the crew expert on air and consumables, announced, "They are on fumes by now."

"Maybe they reached *Luna*," Belka said.

"Then they would be in touch through *Luna*," Grigori said.

Called back to active duty during the Swarm attack, Grigori had flown combat missions in which colleagues were killed. But they were fellow pilots, not his responsibility. Even though he had problems with Terenty and Viktor, and allowing for the danger of a lunar excursion—potentially more deadly than flying combat—he was not prepared to lose one, much less both.

Especially given the way he had summarily ordered them outside to chase a phantom.

Belka latched the helmet.

Twenty minutes of Grigori's two hours was lost waiting for air to bleed out of the air lock. The fabric structure would flap—noiselessly—then go limp, a sign that the air was gone and that it was okay to open the outer door.

Which he did, stepping onto the dark gray lunar soil.

His first goal was to follow Terenty and Viktor's tracks while also searching for any sign of the Moon Maid. The arms of the lunar hillside that embraced the tent and cave site allowed for a widening cone of access—perhaps a hundred degrees right in front of the air lock, broadening to 180 and more after you walked a dozen meters.

Grigori conducted a visual scan and saw nothing but the now-familiar cluster of boot prints he, Terenty, and Viktor had left over the weeks.

Moving out, he immediately and automatically fell into a shuffling gait as he followed the power and fuel lines leading to the lander a thousand meters away and considered the possibility that he might have to complete the mission with only his two joker crewmates.

Belka's path to the lunar mission had originated within the Communist Party apparatus: the small joker had actually been a Party representative at the Bauman Technical School, then at the design bureau that developed Soviet space vehicles.

When a joker department was created within the cosmonaut corps, due to his education, his undoubted skills with equipment repair, his size, and his family connections (his father was high up in the Ministry of General Machine-Building), Belka was an obvious choice.

Sergei had been found in the Gulag within weeks of the Swarm invasion, when the Soviet military put aside its habitual hatred for jokers and, as it had done with proscribed political prisoners during the Great Patriotic War, decided to make use of them.

Grigori could only imagine the harsh methods used to identify these individuals. Four of them, including Sergei, had joined the cosmonaut team in 1986.

It had taken three times as long to prepare these souls—who saw an opportunity for death and glory in space as opposed to mere death in Siberia—to be useful as crewmembers.

As the *Luna* mission grew more real, and the limitations on supplies and equipment more obvious, the utility of cosmo-jokers was inescapable. Grigori found his pair to be far more valuable than jet jockeys like Terenty, or even an aerospace engineer like Viktor—typical nat cosmonauts.

After all, a joker who transformed carbon dioxide into oxygen was invaluable in a space crew.

But why Grigori Florianovich Kolesnikov? Of the five, he was the most experienced cosmonaut, having earned selection at the young age of twenty-seven in 1974 after spending five years flying jets in various Central Asian locales. He had made one spaceflight in 1980, piloting a Sever spacecraft to a docking with the first of the *Zarya* series of space stations to serve a sixty-day tour with two other cosmonauts.

The mission was intended to facilitate spying on the United States and Europe. But one day Grigori had been alerted to the approach of an American Hornet spaceplane. In itself this was not unusual—both sides spied on each other. But with the close encounter his orders were to activate the Nudelman cannon mounted on the underside of the Zarya.

And when the teardrop-shaped Hornet hove into view, Grigori had uncaged the cannon and fired a shot in its general direction. It was only one, and it missed the Hornet by a substantial distance.

But the shot forced the Hornet to divert and move off, and Soviet officials trumpeted Grigori's automatic and ineffectual actions as a heroic attack on the forces of imperialism!

Grigori knew better, but saw no reason not to go along with the *Pravda*. As a result, he had volunteered for *Luna*—and won the assignment.

Aside from his orbital "heroics," what Grigori brought to the lunar trio was Soviet purity—he was a Russian Russian from the Smolensk region west of Moscow, specifically the town of Vyazma. His father, a millworker who had served honorably in the Great Patriotic War, had the ideal proletarian background. His mother was an elementary school teacher.

There were no political unreliables in his immediate or even larger family.

And no jokers.

He had also conducted his personal life "in accordance with Party norms," at least in public. He was married, though his relationship with Maya was frequently as frosty as that between the U.S.S.R. and U.S.A., and father to a budding "Young Pioneer," eight-year-old Nadezhda.

Also helpful was his fluency, at least by Soviet military standards, in English. That was due to his mother, Irina, who had some English herself, and knew that it would be helpful. Grigori had excelled in secondary school English, then finished first in his Air Force school language program, too.

His relative fluency helped with his selection as a cosmonaut—and the assignment to the Zarya mission, since so much of the work involved listening in on American military transmissions. It might also have been the key factor in his selection to lead the *Luna* mission, with its need for global publicity.

What Grigori preferred to believe he brought to the crew was the experience of spaceflight—the realization that the day-to-day work of any mission was a three-way split between maintaining the human organism (eating, exercising), maintaining the vehicle itself, and then performing the primary tasks.

On Zarya, the task had been aiming cameras and radio collectors at a list of American targets. On *Luna* it was to carve out a preliminary habitat and prove that it was possible to convert lunar rock to water and oxygen.

Of course, today, it was to save his crew.

Grigori's helmet was equipped with one light on each side, but the left one had failed in the first week, so since his visibility was limited to a few meters on his right, he trod carefully, keeping close to the fuel line near his left foot.

Growing up in Vyazma, he had never fantasized about the Moon, or other planets in the solar system. He and his friends had occasional adventures on Takis, of course, when they weren't pretending to be heroic partisans killing Nazis.

It was only on night flights in his MiG that Grigori was struck by the Moon, its immense brightness over a low deck of clouds. For one moment he wondered what it might be like to go there—to visit some world free from Communists versus capitalists, jokers versus nats. But the moment never lasted—he was too busy either trying to drop bombs on insurgents or flying an aircraft with faulty instruments.

Yet, now, here he was—two months a lunar resident, with no departure in sight.

Slip, slide. Hear the hiss of the oxygen pump in his backpack. The tips of his fingers felt cold, and so did his toes. The lunar excursion suit provided survivability in the extreme environment, but not comfort—and its thermal controls were limited. To be fair—though why should Grigori want to be fair—it had only been designed to operate for a score of hours, in early planning for short lunar missions.

Once the *Luna* mission was approved, knowing that the desired operational lifetime was now some multiple of the original twenty hours, the teams at the factory had tried to add insulation and redundancy to the suits.

Well, so far the hinges worked, the pressure seal held, and the helmet—though the tinted faceplate was no longer gold but greenish—continued to function. But Grigori and especially Belka, with his smaller model, had experienced nerve-wracking temperatures on their extremities. Yes, there was some insulation—or Grigori's fingers and toes would have cracked and fallen off.

Just not enough.

Within fifteen minutes, exchanging routine and largely audible messages with Sergei, Grigori had traversed the entire length of the pipeline, passing the link to the science station, but seen no sign of Terenty and Viktor.

And no damage and no unusual tracks.

The *Luna* vehicle rose in the distance like a lighthouse, four stories tall, a skeletal structure now that tanks and modules had been removed, but still imposing. Small lights on the crew return vehicle at the top and near the base provided the only illumination other than starlight.

Grigori was struck again by the improbability of their survival: In the darkness, stripped like this, its four solar panels drooping, the lander looked frail and old. *Babushka* was what Sergei had called it upon departure. A good thing there was no wind on the Moon; the vehicle looked as though it would blow over.

His first inspection, slip-sliding in the churned-up soil around the landing legs, showed him that all hoses and power lines were attached as before. Yet something felt wrong. The darkness and limited light contributed to a sense of menace.

That, and the absence of any sign of Terenty and Viktor.

Grigori chose to retrace his route back toward the tents, this time letting his functioning light play across the lines and hoses. And halfway back he saw it—obvious damage, strips of insulation had been peeled off the pipeline! How the hell had he missed that on his outward journey? Damn the lunar night and his failed helmet lamp.

For a moment Grigori thought the damage was serious enough to compromise the unit, and felt his heart rate spike to levels not approached since the landing.

"What did you find?" Sergei's voice was suddenly clear in his headphones.

"What are you talking about?" Grigori had said nothing.

"You groaned."

Grigori knelt and carefully fingered the loose material with his thick gloved fingers. "All right. There is damage here, two hundred meters from *Luna,* but the underlying plastic is still intact."

Which left him examining the flaps of insulation. This section of the pipe lay straight and flat on the dark gray soil—there was no reason it might flex and bend with insulation tears due to extreme temperatures.

Grigori stepped back to look at the dirt . . . and now he could clearly see several boot prints, most of them likely to have been made by Viktor and Terenty, and, given their sharp edges, recently.

He tried a radio call to Terenty, then Viktor. He heard nothing but a faint, crackly reply from Sergei: "Did you find them?"

"Their tracks. So we know they made it this far."

Grigori triggered the camera mounted on his chest pack and clicked off several images on the unlikely assumption that he and his crew would have the time or bandwidth to share them with Control. Then, as best he could with thick fingers and tape that seemed to harden at his touch, he tried to repair the damage.

That accomplished, he performed another walk-around, noting that Terenty and Viktor's tracks seemed to lead to the north, at least for the ten meters Grigori could see.

"Sergei, Belka, how much time do I have?"

"Under one hour," Sergei said. "Come back. They can't possibly be alive after all this time."

True, but that wouldn't stop him. He plunged into the dust, following the tracks. Over a rise, over another rise, tents and *Luna* out of sight. The tracks were easy to follow now, and the wide spacing suggested that the cosmonauts had been in a hurry . . . chasing the Moon Maid? The Moon Maid who left no tracks?

Since it was clearly out of line-of-sight communication, none of the cosmonauts had ventured in this direction. Grigori kept a moderate pace: no leaping steps.

A good thing, too: as he crested a low rise just south of the lunar hills, Grigori discovered what looked like a shallow pond of lunar dust.

The crew had been warned about such features by Musa, one of their geologists—but only one, since the others dismissed the idea. "I call them gold dust," Musa had said. "An American astronomer named Gold thinks the Moon's surface is all dust, that spacecraft will sink into it.

"I don't believe that, and our landers have not disappeared. But I think that you might find these gold dust ponds and if you do, be careful. They might be very deep."

Both sets of boot prints ran directly into the pond, where they vanished. The surface of the pond seemed untouched.

The feature was perhaps thirty meters across. On the other side was typical lunar soil . . . with no boot prints that Grigori could see. He stood at the edge, brushing the toe of his boot in the dust, which seemed light and fluffy.

He found a rock and chucked it underhand into the pond, where it vanished without a ripple.

Now what? He was looking to his right, searching for a way around the pond, calculating how much time he had left before he would have to turn back.

Then, like a breaching whale, a suited cosmonaut popped out of the gold dust pond.

Red ID stripes on the suit's arms told Grigori who it was. "Viktor!" Grigori shouted, realizing that he was wasting his breath—the signal from his suit would have to travel to *Luna* before bouncing back to the pond, and *Luna* was hidden behind hills.

He waited, vainly, for Viktor to move, to swim, to do something. But the cosmonaut just lay, almost floating, in the dust. Grigori would have to pull him out. On Earth, confronted with a comrade in quicksand, he might have used a branch, or a rope. Here, he had nothing.

Nothing but his hands, that is. He would have to wade into this pond of dust and pull Viktor out. There was no way to anchor himself . . . and he was top-heavy in lunar gravity, lacking in traction even on normal soil. But the choice was brutally stark: go in or leave Viktor.

Grigori tried to put weight on his heels, to remain upright, as he took one step into the pond. His boot sank half a dozen centimeters, in dust above his ankle. But there was something solid beneath, enough that Grigori risked a second step. Now he was up to his knees in dust. And Viktor was still several meters away, out of reach. Well, there was no going back. Grigori wondered how long Belka and Sergei would survive without him—

Another step took him waist-deep and sliding, sliding. For a sick moment he thought he was going to topple backward and vanish under the dust. Somehow he managed to right himself, but his thrashing triggered a wave in the dust.

And Viktor sank out of sight.

Grigori looked at the spot, two meters in front of him, and wanted to weep. Worse yet, his head began to ache, a sign that carbon dioxide was building up in his suit.

He had to go back.

Rather than turn, and risk falling, he tried to step back. One, good. Two—

Something grabbed his right boot.

He tried to shake it off but even as he raised his right leg he saw that it was Viktor, somehow clutching him in a deathlike grip.

Grigori was able to pull himself to the "shore" of the dust pond, dragging Viktor with him. Once he had firm footing, he kicked free, then dragged his fellow cosmonaut to relative safety. He lowered his helmet so it was touching Viktor's, hoping to use that method of communication, calling . . . but no answer.

Through the faceplate Viktor's eyes were closed. He was unconscious at best. As for Terenty, Grigori could only assume he was lost in the gold dust pond.

He was out of time. But lunar gravity allowed him to drag Viktor back toward the tents with relative ease.

Just this once, the Moon was a helpful mistress.

"He's breathing, but his vitals are all over the place," Belka said.

Grigori had brought Viktor through the air lock into the hab tent, where Belka and Sergei had assisted in first removing the helmet, then laboriously extracting him through the back of the suit.

The job was complicated by sheer lack of space. Grigori had had to move into the support tent in order to shed his own suit.

"What does that mean?" he asked Belka.

"His temperature is low—feel his forehead. Heart rate is present, but irregular."

"Is he in a coma?" Sergei asked.

"He's suffering from lack of oxygen," Belka said. "He may be brain-dead."

"Then what do we do?" The birdlike joker was about to panic.

"We wait," Grigori said. "When we talk to Control we'll tell them what happened, how he is, and see what the doctors say."

"Our fucking doctors? Good luck," Belka said. Soviet space doctors were chosen for their willingness to adjust diagnoses to meet political ends.

At moments like this, Grigori missed the warming properties of vodka. Soviet cosmonauts—like everyone in the Soviet military, or the entire U.S.S.R., for that matter—drank like peasants of the fifteenth century: Given access to alcohol, they would ingest as much as possible as quickly as possible. The purpose, Grigori realized long ago, was to deaden the pain and misery of Soviet life.

Grigori was not that bad, but given free time or the right occasion—that being any evening or group meal—he would happily knock back three or four shots just to feel brighter.

The drinks made his male companions funnier, and the female ones prettier—and much friendlier.

These lunar nights, and days, the few moments not spent listening for equipment breakdowns, then performing repairs, would have been more tolerable had any of them been able to drink. But they had only been able to smuggle a small bottle of champagne aboard, and that had been consumed in celebration of the landing.

Should he survive, should he have the chance to perform an honest debrief, he would tell his bosses to give cosmonauts their liquor ration. Sailors had it; missions to the Moon were more like sea voyages than airplane flights.

Of course, that was merely one in a long list of complaints he had for his bosses.

"We have to tell Control what happened," Sergei said.

"Go ahead and try," Grigori told him. He wasn't eager to explain how he had lost forty percent of his crew to a Moon Maid, but was too dehydrated, hungry, and exhausted to worry.

When Sergei failed to reach Control, Grigori actually felt disappointed. Clearly he was ready for a fight, or just an end to this godforsaken mission.

In order to keep watch on Viktor, the three decided to sleep in shifts. Grigori, the most exhausted, would rest first, in the cave. Sergei would remain in the support tent. Belka would take the first watch.

All too aware of the different sounds and smells of the cave, Grigori tried to get comfortable on the mat that formerly belonged to Terenty, and cursed again the wrongheaded decisions that brought him and his crew to the Moon.

Even before his recent troubles, Grigori had grown tired of the one-upsmanship, the desire to simply outdo the United States, that had driven Soviet space efforts since the 1950s—each nation using its missile technology to place humans in orbit in small vehicles, then more humans in larger, more capable craft, including winged ships that landed on ordinary runways.

Prior to the invasion by the Swarm the U.S.S.R. had already orbited the Zarya space surveillance station as well as an orbital missile system, a space tracking and alert network.

The *Luna* mission had hoped to expand that system while garnering global praise. Now . . . well, now the goal for *Luna* was to survive until resupply.

Grigori thought he was experiencing a moonquake, but it was only Belka shaking him awake. "Your shift. Sorry, but you gave me orders."

"I did." Stiff and aching from yesterday's exertions, Grigori accepted a nutrient bag from Belka, then followed the little joker through the support tent, where Sergei slept peacefully, it seemed, even though he was sitting up. "I always expect to find him perched like a crow," Belka said, once he and Grigori were back in the hab tent.

There had been no change in Viktor's condition. "He's still breathing very raggedly," Belka said. "What are you going to tell Control?"

"That Terenty was killed when his space suit failed, and Viktor left in this sorry condition because he tried to save him."

"No ghosts, I take it."

"What do you think?"

Belka laughed and departed for his time in the cave.

After his breakfast, Grigori took up his position bedside. To fill the time he recorded power, water, and oxygen levels, and did another pointless inventory of the food supplies.

Then Viktor sat up, eyes open. He seemed confused, awkward.

Grigori gently set aside his clipboard. "Be careful, Viktor," he said.

Viktor's head snapped around, facing him. He opened his mouth, closed it, swallowed, then opened it again. And spoke several words, which sounded like, "*Ya chagha chodo.*"

Viktor's posture, voice, expression—none of it was Viktor's. Grigori wondered if this was what happened when a brain was oxygen-starved. How much of Viktor remained?

Carefully, Grigori answered in Russian. "I don't understand."

Viktor repeated the phrase. Grigori shook his head, spread his hands. He knew how to express linguistic incapacity in French and German, so tried that.

Nothing. Then he said it in English.

And Viktor reacted with a jerky nod. Then he said, "Leave this place."

"Why are you saying this? What's wrong?"

Viktor was trying to get to his feet, and pulled over an oxygen tank. It was as if he had no idea where he was. It didn't seem to matter. Unsteady on his feet, Viktor again said, "Leave this place!"

"Who is speaking?"

The reply was a word or name, two syllables: "Aarti."

"Aarti, then. Why do you want us to leave?"

"This is my home."

"We didn't know. Forgive the intrusion. But we are scientists." That was a total lie, but they were hardly invaders—at worst, unwitting vandals. "And who are you? Are you a ghost?"

Belka arrived at that moment, with Sergei over his shoulder. The interruption frightened Viktor, who plunged through the unzipped curtain into the air lock, then began scrabbling at the hatch.

"Where's he going?" Sergei asked.

Belka, meanwhile, was trying to brandish a shovel that was too big for him. "Someone take this!"

Grigori, however, realized that Viktor was about to open the outer air lock door. He frantically zipped the inner curtain shut—

—just as Viktor wrenched the outer door open.

The air inside the air lock exploded outward, flapping the inner curtain so violently that Grigori thought it would tear, and flinging Viktor outside on his face in the lunar soil.

"What's going on?" Belka said, crowding Grigori as he tried to peer through the plastic window. "Is he dead?"

"Not remotely."

In fact, Grigori watched the thing that looked like Viktor pick himself up. He was covered in lunar dirt, but made no attempt to brush off. He simply looked back at the hab, then turned and began to walk away in his long undergarment.

Before the creature had taken a dozen steps, it stopped and looked back again.

Then vanished in a cloud of dust that quickly settled to the ground.

"He had to be some kind of joker," Sergei said.

They were in the support tent examining their space suits, since the damaged air lock meant that any exit required all members of the crew to be suited. At least until the air lock was repaired.

"From where?" Belka said.

Grigori said, "There are jokers and aces who can go places nats can't. They don't even need spaceships."

"Then why aren't they doing this fucking mission?" To the extent that he could, Belka stomped out of the hab tent and back into the cave.

"Why don't we just go home?" Sergei said, his voice pitifully plaintive.

"We haven't completed the mission. There will be consequences."

"Worse than this?"

"Our families will be punished, too. And they don't deserve this. And besides"—this thought had not crystallized in Grigori's mind until now—"I will not be pushed around by a ghost."

"That was more than a ghost."

"Whatever it was, it's not terminating my mission!" His voice seemed to echo in the tight quarters.

"Now what?" Sergei said.

"It's time to call Control," Grigori said.

It took the better part of an hour for Sergei, calling in the blind, to make a connection. But finally the planets aligned and Control responded.

Grigori took the microphone from Sergei. "This is Kolesnikov. Who is on duty?"

Sergei said, "Pavlov," which Grigori could have guessed. He pictured Pavlov and a group of his deputies clustered around a console at the Crimean Station—exchanging worried glances.

After the lag: "Greetings, Comrade Commander! This is Control Twenty"—for security reasons, all Crimean operators were identified by number; twenty was indeed Pavlov—"so nice to hear your voice! We were afraid you were . . . ill."

He meant "unhappy with us," which was obvious. "Greetings, Twenty," Grigori said, in his most professional voice. "Please shift to channel two." Channel two was an encrypted link available to Crimea and the cosmonauts.

"This is Kolesnikov. Viktor and Terenty are dead." Allowing for the lag and the dire nature of the news, Grigori gave the basic details, which were naturally shocking to Control. "The circumstances will be less mysterious if we can all speak to Comrade Polyakov of State Security."

A long lag, and then these words: "He is standing by, as you requested."

Then Grigori heard a new voice, patched in. Polyakov.

Grigori quickly recounted the appearance of the Moon Maid, and the events with Viktor . . . or Aarti, whoever that was.

Polyakov accepted the bizarre narrative without apparent surprise and with few comments. Grigori wondered how many similar stories the wild card spy had lived through. "I have no idea how to fight a phantom who has already killed two of my men and wants to terminate my mission," he told Polyakov.

"You are in a unique situation," Polyakov said.

That was worse than useless. He had discerned that much by himself.

"Is it possible this phantom is an alien? A Swarm remnant, or even a Takisian of some sort?"

"Possibly," said Grigori. "Some of the Swarmlings took on human form. This thing looked like Viktor. Sergei saw a woman. Beautiful, with dark hair, wearing a sari. Did the Swarmlings wear saris?"

"It is possible a Swarm bud landed in India. We will need to make further inquiries. It is also possible you are dealing with an ace of some sort. Some of the American aces are capable of flying through space. We have files on Pulse and Starshine. This may be another. A new one, possibly Indian."

"Viktor did not fly away. He turned to dust."

Pavlov must have taken the microphone. "This is Twenty again. Whether this creature is an alien or a powerful ace, it is an enemy of the Soviet Union. If it appears again, you are authorized to capture or kill it, whichever seems most practical. We are prepared to declare the mission a success and allow you to lift off at the first opportunity."

"Understood," Grigori said. And then, as the link faded, "Kolesnikov, out."

"There's a launch window every twenty-four hours," Sergei said moments later.

"To get us back to Earth in one piece, yes," Grigori said. "But we could land in the Himalayas, or the middle of the Pacific."

"Or in Washington, D.C.," Belka said, smiling wickedly.

"Only once a week do we have windows that would get us to landing zones in Russia."

"When is the next one?"

"Tomorrow," Belka said. He held up a notepad.

Happier than he'd seemed in two months, Sergei slid off his perch. "Then let's listen to Control, and go home!"

"No," Grigori said.

Before he could drive home the message, Belka spoke up. "How can we leave while that thing is outside?"

"What other choice do we have?"

Grigori poked Sergei in the shoulder. "We're soldiers, aren't we?"

"You might be," Sergei said. "You're trying to protect your bonus even if it kills us!"

Grigori was stunned by this statement, partly because it showed that Sergei was fighting back. But also because it was true. Maya had resisted the idea of Grigori's participation in the *Luna* mission until learning that the bonus for it was 100,000 rubles—twenty years' income. Suddenly there were no more complaints about Grigori's travel for training, the trips to Kazakhstan that she mistakenly believed to involve sexy local women. "You have your own bonuses and rewards. If not money, then a flat, a car, prizes—"

Belka ended the argument. "Toys and money won't matter if we don't figure out how to destroy this thing."

Sergei couldn't continue to argue.

Fighting a phantom left few options, given their limited equipment. "If she was truly a ghost, there wouldn't be anything we could do," Grigori said.

"And we wouldn't have a problem," Belka said. "A physical presence means she is vulnerable to physical actions."

"Even so," Grigori said, "we can't shoot her because we don't have guns." He ticked off the options aloud in the hopes that one of the trio might have a solution. "We have no explosives, and no chemicals we could even mix into explosives or flammables, so we can't bomb her. She doesn't appear to need oxygen, so we can't trap her and suffocate her." He happened to glance at the nutrient bags. "Maybe we could poison her."

"She talks," Belka said. "Sergei could bore her to death." Sergei ignored the insult, which Grigori took as a sign that he was concentrating on solutions.

"I'm thinking heat," Grigori said, "or electricity."

Then they heard a sad pop from somewhere beyond the support tent. Lights and power died.

Grigori's first fear was that Aarti had returned and was on the attack. But then he glanced at the patch panel and saw flipped fuses. Their systems were failing, as usual.

During his Zarya orbital mission, Grigori had experienced a similar event when fuses blew on a panel and left the station powerless, dark, and potentially adrift. The same thing could have happened in his flat near Moscow, but there a few minutes or even hours without power was only a common inconvenience.

On Zarya, every minute without power brought the cosmonauts a minute closer to suffocation. That danger existed here, though Sergei's unique oxygen-generating ability meant that Grigori and Belka, and Sergei, were more likely to freeze first.

Without being told, within minutes, working skillfully in the all-too-silent dark, Belka was able to power up lights and an air pump. "But we're on batteries now," he said.

Sergei was understandably agitated. "How long will they work?"

"Four hours, maybe six if the commander and I are not here."

"Now we have to move to *Luna*."

"Pack up," Grigori said. "Meanwhile, Belka and I will deal with our phantom. We will be ready to launch at the first opportunity."

Over the next two hours, mindful of the clock ticking toward Aarti's potential return five hours hence, Grigori and Belka went through their suiting, with Sergei's help.

Finally all three were suited, though Sergei still had his helmet off, since he would be breathing residual CO_2 as he closed up a pair of equipment cases. As Belka headed to the air lock, Grigori said, "Wait." He took Belka's and Sergei's hands. "We sit."

Neither joker had to be reminded of the tradition, especially in these circumstances. They joined Grigori in sitting on the hard-packed floor for a moment, in silence.

Then Grigori rose. "Good luck to all of us."

Grigori and Belka stepped into the patched air lock and started the depress.

As they made their way, slip-sliding up the pipeline, then left toward the science station, Grigori realized that half-sized Belka seemed born for Moon excursions. In spite of the grim circumstances, the little joker skipped and loped with an ease Grigori could only envy. Of course, Grigori's suit weighed three times what Belka's did—and Grigori was still exhausted from the prior excursion. But it seemed that the Moon might be a better home for jokers than for nats.

Belka was clearly feeling it, too. "It feels good to get out of the tents. I should have done this more often."

Then, in his peripheral vision, Grigori saw Belka stop.

"It's a fucking banyan tree." He pointed.

Grigori raised his head and squinted.

It was indeed a tree, and a strange, multibranched sort. Typical of Belka to know that; even though Grigori had orbited the Earth for months, he had never been out of the Soviet Union except to fly missions over Bulgaria.

As they got closer, it proved to be more of a three-dimensional sketch of a banyan, in bold, primary colors, than a "real" one. And yet—

"It's not an illusion," Belka said, brushing aside several branches and tapping on the trunk.

"Can you explain this?"

"I have a sad Soviet imagination, sorry." Belka tried to push the banyan over with his shoulder. "Roots, too."

"Our phantom has other powers."

"We might have expected that."

Grigori felt sick. "Could this Indian ghost be the work of the Swarm?"

"Viktor would have known," Belka said, a revelation that surprised Grigori, but shouldn't have. "But I suspect not. This . . ." Belka waved at the tree. "This is just deranged art."

"I'll take a picture. You get samples."

Belka was preparing to do just that.

It was a struggle for Grigori just to reach, then raise the camera. He hoped that the charged-coupled-device card could still collect an image. *Click click* on the banyan as Belka scraped pieces of bark into a bag. "Now what?"

"We set our trap."

The science station was just ahead.

The work was simple in theory, but even spreading the mesh took more time than Grigori would have believed. Belka found it difficult to reroute the leads on the power system as Grigori struggled just spreading soil over the mesh to hide it.

"Done," Belka said, finally.

Grigori was on his hands and knees. Hearing Belka's announcement, he literally lowered his helmet faceplate to the ground, collapsing for a moment.

"Careful, Commander. The grid is hot."

"Maybe I was hoping to test it." He had thought about death many times in his career, from his first solo flight in a Yak-11 through every combat assignment, and especially the night before he launched on his Zarya mission.

On the Moon he'd been so exhausted that the possibility of death seemed welcome. Not today: he wanted to kill this Indian avatar then go home.

With Belka following, Grigori headed back toward the pipeline and was within a few meters—within sight of both *Luna* to their left and the hab to their right—when he stumbled. It was strange, because he was standing still.

And then the whole Moon seemed to shudder and shake. Grigori felt like a sailor on a ship's deck in a storm, rising and falling. Only the rigidity of the suit kept him from pitching forward.

"Belka!"

"Behind you!"

Then it was over. Grigori turned to ensure that Belka was still upright, which he was. Then: "Sergei, did you feel that?"

There was no answer, only static.

And then he saw it striding past, no more than a hundred meters away.

This being was taller than a human by at least a head, and bulky enough to weigh 150 kilograms on Earth. It was wearing a blouse and a vest of armor.

"Do you see that?" Grigori asked.

"Yes."

"What is it?"

"If I remember correctly, some kind of Hindu demon. Rakshasa."

"Our Indian ace." He felt as much anger as he did fear.

To Grigori's horror, the Hindu demon strode directly toward the hab tents. "Sergei! It's coming your way!"

But now his headphones filled with popping as the demon attacked the hab tent, literally ripping it open. The whole structure collapsed as if squashed by a giant hand.

The demon waded into the wreckage, throwing their precious tanks and instruments over his shoulder.

A helmet landed at Grigori's feet. Sergei's.

Grigori could see into the support tent, still a bright spot against the dark gray moonscape—and there was Sergei, helmetless, arms wrapped around himself as if battling a gust of cold wind.

Which he was. The protective covering simply flew off, torn by the escaping air, which left Sergei completely exposed, along with all their equipment.

The flap to the cave tore loose, too.

Now Sergei stood, frozen, eyes wide—like a Gulag prisoner in a Siberian winter. Dead, of course.

And the demon rooted around in the wreckage like a boar.

Grigori wanted to take his shovel and attack the creature, but knew he would fail. To Belka he said, "Get to *Luna.* Start the prelaunch checklist."

"What about you?"

"Someone's got to lead that thing to the trap."

"If we both run now, we can get away."

"It will take an hour to prep *Luna,* and the window isn't open yet. There's no point in lifting off only to miss Earth."

Belka seemed unconvinced. Grigori said, "And if we don't eliminate this thing, it will be waiting for the next crew, and the next."

"Special forces will get her."

"Follow my orders."

There was a moment. Then the little joker executed a salute, even though the suit's restrictions prevented his hand from touching his helmet. "As you wish, Comrade Colonel."

Belka turned to go.

Telling himself to concentrate on the task before him, and nothing else, Grigori waved his arms and ran toward the ruined habitation.

Until the Rakshasa saw him and began to extract itself from the tangle of fabric and equipment. Grigori reversed course and headed for the science station. He slipped frequently, falling to his hands and knees at least twice. The second time he risked a glance behind him.

The demon was in motion now, making big strides and gaining on him.

Grigori would have to move faster than ever to reach the station before it caught him.

He pushed off and ran, fell, and stumbled toward the station and the trap. "Belka, do you read?"

"I am in the cabin and working the checklist. We can launch as soon as you get here."

"Can you see the Rakshasa?"

A long pause. Grigori took one, two, three loping steps.

"Yes! Behind you—!"

In the last five meters, he tripped and landed on his face, skidding so close to the electrified mesh that he imagined he could feel a hot surge through his gloves. Wouldn't that have been stupid? To die in his own trap!

Not daring to look back again, Grigori rolled and crab walked to one side, hoping to get to the far side of the web. He had just gotten to his feet and saw the demon looming in front of him, close enough to touch, when there was a flash of light from *Luna*.

For a moment Grigori feared that the demon had thrown something and struck the vehicle.

But no: The Hindu demon stopped its pursuit and stared toward the vehicle. "What happened?" Grigori said as he dragged himself to the other side of the web.

"I fired two steering rockets." Ah, Belka, so smart! One on each side so *Luna* didn't tip over. "We only have sixteen minutes until the window opens."

"Launch when ready."

"I'll launch when you're here!"

"You know the order. Now shut up and let me do my job!" That, after all, was the best a commander could do.

He faced the Rakshasa across the thirty meters of hidden web. The demon glanced at the science packages scattered around the site as if trying to determine what they were. Grigori wished they were laser cannons.

All he had was his shovel.

His head was beginning to hurt.

He waved at the demon. *Come get me!*

It seemed to hesitate. Grigori tried to imagine the entity controlling the demon—could she see through its eyes? Hearing was impossible.

Could she feel?

He hoped so.

He took a step toward the demon, and now it finally seemed to see him.

At that instant there was an arc from one of the instruments. Was the power dying? The web useless?

Grigori no longer cared: he was going to kill this thing if he had to use his hands.

Before he could step on the web, the Rakshasa did.

It was still working. The demon seemed to freeze, shudder. For the first time Grigori could see its face, and what he saw was surprise.

Then the Rakshasa exploded. A ball of white light enveloped them both.

He was on his back. He ached. He smelled something burning, no doubt part of his suit.

His faceplate was clouded, but still intact.

He rolled to one side and, painfully, pushed himself to his feet. The Hindu demon was gone; a rough circle of glazed lunar soil marked where it had been.

Luna was gone.

He had some memory of Belka's voice calling his name over and over again.

So this was it. He was going to die on the Moon. Given the pain in his skull, the ache in every joint, and the ominous sounds from his suit—clearly there was a leak—he was doomed.

The Moon was no place for him, for nats. Leave it to the jokers. He walked back to the dust pond that had swallowed Terenty and Viktor. Pictured Maya, Sasha. Even that was difficult.

Grigori sat down in the dust and began to slide slowly, strangely, almost sweetly into darkness.

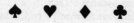

The Moon Maid

PART V

1987

SHE HADN'T MEANT TO kill anyone. That was what Aarti told herself at first.

Aarti had watched the alien Swarm attack in '85 from her house in Bombay, crouched over the small black-and-white TV in the kitchen where Saila liked to watch tearjerker movies while she cooked. Aarti held her breath, terrified that they would come to the Moon, but they had bypassed it entirely, focusing their attention on Earth. When the attack was over, she breathed a sigh of relief.

She should have felt bad for the humans killed in the battle, but those days, it was hard to feel much of anything. Aarti was numb, inside and out. Food held no savor for her, no matter how hard Saila worked to make it appealing. She hadn't taken a ride in the car since Yaj was killed, or gone out to the market. She spent her days dozing in her bed, waiting for the moment when she could wake up on the Moon. Her servants lived their lives, sent their children off to school. Unlike Manju and Yaj, they didn't try to involve Aarti in their days, and Aarti was grateful for that.

Day after day, year after year went by. Aarti counted time from the moment Yaj was murdered by the mob. Nineteen years, all alone. And then the invasion came. Not the Swarm—the invasion of her Moon, by humans.

They were Russians—that much she was able to tell, though she didn't speak the language. Aarti eavesdropped on their conversations, memorized the sound of the words. Then she translated them when she woke in Bombay, arduously bending over a Russian dictionary she'd had Suresh buy for her. Aarti had hoped, at first, that this mission would be like the others, that the Russians would stomp around, collect rocks, set up instruments, and then leave again. Back to the Earth that suited them, that had no place for people like herself.

But these Russians were different. Two of them were clearly wild cards; jokers, she thought, though perhaps possessed of powers. One was so small that at first she mistook him for a child, but no, he was just a joker.

Aarti had never actually met another joker. A small part of her had longed to meet these Russian jokers, to assuage her loneliness with the company of others of her kind. She could paint herself a suit, so as not to frighten them too much, pretend that she was here with an Indian expedition. Perhaps fool them long enough to . . .

But that was where Aarti's fantasy broke down. What did she really want from them? She wanted them to leave her and her Moon to grieve in peace.

Instead, they had built a habitat. It was small and crude, hardly more than a hovel compared to the palace Aarti had built, but still—they clearly meant to stay. Others might come after them and expand their little base or build more besides it. Five men could become fifty, then five hundred, then . . .

Aarti could not allow it. The only question was, how could she stop them?

"Yaj, what should I do?"

It had become a habit of hers. A bad habit, no doubt—any psychiatrist would tell her that she had to let him go. But instead, Aarti held him closer. On the Moon, she had built the figure of her lover, had lovingly painted each feature on Yajnadar's face. Aarti let him age a little, year after year, as if he were still alive on Earth and had simply found a way to finally travel with her. In her moon-palace she'd painted a bed, and there among the silken covers, Yaj made love to her, talked to her, listened to her woes.

She wasn't mad. Aarti knew full well that she was speaking both sides of the conversation. But his voice was more convincing, more consoling. And she knew what he would say, after all. "You should let them be, love. They're far away; they won't bother us. Right now, it's just you and me, alone together." He reached out a gentle hand, traced it down her bare neck.

Aarti pushed herself up on her elbows, shaking her hair loose. "Right now. But what about later? When they spread their way across the Moon, a cancer, a polluting poison . . ."

"Shhh . . . don't we have better things to do?" His hand slipped to the covers now, pulling them down, baring her body. "No need to worry about this now." His mouth followed, tracing a heated path from neck to breast, then farther down.

If only Aarti had listened.

She'd started off just trying to frighten them away. It was her paintings that had given her the idea, her moonscapes full of fabulous figures. If Aarti could create fantastic moon creatures for her own delight, she could as easily paint frightening beasts to terrify the Russians. Moon ghosts—armed with horns and claws and shining teeth, lurking around every corner. She set to work, and within a few nights, she'd painted an array of creatures. Aarti sent them off to haunt the cosmonauts, thinned herself to barest translucency, and followed to watch.

One of her ghost creatures startled a joker so much that he dropped the tray of components he was carrying, scattering them across the lunar surface. Others, tall and gray and twisted, made themselves seen outside the Russian camp, and picked at their pipes and instruments with hard black fingers. But still the cosmonauts did not see, would not believe, would not leave. Stubborn, arrogant, infuriating men.

Frustrated, Aarti had visited their camp once too often, gone too close. She'd been seen, turned, and run away. It was instinct that made Aarti run, and sheer chance that led them to the deep pool of dust—a hazard she never needed to consider, after all, she who walked the Moon on weightless feet.

That was what Aarti told herself at first—but it was a lie. The Moon was her second skin, and she knew its features, had passed that pool a hundred times. No conscious decision to run through it, but hadn't Aarti swerved in her running as she neared it? Headed straight for the center, picked up the pace so that they would run faster, heedlessly, to their doom?

After the first two cosmonauts died, she'd considered it all, in a moment that seemed to stretch endlessly, as long as it needed to. Despair flooded through her, a black river running from head to toe, filling Aarti's arteries and veins with poison—what had she done? What had she become? Yajnadar would not recognize her, would not have believed her capable of this.

Aarti made a decision. There was blood on her hands? She was irrevocably committed, irretrievably lost? Fine. Then something useful would come of it, at least. Aarti let herself sink down into the dust of the pool, found a corpse, took his form. It hadn't been easy, taking on a man's body again, after all this time. But she was determined to do what she needed to destroy them all. One tactic after another, taking care of them, one by one. No turning back now.

When the pain of the electrical net shuddered through her, Aarti woke up, though it was not yet sunrise. Her body arched in agony, and she barely managed to bite back the scream. Somehow, the humans had managed to affect her—Aarti was not wholly invulnerable on her Moon. The shock of that was enough to make her want to vomit.

Still, she'd made sure the last human would die there, cold and alone. Aarti had triumphed. But where was the exhilaration she should rightfully feel? In its place, a cold pit yawned open within her chest, fury and fear mixed together.

Was this what she had wanted?

Aarti rose from her bed and paced the house, resisting the urge to slam doors behind her. When the house felt too confining, she took to the garden. The Moon shone graciously overhead, but it offered her no comfort.

Her family had thought her a monster, a demon, had left her to waste away in this house, like Raksha in his tower. Yaj had tried to convince her that she could have a better life than her parents had left to her. *Society is changing, Aartibai. Jokers aren't as stigmatized as they were when you were young—few wear the cloaks and masks these days. You could go out in the world, live—you could still marry, have children.* Aarti had scorned Yaj's fantasies, and then she'd lost him. Too late for children now, and grandchildren. She hadn't needed them, or at least that was the thought she consoled herself with. Not when she had the Moon, with her palace, her garden, her phantasmagoria of magical creatures. The Moon was hers, and she belonged to the Moon; in the absence of Yaj, it had to be enough.

But now Aarti had turned into the monster her parents had thought her, all their prophecies fulfilled. A murderess. It was no use to plead accident, to say, *I didn't mean to do it!* Aarti felt her soul blackening, shriveling within. Where the

wild card had not broken her, not all the years of living with its legacy, the loneliness, not even Yajnadar's murder—this, this was too much to bear.

Aarti sank to her knees in the garden, amid the sweet scent of night-blooming
jasmine. Bougainvillea arched overhead, hibiscus and passionflower and a dozen
other blooms surrounded her—so much beauty that she did not deserve. Aarti
sobbed, letting loose four decades' worth of tears at once, a wild grief for everything that had been taken from her. For everything she had done or not done.
She dug her nails into the soil, the rich dirt of Earth, wishing that she could sink
into it and disappear.

That night, she returned to the Moon. Aarti summoned Yaj's face and form one
last, desperate time—but he turned away from her, disgusted by what she had become. She let him go. He was right.

Aarti smashed her little palace then, raining rocks onto it until it was shattered into tiny fragments, which dissolved, slowly, into dust. She would not build
it again, nor bring back her lover. She didn't deserve love. The demon form rose
within her, grew huge, crimson and black.

She stalked the Moon's surface, twenty feet tall, three-headed, blood dripping
from her giant fangs. Her clawed feet dragged paths along the dust, and a half-
dozen muscled arms waved gory scimitars at the abyss above. If Aarti were a Rakshasa, a demon from the ancient tales, then the human men had made her thus.

Let the humans dare to come to her again. She'd be waiting.

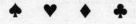

Within That
House Secure

IV

THE COUNTDOWN CLOCK, MADDENINGLY, still read four seconds, as it had for over half an hour now, as if time itself had stopped. Mathilde, maddeningly, had herself been the one to halt the countdown.

Her number two—an on-the-edge-of-elderly Japanese nat man named Ito, who most of the VIPs in attendance believed to be the person actually in charge—typed something on his console. Lines of text appeared at the bottom of one of Mathilde's screens. There is no cause for alarm. You did the right thing to halt and check the coolant system. Also, smoke is rising from your chair.

Mathilde jumped to her feet and kicked her chair back, trying to force calm on herself at the same time. If the chair burst into flames it wouldn't harm her, but her clothing would probably catch on fire, and that would definitely lead to the launch being scrubbed.

Calm down, she thought to herself. This is all going to work out.

A familiar voice came over her headset. "Are we going to go today, Mathilde?"

Theodorus was at home, of course, probably in one of the greenhouses, which all featured nearly as much telecommunications equipment as they did exotic flora or, these days, even more exotic fauna. He kept an engineer on staff specifically to develop means of keeping the equipment running in high-humidity environments. The half-dozen patents that had been generated probably paid for the man's salary and then some.

She keyed the transmit button on the unit at her belt. "Just running some tests on the coolant systems. There was a temperature fluctuation registering in the number three engine, but Captain Harding thinks it's just a glitched sensor, not a real heat spike."

"Captain Harding wants to make sure he's the pilot of record for the first manned Stormwing flight. Don't cut any corners."

That was mildly annoying. "Of course not," she said.

"Of course not," he repeated. "I'll let you work."

Mathilde walked over to the huddle of technicians running temperature and sensor tests, listened in for a moment, and decided that interrupting them wouldn't be productive. They knew their jobs. Everyone in the control tower knew their jobs.

She looked out the window toward the end of the runway, a mile and a half distant, where the Stormwing sat, ready to race its way into the air. There were pairs of Swiss-manufactured binoculars available, so she could have availed herself of a clearer view. She didn't. She knew what a Stormwing looked like. She'd been responsible for much of their design.

The wide-bodied craft could pass for an oversized jetliner to an unschooled viewer, but the humpbacked section that housed the second set of engines—"the business engines," Theodorus called them—and the compact nuclear power plant that drove them, would be obvious to anyone with more than a casual familiarity with aircraft. Not that the Stormwings were technically aircraft. Quite a bit of money, mostly given over to lobbyist fees but also some for settling a lawsuit and even a bit for a public-relations campaign, had ensured that. No, Stormwings weren't aircraft. They were spaceships.

Spaceships that can take off and land at commercial airports, Mathilde reminded herself. *At least at commercial airports that have eight-thousand-foot runways.*

Theodorus was going to make a fortune.

Another one.

She checked her watch, a beautiful and complicated piece of engineering that Malachi had given her when she finished her master's degree, and decided to bust up the huddle running the tests. They saw her coming and rearranged themselves so that a red-eyed young man with a pelt like an otter's was standing in front. He looked back at the other technicians, a mixture of nats and jokers, the betrayal he felt clear on his odd features.

His name was Oliver Taylor, and he was one of the best engineers in her employ, even if he would never believe that himself. She noticed that he wore a lapel pin depicting the silhouette of a squirrel beneath some Cyrillic characters. Mathilde didn't know that alphabet, or indeed, know much Russian, but she knew that the word was *Remember.*

Oliver wasn't the only member of the flight control team who wore such an insignia, a subtle tribute to the Russian cosmonaut Vyacheslav Mikhailovich Kozlov, "Belka," who had died three years earlier when his flight control team had intentionally provided incorrect reentry telemetry, leading to the diminutive joker's fiery death in the upper atmosphere. There were perhaps two dozen people in the world outside the Soviet space apparatus who knew that fact, most of whom were in this room. Theodorus had told them the story. Hell, for all Mathilde knew, Theodorus had provided the lapel pins.

Mathilde snapped her attention back to the engineer, who was looking at her nervously. "Oliver," she said, "I need a determination."

"Yes, well . . . yes."

"Yes?"

"Yes, the captain's feeling that the problem with the sensor is probably correct."

"Probably?"

"Almost certainly."

"Oliver, does that 'almost' cover eight hundred and fifty million dollars' worth of hardware and six human lives?"

The young man looked confused. "The crew complement is five."

She let him think about it for a second, staring at him levelly.

"Oh! You mean me!"

She stared still.

"Would you . . . would you like to look over my data yourself?"

Mathilde considered it. She thought about it like an engineer, and she thought about it like a manager. She turned to Ito, who had been watching the entire exchange, she was sure. She raised her hand, held her thumb upright. Her other thumb pressed the transmit button at her waist. "We're go. We're go. We're go."

There were cheers in the control tower. Over the radio, that familiar voice. "At last."

The automated Stormwings had been in service for just over a year. With the exception of one spectacular failure that Malachi, who was either in the best position to know or the worst, insisted was the result of sabotage, the program had been running smoothly. Malachi's opinion on that failure, Mathilde reminded herself, was shaky judged from an engineering point of view, but pretty sound from a corporate espionage point of view.

Unmanned Stormwings had circled the Earth. Over two spectacular days that Theodorus had spent obscene amounts of money to keep quiet, an unmanned Stormwing had achieved lunar orbit. And returned. To land at a pristine new corporate airfield near Myrtle Beach, South Carolina, something else that had cost obscene amounts of money.

But if there was one thing that Mathilde and Theodorus agreed upon when it came to spaceflight—of course there were dozens of things they agreed upon in that area—it was this. Robots are boring.

"Don't you want to hear a human's voice talking across the void, Mathilde?" Theodorus had asked in the early days of development. "Don't you want to know that there are people out there. People from Earth? People you know?"

Of course she did.

And now five people she knew were hurtling down the runway, fast, but not really that much faster than a commercial liner would have made the same trip. The Stormwing's nose lifted, the fuselage angled up, and then the craft was airborne.

"Showing you a clean set of wheels, Control," said Captain Harding over the radio, still in the affected West Virginia drawl that no one had been able to encourage, coax, or outright order him to abandon. The man was from San Diego.

Ito said, "Nominal across the board."

Mathilde nodded. This was the easy part.

She saw Oliver standing by the window, a pair of those heavy binoculars held an inch or two away from his eyes, tracking the Stormwing south and east and up through the twilight. She looked at her board. About seven minutes until the next crucial point, so she walked back over.

"Not monitoring the sensor suite on engine three?" she asked.

Oliver lowered the glasses quickly and cast a guilty glance back toward his station. "Randy's watching it," he said. "A failure sourced there would have . . . would have manifested already."

By which he meant that if there was going to be a spectacular explosion that was his fault at least, then it would have happened by now.

She nodded. "You knew I wasn't going to check your data," she said.

He shook his head, the gesture obscure. "I believed my data were correct. I believed, I mean, that my interpretation of the data was correct."

"Four minutes," said Ito. Four minutes until business time.

"But you didn't insist on that. You said 'probably.' You said 'almost.' Just now you said 'believed' instead of 'knew.'"

He ran his hand back through that thick pelt. "When you look like me, nobody ever wants you to be too sure of anything."

Mathilde let that hang there. Then she said, "Oliver, I do look like you."

Cahier No. 200
22 September 1990
Myrtle Beach, South Carolina

A spacecraft I helped design is in orbit around the Earth tonight. On television, all of the networks are showing the wreckage of the Brooklyn Bridge.

With today's launch, I have not been following the events in New York City closely, though I know both Malachi and Theodorus have. There is an illegal colony of jokers squatting on Ellis Island, which they've renamed the Rox. They've been there for months, at least. Their leader has incredibly powerful mental powers.

They say he is a child, and physically enormous. No wonder Theodorus is fascinated by him.

Whatever he is, he's earned the enmity of the Great and Powerful Turtle, New York's anonymous hero. The Turtle destroyed the bridge—to save it, no doubt—fighting a joker associated with the terrorist Twisted Fist movement, though what they have to do with the Rox is unclear. All of the news out of New York is unclear.

There are more soldiers in and around the city now than there were during the Swarm invasion five years ago.

However powerful the jokers on the Rox might be, I do not think they will be there much longer.

Within That
House Secure

V

IT WAS IN THE autumn of 1995, when she was twenty-seven years old, that Mathilde Maréchal—engineer, designer, prodigy, mathematical savant, hell, maybe a bona fide genius—learned to read a balance sheet. She did so against her will.

"Don't tell me again what I'm looking at," she told the timid woman who, for some arcane reason having to do with a recent reorganization, technically reported to someone who technically reported to someone who definitely reported to Mathilde. "Tell me why I'm looking at it."

The year's strain of influenza had hit Charleston hard and Witherspoon Aerospace harder. Luckily, jokers seemed immune to it. Unluckily, 50 percent absenteeism meant taking up slack in areas not even tangentially related to Mathilde's usual responsibilities.

"It's the labor and consumables discretionary budget for the Stormwings," the woman said again, as if that wasn't written right across the top of the legal-sized printout she'd placed precisely at the center of the conference table. As if she wasn't repeating herself for the third time since Mathilde had found her skulking in her empty outer office. Mathilde's secretary was home sick, too.

"You just did it again. I told you not to tell me what I'm looking at and you did exactly that."

"I . . . well, that is . . ." The woman took off her glasses and began furiously polishing them with the ragged hem of her sweater.

"Okay, let's start over," Mathilde said, and seeing the woman brighten and point to the identifying line at the top of the ledger again she held up her hand. "Not from the beginning. Well, yes, from the beginning, but we're going to skip some things that have been well covered. What's your name?"

In mute answer, the woman extended her name badge on a retractable line. JESSICA SHERMAN, WITHERSPOON AEROSPACE, EMPLOYEE #1141. And then a series of letters and numbers that probably told people better versed in that sort of thing than Mathilde exactly what department Jessica Sherman worked in.

She nodded, and the woman let go of the badge. It snapped back against her collarbone with an audible *thwack* and she winced.

"Okay, Jessica. The scheduling software routed me your appointment with . . . with whoever it was your appointment was originally with."

"Mr. Baker. This would have been the third time I've taken this to him. He keeps telling me it's nothing."

"Mr. Baker, okay. I don't know Mr. Baker. Is he in accounting?"

Jessica blinked. "He's your accountant. That is to say, he does the internal books for Stormwing Operations. You're the division head of Stormwing Operations."

Mathilde took a deep breath. What the woman said was true, but Mathilde left day-to-days to the organizational whizzes Malachi had hired as her assistants after Theodorus overheard her complaining that she never got to actually engineer anything anymore. "I also lead the speculative design team, and that takes up most of my time."

"You're very busy, everyone says." Jessica spoke in a rush. "But it's the labor and consumables discretionary budget, you see. Mr. Baker won't hear me out and the discrepancy is getting larger every month."

"Aha!" Mathilde said, admittedly a bit loudly, and Jessica jumped in her chair. "Sorry," she added. "But we're finally getting somewhere. There's a discrepancy. So something is operating outside of tolerances or however you money people put it."

Jessica brightened. "Yes! Well, no, that's not a particularly apt analogy, but yes, there's a discrepancy!"

"And it's getting larger every month."

"Yes!" said Jessica. She seemed genuinely happy.

"And what is the discrepancy?"

Jessica leaned in, as if she were about to share a secret. "It's actually quite mysterious."

"I do love a mystery," Mathilde lied. "Do we have any suspects? Do we think Mr. Baker is cooking the books? Skimming?" She'd reached the edge of her appropriate vocabulary. "Erm, looting?"

Now Jessica looked shocked. "Oh, no, I'm sure there's nothing like that going on. Everything balances out at the bottom, of course, and the affected vendors say we're paid up, and nobody has complained to payroll, though of course, why would they complain because if anything the technicians are getting paid more than is budgeted, but then that raises the question of how since the budget didn't account for their overtime but there's no shortfall recorded so—"

Mathilde reached over, pulled Jessica's name badge to the limit of its retractable line, and let it go. *Thwack.* "Vendors are being paid," she said. "Technicians are being paid. Nobody is complaining. What's the problem?"

Jessica rubbed her collarbone, her lower lip sticking out just a bit. "It's what they're being paid for. As near as I can tell, we're buying more fuel than is accounted for in the budget, and paying technicians to use that fuel . . . somewhere. But their pay for using it isn't in the budget, either. And even though those costs add up to some pretty significant amounts, there haven't been any shortfalls. It's like money is magically appearing to cover work nobody is doing using supplies nobody purchased."

Well, that . . . that was interesting, in fact.

"You make it sound like the Stormwings are being used for unscheduled flights."

Jessica shrugged. "That would seem to be the most logical explanation, if the only discrepancy was in their operational budgets."

Mathilde felt like the meeting could be going better, but she didn't know exactly how.

"There's another discrepancy?" she asked.

"Oh, my, yes, quite a large one," said Jessica. "An expenditure. It's been accounted for, but it's not been explained. At least, not in a way that I understand."

"Lack of understanding seems to be going around," said Mathilde. "Why don't you show me this other discrepancy. Maybe I can explain it." Who knew? Maybe she could.

Jessica reached into the overstuffed valise in the next chair over and brought out an overstuffed portfolio. As she started to open it, it slipped from her grasp and a sheaf of papers spread across the gleaming conference room table like a deck of cards dealt by a careless magician. Jessica gasped and began gathering the papers, giving each a glance as she did so, murmuring apologies.

While she waited, Mathilde idly picked up the sheet closest to her and ran her eyes down the columns, across the rows. This one was labeled MISCELLANEOUS and one entry had been highlighted in yellow by someone who wasn't particular about drawing straight lines. Slightly annoyed by the imprecision—imprecision always annoyed Mathilde at least slightly—she started to hand the paper over to Jessica, who was now going through the stack in front of her in some confusion. But then Mathilde stopped, actually reading the entry.

Flavian Finnegan Mitchell. $1,000,000.00. Extraterrestrial real estate.

"Is this it?" Mathilde asked. "Does this mean somebody spent a million dollars out of my budget on whatever 'extraterrestrial real estate' is supposed to mean, and hid it in miscellaneous expenditures?"

Jessica brightened. "Yes! Yes, that's it! And *extraterrestrial* means off the planet, so—"

Mathilde held up a warning hand. "You know I'm a rocket scientist, right?"

Jessica nodded, clamping her mouth shut.

"So odds are pretty good that I know what the word *extraterrestrial* means, right?"

Jessica nodded again.

"But I did not know that there was such a thing as an extraterrestrial real estate transaction. For such a transaction to take place, someone would have to own some off-planet real estate in the first place, and as far as I know, nobody does." *Yet,* she added to herself.

"I researched that!" exclaimed Jessica. "You're absolutely right. There's no governing body of law for such a transaction. So it must mean something else."

"Maybe," said Mathilde. "Did you happen to research this Flavian character who sold us this mysterious property? Do you know who he is?"

"I did!" said Jessica happily. "Though it took some doing. As far as I know, his birth name only shows up on his birth certificate, on his driver's license, and in this ledger entry. I, um . . ." She colored, apparently embarrassed by something. "I had to ask Trevor, one of the security people, for help with that part. Trevor's terribly nice, but kind of shy, and—"

A warning hand. "Who is Flavian Finnegan Mitchell?"

Jessica collected herself. "He's Cash Mitchell. The man who flew to the Moon."

Entering her code at the entry chamber of the greenhouses should have been enough to alert Theodorus that she had arrived, but Mathilde called out anyway.

"Hey! Tell your pets that I'm coming through and that I'm carrying a very large shaker of salt!"

Theodorus's voice replied from a speaker mounted amid a stand of Chinese fan palms. That was a new addition. "They're not pets. And none of them are in this wing at the moment. I'm by the strangler fig."

Making her way through the enlarged greenhouse was like trailblazing through some impossible jungle. Plants from South America, Africa, the Indian subcontinent, and Southeast Asia crowded the narrow walkway she followed. Despite Theodorus's assurances, she kept glancing left and right for any sign of giant mutant molluscs. The damned things were quiet to be so big.

It was hard to tell when Theodorus was relaxing. He couldn't exactly recline in a lounge chair or hit the hot tub. Though he did, she happened to know, have a weak spot for piña coladas. The image of her friend wearing a tropical print shirt and sipping a rum drink from a coconut came to her mind, and Mathilde almost grinned. Almost. She was too angry with him to get distracted, despite whatever her subconscious was trying to tell her.

If Theodorus wasn't relaxing, though, he wasn't tense, either. Unusually, he wasn't even working. There were no gardening tools nearby, and the specialized rolling rig of keyboards and monitors he used to keep up with his multifarious interests wasn't in evidence, either.

"Hello," he said when she entered the clearing. "I didn't know you were visiting today."

"Something you don't know. That must be pretty unusual for you."

He'd been looking up at the tree that dominated this end of the greenhouse, but now he turned to her. "What is it?" he asked, simply.

No preambles, then. Well, she hadn't wanted any. "What are you sending into space, Theodorus?"

If she hadn't known how carefully he arranged every expression, she might have thought he looked genuinely confused. "Satellites. Probes. Commercial payloads. Sensor suites bound for the Lagrange points and science packages bound for the asteroid belt. Why are you asking me this? It's you I depend on to do the sending."

She sighed, disappointed. She shook her head, not breaking eye contact with him. "And you think you bought the Moon."

His expression changed to something more neutral. "I see," he said. "Was it

Baker? Malachi said from the beginning that hiding the money trail would be the hardest part."

"Malachi is in on it?" she asked. "Wait, don't answer that, of course he is. But no, your Mr. Baker is home with the flu like everybody else. The money trail was uncovered by a woman who works for him, or maybe works for somebody who works for him, or used to anyway, because she just got a promotion and a raise."

"Malachi won't be pleased about that. He's trying to control personnel costs."

"Oh, just shut up, will you, Theodorus? At least shut up with the . . . the prevarications. You've been using the Stormwings, for years apparently, to boost God-knows-what everywhere in the solar system we send cargo and craft. And you're right, you have depended on me to do the sending. And you depended on me to not notice whatever the hell it is you're up to, as well, even when you spend a million dollars on a completely specious real estate transaction."

"I was going to tell you," he said. "Quite soon. In the next few weeks, in fact. It's all scheduled."

"Scheduled? You're keeping a schedule of when to reveal your betrayals?"

"I wasn't betraying you. I was protecting you."

"Shut up!" she said, shocked to hear her voice crack, angry to feel hot tears at the corners of her eyes. "I don't want to hear any more lies! This was my work, Theodorus. My work."

His great bulk shifted, and for a moment, she thought he was going to approach her, reach out to her. But no, he was turning back to the tree.

"Did you follow the news from Vietnam last year?" he asked.

She wiped her eyes and didn't answer. She recognized his tone, his teaching voice. It meant that he was about to tell her what she'd come to learn. Just not in the way she'd want to hear it. Not in a direct way, no, never that.

"I'm sure you did. They almost—well, I thought they almost had a chance. A joker homeland. A paradise. But the world wouldn't let it last, not in Vietnam. Not anywhere. It was always a long shot there, there's been so much hatred and bloodshed over the centuries. The French against the Vietnamese. The Communists against the colonialists. The Catholics against the Buddhists." He stretched his arm out and out and out, far longer than a nat could. He rested his hand on the tree.

"The strangler fig. Ficus religiosa. Sacred to the Buddhists, in fact. They believe the Buddha sat beneath one once and meditated. Didn't I give you a book with some of his teachings?"

Mathilde shrugged. She didn't remember. He gave her books all the time.

"Quotes the whole way through of course, but here's one of my favorites. 'No one saves us but ourselves.' Isn't that lovely?"

"It's terrifying," Mathilde said. "What about people who can't feed themselves much less save themselves? What about people who can't even walk? Or speak?"

"Yes. Yes, what about them? And what about people who aren't allowed to save themselves?"

For the first time, she realized that one of the things that frightened her about uncovering Theodorus's hidden program with the launches was its scope. It wasn't just that he was doing something that affected her. He was doing something that could conceivably—potentially, probably—affect everyone. And she knew how to answer him.

"Well, I guess you'll save them, right?"

And the gleam in his eye and the tremble in his voice were terrible when he said, "Yes. Yes, I will."

Within That
House Secure

VI

IN THE THREE YEARS since she'd learned about Joker Moon—since she'd been co-opted by it, since she'd joined a conspiracy to found a homeland for jokers on another world—Mathilde had traveled to, at last count, forty-four countries. She had been to installations both secret and public on five continents (annoyingly, she'd somehow never made it to Australia, and while Theodorus had interests in Antarctica they weren't directly related to the Project). Her French, which she had let atrophy over the years, was now once again perfect, which came in handy in the distressing number of places in the world where the French had once ruled colonial outposts.

She had been to Russia and China and every major European capital. She had been to all eleven nations traversed by the equator, and a double dozen nations close to the equator, spending enormous amounts of money, buying vast tracts of real estate, making contacts within high-tech industries and research universities.

She'd even been to this three-mile-long rock in the South Atlantic before, more than once.

Stepping off the cargo plane—since every passenger jet in Theodorus's fleet was busy ferrying people to this meeting, she'd hitched a ride with a load of heavy construction equipment—she looked around and idly wondered about the island's cartographical status. She herself made few gestures toward keeping her activities secret—that was Malachi's department—but she was well aware that the true purposes of Witherspoon Aerospace's enormous flurry of activity over the last few years were well obfuscated. So, the island. Did it still appear on any maps?

It would appear on old maps, of course, but increasingly, maps were digital. It would probably be impossible to alter or destroy the charts in every library, government office, and shipping company in the world, but Theodorus had people working for him who were very adept indeed at altering and destroying digital information.

There are probably still plenty of old sailors in this part of the world who know all these lonely islands from memory, she thought. Then, *And they're probably all on Malachi's payroll.*

The cargo plane had taxied to a hangar far from the hub of the compound before its belly had opened up to let her out and the first of several waiting forklifts on. She looked around for transport and spotted an unattended Jeep. She threw her rucksack in the passenger seat and slid behind the wheel and thought about the last time she was in a Jeep. She wondered if Croyd Crenson was still alive, and thought that he probably was.

Theodorus wouldn't stop talking about his trip from Charleston.

"The flight crew was fantastic," he said. "I was listening in the whole time, and when they got the weather bulletin about storm activity along our path, I was worried. But they made adjustments and rerouted without even talking about it. I had the navigator's instrumentation mirrored on my panel in the passenger compartment, of course, and it was just one, two, three—new route. So elegant."

Mathilde had been with Theodorus the last time he'd flown. She'd been eleven years old, and it had been in an alien spacecraft. Other than that strange trip, he hadn't left Charleston since his card turned. Hell, he'd barely left his house since then.

But this meeting, he thought—they all thought—was important enough that extraordinary lengths had been gone to. And it had taken an extraordinary amount of planning and scheduling to get Theodorus from his home to this base in the South Atlantic. It had even taken a little bit of engineering, which Mathilde had seen to herself. Corporate jets didn't roll off the line equipped to handle passengers with Theodorus's unique requirements, and the Stormwings were just too conspicuous.

And it had taken a lot of money, of course. Malachi wouldn't let them forget how much all of this was costing.

Somehow, over the years, Theodorus had gone from being the richest man in South Carolina to being the richest joker in the United States to being the fourth richest person of any description in the world. So he wasn't concerned about how much anything cost. Whenever Malachi brought it up, he would just ask, "Am I still the fourth richest person in the world?"

And Malachi would grumble something about what a long drop it was down to fifth place, and Theodorus would happily sign whatever check needed signing. Metaphorically, at least. Mathilde doubted Theodorus's signature was on any paperwork related to Joker Moon at all. Not yet. He promised that he would make everything public at some point, but for now, for years now, it was always, "Not yet."

Before he could begin describing the modified technical specifications of the plane—the very specifications she had modified—Mathilde asked, "Are they all here?"

"Still waiting on the delegation from Northern Ireland."

Still waiting on the terrorists of the Twisted Fist, then.

"We don't need them," she said, not putting much into it. She'd said it more forcefully before, more than once. If she pushed, Theodorus would just remind her that she'd been outvoted, and then she would say that no, she'd been overruled, and however long they argued the Twisted Fists would still attend the summit.

Telling women and men wanted by governments around the world about the project seemed like a huge risk to Mathilde. But then, telling anyone about it at this point was a risk, and the number who knew parts of the whole, a few details, was growing daily. They were undertaking, Theodorus said, and Mathilde agreed with him, the greatest project in human history, and they were trying to do so, for now, in secret.

"Secrecy will soon be impossible," Theodorus had said. "And it's pointless to build a home world for jokers if no jokers populate it. We have to bring some people in."

So Malachi had made the arrangements, and now joker leaders from across the globe were descending upon a windswept island claimed by no nation and owned outright, if through a chain of obscuring holding companies, by one of the more famous jokers in the world. Some of them were legitimate government officials in their homelands, minor functionaries benefitting from tokenism in most cases, but there was one fairly high-placed operative from the U.S.A.'s Democratic Party. There were spiritual leaders, business leaders—one or two of these were somewhat shady—a couple of journalists, even a poet, this last being a late addition of Malachi's, naturally.

And there were terrorists.

The conference room featured a large U-shaped table. Theodorus, who didn't need a place to sit and who was by far the largest individual present, would stand in the open end of the U. The seats were assigned, and the chairs were all specially built, designed to accommodate the anatomies of the dozen or so people who would sit in them.

Mathilde didn't have a place at the table. She sat along one wall off Theodorus' right shoulder, perched on a stool next to Malachi. They could see the faces of everyone at the meeting that way. Everyone but Theodorus himself.

Those faces represented the great variety of jokerdom. Furred, feathered, tentacled, and green, the people around the table, to a one, could not conceal what they were. The people around the table, to a one, could not conceal their shock.

"The U.S. government knows nothing about this?" asked Matt Wilhelm. He was the Democratic Party operative from the States. Even as he spoke he was taking notes on a legal pad, and Mathilde wondered if the fur-faced man imagined he'd be allowed to take them away from the island with him.

"There are . . . elements . . . in government who know parts of what's happening," Theodorus replied smoothly. "There are individuals. Not just the U.S. government, though."

Two or three people spoke at once in response, and Mathilde couldn't make sense of the babble. They weren't all speaking English. Or French.

"Why the Moon?" This was the masked man from England. The Twisted Fist representative, the self-styled "Green Man." "If you think you can change that rock into someplace we can live, then why not just change this rock? That's what the rest of us have been doing."

The famous Jokertown priest, Father Squid, was seated directly across from the Englishman. "Yours have hardly been changes for the better," he said gently, if firmly.

The Green Man stared through the eyeholes of his mask. "Ah, Robert. The Black Dog once told me you used to have guts."

This prompted more cross talk and Malachi leaned over to whisper an explanation. "He was one of them. Father Squid fought with the Twisted Fists in the seventies, before he joined his cult."

Malachi was not a particular fan of religion.

"But it is a good point," said Thoth, the representative of Egypt's Living Gods. Another cult, Malachi would have said. "The Moon is barren, devoid of any life. My kinsman Khonsu rules the Moon, but even he does not live there."

"Who's Khonsu?" Mathilde whispered.

"Who knows?" answered Malachi. "One of the Living Gods, probably. Some joker with a round white head or something. There were apparently exactly as many Egyptian gods as there are Egyptian jokers."

Mathilde was pretty sure that wasn't true, but she turned her attention back to the contentious meeting.

A man in an elegant suit stood. At first, Mathilde thought he was wearing a mask as well, but then she realized that his skeletal visage was, in fact, his face. The room quieted, so Mathilde guessed that he must command some respect even across the broad swath of interests represented at the table.

"Mr. Witherspoon," said the skull-faced man. "To my way of thinking you've already accomplished a great deal even bringing this group together in a relatively peaceable fashion."

Theodorus nodded. "Thank you, Mr. Dutton. Your aid was, of course, invaluable in arranging this meeting."

"Charles Dutton," whispered Malachi. "Not well known outside Jokertown among the general public, but very well connected and quite wealthy. For an entrepreneur."

To judge by his tone, Mathilde thought Malachi might as well have said *for an arriviste*.

"Even knowing as little as I did about your intentions," said Dutton, "I sensed that this would be an important gathering. A very important gathering, indeed."

"I think it is," said Theodorus. "Now that you know more of my intentions—now that you know, essentially, all that is important to know, what do you think?"

There was a brief pause. Then Dutton said, "I believe that this project is the answer to our problems and our prayers."

He seemed to be about to say something more, but then a dissolute-looking man in stained Edwardian costume stood up. He posed dramatically, the mess of tentacles that took the place of one of his hands writhing against his forehead. "I have composed a few couplets that I believe to be germane," he said. He sounded drunk.

"Did he just say couplets?" Mathilde asked.

"Shhh," Malachi replied, leaning forward. "I want to hear this."

The man may have been inebriated, and his voice, for a certainty, was ragged. But somehow his words took on a hypnotic power when he recited:

> Despised and spat on, hated and cursed,
> The poorest, the sickest, the dregs of the earth.
> Does the spiral helix, in us askew,
> Doom all us freaks, unless we few . . .
> Follow a dream that is doomed to fail?
> Cast in our lot with a fool of a snail?

The Green Man's laugh was low-pitched. He was the only one who reacted aloud.

Mathilde looked over at Malachi. He was shaking his head. "Doggerel. The man once won a Pulitzer Prize and he gives us doggerel."

"Why is he even here?" she asked.

Malachi said, "Because I'd hoped for better."

The three of them were alone in the conference room. There was an odd curve to the chair Mathilde sat in, causing her to lean forward at an uncomfortable angle.

"That could have gone better," said Theodorus.

"Some of them will help when the time comes," Malachi said. "And I think the . . . inducements we offered them each privately were enough to ensure their silence. At least for now."

"What inducements? What are you talking about?" asked Mathilde. "Bribes?"

"In some cases," said Malachi.

Mathilde started to ask more, but Theodorus said, "What about the poet?"

"Who ever listens to poets?" asked Malachi.

"You listen to poets," said Theodorus at the same time Mathilde said, "You do."

"I admit it was a mistake to bring him here," said Malachi. "I guess I thought he could, I don't know, record our grave deeds or something."

"Even I don't believe we have the power to dictate how people are going to remember what we're doing here," said Theodorus.

"No," said Mathilde. "But you still believe you have the power to dictate whether they remember it. Or whether they know about it, anyway."

A woman wearing a headset appeared in the doorway, wringing a sheet of paper in her hands. Malachi waved her in. "What is it?" he asked.

"One of the planes," she said. "One of the planes carrying the dignitaries has gone down. We can't raise it on the radio and the radar is clear."

Mathilde held out her hand and the woman handed over the paper before departing.

Theodorus, his voice stricken, said, "How is this possible? Was it a rogue lightning bolt?"

Mathilde shook her head and smoothed the paper on the table. There was nothing written there that explained why the plane carrying the poet, Dorian Wilde, had disappeared into the sea. Looking over at her father, she wondered if anything ever would.

The Moon Maid

PART VI

2003

AARTI HAD, PERHAPS, GONE a little mad.

Fourteen years ago, she'd been transformed by the evil acts she'd committed. She'd abandoned the demon form after a few months—rage was hard to sustain in silence. Aarti let herself go gaunt. Eating often seemed more trouble than it was worth, and her servants—busy with their own lives, educating their children, marrying them off, celebrating grandchildren—didn't care enough to coax her. Aarti subsisted on a little rice and lentils, and her gray Moon face was sunken. Her ribs grew prominent; her breasts sagged and fell. At seventy-five, she looked decades older, aged by grief and guilt. When Aarti floated across the Moon, it was as a wraith, gray hair streaming behind her. She did not paint.

On Earth, the joker situation ebbed and flowed. The Indian government gave jokers rights and then took them away again . . . almost at whim, it seemed. Some jokers made attempts at a joker homeland; the Rox was created and then destroyed, and Free Vietnam met a similar fate. Aarti watched the news online; the internet had given her access to the world again, first on BBSs and then newsgroups and finally the World Wide Web. She watched, but couldn't bring herself to care.

Aarti might have gone on that way until her death—but two things happened in her seventy-fifth year. Saila's grandchild, a winsome little girl of five, was struck with the virus. Rich brown skin went iridescent blue, a hard carapace formed on her back, and four spindly legs grew from her hips. Little Anjali looked something like a beetle—lovely in her own way, but an outcast now. Jokers currently weren't allowed in Indian public schools, though that could change again tomorrow.

Her parents let her scuttle freely in the house and garden; all their conversations turned to what would become of Anjali. "*Aiyo!* No husband, no schooling. Her sister, so, so smart; I'm sure she will be a doctor! But this one . . ." Then Saila's daughter broke down in tears again, and her husband patted her hand helplessly.

Aarti didn't get involved—she'd been a ghost in that house for long enough that her intervention would likely only upset them further. But a spark of sympathy had lit within her. She left sweets on the little girl's pillow when no one would notice, and checked her own accounts—her investments were doing well, and there was plenty to hire a tutor if needed, though that would be a lonely road. Aarti could even send Anjali to one of the two exclusive private schools that had sprung up in Bombay for joker children of the wealthy—would the girl be happier among her own kind? What would become of her? Aarti fretted, deep into the night.

A few months later, more ships arrived on the Moon.

They looked almost like large airplanes, but more bulbous in the back, clearly designed with larger engines. Well, they'd need them, wouldn't they, to traverse space? These spaceplanes came, one after another, depositing massive numbers of jokers, who began repairing and enlarging the base, building a landing strip. Overnight, it seemed, new shelters sprang up on the surface, tiny pods and bigger ones, chosen, it seemed, for the size and shape of the jokers who would inhabit them. Her quiet Moon had been invaded by a horde of Earthlings. Within Aarti's chest, the Rakshasa stirred, its clawed hands reaching out, its demon teeth bloody. She could rain a hail of asteroids down to destroy them all! Set a fire raging, to burn them out, or crack open the surface, and let them tumble down.

But Aarti was tired. As her human body failed back in Bombay, it took more and more effort these days to paint her fantasies. She hardly painted at all these days, on Earth or the Moon. The canvases stayed white and blank.

She didn't want to murder again. The screams of the dying cosmonauts still haunted her dreams. Gray dust surrounded her, grabbing at her, pulling her down into the depths. Her breath was sucked away, her mouth and nose and eyes buried in an endless stream of dust. Arms reaching up, helplessly, for the unforgiving sky. Aarti drowned in moondust, over and over again, and woke screaming. Suresh and Saila, even the children, had learned to ignore the screams. Should she pile more nightmares atop the ones she already carried?

Once Aarti had thought murder and monsterdom was like flipping a switch—you were good or evil, nothing in between. But perhaps wickedness was more like love than not. Yaj had said, *We build our love anew, every day. Every day, you decide to commit to your beloved, to try to be your best self. Sometimes you fail, but then you try harder, the next day.*

Aarti had taken to reading, these last few years. Her body was too tired to pace the halls all day, or work in the garden. But she could lie in bed and lose herself in other worlds for hours upon end. Tolkien and Lewis, her old acquaintances, had gone on to fame beyond anything she might have dreamt of. She read their work, and that of other fantasists and science fictioneers. They got the Moon so wrong, those writers. But still, they tried, and she loved them for the attempt.

Essays helped, too. Emerson had written, "Finish each day and be done with it. You have done what you could. Some blunders and absurdities no doubt crept in; forget them as soon as you can. Tomorrow is a new day. You shall begin it serenely and with too high a spirit to be encumbered with your old nonsense." Yaj hadn't read English, but he would have loved that. Aarti could not count her murders as mere blunder, absurdity, and old nonsense—but she could, at least, refrain from killing again.

So she would be a murderer no more. Not of one or two Earthlings, and certainly not hundreds. Soon thousands—Aarti had taken her old form again, the eighteen-year-old girl, and slipped close enough to overhear. They were planning to make a nation of jokers up here. There might be a place for her little Anjali on the Moon, and the thought of that stirred her heart.

But the jokers would transform her Moon utterly in the process. Already their machines were doing that work, gouging great holes in Her surface. Aarti could not stand by and simply let the invaders in. Her body was still as young as she needed it to be on the Moon. The base's commander was a handsome man; Aarti toyed with the idea of making herself impossibly beautiful, seducing him into leaving the Moon. She remembered, sharply, the pleasure one could find when two bodies come together. Aarti could take that, use it.

Aarti lengthened her hair and darkened it to glossy black, sent it rippling down to her bare feet. She gave herself large breasts, a tiny waist, swelling hips—like the women in the movies, the fantasies of men, who sang of betrayal under waterfalls, or in pounding monsoon storms. Lips reddened, eyes kohl-darkened. She turned herself into a siren of the Moon, enough to break a man's heart—break dozens! (Though she knew that Yaj, at least, had preferred her as she was.)

This was ridiculous—she couldn't possibly appear as a gorgeous human. This shape would be suspicious to any joker on the Moon, or really, to anyone. Aarti let that false body slip away. The act would be hard enough to perform in her joker shape, one that she didn't have to think to maintain. The sores were mostly healed these days, so the only obvious legacy of the virus was her large, lunar head, cratered. Her body was lean and lithe, especially in her favored eighteen-year-old form. Perhaps it was seductive enough for a lonely man, isolated on the Moon.

His name, she'd learned, was Mike Sampson. His skin was pale pinky-white, that flushed red when he got excited or angry, which seemed to happen easily. Tall, clean-shaven, with bushy white eyebrows and a shaved-bald head. About her own age, but strong and fit still; he spent hours in the gym each day, maintaining muscle tone in lunar gravity. Aarti thinned herself to translucency and carefully observed him for a few days before making her move.

She bumped into him in a corridor, her bulbous gray head deliberately bent over a tablet. "Oh, sorry! My big, bald head!" She was careful to inject some extra dismay into her voice. Damsel in distress, that was what she wanted him to hear.

He chuckled. "No balder than mine—once your hairline recedes enough, you know it's time to just let it go." Then he frowned. "We haven't met?"

She shook her head, then shifted, mirroring his stance. A sign of sexual interest, she'd read on her computer back in Bombay—the World Wide Web had offered several "tips" on seducing a man. "I just arrived on this morning's transport. You'll find me on the manifest."

"People are coming through so fast these days." His brow was furrowed. "I don't remember . . ."

"Anya Chakraborty." She'd gleaned the name from the morning's manifest list and checked it against the news. A wave of anti-joker sentiment had recently erupted in Delhi; blood had run on the dusty streets.

"Oh, yes. I remember that name. Well, welcome to our glorious joker paradise." Plenty of irony loaded into that as his hand extended to encompass the cramped hallway.

"It seems pretty glorious to me, actually," Aarti said, smiling through what she hoped looked like remembered pain. She really had no practice at acting, or even talking much to other people. Aarti shifted a little closer to him. The corridor was so small, after all. "Much more peaceful than Delhi."

His eyes darkened. "I was sorry to hear about what happened there. You'll be safe here."

Sampson assumed that she'd come because of the killings, that she was one who had narrowly escaped. Aarti let her voice tremble a little as she said, "Honestly, I still can't sleep at night. And I get so confused—" She let out a little laugh as she put her fingertips on his arm. "—I'm not even sure where my shelter is. Last night, I ended up sleeping on a couch in the common room."

"Well, we can't have that." Sampson leaned closer, his hands reaching for her pad. A few taps, and a map came up. "There, see where it is?"

How dumb could Aarti pretend to be? "I think so—thank you." She couldn't manage an eyelash flutter, she really couldn't. "You've been so helpful. I'm very grateful."

"It's my job to take care of all of you." Sampson smiled, and then his eyes widened as she held his gaze for a little too long. Her fingers were still somehow on his arm, and they were a breath away from each other. "Maybe—maybe I should show you the way?"

"If you're not too busy, that would be wonderful," she breathed.

"Not at all. After you, Miss Chakraborty."

After that, it was almost too easy.

He'd seemed oddly unsurprised that an eighteen-year-old girl would have any interest in an old man. Was he just arrogant, or did Sampson have this sort of thing happen to him all the time? Aarti supposed she should call him Mike now, after what they'd done together. His fingers tracing paths along her skin, and she was now practiced enough at simulated lunar sex that memory was enough to convince her Moon body that this felt good, though strange. No man had touched her since Yajnadar. No one had touched her at all, in fact. Was there such a thing as skin-hunger? Mike had dozed off, exhausted from their joint efforts, but Aarti wanted to wake him. She craved his touch.

Maybe she'd made a mistake, shutting herself away from the world all these years. If Aarti had gone out among them, sought out other jokers, might she have had a different, richer life? Might she have had a host of lovers, married, had children and grandchildren of her own?

And why had she let herself give up her work? She could have showed her paintings, even taken up the study of astronomy again. Instead of locking herself away from it all, rejecting the world because it had, for a little while, rejected her . . .

Oh, this was foolish! She was no girl now, to be daydreaming away in might-have-beens. Aarti had come here with a mission, to learn what she could from the commander. What was there to learn, really? Her prior qualms seemed insignificant now; she should just kill him and be done with it. Aarti lay her fingers across his sleeping throat, let them sharpen to razor edges. The work of a moment to slice through the carotid artery, so that Mike's blood would pulse out, falling as tribute on the Moon's surface . . .

. . . well, on the floor of the shelter, anyway. The symbolism was muddied a bit. And Aarti was distracted again, her fingers refusing to make those small motions. Mike had been sweet with her, tender. His eyes bright, delighted that this girl, bulging gray head and all, was willing to lie down with him in the dim lights of her room. And wasn't she lucky that the real Anya Chakraborty hadn't walked in yet? Mike had been so happy that Aarti had offered her young body to his eager touch. For that, did he deserve to die? Would she kill Anya if the girl came in, a joker girl who had committed no crime at all?

No. Aarti began carefully extricating herself from under his outstretched arm, and then caught herself, smothering a laugh. How long had it been since she'd laughed?

For a little while, Aarti had almost forgotten who and what she was. She let herself dissolve—Mike would wake to find a pleasant memory and a scattering of moondust in his arms. As for Aarti, she'd go back to simpler methods. These jokers were reliant on their machines that sheltered them from the Moon's harsh realities. If those machines failed, surely they would give up and go home again? It was worth a try.

With that decision, a strange peace descended. Something that was wrong had gone right.

Maybe now, Aarti could paint again.

Within That
House Secure

VII

MATHILDE WATCHED A SNAIL with a shell the circumference of a dinner plate crawl up the wall beside the security door. Its size, of course, did not discomfit her. She was used to large snails, after all. The speed with which it moved along the vertical surface, on the other hand, was disturbing. It was fast.

The snail stopped at the keypad mounted next to the door. There were more sophisticated locking mechanisms available, such as those which read fingerprints or even performed retinal scans, and those types were in widespread use at Witherspoon Aerospace headquarters and others of Theodorus's companies. Here on the estate, however, they made do with the numeric keypads. Theodorus did not have fingerprints, and the specialized anatomical structures within his eyes stymied most machine readers.

The snail extruded a calcium spike from near its sensory organs, something else that happened at a pace that disturbed Mathilde. The spike grazed the keypad once, twice, a third time. Then the snail moved again, completely engulfing the mechanism.

"What's it doing?" she asked.

"Wait," replied Theodorus. "Watch."

The status light above the door flashed colors, flickering between the red that signaled that the door was closed and the amber that shone when a code was being entered. Then the light turned green and, with an audible clicking noise, the door unlocked itself and swung open. Slowly, Mathilde was glad to see, though that was hardly a comfort.

"You've trained a snail to be a locksmith?" she asked. She knew she was being reductive.

"Trained is hardly the right word," Theodorus replied. He didn't sound offended. He was, in fact, positively jolly, clearly pleased that the demonstration had worked as he'd planned.

The locksmith snail detached itself from the keypad and slid back down the wall, leaving a trail that glistened in the green light of the door's status signal. It stopped once it reached the floor and moved its head back and forth.

"What's it doing now?" asked Mathilde.

"Respectfully awaiting further instructions in a patient manner. A model employee, wouldn't you say?"

Mathilde ignored the jab. "And you communicate with it telepathically some-how? Like with the other . . . varieties?"

Theodorus nodded. The locksmith snail glided off in the direction of the near-est greenhouse.

Eyeing the slime left on the keypad, Mathilde said, "You know, I could have unlocked that myself without all the mess."

"Hardly as impressive, though, is it?" said Theodorus. "You know the code."

Which was a fair point, but Mathilde habitually carried a few tools around, and she was certain she could use them to open any door on the estate, though she couldn't think of any she didn't have the passcode for. She decided not to tell Theodorus any of that. Well, he knew about the tools. He'd funded the design and manufacture of more than one of them.

A staffer came along with a cart of cleaning supplies. "Yes, Mr. Witherspoon?" he asked. Mathilde was about to ask how Theodorus had signaled for the man but then she recognized him.

"Amos! It's been forever!" she said.

The man had scaly skin over a vaguely porcine face and was thus apparently incapable of blushing. Mathilde sensed that he would have been, though, had he been able.

"Theodorus still has you cleaning up after his messes after all these years, does he?" she said, trying to find a way to make him comfortable. "How long have you been working here now?"

"Not really sure, Miss," he said. "A pretty long time."

"You can call up your hire date on the house system anytime," said Theodorus, and Mathilde supposed he thought he was being helpful. She changed the subject.

"And how are things going for Orson in the archives?"

Amos shot a guarded look at Theodorus. "He's not there anymore. He's with all of them up there. Up on the Moon." His voice nearly cracked on the last word.

"We'll leave you to your work," Theodorus said, and began gliding away. Mathilde waited a moment before following him, wanting to say something more to Amos, not being able to think of anything.

When she caught up with him, she said, "I can't believe you split them up."

Theodorus said, "Orson has skills that are applicable to the current phase. Or at least adaptable."

Mathilde started to say something acid, but Theodorus went on.

"And he was dying. He spent his entire life being slowly crushed by the rocky weight of his own body. Now he doesn't have to worry about that anymore."

Mathilde wondered when a phase would come around that would require, or at least support, Amos's skills. That, she supposed, was the question they were all working on answering.

In recent years, as Theodorus had simultaneously grown more insular and work on the Moon project expanded, he had paid less and less attention to any-thing not directly related to the work. Setting aside, for now, thoughts of Amos and Orson, Mathilde realized she was glad to see that Theodorus had taken the time to design a snail that did something so relatively prosaic as open a door. His developing wild card power seemingly allowed him to coax snails into any task, at any size, and, now it seemed, with any speed. "That was a pretty fast one," she said. They were moving toward Theodorus's greenhouse lair now themselves.

"Hmmmm?" Theodorus responded. "Yes, I suppose. For one of the terrestrial varieties, anyway. I'm working on speed right now."

This was a reference to the fifty or so gigantic snails Theodorus was slowly bringing along as part of the great work. If everything went as planned, those would ultimately prove far faster than any natural biological organism had ever been before. And they certainly wouldn't be "terrestrial."

"We're maintaining a pretty stately pace right now," said Mathilde. She was raising a subject Theodorus didn't like raised.

"My power does not work on myself. I've told you this many times."

"Theodorus, you didn't even discover you had a wild card power until after you were an adult, and as you just demonstrated, you're still figuring out different things to do with it. I remember when you started experimenting with the snails, and I know you haven't ever tried using it on yourself. I know you better than anyone. I know you're afraid."

They came to the complex air lock that led into the greenhouse. Theodorus did not answer her, but gestured at the keypad, indicating that she should enter the code.

She couldn't remember it.

♥

Cahier No. 371
14 July 2005
Charleston, South Carolina

In France, they are celebrating Bastille Day. Once, I would have written "at home" instead of "in France," but now, so long an American, I am afraid my erstwhile countrymen would look at me askance as much for my atrophied accent as they would for the color of my skin. I am still, technically, a citizen of France. I am without a doubt a citizen of the United States of America. But more and more, I think of myself as a citizen of something else, someplace else. The Moon. Everyone and everything about me is now bent toward the Moon.

There was a celebration at the estate today, as well. Theodorus announced that his preparations for the launches to the asteroid belt are complete. We await only their specific destinations, proof that bodies of the composition we need are out there somewhere. So much work has been based on the assumption that there are acceptable bodies.

I have just looked at those last two words for twenty minutes, pen in hand.

"Acceptable bodies."

That is what this is all about. I must remember that. Theodorus certainly never forgets it. We—all us jokers—have been made, or rather remade into unacceptable bodies. We inhabit physiologies that draw down hatred and violence that seems almost instinctive in the massive run of humanity. The astronomers and geologists tell us that the asteroids we're looking for are, statistically, almost certain to exist.

Theodorus has chosen to ignore the word "almost" in this case. More and more, he is a dealer in absolutes.

Since he believes, absolutely, that we face eventual genocide, then I suppose I can't blame him. Since I believe the same thing, I suppose I can't blame myself. For whatever happens.

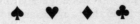

The Sands of Mourning

by Caroline Spector

PART 1

2007

IT WAS HOT. NOT in a San-Diego-Hey-we're-having-a-heat-wave-and-it's-80-degrees way. More in a Jesus-it's-130-degrees-in-the-shade kind of way.

Michelle stared across the ocher desert. Heat radiated off it. She had had an ophthalmic migraine once and that's how the air above the sand looked. Shimmery and wavy—a trick of the eye. Sometimes she thought she saw enemy forces advancing, but mostly it just hurt her eyes.

A siren went off. Her heart started racing and her stomach knotted. They were under attack—again. Soldiers, Living Gods, jokers, and nats ran past her, cursing as they streamed by.

"Bubbles! We have to get moving!"

It was Curveball. She, Earth Witch, and Simoon were already racing past Michelle toward the end of camp where jeeps were parked. In the distance, the desert now had a smog-like haze above it.

Michelle closed her eyes then opened them again, wanting to see anything other than the relentless desert and the oncoming pain. But she couldn't escape it, so instead she dashed after the others as fast as she could, given her current size. The four of them were only teenagers on *American Hero,* but the softness of their youth had left them. Egypt and the war had made them harder people in just a few weeks.

Michelle caught up with the others and tried to lug herself into the jeep they'd commandeered. It tilted to one side from her girth. "Shit! I'm too fat right now," she said angrily as she started to climb out.

"No, you're not," replied Curveball, impatience in her voice. "We need you! And we need you fat! You're not going to make anything go boom if you're skinny."

Michelle nodded, then stuffed herself into the back seat. She ooched over until she was in the middle, her enormous girth spreading out. Simoon squeezed past Michelle's knees and squatted in the middle of the front seats, and the jeep evened out some. Earth Witch slammed it into gear and it lurched forward. There was a shitty road half-covered in sand. It ran along the camp and Earth Witch headed for it. An army camp was just an army camp, even with Living Gods residing there.

This wasn't what Michelle thought being a hero was all about. It wasn't supposed to be grit in your eyes and in your ass crack because sand went everywhere and got into every crevice of your body. Michelle was keeping as much fat on as she could and that made a lot more places for the sand to go and rub you raw.

The war had been raging since before the group from *American Hero* had arrived in Egypt. She'd thought she was going to do good with her power, but so far, she'd only managed to blow shit up. She knew there was more she could do with her bubbles, but when the fighting came—and it did with mind-numbing regularity—her fallback was always making things go boom. And when things went boom, people died.

Michelle closed her eyes and the memory of the first time she'd killed someone with her power replayed. The bubbles she had released then had risen glistening and iridescent in the sun. They were pretty, looking as delicate as Christmas ornaments and appearing as harmless . . . right until the moment they hit the Halo helicopter she'd aimed them at. Those beautiful bubbles touched the exterior.

And they went boom.

The left side of the copter exploded, sending pieces of half its occupants into the air. She could see through the gaping hole she'd made that the rest of the men were still belted into their seats. She distinctly remembered them wearing desert camouflage. At the time, she hadn't even known there was such a thing as desert camouflage and for a moment, she thought, *Huh, how about that?*

Looking back, it was a horrible thing to think while she was killing them. But everything about what had happened then had been weird, monstrous, and horrifying.

Her second bubble hit.

Most of the remaining soldiers died immediately, but a couple sped toward the ground, trapped by their seat belts. She couldn't hear them, but she knew instinctively that they were begging Allah, or maybe the Living Gods, to save them. They died screaming as the ground rushed up to meet them.

And that sound they made as they hit—that sickening crunch muffled by the sand. She was rooted, thinking it must be over. It had to be over because she couldn't do that again. Intellectually, she'd known that her power was dangerous. And though she knew preventing the Living Gods and their worshippers from being slaughtered was a noble goal, it didn't matter as she fell to her knees and began puking.

That had been weeks ago. In the interim, she'd become numb to it all. The dying. The destruction. And they never learned. They shot her and tried to blow her up, which only made her fatter and more powerful.

And that felt good.

She opened her eyes. Nothing had changed, but now there was a tremor in her hands. That had started recently. So had the nightmares, but she'd kept those to herself.

The jeep was plugging along, but Michelle knew they'd be damn fast without her. A personnel truck carrying jokers came up beside them. She waved at the driver and the truck began to slow. "I'll catch up!" she yelled over the noise of the jeep and the truck. "Go on ahead of me."

"It's okay! Stay with us!" she heard Simoon calling, but by then Michelle was already crawling out the back of the jeep. The fall gave her more fat. It was delicious. The truck slowed to a crawl and she lumbered to the back of it, grabbed hold of the back gate, and swung herself up. At least she tried to. She got stuck with one leg up and one leg hanging off the back. The jokers helped roll her onboard.

"*Shukran*," she said breathlessly.

They stared down at her. Some were Living Gods and she recognized her new tentmate, Bastet, among them. Bastet sported a cat's head larger than her real head had been. They'd barely said hello to each other before Bastet was called off to some Living Gods' meeting.

Sobek gave Michelle a smile. At least she thought it was a smile. His head was that of a crocodile and he pretty much always had a creepy grin on his face. She wondered how many shitty Turkish cigarettes it had taken to turn those teeth such a delightful shade of cat-shit brown.

"Bubbles," he said. Sobek didn't think much of some of the *American Hero* contestants, but he'd asked Michelle to bunk with Bastet as a personal favor. "She's not handling the fighting well" was his only explanation. "This should be the last of these battles. Bugsy says they're weakening."

The other soldiers nodded. In this truck there were mainly Living Gods: Hathor, Seth, and Amun were the ones Michelle recognized. There were a couple she wasn't sure were Living Gods rather than just run-of-the-mill jokers. Any one of them could be some obscure god she didn't know about. The ancient Egyptians had a lot of gods.

The truck rattled down the sandy road kicking up dust. The other people in the truck were dirty and looked as tired as she felt. "Hey, Bastet," Michelle said as she sat down between Bastet and a joker who had the head of a baboon. *A really mean baboon.* He glowered at her, then got up and sat on the other side of the truck.

"I'm ready for the war to be over and we can decide what we're going to do with our lives," Sobek said as he settled down on the other side of Michelle, forcing another joker to move. "Maybe I will go live in Las Vegas with the Gods living there."

Bastet gave him a baleful look, then patted her rifle as if it gave her some comfort. "Why would you go? Would you leave your home? Your people?"

"My people? I'm a joker, little one. There's no country for us. And this," he said, making a sweeping gesture. "We're fighting over a scrap of land and who to pray to. As if either made any difference."

"They say Mohammed is greater than all the Living Gods," one of the other jokers interjected. She was naked and her body was a deep navy color with silver stars covering it. She wore a traditional short-cropped wig with bangs. Lying on the floor at her feet was a man, also naked, his arms outstretched to her. There was a snake coiled around his brow. He held a goose in one hand and a gun in the other.

"Sweet wife and dear sister, Nut, fear not," he said, smiling at her. "I am creator of all things. Despite what those damned upstart children of mine say. We shall destroy the new god, Mohammed. An invisible god is no god at all."

Sobek rolled his eyes, then said, "Yes. Yes. We are the visible Gods! And we will prevail!" His voice was suddenly rousing as he leapt to his feet, adopting a heroic pose.

Abruptly, he sat down again. Michelle leaned over and hissed, "What the hell was that all about?"

"Look at them," he replied, nodding at the others. His voice was sad and tired. "Look at you. Everyone is exhausted and still we must fight. There is no other choice. You know this. Fight or they will kill us all."

There was a whistling noise that Michelle recognized. *Missile,* she thought, just as it hit. The truck was slammed sideways, throwing its passengers willy-nilly. Bastet shrieked and sailed past Michelle. Sobek's head hit Michelle in the face, then he was tossed out of the truck as well.

Michelle hit the ground and got a nice zing of fat. She wasn't sure what the limits to her ability to take damage were yet, but so far she had the feeling that she hadn't come close.

"Bastet?!" Michelle yelled. There was a ringing in her ears from the missile strike. *Jesus,* she thought. *By the time this is all over I'm going to be deaf.*

"Over here," Bastet said with a quaver in her voice. Dirt and smoke hung in the air, obscuring Michelle's view.

"You hurt?"

"No, just tired of all of this. And I'm going to be bruised all over. That's nothing new." There was a snarl in her voice. "Let's go."

The smoke cleared enough that Michelle could see Bastet. Michelle staggered to her feet, then grabbed Bastet by the hand and pulled her up to where she stood unsteadily.

Michelle didn't have time to see who had survived the missile and she couldn't stay to find out. She could hear the wail of an ambulance. Another convoy truck slowed to a stop. As Michelle and Bastet were climbing aboard, Sobek appeared out of the smoke. There was a nasty burn down the right side of his snout and burns on his chest where his shirt hung in tatters.

"Are you sure you're good to go?" Michelle asked as he pulled himself into the truck. It jerked into gear and started toward the battle.

He shrugged. "My skin is tough," he said tersely.

Curveball was throwing rocks as fast as she could. Bright crimson blood bloomed on enemy flesh as her projectiles found their targets. Simoon started spinning slowly, then sped up. A tornado of fine sand whirled around her. She moved toward the enemy forces, and as she passed by, her sands shredded their skin while pulling them into her whirling vortex. After a moment, the whirlwind spat them out. Earth Witch squatted and laid her hands on the ground. She closed her eyes and the sand began to tremble as the ground beneath it bent to her will.

There was the usual chaos of fighting, and Michelle felt her heart beating faster, but it wasn't from fear, at least not fear for herself. The fear of what she was about to do was like alum on her tongue.

Bubbles formed in her hands. They floated up. She looked across the battlefield and in one horrible moment she thought, *Fuck it. Sobek was right. This has to end. No matter what.*

The bubbles flew. They zoomed past Curveball as she threw rock after rock after rock. Simoon's whirlwind didn't touch her bubbles as they blazed through.

Let's finish this.

Bullet-sized bubbles smashed into soldiers, shattering bones and ripping apart organs. There were bubbles in as many destructive forms as Michelle could imagine—she was getting more inventive as time wore on. Her fat melted off, but she knew it didn't matter because she was a target now. And every shot that struck her just made her more powerful.

Michelle headed back to her tent. Sand, layered with dirt and sweat, was making her skin itch. Her platinum hair had gone a nasty shade of yellow and there were purple hollows under her eyes from lack of sleep.

Inside, Bastet was lying on her cot staring upward.

"Bubbles," Bastet said dully. Her black fur was covered in dust, turning it a dingy gray. "Sobek asked you to look after me, yes?"

Michelle nodded. "Yes." It was miserably hot and she was too tired to pretend otherwise. The end flaps of the tent were open and an anemic whisper of wind blew through them.

"It's ridiculous." Bastet sat up, grabbed her canteen, and took a long swallow. Some of the water trickled out the side of her mouth. She held the canteen out to Michelle, who took it and drank, too. "I'm here doing what needs to be done. My people are dying for the sin of changing into something others can't understand."

"I'm here because I was on some stupid TV show doing nothing useful at all," Michelle said.

"You could have stayed in America," Bastet said. "You don't need to be here."

"At the end of the day, if they come for you, they'll come for me, too."

"I daresay they wouldn't," said Bastet, then suddenly, "I'm so tired." Her shoulders slumped and her head dropped into her hands.

Michelle reached out and patted her arm. "It's okay," she said softly. "None of us are doing that great right now."

Bastet nodded. "I hate all this killing. It seems like you're not affected by it at all."

Michelle drew back as Bastet looked up at her. "I am," Michelle replied, trying to keep her voice neutral. She could tell Bastet was suffering, but her words had wounded. "It's awful, but they've left us no other choice. Sometimes there aren't any good choices."

"Do you suppose you would have come here were it not for the war?" Bastet rocked back and pulled her knees to her chest. "Would you have cared about us?"

"I don't know," Michelle allowed. "I wasn't exactly political before my card turned, but now that it has, I'm not sure I have a choice."

Bastet nodded. "Maybe none of us has a choice anymore."

Michelle sighed. "Especially jokers." She couldn't figure out why someone would care about Bastet's joker anyway. Her head was only a little larger than normal size, not the size of a real cat's head, which would have been deeply odd on her average-human-sized body.

"I'm not a joker," Bastet said huffily, glowering at Michelle. "I'm a God."

The way she said it made Michelle want to laugh, but she couldn't blame the Living Gods for choosing to be called gods. Given the choice between being a god—including having actual followers—and being just a joker, well, Michelle knew which end of that equation she would be on.

"I'm sorry." Michelle smoothed her dirty khaki-colored pants. "I don't know much about any of the jok . . . Living Gods. And I don't know anything about you at all. I'll tell you my story if you tell me yours."

Bastet eyed Michelle warily and then stretched and settled into a cross-legged position. "My mother was a Coptic Christian and my father was a Muslim. They never could decide how I was to be raised. So I was neither one thing nor another." There was a decidedly sad note in Bastet's voice, but her face was inscrutable. Or maybe that was just the default cat expression. Either way, Michelle liked it.

"But didn't that mean you got to decide what you were?" Michelle asked. Michelle's parents were indifferent to any kind of religious upbringing, even though her mother was Jewish.

Bastet shrugged. "I never wanted to disappoint either of them, so I just didn't choose. Eventually, I ended up at University College London researching the Bast cults even though my interest was the Amarna Period."

"I don't know anything about the history of Egypt," Michelle said, embarrassed about her lack of education.

"I'll give you a list of things to read," Bastet said eagerly. A sad expression crossed her face. "If we get through this, that is."

"We're going to be fine. Tell me about your card turning."

Bastet shrugged. "There was no trauma, I just woke up and I knew I'd changed." She patted her face as if feeling it for the first time. "The college asked me to leave; they were very polite about it. My parents were polite, but distant. Eventually, I gave up and came here. I didn't fully admit what I'd become until the fighting began."

"I'm sorry about your parents," Michelle said. "But godwise, you could have done a lot worse. You could have gotten Sobek's joker and you'd be all, 'I'm the Crocodile God. Grrrrrr.'"

Bastet, who had been taking a drink from the canteen, snorted, then wiped her nose on the back of her sleeve. "You did that on purpose!" she said with fake anger, shaking her index finger at Michelle. "Water! Out of my nose!"

"I'm sorry," Michelle replied with a hint of contrition.

"My parents tried," Bastet said, suddenly serious again. "They really did."

Michelle was feeling a little jealous. "Mine just stole my money. They're in Paris now living off it. They really are a couple of first-class assholes."

"They sound like it. But now, I'm a God, and you are very tough. Not too bad as wild cards go."

"I'm not as tough as Golden Boy." She was still smarting at her defeat at his hands on *American Hero*. "He was—"

"A jerk," said Bastet, finishing Michelle's sentence.

"Wait, you saw *American Hero?*" Michelle was surprised. Bastet didn't seem like the reality show type.

"There are clips online. You were most impressive."

Michelle could feel her face getting red. "I loved getting my ass handed to me on national TV."

"Oh, international," Bastet said with a grin. If she'd had human teeth it would have been in Cheshire Cat country. Michelle liked it. "And with the internet it'll be with you forever," she finished, clearly tickled by Michelle's embarrassment. "The only thing I can do is turn into a house cat." In a flash, Michelle was looking at a small black cat where Bastet had been. It jumped onto Michelle's lap. The cat started purring and Michelle scratched it behind its ears.

The cat jumped back to Bastet's cot and in the blink of an eye, Bastet was back. "I'm useless in battle."

"You're a dead shot with a Light Fifty," Michelle replied. It bugged her that Bastet didn't think she was adding anything significant to the fight. "That's better than plenty of people."

"You've got a bubble going." Bastet pointed at Michelle's hand.

"Oh, shit, I didn't realize it." Michelle let the bubble pop. "You know, you could do that cat trick on TV."

"Yes, that would help our cause." Bastet's accent got a little thicker. "People are stupid, Michelle. There are conspiracy theories surrounding us. And the internet doesn't help. Do a search on 'Living Gods' and the amount of insanity you'll find online will astonish you."

"Yeah, I don't think so," Michelle replied. She grabbed her tummy where a little roll of fat still pooched out. It jiggled in a satisfying way. "You should see the stuff they say about me. It's both horrible and hilarious."

"What they say about the Living Gods is worse."

"Nope. Not a chance." Michelle shook her head. Her dirty, almost ass-length hair got stuck on her sweaty neck. "I'm fat, a woman, and gay. If I weren't white, I'd get all the bonus points."

"Who gives out these bonus points?" Bastet asked, a sneaky smile crossing her face.

"Now I know you're being goofy," Michelle said, giving Bastet an aren't-you-a-funny-girl look. "Bugsy has an internet connection—I'm not sure how. We'll ask him to Google 'Living Gods' and 'Amazing Bubbles' and see what comes up. I'll bet you I get shittier hits than you do."

"You're turning people hating you into a competition?" Bastet asked with dismay.

Michelle cocked her head to one side and said, "Of course! Doesn't everyone?"

Bastet won the "Who has shittier press on the internet" competition handily.

It was supposed to be over. The Egyptian Army had been routed. They were no match for aces, jokers, and a desperate people protecting their beliefs. But now it was done and life could start getting back to normal. Or as normal as anything could be after that sort of thing.

Except that didn't happen.

What happened was the Army of the Caliphate—and they had the Righteous Djinn.

Curveball, Simoon, Earth Witch, John Fortune, Drummer Boy, Bugsy, and Michelle were jammed into the command tent with a small group of Living Gods. They were trying to work out what to do now that everything had gone to shit again. Michelle decided she didn't have anything of use to add and slipped out, heading back to her own tent.

Bastet was napping inside, and it was remarkably quiet in the camp. Michelle began to sit down on her own cot when a missile hit nearby. The ground shuddered and Bastet jerked awake.

"C'mon," Michelle said urgently. "Jesus! Bastet, move!" But Bastet didn't move; she just sat there frozen, a terrified look on her face. Michelle grabbed Bastet's arm and yanked her to the floor. "Stay down!" she said. Bastet grabbed hold of Michelle and held her close, body trembling. "It's okay," Michelle said, patting Bastet's back. "It's going to be okay." She started to pull away, but Bastet tightened her grip.

"Don't leave me," she hissed. The lilting, almost purring quality of her voice was gone. Now it was filled with simple human fear. "I thought we were done with the fighting!"

Michelle took Bastet's head between her hands and stroked the fur between her eyes. "Look at me," Michelle said. Bastet jerked her head away. Michelle took it again. "Look at me! I'm not going to be gone long! I promise. I'm just going to take care of what's going on out there."

"You won't come back," Bastet said in a small, whispery voice.

"Really?! Have you seen me?" Michelle would have laughed but inside, she was just as afraid as Bastet. It wasn't from being hurt. She'd heard about the Righteous Djinn. The thought of him taking her power was terrifying. "I absorb missiles for breakfast!" she said with false cheerfulness. It sounded horrible, but missiles, missiles were easy.

"You're going to kill someone again," Bastet said miserably. "I don't want you killing anyone. I don't want to kill anyone any more. Don't go. Say you won't go!"

"I'm sorry," Michelle replied sadly. "It's what I do now."

Michelle stood with her feet planted wide, bubbles streaming from her hands toward the Caliphate Army. Bastet's words were with her. *You're going to kill someone.*

No, Michelle thought. *I'm going to kill a lot of someones.*

Parts of the Caliphate forces were positioned on either side of the Righteous Djinn. Rusty was to her left and Drummer Boy somewhere off to her right. Simoon had turned herself into a whirling dust devil, her form spinning tighter and tighter. She moved toward the Djinn and her sand began flaying his flesh.

He screamed. She spun closer to him until the center of her dervish engulfed his body.

Michelle heard Kate scream, "NO!"

But it was too late, the Righteous Djinn had grabbed Simoon, and Michelle watched in horror as he drained her power. She reverted to her human form . . . and, in one simple move, he ripped her in two.

Michelle felt as if she'd been punched in the chest. Suddenly, she couldn't breathe. Drummer Boy was mute for the first time ever, but Rusty kept saying over and over, "He killed her. Cripes, he killed her." Sobek cursed in a stream of several different languages. Then they just stared, stupidly, at the tragedy before them.

It was Curveball screaming that snapped them out of it. She was throwing her tiny missiles at the Djinn. Sekhmet jumped at him, her body aflame, fire sizzling all around her. The Djinn brushed Sekhmet aside and she spun through the air, landing heavily. He went for Lohengrin, who managed to avoid being touched by slicing off one of the Djinn's hands.

Michelle watched in amazement as the Living Gods began running for the Djinn, led by Sobek. It was madness. They were bound to die. If they possessed any powers, he would suck them dry. Drummer Boy yelled something at her, and Rusty started running toward the Djinn, too.

A furious scream clawed its way out of her. Then she assumed her pose and began streaming the most destructive bubbles she could think of at the Djinn. Her fat dwindled at an alarming rate. Her bubbles hit him and blew up with as much anger and power as she could put in them. The Djinn continued taking enormous damage from all sides, but nothing seemed to faze him.

It was Drummer Boy who finally stopped the Djinn. While the Djinn was dealing with everyone else's attacks, Drummer Boy began pounding on his chest, sending sound waves across the desert that exploded the Djinn's head like a soprano shattering a wineglass. Brains, bone, and ichor covered the ground and were strewn across both jokers and Caliphate forces. It seemed fitting that in a place where jokers held sway, a joker had saved them.

But there was no celebration for Michelle. She ran down the embankment toward Simoon's body. Lohengrin, Drummer Boy, Curveball, and Sobek were already there.

Simoon's body lay bloody and rent. Michelle didn't have much fat at the moment, but she had enough to send a bubble wafting over to encase Simoon's body. It took barely a thought to lift her. Michelle turned and started back to camp.

Drummer Boy picked up John Fortune and, with Curveball at his side, dashed past Michelle. Michelle didn't care. Slowly, the Living Gods began walking beside the bubble carrying Simoon. They surrounded her so no one could see her naked, brutalized body. Simoon was the daughter of Isis and Osiris, and that gave her special meaning to the Living Gods. She was one of them.

"Who is going to tell her parents?" Michelle asked. Sobek was on her right, his rifle slung across his back.

"It's for me to do," he said, a tear slipping down his cheek. "I know them. It'll be easier to hear it from me. As if something like this can ever be easy."

Michelle hadn't known Simoon well, but they'd been part of something. Something bigger than themselves. And Simoon had been fearless in fighting for it. Michelle thought about the other lives that had been lost—King Cobalt and Hardhat had died early and the shock of that was still fresh—and the reason why, and a wellspring of sorrow filled her that would never run dry.

After Michelle turned Simoon's body over to the Living Gods, she went looking for Bastet. She found her staring at the battlefield where the Righteous Djinn's enormous body lay. Around him were scores and scores of dead Caliphate soldiers, many of whom Michelle had killed.

"I'm glad you killed them," Bastet said. Her voice was icy, her body rigid. This wasn't the Bastet Michelle knew. "Look at what they've done. They will never stop coming for us. We should have killed them all so they will never come back. So their blood will soak into this place as a reminder of who we are and what we will do to them every time they come for us."

"But I thought you didn't want to kill anyone," Michelle said. "I thought that you were sick of the killing. If they come back, you'll have to kill more of them."

"Good," Bastet said. Then she turned and walked to camp without a single glance back.

But Michelle stayed and stared at the carnage.

She couldn't look away.

Within That
House Secure

VIII

MATHILDE CONSIDERED THEODORUS AND Malachi. She had never developed the habit of taking or keeping photographs when she was younger, and so hadn't adopted the new fashion of snapping pictures of everything in sight with her phone, even though it was always to hand.

But to judge by her memory, which was she thought trustworthy, which she was pretty proud of, in fact, neither of the two of them looked appreciably different today than they had ten or even twenty years ago. Could that be true?

There was Theodorus, resplendent in a white lab jacket, shell burnished and gleaming. The last time he'd agreed to be weighed that Mathilde knew of was when he'd flown to that first meeting of joker leaders at Base One almost ten years ago. Then, he'd weighed about three thousand pounds, which was more or less what he'd told her he weighed after his card turned, at some point during their childhood. When had then been exactly? Why did it make her think of wooden elephants?

Malachi was now seventy years old, but how could anyone tell? His skin, for all that it was light gray, was smooth. The fringe of hair around the dome of his skull was white, but it had been for as long as she had known him. With his hunched back, he'd never been spry, but he seemed to move as well as ever.

The wild card took away, it could not be denied. But sometimes it gave, and in the case of these two men, at least, it seemed to have given in the form of longevity and vitality.

Mathilde herself was now forty years old, and didn't think she'd been gifted the same way her father and her friend had. She spent more time now than she ever had before in her life actually paying attention to her own body. A little thickness in the middle didn't bother her—it didn't seem to bother Oliver, either, or at least he'd never said anything—but even after all these years her one vanity was clothing, and the designers who made her outfits in New York and Paris on semiannual trips hadn't been shy about pointing out that she was no longer a svelte twentysomething. "*Vous avez un petit ventre*," her old friend Lars had admonished her, the last time he'd measured her in his workshop in the Seventh Arrondissement. He'd even poked her in the stomach. It hardly seemed fair. But then, what was?

The hiss of the automated watering system sounded, and suddenly Malachi put the lie to her thoughts about him not being spry. He jumped up from the canvas chair where he'd been reading, whirled to hold his folded newspaper between him and the nutrient-rich water gently misting the foliage he'd been reclining under, and sputtered, "Must this happen every time?"

His paper, Mathilde thought, was barely damp, but Malachi made a great show of holding it out at arm's length and flapping it back and forth as if it were sodden. When neither Theodorus nor she offered him any sympathy, he harrumphed and dropped the paper to the greenhouse floor. "Now, would you just throw your newspaper on the floor if we were in someone's library?" Mathilde chided.

"I've never been in a library where water was sprayed all over me," Malachi said.

"You should use one of the tablets," Theodorus said, lifting up his own wireless data pad. "There's nothing in that paper that isn't available on the network. And what's on the network is more up-to-date. Real-time stock data, Malachi. I still can't believe you aren't hooked into a feed of that around the clock."

Malachi made an obscure gesture at the tablet. "Connectivity has costs," he said.

Mathilde looked at her own tablet. There were, in fact, columns of numbers running down one side of the display, but they didn't show stock prices. Instead, the numbers, along with other data on the screen, reflected all the information that would have been at her fingertips if she had been sitting in the controller's chair of a Stormwing launch facility. Actually, it was the data from three Stormwing launch facilities, one each in the Marshall Islands, the Maldives, and along the border of Colombia and Brazil. Eighteen years after she'd run the first manned Stormwing launch from a facility packed with personnel and equipment less than twenty miles from Theodorus's home, she was running the launch of a trio of much-updated Stormwings simultaneously around the globe from a device the size and shape of a fashion magazine.

While sitting in a canvas chair carefully positioned clear of any automated misters and keeping an eye out for any of Theodorus's giant "security snails."

"Nevertheless," Theodorus said—they were still talking about connectivity, apparently—"you're going to have to get over your technophobia sometime."

"Sometime," said Malachi. "How much longer now?"

"A few minutes," said Mathilde. "Everything is running smoothly at all three facilities. The information we're getting from our satellites and from the Stormwing already in orbit indicate everything is ready to go. The 'wings will be up there in less than an hour, and three hours after that, they'll launch the packages, and—"

"And we'll have well and truly begun the terraforming of the Moon," Theodorus interrupted. He sounded delighted.

"Yes, well, so long as everything works the way it's supposed to," said Malachi. He was digging in his briefcase for another newspaper. Mathilde wondered if it was a copy of the same one he'd dropped, whether he kept a backup, just in case.

She understood the impulse. Backups were part of the philosophy of spaceflight, too. Thus three probes bound for the asteroid belt and the icy bodies Theodorus's contacts in the Chinese space service had located several years before. Not that these three were redundant to one another. They would need a lot more than three ice asteroids before they were done.

"Everything will be fine. Mathilde's teams are the best in the world at this kind of work."

Mathilde let a rueful grin spread across her face. Her teams were pretty much the only people in the world doing this kind of work. At least they all hoped so.

"It's not them and their machines I'm worried about. It's your contribution," Malachi said. "The one we haven't been able to test."

"Ah," said Theodorus, but his enthusiasm was undimmed. "The rocket snails are already at twenty percent of their growth, hitting the projected rate exactly. By the time the probes latch on to the ice asteroids and they come out of dormancy, they'll be among the largest living things ever born on Earth."

"On Earth, maybe," said Malachi, "but not of Earth, not entirely. Your way of tailoring and growing all these specialized enormous snails is about the damned oddest ace power I've ever heard of, even without adding in the Swarm component, and I acknowledge that it's been a boon for the project. I shudder to think what a purely technological solution to getting the asteroids back here would have cost—"

"If we could even have engineered such," said Mathilde.

"If you could even have engineered such, yes," Malachi rolled on, "but I wish you'd have come up with some way of running tests instead of simulations."

"It will work," Theodorus said confidently. "The snails will come out of dormancy, convert the probes to the hardware components of their hybrid selves, and then pilot the asteroids back to the Moon. It will be a most impressive sight, I think."

Mathilde glanced at her tablet. "Well, whatever misgivings we may still hold, it's too late now. Launch is in less than one minute."

"This is it, friends," said Theodorus. "When joker historians on the Moon tell the story of our new world, they will say it began on the second day of July in 2008. As time was reckoned on Earth."

"'As time was reckoned on Earth'?" Malachi repeated in a disbelieving tone. "Have you been reading science fiction novels again?"

"Takeoff!" said Mathilde. Even after all these years, even though she was thousands of miles from the actual events, she still felt the old thrill.

"Does everything look good?" asked Theodorus. He was holding his tablet up close to his eyes, and she knew that he understood everything on it just as well as she did. *Or nearly as well, anyway,* a petulant part of her added silently.

"Green across the board," she said. Then a dialogue box she'd never seen during an actual launch opened up on the screen. Simultaneously, her phone rang, and a low buzzing sounded from Theodorus's nearby workstation.

"What is it?" Malachi asked. He may not have known machines, but he could sense trouble as well as anyone. "What's going on?"

"It's the Marshall Islands launch," Mathilde said, reading rapidly, now cursing the interface she'd been so happy with a few minutes before. She wanted to be doing something with her hands. "There was . . . something else launched from offshore immediately after the Stormwing. But we checked for naval craft."

"Submarine, then," said Malachi. He walked over, looked over her shoulder. "Probably the same damned Chinese we bought the location of the ice asteroids off of." He pulled out his telephone—the latest and most sophisticated available, despite how Theodorus had teased him, and went back to his chair. In a moment, he was speaking Mandarin in a low, angry voice.

"He's right," said Theodorus. "That's a missile launch. Somebody's trying to shoot the 'wing out of the sky!"

They were helpless, hopeless. The Stormwing was already accelerating at full thrust and its maneuverability was limited at this point. It would, in fact, soon begin slowing down as it prepared to switch from its atmospheric to its more powerful nuclear engines.

She called up a simple plot showing two lines racing upward, lines rapidly coming together.

"Malachi!" Theodorus shouted, panicked.

Mathilde looked over. Malachi was on the floor, his chair knocked over beside him. One hand clawed at the damp concrete and the other clutched his phone in a white-knuckle grip. His humped back was arched in a painful-looking convulsion, his head bent back so far that she couldn't see his face from where she stood.

There were four people on the Marshall Islands Stormwing. She'd known them all for years.

Malachi was her father.

She dropped the tablet and shouted, "Tell them to cut the atmospheric engines now! Maybe it'll overshoot!" She ran to Malachi's side.

And as she went, she slowed to an inexorable crawl.

People in Witherspoon Security uniforms rushed past her. She couldn't tell if they were moving at supernatural speed or if the molasses pace she found herself keeping just made it seem that way. Then she saw Throttle, Clifford Bell, Theodorus's ace head of security, and knew that it was both.

A pair of guards crouched on either side of Malachi, not touching him but giving every appearance of attending him. Mathilde felt herself returning to normal speed and shot a furious look at Bell. He walked over, hands held apart in a gesture of peace.

"I'm sorry, Ms. Maréchal, but I saw what was happening on the cameras and came at once. Mr. Schwartz has standing orders for this situation and has made it crystal clear that we're to follow his protocol when he seizes."

"When he seizes? Malachi's not epileptic!"

"It blew up!" Theodorus interjected. "Even before I could tell them to cut the engines the missile blew up short of them! They're safe!"

And then Malachi was shaking off the guards, trying to stand. Too much was happening at once. "What's going on?" Mathilde shouldered the guards aside and helped Malachi to his feet. "Are you all right? What was that? Why does Cliff know about this and I don't?"

Malachi mimed taking a drink of something, and Bell spoke to one of the guards. "Go to the kitchens and get one of the electrolyte drinks Virginia brought." The woman took off at tremendous speed, obviously still under the influence of Bell's ace "throttle" power, which allowed him to gift others with super-speed, or, as had just happened to Mathilde, rob them of any speed at all. Mathilde watched her go, wondering through her shock if "Virginia" was Virginia Matuszczak, Malachi's relatively new secretary.

The guard returned in an instant, and Malachi nodded his thanks. He now held a clear plastic container shaped and sized like a water bottle found in any service station drinks cooler. This bottle, though, was pasted with a pharmacy's prescription label, and the murky contents clearly weren't water. Malachi made a feeble attempt at unscrewing the sealed bottle cap, and Mathilde snatched it from him, opened it, and handed it back. "Drink!" she said.

He did, draining the bottle in three long draughts. Then he took a deep breath and said, "To answer your questions from earlier, I am now fine, that was a sort of seizure, and Mr. Bell knows about it because he knows what I want done when it occurs and will do it. If it were up to you there would be an ambulance on the way here now and soon there'd be outsiders tromping through the House Secure."

The House Secure was what Theodorus had rechristened the Witherspoon estate a few years earlier, after Malachi had found a poem for him that Theodorus particularly liked. Mathilde wasn't overly fond of the name or the poem.

"How long has this been happening?" Theodorus asked.

Malachi looked between the two of them. Then he said, "For fifty-five years."

Fifty-five years?

Theodorus said, "Ah, well, then you clearly know what you're doing."

Mathilde couldn't believe it. She watched Theodorus turn back to his tablet, watched Malachi straighten his jacket and dismiss Bell and his guards. *They're both so good at keeping secrets that revelations don't phase them,* she thought. But that, she realized, heart stricken, was hardly a revelation itself.

Diggers

by David D. Levine

PART ONE

BRICK BY BRICK, GIRDER by girder, Tiago Gonçalves was putting himself back together. It wasn't working.

He kept at it anyway. He didn't know what else to do.

"More concrete!" he called to Salpicado, holding up a three-story-tall steel pillar that wanted nothing more than to fall over. They were all amateurs here, but he hoped that with enough steel and enough concrete they would be able to make something that lasted.

Tiago was about five meters tall at the moment, a man-shaped sculpture of batten, board, and broken concrete at the heart of which was a trembling, sweating twenty-six-year-old *curinga* whose skin was a jigsaw patchwork of shades from ebony to alabaster. When the wild card virus had dealt him a joker—had it been nearly ten years, now?—it had made him a collage, a messy assemblage of all humanity's skin tones and textures. Even his eyes were two different colors.

But the virus, always capricious, had also dealt him an ace: the ability to draw to himself any bits of junk or trash in the vicinity. These objects, upon touching his skin directly or indirectly, became part of his body, and through them he could feel, see, touch, and even taste; the more junk he piled onto himself the larger and stronger he became. It worked, the UN scientists had told him, on any "organic" substance—which meant, in their strange lingo, not healthy and pesticide-free but something about the elements of which they were composed. Wood, plastic, meat, and bone yes; metal, stone, and glass no. This ability had earned him a spot on *Heróis Brazil,* the name the Recycler, membership in the Committee . . . and a trip to Hell.

It was only by blind chance and good fortune that he had escaped Kazakhstan with his life, and even so—even with the help of some of the UN's finest therapists—he sometimes wondered if the thousands who had died had gotten off more easily. Memories of his time as a horrific golem of rotting, pustulent flesh, slaughtering friends and strangers with unthinking cruelty, haunted him day and night.

It was Horrorshow who had performed those atrocities, he knew, not truly him—he had been only a tool, an extension of Horrorshow's twisted soul with no more volition than the bits of wood and string that made up his gigantic extended body at the moment. No normal mind, and very few extraordinary ones, could possibly have resisted that malefic influence, and he needed to forgive himself, to stop flogging himself for failing to achieve the impossible.

But it was his hands that had torn out those throats, his eyes that had looked on the slaughter with gleeful malice, his mouth that had laughed and sneered and cursed the blameless victims even as they bled out on the shuddering fleshground at his feet. He could never forget how satisfied he had been at the carnage, and though time and therapy and hypnosis had blunted the pain of those memories, they would always be a part of him.

The pillar shifted, and he put his wooden shoulder against it to steady it. "Hurry!" he called to Salpicado, a *curinga* whose spongy body exuded water in seemingly endless quantities. Even now he was wringing his hands together, squishing out liters of water into the trough where two young men from the favela—part of the community that would be served by the hospital they were building, if they ever finished it—mixed it together with cement and rocks to form concrete. "That's enough!" Tiago shouted as the pillar shifted again, this time trying to fall in the opposite direction, and even as he struggled to right it he reached out with his power, pulling bits of rubber hose and scrap wood from the trash heap nearby onto his body, trying to make himself big and strong enough to hold this three-story steel stick vertical until the tardy concrete could be poured.

Trying . . . and failing. Despite his best efforts, the pillar kept tipping, painfully tearing bits of plywood and drywall from Tiago's straining fingers. "Look out!" he cried, his powerful voice grating oddly from a throat built of rope and cardboard. Nats and *curingas* alike scattered from the falling pillar as it toppled, smashing the foundation form in which it stood and turning a tidy pile of cinder blocks into shattered rubble. When the dust cleared, the pillar—which, together with three others, was intended to form the hospital's sturdy spine—was bent and twisted to uselessness.

"*Droga!*" he swore, relaxing his power. The giant man, the Recycler, gradually collapsed, leaving in its place Tiago Gonçalves: a trembling, sweating skinny kid with ugly patchwork skin, standing in soaking jeans and a T-shirt in a heap of shattered junk. He stood bent over, hands on knees, panting and gasping from effort and frustration. "Damn it," he swore again, in English this time—it was a habit he'd picked up in the Committee.

"*Está bem,*" Salpicado reassured him, placing a damp and squidgy hand on his shoulder. "We can try again tomorrow."

"But look at the pillar!" Tiago cried, flinging a hand at the twisted, useless thing. He was near tears, he realized, and tried to calm himself, closing his eyes and focusing on his breathing as his therapist had taught him. *We can buy another pillar,* he told himself. No one was hurt. He had done his best. But what he said aloud was, "Everything I touch winds up broken."

Now the tears did come, and he turned away from Salpicado and the other workers—nats and *curingas* working together to build a hospital for the favela, people he himself had brought together . . . and failed. Wiping his eyes and his running nose, he stumbled blindly away downhill.

Poor people, nats and *curingas* alike, lived up in the *morro,* or hills, while rich people lived down on the flats, the *asfalto.* Tiago slept in a hotel by the beach, with a soft enormous bed, air-conditioning, and room service, all paid for by

Committee money. The UN had been generous to him in the wake of the Kazakhstan disaster. But nothing—not his money, not his determination, not his wild card power—could remedy Rio's poverty or assuage his guilt for Kazakhstan.

He was doing everything he could, and it wasn't enough.

"Senhor Gonçalves!" called the front desk clerk as Tiago dragged himself despondently through the revolving door into the hotel's cool, scented lobby. Being addressed by that name still surprised him every time. "There's a message for you, sir! It's urgent!"

Politeness and curiosity overcame Tiago's weariness and despair, and he accepted the proffered envelope with a nod and a small tip.

Within the hotel's envelope was a second, smaller envelope, heavy cream-colored paper with a gold embossed logo: Witherspoon Holdings do Brasil Ltda. Within was a note, handwritten in looping, elegant curves. He stared at the rich paper and deep black ink for some time.

Shame suffused Tiago's chest as he handed the note back to the desk clerk. "Could you read this to me, please?" he said. "I . . . I forgot my reading glasses." In truth, he could not read cursive. Indeed, it was only by dint of intensive hypnotic training that he could read at all, or speak English. Neither of these skills had been necessary for a child of the favelas, and his life since escaping the slums had been far too chaotic for a normal education.

The clerk's skepticism about Tiago's reading glasses was clear, but he took the note back and read aloud: "'Senhor Fernando Suzuki, personal representative in Brazil of Theodorus Witherspoon, sends greetings to Senhor Tiago Gonçalves, also known as O Reciclador. He desires a personal meeting with you at your earliest convenience on a matter of utmost urgency and confidentiality.' There's a phone number." He looked up. "Would you like me to dial it for you?"

Anger joined the shame. "I can dial my own phone, thank you. Just write the number out clearly for me." Then, belatedly remembering his excuse, "And large." He handed over another tip, much bigger than the first.

The clerk nodded and returned the original letter with the number written in huge, childish numerals at the bottom. "Will there be anything else, Senhor?"

"No, thank you."

Fernando Suzuki, whose cultured Brazilian Portuguese on the phone had been completely without accent, had the Japanese facial features his last name suggested. He was also a *curinga,* having a second pair of arms in place of his legs. He walked on all fours, his hands protected by fashionable black leather gloves, and wore a suit whose exquisite tailoring managed to make him look like the lawyer he was rather than a dressed-up dog. "So pleased you could see me on such short notice," he said, stripping off his right fore-hand glove and reaching up to take Tiago's hand. His grip was firm, his palm surprisingly soft. A nat assistant, also wearing a suit though not quite so finely made, carried his briefcase.

They had met in the hotel bar, and Suzuki clambered up into a booth without a trace of awkwardness. Tiago took the seat across from him; with Suzuki's lower limbs hidden by the tabletop, he seemed merely somewhat short. The lawyer folded his delicately manicured fingers before himself as the assistant—silent and not introduced—sat down beside him. "You are familiar with Theodorus Witherspoon, I trust?"

"I've heard the name. Joker? Rich guy?" Tiago recalled pictures of a giant snail-centaur on the covers of the magazines behind the counter at the convenience store, usually seen in the company of beautiful blonde women.

"Fourth richest person in the world. Also the developer of the Stormwing." Seeing Tiago's blank look, Suzuki clarified, "It's a spaceplane that can take off and land at any major airport. Single stage to orbit."

Tiago shrugged. "That's nice. What does this have to do with me?"

Suzuki leaned forward over his folded hands. "As I said on the phone, this is a highly confidential matter. Before we proceed I must ask you to sign this nondisclosure agreement." Without prompting, the assistant drew from his briefcase a fat sheaf of papers, dense with text.

Tiago made a show of looking over the papers, but he could barely understand one word in three. "So, bottom line," he said—it was a phrase he'd heard often from the producers of *Heróis Brazil*—"this means that if I tell anyone what you're about to tell me, very bad things will happen. To me."

"Precisely." Suzuki took a pen from his own pocket. It was warm and very heavy in Tiago's fingers.

Tiago signed.

Suzuki bowed his head as he took the signed agreement back from Tiago, then handed it to his assistant. The assistant tucked it into the briefcase, then brought out a slim metallic device, placed it on the table, and pressed a button. A thin whine, almost too high to hear, came from it, and at once the voices of the other patrons of the restaurant dimmed to a low incomprehensible mumble. "We can speak privately now," Suzuki said, his voice slightly muffled and echoey, "but I must remind you that we can still be seen. Do not make any sudden or dramatic gestures."

"All right." Tiago folded his hands on the table before him, mirroring Suzuki, but his ugly patchwork skin and ragged fingernails made the gesture more a parody than a reflection.

"You may be aware that Mr. Witherspoon is a strong proponent of jokers' rights," Suzuki said. Tiago shrugged. "However, in addition to his public persona, Mr. Witherspoon has for many years been pursuing a personal project of dramatic scope, one which will immensely improve the lives of jokers around the world. That project has now reached a critical new stage, and we have an immediate need for a great many talented jokers—jokers such as yourself."

"Go on."

"The Stormwing is not merely an orbital craft," Suzuki explained then, for no apparent reason. "It is capable of reaching the Moon, and has been for over ten years. And Mr. Witherspoon has been using his fleet of Stormwings—which includes, by the way, many more craft than are publicly known—to construct a homeland for jokers on the lunar far side."

Tiago clutched his hands together, reminding himself not to make any sudden or dramatic gestures. "You're shitting me."

"I am not shitting you, Senhor Gonçalves. And this homeland, which currently consists of just a few hundred hardy jokers, is about to expand dramatically. Beginning in 2020, and continuing for many years more, a barrage of water-ice asteroids will impact the lunar surface. This influx of volatiles—forgive me, water and gases—will, over the course of the next few decades, transform the Moon from a barren rock into a livable planet. But in order for this project to succeed, the population of the joker homeland will need to increase by a factor of one hundred or more—tens of thousands of jokers with the specialized scientific, engineering, and technological skills needed to manage the transformation."

Tiago blinked, then slowly spread his hands. "I . . . I appreciate your confidence in me, Senhor. But I have no such skills."

Suzuki inclined his head in acknowledgment. "But these highly skilled individuals will need a place to live. And you, with your particular abilities, experience, and motivations, are perfectly suited for the job." He held out a hand and the assistant placed in it a tablet computer, which Suzuki switched on and turned to face Tiago. The screen, Tiago noted, was built for privacy—it appeared black unless it was pointed directly toward the viewer.

The image on the screen was a drawing of a giant robot—a humanoid form, clean and white and shiny, with clever jointed fingers and a smooth head, noseless and mouthless, that suggested rather than depicted a human face. A human figure drawn next to it showed that it was about three and a half meters tall. "What is this?" he asked Suzuki.

"You." Suzuki touched the screen and a third human form, this one skinny and colored in a patchwork of browns, faded into view in the middle of the giant robot's torso. In case there were any doubt, it had Tiago's face and hair.

"I couldn't possibly assemble something like that. I don't have that kind of control."

Suzuki shook his head. "We will build it for you. It will be custom fitted, very comfortable, and airtight. But as it is built entirely of plastic and will be in contact with your skin, because of your unique abilities it will also be an extension of your body. With this suit you will be stronger than any space-suited astronaut, and also able to manipulate and feel objects in vacuum as well as an ungloved human hand. A perfect lunar construction machine."

Tiago stared hard at the illustration, trying to imagine himself within it. With this suit he could walk upon the Moon—the Moon!—and feel the lunar rock beneath his feet, as no one else had ever done. Those fingers, carefully crafted and machined, would surely be stronger and more precise than any he'd ever formed of junk. And he would be helping to build a homeland for jokers. "What's the catch?" he said.

"You will need to depart immediately—as in, right this minute. You can't tell anyone where you are going, and you won't be able to communicate with anyone on Earth while you are on the Moon. We will take care of your affairs and make sure your friends and relatives don't worry about you, but no one can know about this project until it is much further along."

"I don't have any relatives." Even his friends, he realized, were not close . . . most of his best friends, those he had made on the Committee and, before that, in the landfills of Rio, were dead or missing. "But I couldn't possibly. I'm building a hospital."

"We are aware of this, and I have been authorized to make a substantial donation—a very substantial donation—to the project. Anonymous, of course, but it should be sufficient to complete the project in your absence."

Tiago drummed his fingers on the table. "Enough to pay for a real architect and proper construction equipment?"

Suzuki gazed at him levelly. "Enough to make it the finest hospital in Rio. If you join our project."

The two *curingas* studied each other for a time. "I don't understand," Tiago said. "There must be a hundred jokers in the world better suited to this project. Why is Witherspoon that desperate to hire me?"

Suzuki tilted his head, his expression softening. "It's not Mr. Witherspoon," he said, "but Mr. Schwartz, the project manager, who specifically requested that I approach you. And, frankly, I don't know why." He folded his hands on the table and leaned forward over them. "As I'm sure you can understand, most of the people involved in this project are what you might call 'true believers.' Usually new recruits spend a considerable time—years—volunteering, or working in more peripheral roles, before being offered an on-site position like this. This is an extremely unusual opportunity, Senhor Gonçalves, and I strongly encourage you to accept it."

Something about the deal smelled, Tiago thought. But still . . . it was an extremely unusual opportunity, indeed the opportunity of a lifetime. And what would he be giving up to do it? The hospital? The hospital whose spine he had just broken, through inexperience and inadequacy?

They would be better off without him.

Tiago hesitated a moment longer, then stuck out a grubby patchwork hand. "I'm in."

The silent assistant accompanied Tiago up to his room and helped him to pack his few things while Suzuki paid the hotel bar bill. They walked out the door and right into Suzuki's waiting car—not a limousine as Tiago had expected, but a BMW sedan, black and powerful and luxurious, with a customized driver's seat and controls so that Suzuki could drive. Tiago sat in the passenger seat, clutching his backpack to his chest, and watched in silent terror as Suzuki zipped through Rio's traffic like a football star dodging defenders on his way to the goal. He was beginning to wonder what he had gotten himself into.

Soon they arrived at the airport, where they drove directly onto the tarmac, parking next to a private jet with Witherspoon's logo on the tail—there wasn't even any security or passport control. "The air hosts will take care of your needs from here," Suzuki said, shaking Tiago's hand as the assistant carried Tiago's bags to the plane. "Thank you again for agreeing to join our team. I'm certain you will be very happy with your decision."

"I'm glad someone is."

Suzuki pulled down the wraparound sunglasses he had donned for the drive, peering at Tiago over their black horizon. "Please give my regards to Mr. Schwartz when you see him," he said with what Tiago thought was a rather ambiguous expression. The assistant held the passenger door open, giving Tiago a very slight bow, then climbed into the passenger seat after Tiago vacated it.

"Good luck!" Suzuki called cheerily, then waved and pulled away. The car's engine had a low growl like some powerful forest cat.

Tiago swallowed, turned away from the receding BMW, and allowed the air hosts—there were two of them, identical, with bright blue crystalline skin—to escort him aboard the plane. Within minutes they were airborne.

Even Witherspoon's money couldn't make the thousands of kilometers between Rio and the House Secure, Witherspoon's home and headquarters in Charleston, South Carolina, disappear. But the plane, though smaller than Tiago's Rio hotel room, was even better appointed; all manner of food and drink was available for the asking, and Tiago's seat folded out into a quite comfortable bed. He was also kept busy filling out forms, answering questions, and recording reassuring videos for his friends and associates so Witherspoon Holdings could manage his affairs while he was away. By the time they landed in the United States he was certain the air hosts knew more about his finances and other aspects of his personal life than he himself did.

Tiago stared amazed at the sleek, gigantic aircraft parked on either side as he staggered, exhausted, down the jet's rickety aluminum stairway. Witherspoon's private "airstrip" was actually a full-sized airport, where dozens of enormous delta-winged Stormwings were being serviced, little electric Jeeps zipping back and forth towing trains full of five-sided silver cargo modules. All the modules were heavily scarred, obviously veterans of many, many trips. To the Moon? Tiago had no way of knowing.

Again, there was no passport control. Tiago and his bags were ushered into the house—it appeared from a distance to be an American plantation house like the one in *Gone with the Wind,* but up close it was more like an office building, seven or eight stories tall and clad in white-enameled metal—and up to a luxurious suite where he collapsed on the bed and fell asleep without even removing his clothes.

Tiago awoke wearing soft white pajamas. While he had slept, his clothes had been removed, cleaned, and folded, and were now lying on a chair next to the bed. He was both amazed at the level of service and disturbed that it had been performed while he was unconscious. Exactly as he finished dressing, a gentle knock at the door announced the arrival of an attendant wearing an expensive-looking suitdress that nicely accommodated her enormous, misshapen legs, who escorted him downstairs to a conference room set with round tables and a breakfast buffet. It smelled delicious, and Tiago realized he was ravenous.

Several more people, all jokers of one sort or another, entered the room as Tiago filled his plate from the buffet. One of the last to arrive was enormous—he had to duck under the doorframe, and barely fit through the double doorway. His skin was hard and gray, resembling rough-hewn rock or rhinoceros hide, and each of his arms was the size of a big man. "You can call me Hardbody!" he boomed, waving one enormous hand—it was bigger than a car tire, with rough gray nails resembling horses' hooves. Tiago was annoyed by the man's thoughtless commandeering of the room, stilling every conversation and drawing every eye to himself with his imposing size and the raw power of his voice.

Hardbody, Tiago noted, required the assistance of two attendants to fill his plate and ate with a special utensil, a small metal shovel. Huge and powerful he might be, but those gigantic hands were not at all suited to fine work.

After everyone had seated themselves, another elegantly dressed joker—a gray-haired gentleman whose head, torso, and limbs were drastically elongated—stepped to the lectern at the front of the room. Steel-rimmed spectacles perched at the top of his long, horsey face. "I'd like to welcome you all to the House Secure and the Joker Homeland Project," he said. The projection screen behind him lit up with the Witherspoon logo, which was then replaced with an image of the Moon.

For two hours he spoke, explaining the history, goals, and status of the project. The current habitation, housing a little under three hundred people, was about half prefabricated modules and half dug under the lunar surface, or "regolith." The additional space needed by the thousands slated to arrive soon would be mostly underground—it was safer from radiation and micrometeoroids, and much larger spaces could be enclosed without the enormous costs of bringing materials up from Earth. "When I say 'costs,'" the lecturer clarified, "you must understand that these include costs in energy, fuel, time, and opportunity as well as money . . . which, even for Mr. Witherspoon, is not unlimited." The current group of new recruits, of which this roomful was just a small part, had been selected for their particular skills in subsurface excavation and construction, and would be going to the Moon as soon as the rest of the group had assembled—a matter of days, it was hoped.

At the end of the briefing, one of the attendants—a bullet-headed man with a blubbery shape, but whose movements showed that the blubber was in fact solid muscle—touched his earpiece and came over to Tiago. "I've been asked to bring you to Mr. Schwartz," he said. The stress he placed on the words *Mr. Schwartz* showed a great deal of respect, and also some surprise at the personal attention Tiago was receiving.

Mr. Schwartz's office suite occupied an entire floor at the top of an elevator that required the attendant's fingerprint. It was a hushed space of thick carpet, wood paneling, and panoramic views over the airfield to one side and piney woods to the other. "Mr. Gonçalves!" said the occupant as he waddled across the carpet toward Tiago, extending a pudgy hand. "Malachi Schwartz. I am so delighted that you have agreed to join our project, and I wished to extend my personal welcome to you."

Schwartz was not an attractive man. Shorter than Tiago, he was hunched and round and bald, with gray skin, black lips, and no nose. His arms and legs were short and swollen, and his hand in Tiago's was lax and spongy. But the nails were neatly manicured, his voice was smooth and reassuring, and his suit was impeccable. "Pleased to meet you, sir," Tiago said. "I understand that you are personally responsible for my presence here?"

"I am indeed!" Schwartz replied, touching his fingertips together and backing away to inspect Tiago from head to toe. "I have been watching your career closely, young man, and I must say I have been very impressed with what you have been able to accomplish in such a short time."

Tiago pulled his gaze back from the depths of the man's black eyes. "It doesn't feel like so very much, sir."

"The best lack all conviction," Schwartz pronounced, shaking his head, "while the worst are full of passionate intensity." The way he said it made it sound like a quote, though Tiago didn't recognize the source. "Come, come, dear boy, have some confidence in yourself! Your unique abilities, properly nurtured, could make you a force to be reckoned with!"

"Thank you, sir." But by comparison with the spaceplanes, extensive facilities, and tidy gardens visible through the broad windows, the ability to turn himself into a walking trash heap didn't seem very significant.

"We spend our days surrounded by things, Mr. Gonçalves, as well as people." Schwartz touched Tiago's elbow and looked up into his eyes with deep sincerity. "The man who can bend the inanimate to his will, as you can, has many more allies than most. Do not forget this."

"I will try not to, sir." Though Schwartz's touch was surely meant to be reassuring, and was not at all sexual, Tiago still found it somewhat disturbing.

Schwartz released Tiago's elbow and stepped back. "Thank you for coming to visit me in my luxurious prison." He gestured at the office. "However, we are both busy men, and I won't take up any more of your time. But I will be keeping an eye on your progress, and I will be joining you on the Moon in a few weeks. Until then, if there is anything I can do for you, do not hesitate to ask."

"Thank you, sir." Again he shook the flabby hand, and the attendant, who had remained discreetly by the door during their conversation, ushered him to the elevator.

As he descended to the ground level, Tiago considered what Schwartz had said. He had confidence in Tiago, even if Tiago himself did not, and as the one in charge of this whole impossibly ambitious operation he was obviously smart, influential, and powerful. If Tiago were smart he would not decline this man's favor; he should, instead, work hard to fulfill his high expectations.

Tiago may have failed at everything else he had ever attempted, broken everything else he had ever touched. But this time—this time, everything would work out for the best. And he would give every particle of his being to make sure it did.

The next few days were extremely busy, with training, paperwork, exercise, medical exams, and fittings for space suits. The last of these was an interesting challenge for the engineers, as many jokers required a custom suit to accommodate their unique physique. Hardbody's rock-hard skin was vacuum-proof, but he received a bubble helmet, cemented to his neck, so he could breathe. Tiago, who had spent much of his life building beautiful and useful things from whatever came to hand, was fascinated by the process, but his own suit, which he received in addition to the giant plastic body that was being fabricated for him on the Moon, was completely off-the-shelf.

There was not much conversation during this time—they were all exhausted when they were not occupied, and even at mealtimes they were all too busy shoveling food into their mouths for chat—but when they did talk among themselves, Tiago felt himself the odd man out. Everyone else was excited about the project, all looking forward to the challenges that awaited them, all fully committed to building a homeland for jokers. They acknowledged that there was danger, but they were all certain the project's scientists and engineers had done all they could to reduce it, and even if injury or death might await them they were prepared to take that risk.

For his part, Tiago was much less sanguine. Although he agreed, in theory, that jokers deserved their own homeland, one designed and built for them and by them and separated from the nats and their mundane concerns, the technical difficulties of the project were daunting and the politics were worrisome. Even if they could manage to build a safe haven on the Moon, and keep it safe, how would the world react when they learned that an independent nation of jokers was literally hanging over their heads? Would there be opposition? Hostility? Even retaliation?

Tiago's negative attitude, he told himself, could almost certainly be chalked up to his deprived childhood and traumatic experiences in Kazakhstan. Of course he was reluctant to trust anyone, even a philanthropist like Witherspoon; of course he was worried about backlash from the nats. But with Witherspoon's money and organizational skills, everything would work out well.

And so he kept his concerns to himself. But still, during the brief moments between crawling into his luxurious bed and falling asleep, he worried.

Then came the morning they were all awoken early and herded onto one of the Stormwings for the trip to the Moon. Each of them donned their space suit, settled into the seat, cradle, or rack that had been customized for them, and awaited launch. But the Stormwing launch was not nearly as dramatic as the nuclear-thermal rocket blastoffs Tiago had seen on television and in movies . . . the giant plane merely taxied down the runway and took off like a passenger jet, albeit faster, rougher, and noisier. But the thrust against Tiago's back did not stop when they reached cruising altitude, instead going on and on for hours. Soon the blue sky outside the tiny round windows faded to black, and not long after that the ends of safety belts and other small unsecured objects began to float about the cabin. A few people threw up, and attendants came to their aid, but in general everyone remained secured in their places for their voyage, using the facilities for eating and elimination built into their suits. Large as it was on the outside, the spaceplane's interior was much tighter than any commercial airliner; there wasn't any spare space for wandering around, especially with everyone in bulky space suits.

They all dozed on and off or listened to technical information on their headsets until the Stormwing entered lunar orbit. The change was nearly imperceptible to the passengers, except that there was half an hour or so of thrust, following which the craters of the Moon filled the tiny windows every few minutes as the craft rotated in "barbecue mode." Some hours later there was another period of thrust, this one much shorter. "Deorbit burn complete," came the announcement in Tiago's headset.

Tiago knew from his training that the Stormwing, its great delta wings useless in the Moon's lack of atmosphere, was now falling toward the lunar surface like a rock. At the very last minute landing rockets would fire, permitting a gentle tail-first touchdown on a concrete pad near the joker habitat. It was something Witherspoon Holdings had done hundreds or thousands of times before, though the public knew nothing of this, but it still seemed risky. "How many of these landings have failed?" Tiago had asked during training.

"Hardly any," had been the response.

"All hands brace for landing burn," came the voice, entirely too calmly in Tiago's opinion.

The rumbling shove against Tiago's back was more sudden, harsher, and stronger than the gentle push of takeoff, and his heart leapt into his mouth. But it lasted less than a minute, and then faded away, ending with a gentle thump followed by the steady light pressure of lunar gravity.

"Secure and cross-check all systems for debarkation," the voice said then, stated less as a command than as a simple statement of fact. Then, with a bit more animation: "Welcome home, jokers."

Home, perhaps, but not very homey. The new arrivals were issued coveralls in a rough gray fabric that looked and felt like something made from moon rocks, which is what it was. When those got dirty or wore out, they were to be returned to be recycled into new fabric; water was at a premium. Tiago was also given a tiny cabin, just tall enough to stand, wide enough to dress, and long enough for a bunk, which was set into the wall at the top of a short ladder. Behind the blank wall below Tiago's bed was the bunk below, in the cabin next door.

There was quite a variety of cabins, to suit the highly varied needs of a population of jokers, but Tiago didn't envy those whose quarters were larger; no one had more space than they needed to turn around and lie down. The watchword was "equity" rather than "equality"; the ideal was to accommodate everyone's unique requirements rather than trying, as the nat world did, to hammer every round, hexagonal, or amoeba-shaped peg into the same square hole.

Even the administrative personnel, no matter how highly placed, had the same Spartan quarters and bland nutritious diet as everyone else. At least, so they were told; the administrators were housed underground, while the new arrivals' quarters were located in the prefabricated modules on the surface. These modules were the oldest part of the settlement, their plastic and metal scuffed and worn, and those who lived there were exposed to more radiation and greater danger of decompression than those who lived belowground. But, they were assured, this situation was temporary, and they would be moved below as soon as more space was available. Which was, after all, the reason they were all here.

After breakfast on his first full day on the Moon—meals were communal and utilitarian, as were the bathrooms, which were segregated by size rather than by sex—Tiago was intercepted by a couple of technicians and taken to receive what he thought of as his "giant robot suit." Walking in the low lunar gravity didn't require a lot of effort, but it wasn't exactly easy . . . the instincts Tiago had developed in a lifetime on Earth were all wrong now, and he tried to match the technicians' shuffling gait so as to avoid caroming off the walls and ceiling. At least it didn't hurt when he fell, which was often.

The thing that was most surprising to Tiago was that working in lunar gravity wasn't slow motion, the way it looked on TV . . . everything moved at the same speed as ever, except for the falling part. It wasn't like moving underwater, it wasn't like swimming, it wasn't like flying, it was just weird and disorienting and a lot harder to get used to than he'd expected.

The corridor was much broader and higher than Tiago would have expected, given the tightness of his own quarters, but he realized as a walrus-like woman humped into the elevator along with them that this was necessary to accommodate jokers of widely varied sizes who walked, rolled, or slithered in many different ways. The very large elevator also accepted speech commands, and had panels of buttons near the floor and ceiling as well as the usual buttons at Tiago's chest level.

Five levels down they found a large, chill workroom crowded with tools and equipment. Lying on a table under bright work lights were the pieces of Tiago's giant robot suit. "It's huge," he said.

"It's actually smaller than your typical junk body," said one of the techs with a small self-satisfied smile. Her name tag read SUMA and she had dark brown skin, wavy black hair, and five soulful brown eyes. "You've just never seen yourself from outside before."

Every piece of the suit, Suma explained as she snapped the two halves of the suit's lower torso around his body, had been computer-designed and 3D-printed to fit his body exactly. This was standard procedure for joker space suits, but the fabrication of Tiago's suit had been both more difficult, because it had to be skin-tight, and easier, because many of the joints and fittings that were the most finicky parts of the suits could be left loose, leaving the details up to Tiago's power.

Tiago slipped his hand into the suit's giant arm. His own arm reached only as far as the suit's elbow; beyond that was solid plastic, with ball-and-socket joints at the elbow, wrist, and fingers like a larger-than-life-sized artist's model. As soon as the plastic touched his skin it became a part of him, and he raised and flexed the hand. The joints squeaked a little, but he'd never felt anything so smooth and clean. "This is amazing." He tapped each fingertip rapidly against his thumb tip. "I could play the piano with this!"

"We don't have a piano that big." Suma fastened the seal where the arm met the torso.

"That's okay, I don't know how to play anyway."

The other arm and the legs were the same, but the head and upper torso proved a little more problematic. "It seems . . . claustrophobic," he said, peering dubiously into the black padded opening. Once he had donned it, his head would be completely surrounded and he wouldn't be able to move it at all.

"Isn't this what you are used to?" Suma was looking up at him now. With the legs on, his head nearly touched the workroom's high ceiling.

"Sort of. It's different when I do it." He usually started by pulling small bits of material onto his head, he realized, covering his face with leaves or scraps of paper before adding larger pieces. It took only a few seconds, but doing it all at once like this seemed weird and frightening.

"Well . . . close your eyes, hold your breath, and just do it. I'll be here if you run into trouble."

"Okay . . ." He gripped the suit's upper torso unit with his giant plastic fingers, closed his eyes, held his breath, and jammed it onto his head. For a scary, disorienting moment he couldn't see, couldn't breathe . . . and then his senses extended into the head, his plastic eyes opened, and he felt the antennae on the back of his head scraping the ceiling. The suit's air smelled like metal and fresh plastic. "That wasn't too bad," he said with relief. Unlike his usual trash body, the suit had no mouth; instead, the voice of his flesh-and-blood mouth was relayed to a speaker in the chest. In vacuum it would be transmitted by radio to his coworkers.

"That's great," said Suma, and he heard the sound both with the suit's plastic ears and through a headset built into the upper torso unit. "Try moving around."

There were a few hiccups—some joints had to be adjusted, and Tiago found the suit's radio, air supply, and other technicalities less than intuitive—but after a couple of hours Suma pronounced Tiago good to go. "Okay, just one more thing. Feel this." She picked a half-meter length of I beam off a shelf and tossed it to him.

Still unused to the lunar gravity, he fumbled the thing several times before managing to grab hold of it. It was very light—some kind of plastic rather than metal—but as it touched his plastic hands it felt very strange. His sense of touch extended through it, as it did with most plastics, but the feeling was odd and tingly. "This feels weird," he said. "What kind of plastic is it?"

"We call it *regolene*," she said. "It's not technically a plastic, but a rigidized polysiloxane . . . its chemical backbone is based on silicon, rather than carbon as in true plastics. There aren't any hydrocarbons on the Moon, but we've figured out how to make a strong, flexible structural material from local resources. Most of the base is made out of it. Now the question is whether its chemical structure is similar enough to ordinary plastics for your powers to work on it." She tapped the I beam's end. "Can you feel that?"

He could, but it felt more like a spark of static electricity than the tap of a fingertip. "Sort of."

"Hmm. Come over here." She walked him over to where another beam, this one about two meters long, was clamped in a device that seemed designed to test its tensile strength. "Touch this. Can you feel the strain it's under?"

Cautiously he laid a giant plastic hand on the beam. "I can," he said. "It kind of . . . aches."

"Now try this." Suma pressed a button; an electric motor whirred and the beam flexed.

"*Ai!*" Tiago cried, jerking his hand away. The feeling had been as though someone very strong were trying to bend his arm bone in the middle.

Suma frowned. "That was only three pascals of pressure." She tapped her chin. "Still, at least we know you can do the job. We'll . . . we'll figure out how to make it more comfortable for you." She didn't seem entirely convinced. "In the meantime, you're good to go. Report to air lock seven at 0800 tomorrow."

◆

The next morning Tiago reported to air lock seven, where he found a work crew of jokers, all of them ready to do heavy construction work in vacuum. In addition to Tiago and Hardbody—who scratched himself disgustingly, sending hard gray flakes of skin drifting to the floor as the suit techs glued his helmet to his neck—there was a crab-like individual one meter high and three wide who didn't need to breathe at all, a metal woman resembling a shipyard crane whose oxygen needs were provided by a small tank welded to the small of her back, and a burly misshapen dwarf whose telekinetic powers held an envelope of air near his body as well as giving him enormous strength. In this group Tiago was keenly aware that, although his parti-colored skin alienated him from society, his shape, size, and physical abilities were entirely within the norm—by comparison with his co-workers he was practically a nat. But once he had donned his suit he fit right in, and furthermore the air lock and other fittings were all oversized and designed to accommodate a wide variety of shapes, sizes, and abilities, so he didn't have to watch his back and his feet all the time the way he usually did. For perhaps the first time in his life he did feel truly at home.

"I'd like to welcome two new diggers to the team," said the crab, whose name was Mike, gesturing with a claw to Tiago and Hardbody. His voice came from a small box glued to the shell behind his eyes. He sounded like the digital assistant on the smartphone Tiago had had back in Brazil.

"It'll be good to have you on-board," said the dwarf. He had introduced himself as Beauregard but everyone called him Bo. "We've been understaffed ever since we lost Margot."

"What happened to Margot?" Tiago asked.

"Ceiling cave-in," said Mike, his eyestalks bending downward. "But sacrifices have to be made."

Tiago kept his opinions on that to himself.

Once they had all been briefed on the day's work and their suits, or equivalent, double-checked, the techs left the air lock and the large inner door swung closed with a definitive bang. Air pumps immediately began chugging away, and Tiago felt his ears pop as the pressure dropped. His plastic suit, too, felt the change, which came to him as a strange tightness in the skin. Tiago's heart thudded—he trusted the techs, but no one had ever actually worn this particular suit in vacuum before and he knew that nothing mechanical worked 100 percent right the first time you used it—but though various parts creaked alarmingly as the suit settled into the lunar environment, all the seals held, and soon Tiago found himself standing in the dead silence of vacuum. "Radio check," said Mike, his voice now sounding directly in Tiago's ears, as did everyone else's. "All right, let's go."

The crane woman undogged the outer door and swung it open—Tiago felt the metallic screech of its hinges in his feet rather than hearing it with his ears—and they all trudged out in silence. The construction zone immediately outside the air lock resembled the corridor just inside it, with workers spraying new plastic onto the walls just beyond that, but as they shuffled and bounced along the tunnel it rapidly changed character from "construction site" to "hard rock mine." Half an hour's walk brought them to a place where the walls were of rough broken rock, the lights were few and harsh, and thick dust lay everywhere. Space-suited jokers with grinding machines worked to smooth the walls, spewing chips everywhere in eerie silence. The air, strangely, was completely free of dust . . . and after a moment's thought Tiago realized it was also completely free of air.

At Mike's direction the team distributed themselves along the tunnel face, each working to extend the tunnel according to their particular abilities. The diggers had a few machines to help with the work—automated forklifts to do some of the heaviest lifting, and miniature self-driving dump trucks to haul rubble away—but they were only supplemental. Mike explained that they had tried robots, but they broke down frequently and were not very good at adapting to the constantly changing circumstances. Despite the expense of keeping human beings alive, jokers were better suited to this work than robots.

Hardbody was clearly in his element, smashing the wall with his enormous fists and clawing the broken rock down and away with his shovel-sized fingernails. His great strength and size were complemented by an ace ability: anything he destroyed with his hands crumbled away to nothing, leaving almost no rubble to be hauled off. It was, Tiago reflected, a formidable and yet rather depressing ability—a power useful only for destruction, not creation, but one in which Hardbody clearly took considerable pleasure. It was good that the joker homeland had found a way to use this power for productive ends.

Tiago's role was to clear away rubble, shift equipment as needed, and shore up the ceiling and walls as his colleagues extended the tunnel. For the latter task he was provided with beams and girders formed of tough gray regolene, which he could feel fitting into place as he jammed them into position with his plastic fingers. Here, too, he realized, the homeland's administrators had found a way to use everyone's particular abilities to benefit all jokerkind, and though the stresses and strains he felt in the plastic were actually quite painful, he tried to take pleasure in being uniquely useful.

After two hours of this Tiago was tired and aching. After four hours he was more than ready for a break—which came at five hours, but proved to be extremely brief, little more than a momentary lie-down on the hard, rubble-strewn floor and a drink of glucose and electrolytes from a tube near his mouth. Six, eight, nine hours . . . Tiago kept working diligently, egged on by his comrades' tireless efforts and constant radio encouragement from Mike, who was also working as hard as anyone. Finally, at 1800, after ten hours of continuous grueling labor, Mike told them to knock off . . . which meant another forty-five minutes of cleanup and inspection to be sure nothing would collapse overnight and they'd be ready to go in the morning.

Half-dead from exhaustion, Tiago dragged himself to the commissary and wolfed down a tasteless meal before collapsing onto his hard little bed.

And then the alarm rang and he had to get up and do it again.

Within That
House Secure

IX

WHEN SHE WAS FORTY-FIVE years old, Mathilde Maréchal became somewhere around the 150th person to step foot on the Moon. Records of early attempts—the two landings of Cash Mitchell's *Quicksilver*, the failed Russian attempt—were sketchy, at least compared to Witherspoon Aerospace personnel assignment files. If she wanted, she could call up the numbers and determine exactly how many of Theodorus's employees had been up here before her, though she knew off the top of her head that there were about seventy on-site with her right now.

She didn't bother checking. She was busy. She was gloriously busy.

The pump she was working on, its protective cladding folded back, was proving recalcitrant. She hadn't yet been able to chase down the source of the blockage that had caused it to freeze up; she didn't have one of the tools she needed, because, she now saw, the subcontractor who had manufactured the stubborn device hadn't followed specifications in the type of closures that held its main body together; and, advanced and supple as the gloves of her suit were, she was still having trouble with fine manipulations. She'd never been happier.

"Mathilde, are you finishing up out there?" The speakers built into her helmet were among the most advanced ever manufactured. It sounded like Oliver was standing right next to her. Early on, before people had complained about it sounding like callers were literally inside their ears, the fidelity had been even higher.

"Not really," she replied cheerfully. "Say, you wouldn't want to run some hex key wrenches out here, would you?" She knew he'd say no. Oliver had agreed to come on this deployment because, he said, they never got to spend any time together on Earth, but he claimed he didn't like the fit of the suit that had been specially built for him. Mathilde suspected he was a bit agoraphobic, uncomfortable under the starlit dome of the sky. He'd spent most of the time these first two weeks helping the teams running atmosphere to the new sublunar excavations that were being dug at a steady rate.

"I think you might need to button that pump up and come on in," Oliver said. "I've got something here I think you need to take a look at."

All these years later, and he was still couching his phrases. *I think. I think.* Of course, she was quite a bit higher up the corporate ladder than he was, though they had long since taken steps to ensure she would never be in a direct supervisory role over him.

Not that that many people reported to her. It had taken quite a bit of negotiation and even a bit of intrigue to ensure that she still spent most of her time doing what she thought of as real work instead of "managing." Theodorus and Malachi had, for once, been on opposite sides of that particular contretemps, and eventually Malachi threw up his hands, saying he had taught them both too well.

"Will I get to use a hex key wrench on whatever you want me to look at?" she asked.

"If you can find one big enough," Oliver replied.

Mathilde sighed. She stared down at the pump for a moment. Then, careful to balance herself in the still-unfamiliar light gravity, she gave it a kick. Her entire body rebounded, and she arced a few feet backward to land inelegantly on her backside. A tone sounded from the diagnostic program running on her wrist computer. The pump had unjammed.

If only all my problems could be solved that way, she thought.

Oliver was in the office suite somewhat grandiosely labeled COLONY CONTROL on the base schematics. It was in one of the first bunkers dug out by the teleoperated heavy tractors that Witherspoon Aerospace had been covertly delivering to Crater Mandel'shtam for almost three years. Which meant that the ceiling felt a little low. For all that the specifications for the bunkers had been planned out down to the micron and for all that the smart systems that directed most of the digging were among the most advanced in the world, it had taken actual people inhabiting the bunkers, working in them, living in them, to get a real feel for what was going to be needed up here in terms of physical space.

Crater Mandel'shtam wasn't that easy a place to define, consisting as it did of many overlapping and interpenetrating craters. But the overall area, the notional near-circle labeled on lunar maps with that name, was nearly two hundred kilometers in diameter, located 5.4 degrees north of the lunar equator on the Moon's far side.

As she stepped out of the shadow of the equipment node that housed the pump, Mathilde's visor polarized against the battering sunlight. She reminded herself to pull a still frame from her suit's video feed later to send down to Malachi, the latest salvo in her doomed battle to convince him to stop referring to the hidden base's location as being on "the dark side."

If she did, though, he would just send her an audio file of that damned album again.

"Are you humming 'The Great Gig in the Sky' to yourself?" asked Oliver as she walked into the office an hour later.

"I really have no idea," Mathilde said. "It's just some prog rock thing Malachi keeps sending me."

"I will now refrain from talking about the difference between psychedelic rock and prog rock," said Oliver, "in favor of expressing my amazement that Malachi listens to either."

"Oh, he doesn't," said Mathilde. "He just knows I won't read any more poems about the Moon if he sends me those."

"Fair enough. That particular track is a little . . . lyrically underdeveloped for Malachi anyway."

Mathilde thought about what she'd been humming. "Oh! It's the one that's just screeching all the way through."

Oliver was yet another joker man in Mathilde's life who seemed ageless. Except for what she personally thought was a rather rakish white stripe in the thick fur running from his right eyebrow back over his flat head, he'd hardly changed at all since they started working together, back at the beginning of the company.

"And this is where I refrain from saying something about you being your father's daughter and apples not falling far from trees. 'Screeching' is hardly fair. In fact—" He broke off and looked at her, then chuckled. "Okay, yes, it's that one. Nice title though, you have to admit."

He was seated at a work console, so for once she had a couple of inches on him. She leaned over and kissed the top of his head, breathed in his scent. "I so admit," she said. "Now, why did you call me in?"

"I've been running some numbers," he said, turning back to the console, waving her to a chair beside him.

"'Running Some Numbers,' the Oliver Taylor story," she said, but she looked at the screens he was pulling up. "What is that, a statistical forecast of some kind? Come on, babe, run some engineering numbers!"

"Kicking that pump really put you in a good mood, didn't it?" he said. "Yes, it's a statistical forecast, and you're not going to like what it says."

She turned away from the screen, took hold of the arm of his chair, and spun him to face her. "And what does it say?"

He glanced back at the screen. "I believe what it says—"

She gave him a warning look.

He nodded. "Okay. Okay. I know what it says is that we're not going to meet Theodorus's timeline for construction of this base. Or for the subsequent bases."

Mathilde was confused. "This was all worked out. There's plenty of time built into the schedule. We just need to have everything in place when the first ice asteroids hit, and that's seven years from now. Hell, we could build everything twice in that time, according to our estimates."

Oliver said, "I know what the estimates say. I helped prepare them. But since we've been up here, I've been noticing things. Time slippages. Performance shortfalls."

She knew him very well. "And once you noticed a few of those things, you went looking for more. Then you developed a theory on what was happening and why, and tested it against our forecasts and probably against two or three other models you wrote up during my naps. And finally, you built a big old statistical forecasting program that proves . . . what?"

"It proves we overlooked something."

"Tell me."

"We overlooked the Moon."

"Put that in a haiku and send it to Malachi. Tell me what you mean."

"Okay, at bottom, it's the same problem you were addressing out there with the pump. The problem you didn't have the tools to fix, which is also germane, actually. That pump was designed, manufactured, and tested in a terrestrial environment."

"Designed with lunar deployment in mind, manufactured to the most exacting standards, and tested, to be precise, in vacuum and in microgravity on one of our orbital stations."

"Yes, but all of that was still done from a terrestrial perspective. Setting aside the fact that microgravity isn't the same thing as one-sixth gravity—which is, by the way, the problem with that pump and with all the fluidics up here—all of these small delivery delays and unforeseen deployment problems can be explained by the fact that we underestimated the hostility of this environment. We also overestimated our ability to be agile in addressing problems and we are vastly underperforming against the timelines we set up for ourselves. I don't know why I'm the first person to notice this. I don't even know how I can be the first person to notice this."

What Mathilde had noticed was that he hadn't said that he'd thought the problem with the pump was the gravity difference. He'd stated it outright. He'd known.

"Okay," she said. "I guess I know what we have to do."

"What?" he asked.

"We have to set up a goddamned meeting," she said.

"No," said Clifford Bell. "Not her, absolutely not."

"I find that I'm in agreement," said Malachi. His copy of the dossier, of course, provided by his ever-present secretary, the elfin-eared Virginia, was a physical folder consisting of dozens of top-bound pages that he was flipping through like a detective on a procedural show. He even had an eight-by-ten glossy photograph sitting to one side. It showed a plump young white woman with curling red hair, dark brown eyes, and a spray of freckles across her nose.

"She's exactly what we've been looking for these past three years," Theodorus insisted, scrolling through the same data on his tablet. "She is not a teleport per se, but the portals she opens are effectively the same thing, allowing near instantaneous passage through folds in space. If there's a limit to the distance she can reach, they have not found it yet. Assuming she can open a portal on the Moon, our delivery times of personnel and material to the lunar bases will be reduced by an order of magnitude."

"Sir," said Cliff, "did you read all of this? The first time she worked for anybody we know about she betrayed them and tried to steal from them. And that was before she got involved in an underground joker fight ring in Kazakhstan. And tried to eat someone's eyebrow."

"And of course she's in federal custody," added Malachi. "Being an international criminal and all."

Theodorus said, "Says the man who once hired a helicopter pilot without a pilot's license who was wanted in six countries."

"She got her license eventually," said Malachi.

"After we pulled some strings. And we can pull strings to get Mollie Steunenberg released as well. We haven't burned all our bridges with the government."

"Not yet," said Malachi. "But why do you want to waste what little capital we have with the van Renssaeler administration on this? There are Stormwings boosting tons of supplies to the Moon every day now. A few delays—"

"A few delays doesn't begin to describe the situation," Theodorus said sharply. "I thought the problems Oliver Taylor identified three years ago were temporary when I noticed them myself earlier, that's why I didn't say anything. But we have a systemic array of difficulties we must overcome if we're going to have the bases in place in time."

Mathilde had not said anything up to this point. She didn't really know why she was in the meeting. She didn't really know why she felt a slight frisson of surprise when Theodorus admitted he'd been covering up the delays Oliver had exposed in his memo from the Moon back in '13. A cover-up, after all, was just Theodorus's style.

She tabbed over to the dossier the others were all studying. It was labeled **TESSERACT**, which she supposed was this Steunenberg woman's ace name. She ran her eyes over the lines of data, paying scant attention. She paused briefly when she saw that the woman, the international criminal, the potential hire, was from Coeur d'Alene, Idaho. She and Oliver had vacationed there once, years before. She remembered all those lakes. She remembered seeing an osprey strike a fish from the water. She set the tablet down.

"What can she do *for us?*" Mathilde interrupted.

Theodorus set his tablet down. "It's all in there. If you'll just review the analysis in the appendix describing her power suite—"

"You said an order of magnitude," Mathilde interrupted again. "Were you being literal?"

Theodorus worked his gray-green lips back and forth. "Quite," he said.

"Then never mind," said Mathilde. "I know what she can do for us."

"Then please," said Malachi, "do share."

Mathilde stood up and headed for the conference room door. "She can save us," she said over her shoulder.

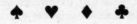

Dreamers of the Day

by Melinda M. Snodgrass

"DAMN IT! I LOOK like a fucking ass!"

My wife of nearly twenty years said, "No, Bradley dear. You have the body of a horse, so ass is not a correct comparison."

I abandoned my attempts to straighten the bow tie and carefully turned to look at Clara. Even with the furniture in the hotel room pushed to the side I still managed to brush an end table with my big horse ass. My tail whipped in agitation and swept a lamp onto the floor.

Fortunately, the Mayflower Hotel had deep carpet. "Clara, I love you, but god damn you are the most pedantic person I know."

"I am not," she said, offended.

Our eldest son (by two minutes) put an arm around his mother's waist and kissed her cheek. "Yeah, Mom, you kinda are," Bryce said.

"In fact you could be the poster child for Asperger's syndrome," Brook, his younger twin brother, added, kissing her other cheek.

"You are both awful," my princess, Caitlyn, declared, shoving both her brothers aside so she could lean against her mother's side.

I smiled fondly at my sixteen-year-old daughter. Caitlyn had inherited my fair hair, though mine was more silver than gold now. The boys took after Clara—tall, dark, and not at all mysterious. In personality they were a lot like me—gregarious, cheerful, popular at school. They were eighteen, in their first year at Harvard, and neither of them was following in Clara's or my footsteps. In fact, I had no Earthly idea what path they were following, but I was willing to give them time to find a direction. Their lack of focus made Clara crazy, but so far she was managing to hide her dismay.

I had known from the first moment I saw *Doogie Howser* that I wanted to be a doctor. My dad, who was still an active Hollywood director, had been grateful I hadn't wanted the film industry; he made it easy for me to get an education, though he had been a bit disappointed when I went for general practice with a focus on joker physiology rather than a more sexy specialty.

Clara was primarily a researcher. The fact her research had almost resulted in my death and the death of every other wild card in the world was something of which we never spoke. Clara had spent twenty-five years trying to atone for what she viewed as her unforgivable sin. I let her; it had been a terrible sin.

That was one of the reasons we hadn't attended her cousin Pauline van Rensaeler's first inauguration back in 2013. Clara's father, Brandon, hadn't attended that one, either; he lived in exile in a country carefully selected because it didn't have an extradition treaty with the United States. It didn't matter. Being around any of her family gave Clara hives, which led to ugly marital spats, so I had let it drop.

But I wasn't going to back down this time, and I had the support of our kids. They had pointed out to their mother that they were unlikely to ever get to attend a presidential inauguration ever again. She was denying them this incredible experience, and hadn't she already gotten her vengeance on her father by marrying a disgusting joker? That had pulled a murmur of protest from me, since I was the disgusting joker to whom they were referring (and truthfully my palomino pony body seemed to be holding up better than my human torso, which was showing a distressing tendency to develop a paunch).

The upshot was that Clara had reluctantly agreed, which was how we now found ourselves in a suite at the Mayflower getting ready to attend an inaugural ball being held in the main hall of the Smithsonian National Air and Space Museum.

Clara set her daughter gently aside. "All right, dear. I know I'm humor impaired. Let me fix that." She tied my bow tie. "Now we'd best go or we'll be late."

As we emerged from the elevator into the lobby we got more than a few looks. Two handsome young men in tuxedos, and my girls looking beautiful in their evening gowns. Caitlyn wore a gauzy lemon-yellow confection—I was sure she was going to freeze in the January weather—and Clara wore a deep emerald gown that brought out her striking green eyes. *And then there's me,* I thought as I gave the gawkers a little wave, *the joker turd in the punch bowl.* I saw a few cell phone cameras being unlimbered and gave them the jaunty grin I'd perfected back when I had been earning money as an extra in Hollywood.

The bellman held the door and we emerged onto the sidewalk. The cold air was like a slap and I felt a few snowflakes hit my cheeks. Their touch set my skin to quivering. The horse part of my body was incredibly sensitive, which made pain worse and sex all the better.

I had wanted to drive my modified van to the site of the ball, but Clara had put her foot down. We would get a limo, one with enough space between the seats to accommodate all four hundred pounds of me. The driver, looking like an undertaker in his cheap black suit, was holding open the back door and was looking dubious. "Don't worry. I'm housebroken," I said, stuffing a C-note in the guy's breast pocket.

"Are you guys going to dance?" Brook asked.

"It is a ball," Caitlyn said with a sniff.

"And I'll have you know that your mom and I have been known to get down," I said.

"Oh, that's going to have the Republicans' eyes popping," Bryce said, his voice catching on a laugh.

"Now, Bryce, Aunt Pauline belongs to the Liberty Party," Clara said.

"As in Republican with twice the crazy," Brook said.

♠

The glass, concrete, and steel didn't do much to absorb the noise of hundreds of people yammering, or the footfalls on the hard floor as they pretended they knew how to ballroom dance. Like most of the van Renssaelers, Pauline was uptight, conservative . . . in short, stuffy . . . so it was a truncated version of the Boston Pops Orchestra providing the music. My kids were appropriately disgusted; they had been hoping for one of the hot new rockabilly bands. I was relieved that their hearing would be preserved for a few more years.

I drained my champagne and was immediately sorry. Apparently "Renewing America" didn't extend to supporting good vineyards. I'd had better champagne at an agency party, and those guys are cheap. Still, that didn't keep me from grabbing another glass from a passing waiter.

The scent of clashing perfumes and the food on the long buffet tables mingled with a faint undertone of male sweat made both of my stomachs a bit queasy. I decided to wait to eat until we got back to the Mayflower to order room service rather than face Swedish meatballs, the ubiquitous veggie platter, chilled salmon to make it seem classy, and various kinds of cheese. Judging from the quality of the champagne, it had all likely been bought at Costco.

Long silken banners screened with pictures of beautiful American landscapes and overlaid with Pauline's campaign slogan—"Renewing America"—hung from the exposed steel girders and brushed the sides of the airplanes and missiles on display. I was using one for cover since I appeared to be the only joker in the joint.

Not that there weren't other wild cards . . . of the ace variety. Mistral was out of her signature bodysuit and wearing a long gown. Cameras were trained on her. Apparently she'd learned from her late father how to be a publicity hound. The Reverend Thaddeus Wintergreen was present, in his massive powered wheelchair. In addition to being a preacher of some fundie Protestant flavor, he had also been a contestant on *American Hero* and a fringe presidential candidate. It looked like he'd thrown in his lot with the Liberty Party. At least he wasn't rolling up in a ball and demonstrating his ace power.

The boys weren't wrong about the Republicans. The attorney general, a former senator from Texas, was oiling his way around the room with that thin pasted-on smile and calculating eyes that had made him (along with his obnoxious personality) the most hated man in the world's most deliberative body. When he spotted me, the smile slipped into an expression of disgust. I gave him a broad smile and held up my glass in a salute. Cruz hurried to the other side of the room.

I scanned the room for Tribe Finn. The boys had already snagged partners, pretty girls in expensive evening gowns, and were dancing. Caitlyn, looking like a nodding daisy, stood in the middle of a circle of admiring young men. I fought off the urge to rush over and make protective daddy noises. *Sixteen. She's sixteen. Not a little girl. Don't embarrass her. The fact that she has a joker for a dad is mortification enough.*

I searched for Clara so she could reinforce my good intentions, but saw her disappearing toward the restroom. That suddenly seemed like a good idea. I finished off the glass and trotted off toward the johns. I really, really hoped there were urinals; stalls are not my friend. I found myself chuckling at my own joke and decided maybe I should slow down on the bubbly. Being the only joker in a room full of rich, predominantly white people had certainly raised my anxiety level. Not so much for me, but for the sake of my kids. They had grown up in Jokertown with occasional visits to that liberal bastion, Hollywood. I didn't want them to hear the crap. With luck, though, this crowd was too well bred to indulge in slurs. And I did have the white, privileged male thing going for me . . . along with my horse's ass.

I pushed into the bathroom. There were a couple of older men at the sinks washing their hands. They gave me a dubious look and hurried to the towel dispensers. As they started to rush out I called, "Don't worry. It's not catching."

There was a long urinal against one wall. I got myself lined up and carefully raised myself so my front hooves were braced against the wall. I struggled to relax and allow my dick to drop but it was hard when I knew that at any moment a nat could walk in and react. It finally dropped and with a groan I released a stream of hot pee.

And right on cue a nat walked in. He took up a position next to me, unzipped, and pulled himself free. When he glanced over at me and couldn't keep his eyes from diving down to my exposed penis, I smiled and said, "Really, don't compare. You'll just feel inadequate."

He surprised me by laughing. "Yes, that is pretty impressive."

I bounced a bit to shake off the final drops, sheathed my penis, then dropped back to the floor and turned to face the man. He was dressed in the expected tux, but I noted the physique beneath the material. The man clearly worked out—a lot—and he held himself like a soldier.

"If this is a proposition, thanks for the compliment but I'm not into boys." I maneuvered around and headed to the sinks.

"You're welcome, and neither am I. I work for General Jack Campbell. He'd like to talk with you tomorrow at nine a.m. West Wing of the White House. Use the Seventeenth Street entrance. A pass will be waiting at the gate."

It took me a second to place the name. Once I did, I blinked a couple of times. "The national security adviser wants to talk to . . . me?"

"Yeah."

"Why?"

"That's above my pay grade. I'm just the messenger. Enjoy the ball."

"Fat chance now," I muttered at the man's departing back.

I returned to the main hall just as the crowd began applauding and cheering as President Pauline van Renssaeler made her entrance, escorted by her longtime business partner turned campaign manager, Steve Wilson. Secret Service agents fanned out, cold eyes flicking across the well-dressed attendees.

She had aces in her security detail as well. I knew one of them. Lady Black and I had crossed paths a few times when she was just an agent. She was now the director of SCARE. She was accompanied by two other aces. Alan Spencer was another *American Hero* alum with rather mediocre cold powers; the show's producers had tried to bolster his badassery by dubbing him Colonel Centigrade. I didn't know the woman flanking him, but I assumed she was also an ace.

Pauline moved through the crowd shaking hands with the men and exchanging hugs and air kisses with the women. When the president reached Clara she gave her a real hug and an actual kiss on the cheek. I started to join them only to find myself blocked by one of the nat agents.

I pointed first at one woman then at the other. "My wife. My cousin. By marriage. May I pass? Not that passing is ever possible for me, but you catch my drift." The guy's stony expression didn't change at my attempt at humor. Nor did he move. I felt the blood rising up my neck and into my face. "Look, pal, I know you've got a job to do, but I'm going to lose my temper pretty damn soon."

Fortunately, Lady Black stepped in before things could escalate. She touched the agent on the elbow with one gloved hand. "Relax."

"He's a joker," the man said.

"No shit," I said at the same time that Lady Black said, "I know him. It's fine."

The agent reluctantly stepped aside, and I joined Clara and Pauline. "Bradley!" the president said with evident pleasure. I couldn't help it; I gave the agent a *see, I told you so, asshole* look. Pauline pressed one powdered cheek against mine, and I noted that her hair contained more gray than when we'd seen her on a campaign stop in New York City back in the summer of 2016. But she still had all the van Renssaeler grace and elegance, the noblesse oblige that typified old money. I might be the son of an enormously successful and wealthy Hollywood director, but I always feel a little grubby and very nouveau riche in the presence of Clara's patrician family.

"Your children are here?" the president asked.

"Yes," Clara said.

"I'll get them," I added. I pulled out my cell phone and started texting. "Easiest way to summon The Young," I explained at Pauline's quizzical expression. "Sometimes I have entire conversations with my children via text when we're all sitting together in the living room."

Within minutes the twins and Caitlyn arrived. I stepped back and enjoyed watching my kids interact with the most powerful woman in the world. I was especially pleased to see that they were neither awkward nor overawed. Clara came to my side. I slipped an arm around her waist and whispered, "We did good."

"Yes, we taught them to be respectful and polite," she said.

"But to know their own worth and never take anything at face value," I added.

Truthfully, I had no idea how my sons or my wife had voted. The presence of Duncan Towers on Pauline's Liberty ticket had made it an easy choice for me. I'd lived in New York City for decades and I knew Towers for the blustering buffoon he was, so it had been a no-brainer to support the Democrat in the three-way race for president. I just prayed that by the end of Pauline's second term, the fever that had gripped the country and brought a rather kooky third party to power would break.

There were four minutes of inconsequential chatter before the chief of staff gently touched Pauline's elbow and said respectfully, "Madam President, I just spotted the Ragsdales. . . ."

Pauline gave us her patented politician smile. "Do excuse me. It's sad when family takes second place to donors, but such are the waters in which we swim." More kisses were exchanged, and she moved away with the perfect smile perfectly in place.

"Well, that was nice of her," Clara remarked.

"Yeah," I said. The interlude had momentarily displaced my bafflement over why the national security adviser wanted to talk with a joker doctor from Manhattan.

Caitlyn spoke up. "May I go? There's a boy who asked me to dance."

"Okay," I said. I then called after her, "But he better not be a Republican or a Libbie." My voice carried more than I expected and a few foul looks were sent my way, along with an exasperated one from my wife. "Just ignore your father, dear," Clara called as Caitlyn gave me the patented teenage eye roll.

"In this crowd it's probably a lead-pipe cinch this guy will be either one or both," Brook said.

"Or she could hit the trifecta," Bryce added. "Republican, Liberty Party, and Libertarian."

"That would be a whole basket of crazy," Brook added.

"Hush, all of you," Clara said. "You're going to get us tossed out."

"We should be so lucky," I grunted. The evening had soured for me after the bathroom exchange. The boys laughed and went off in search of girls, drinks, food, or all three.

"What is wrong with you?" Clara asked in an undertone. "You're the one who pushed me to attend."

"Something weird happened. I'll tell you back at the hotel."

"I hate weird. Weird is never good," Clara said.

"Ain't that the truth."

It was a good thing the Mayflower was within walking distance of the White House. Otherwise, unless I hired another limo, I would have had no way to get there without my customized van. As I trotted up the driveway to the guardhouse, I couldn't help feeling a surge of awe and excitement. I'd never been to the White House. I'd attended the Kennedy Center Honors a few years ago when Dad had been honored, but this was quantitatively different. A few years back when JFK, Jr., was president we had thought my dad might get the Presidential Medal of Freedom, but it hadn't happened, and given the recent direction of the country I doubted it was going to happen anytime soon.

I dredged up some history from a long-ago class and recalled that John Adams had been the first president to live in the White House. Since then it had seen its share of statesmen and scoundrels, but it was still the house where Lincoln had crafted the Emancipation Proclamation, FDR had saved the country from the Depression and the world from fascism, and the first Kennedy had kept the world from dying in nuclear fire.

As I pulled out my driver's license to present to the guard I found myself thinking about John Adams's prayer, written in a letter to his wife and now engraved on a mantel in the State Dining Room—"I pray Heaven to bestow the best of Blessings on this House and all that shall hereafter Inhabit it. May none but honest and wise Men ever rule under this roof." I wondered how old Adams would have handled the fact that it was now a woman who ruled. I had a feeling Abigail would have approved.

It seemed to be a requirement that all security guards look surly and the two in the guardhouse were no exception. I felt like I was coming in for extra scrutiny when the wait time stretched into minutes as the guards looked at my license with suspicion, checked the logbook, checked the license again, back to the logbook, stepped aside to mutter to each other. One of them picked up the phone while the other one returned to the counter.

I gestured down the length of my horse body. "Honest, there isn't another guy hiding in back." I didn't even get a smile. If anything, my sally made the guard look even more grim and sour.

The phone talker hung up and returned to his partner. "It's okay. He is actually going to see the general."

"Okay. Go on in. You'll be met," the other guard said.

They handed me a pass and I made my way up to the building. They must have called ahead because the door was already open. The guy from the john was waiting. He led me down several halls. We were passed by intense young people in suits and skirts hustling by, many of them clutching folders. They were certainly focused. I only got a couple of startled looks. It seemed odd to me that only one day after the inauguration everything was up and running. Then I realized that was probably a dumb reaction. This was Pauline's second term. Of course they'd know the way to the bathrooms and how to turn on the lights.

We ended our trek at a conference room where General Campbell was waiting. There were a couple of aides with him. Body Builder settled in a chair next to his boss. Apparently, he was more than mere muscle.

The general stood and held out his hand. "Thank you for coming, Doctor."

"Well, you don't normally turn down an invitation to see the head of National Security at the White House. Of course, I can't help but wonder why."

Out of force of habit Campbell gestured toward a chair. He stopped partway through the gesture and gave me an embarrassed look. "I'm not exactly sure how to make you feel welcome."

"A cup of coffee would go a long way. I was up late last night."

"So were we all, but probably not for the same reasons."

A call was made and a few minutes later a young aide rushed in with a china cup with the seal of the White House on it. I wondered if I could steal it. The general waited for me to take a couple of sips before speaking. "You're probably wondering why I asked you here."

"That would be an understatement. If it had been the surgeon general I would have had some idea, but aren't you like the top spy or something?"

Campbell had a chilly smile. "Not exactly. Though I do talk to a lot of spies. Then I synthesize and inform the president of possible threats against the nation."

"And I fit into this . . . how?"

He deflected instead, asking, "What do you know about Theodorus Witherspoon?" Campbell reacted to my darkling expression. "I take it you aren't a fan."

"He stole away my chief of security," I burst out. "Troll . . . Howard Mueller . . . had worked at the clinic for decades, and suddenly he tells me he's leaving to go work for some billionaire down in South Carolina? Yeah, fuck Howard and fuck Witherspoon, too."

Campbell seemed taken aback. He rolled his chair back from the desk as if to escape my ire. "That might be a problem. I was hoping I could send you to talk with Witherspoon. Joker to joker."

A trickle of ice ran down my human spine. When nats start talking about joker-to-joker conversations, we hear what Black people hear when whites start telling them they need to talk to their communities. They are about to point out to us how we are failing our people and giving nats or white people the sads. "About what?" I asked.

"I need you to get him to tell you what the fuck he's doing out in the asteroid belt."

"Duh fuck?" I asked intelligently.

"Beginning in 2008 and continuing for a number of years thereafter, Witherspoon has been sending ships to the asteroid belt."

"Uh . . . why is he doing that?"

"Well, that's the question. He told us at the time it was for research." The general did air quotes. I didn't kill him for it. "Our long-range scanners indicate that there are presently a shitload of asteroids heading toward the inner solar system, if you will pardon my French. We want to know where they're headed and why. That's where you come in."

"If Witherspoon is on the Moon you can count me right out." Most people don't know that I got teleported to an alien planet a while back and had to spend two fucking years getting back home to Earth. I'd done enough space travel for ten lifetimes.

"He's at his family estate. So will you speak with him?"

"And ask him what . . . exactly?"

"We want access to his flight control so we can be sure none of these bastards hits the Earth. That would be a really fucking bad day."

"Like death-of-the-dinosaurs bad day?"

"Yes."

Not the answer I had wanted. "How do I get the appointment?"

"We'll reach out and get something set up."

Body Builder stood up, indicating the meeting was over. I held up the cup and asked Campbell, "May I?"

He smiled, relieving some of the deep lines in his face. "Wouldn't you rather have a clean one?"

A cup was handed over and we left. As we passed a busy outer office, I spotted Pauline walking toward us. She was murmuring to an intense-looking young woman taking notes on her iPad. Secret Service agents walked behind them. She spotted me and smiled.

"Just one moment, Julie," she said to the younger woman. She came over and gave me a quick hug. "Thank you so much for doing this."

"Wow, news travels fast in this place," I said.

"It has to, given the state of the world. I'd like you and the family to come over to the residence later for tea. Would you like to?"

"Uh, yeah."

"My staff will be in touch." She started to walk away, then turned back. "And thank you again for doing this. I can't think of anyone better to handle it."

I sure as hell can, I thought, but what I said was, "I'll do my best, Madam President."

Clara and I continued to be overawed. My kids, not so much. The boys were busy laying waste to the finger sandwiches, cookies, and petit fours the White House chef had supplied. Caitlyn was nibbling daintily on a cucumber sandwich and gazing at her brothers with the air of a time-traveling anthropologist studying Neanderthals.

The family quarters were surprisingly homey and comfortable, but clearly a space inhabited by a single woman. Pauline had never married or had children. All of her focus had been directed into her career. By doing so she had achieved the pinnacle of power for an American politician. She had a strong resemblance to her grandmother, Blythe van Renssaeler, whose portrait hung in the clinic that bore her name; she was pretty, blonde, and (for a president) relatively young at only forty-nine. She had also been blessed by the Charisma Fairy, which had made her a formidable television journalist. Alas, the fairy had overlooked my wife, but as I gazed at Clara's profile I knew I would take brains and passion over charm any day.

Clara was, however, proving that she wasn't going to curb her tongue just because her cousin was president. "I can't believe you put that dolt on the ticket. You beat him for the Liberty nomination in 2012. Why give him anything this time around?"

"I understand your dismay, but Duncan was able to amass a very large following over the past four years. If I hadn't brought him into the tent—"

"He'd burn down the whole circus . . . or the crazies who support him would," I offered. "Pauline, I know our politics don't align. You're pretty conservative and I'm a flaming Hollywood liberal, but you really tried to weed the truly crazy and offensive out of your party. By bringing in Towers as your running mate you just undid all of that good work."

"If I hadn't, he would have challenged me and probably taken the nomination."

Clara gave a sniff of disdain. "Then Rodham would have beaten him."

"I don't agree. Towers is a buffoon, but anger is a powerful motivator and his supporters have that in spades. Against that, Gramma in a pantsuit wouldn't have had a chance."

Clara began to bristle. I hurried into speech. "Let's not relitigate the entire election, please?" The two women exchanged one final familial glare, then nodded. "Let's just all agree that Towers is a towering fool, but he's also a snake. You should watch your back, Pauline."

"Well, I'm term limited out after this so I'm not worried."

"Just make sure you don't help him follow you into the White House," Clara warned.

After that I went searching for safer topics . . . which wasn't easy in a family with as many secrets and lies as the van Renssaelers. Thank God we had Hollywood to fall back on.

It didn't happen as quickly as I expected. The family returned to New York, the boys headed back to Harvard, Caitlyn went out on way too many dates, and I had way too many patients. I pretty much forgot about the odd request until mid-February, when I got a call from a number I didn't recognize. I answered with my surly voice, assuming it was some kind of telemarketer. Instead I heard a woman's voice asking, "Doctor Bradley Finn?"

"Speaking. What's this is regard to?"

"This is Mathilde Schwartz; I work for Theodorus Witherspoon. The White House contacted us. We understand you wish to meet with Mr. Witherspoon?"

"Uh, yeah."

"Regarding what?"

"I think it better that I discuss that with Mr. Witherspoon directly."

"Then you don't get your meeting."

"Then Mr. Witherspoon doesn't get to hear about my trip back from Takis aboard three different alien spacecraft." I'd done my homework on the big snail since my conversation with Campbell and knew he was space crazy.

"I don't believe you."

"Ask Jay Ackroyd. He sent me to fucking Takis. Ask my wife who had to wait two years for me to get back so we could get married."

"You're serious."

"As the grave."

"I'll get back to you."

She did, in about ten minutes. "Mr. Witherspoon would like to meet you. We'll send a Stormwing for you."

Because that doesn't sound ominous at all. I debated about whether I was giving up too much of my negotiating position by agreeing too quickly. Maybe I should insist on government transport? But I was curious about these spaceships that were threatening to put Boeing and Airbus out of business. "Okay. Where do I grab the ride?"

"Tomlin. The plane will be at Tomlin in an hour."

"I won't. I've got rounds. Give me three."

She hung up. I took that as a yes.

I was standing in the fuselage of the aircraft. It was obvious that seats had been hurriedly unbolted and removed and other accommodations had been made. The fold-down stairs had been covered by a ramp so I didn't have to contend with small steps and squeezing my bulk between handrails. The captain had welcomed me, shaken my hand, and then vanished into the cockpit with his copilot and shut the door.

Left to my own devices I pulled a can of Coke out of the small fridge up near the cockpit and found a drawer filled with bags of chips, nuts, and granola bars. I went for the nacho-flavored Doritos. As I noshed through the orange-colored chips I acknowledged that I was nervous as hell.

The captain's voice came over the intercom telling me to hang on. I grabbed the back of the only remaining chair as the Stormwing catapulted into the air.

The ride was pretty much go straight up, brush the edges of the atmosphere, and dive straight down. In fact I got a brief glimpse of that yawning icy darkness beyond the warm cocoon of atmosphere. I pulled my gaze away and back to the curvature of our beautiful blue marble. There was a storm brewing over Virginia. Which sounded like the start of a particularly ominous country western song.

We landed in an open meadow. In the distance I could see security fencing and beyond it a large Southern plantation. I wondered if the slave quarters were still around, then decided taking that attitude might not be helpful to my assigned task. The ramp was set up and I descended to find a nine-foot-tall joker with warty gray-green skin and large yellow teeth waiting for me. "Hey, Doc," he said, and smiled.

I didn't. "If you're expecting a joyful reunion, Howard, don't. You walked out on us."

He looked hurt, then angry. Considering that even at his age he was one of the strongest men on the planet, it probably wasn't the smartest thing I'd ever done. He shook his head. "You do good work at the clinic, Doc, but Theodorus needs me more than you did. Not to mention, he tripled my salary. The last time I got a raise was when Tach was still in charge. Give Theodorus a—"

There was a loud throat-clearing from an attractive mixed-race man of middle years. "It would be better to let Mr. Witherspoon make his own pitch, Howard," the man said.

Troll throttled whatever he was going to say. "Yes, sir, Mr. Bell."

The man held out his hand. I shook it. "Clifford Bell, head of security for Witherspoon Holdings. I trust your ride was smooth?"

"It was short," I said.

He laughed, and gestured toward an enormous greenhouse that squatted like a translucent mushroom on the verdant grass. He led off and I started to follow.

"Catch you after, Doc?" Troll called.

"I don't think so." I was a little surprised at the intensity of my churning anger, but I couldn't shake it. Troll had been a fixture in Jokertown for decades. Volunteering at career days at the local high school, taking part in the food and gift drive led by the Church of Jesus Christ, Joker every holiday season.

"Why you busting my balls, Doctor?"

I stormed back to him. My tail was stiffly upright with outrage. "You were a role model to younger jokers. And you abandoned our people to live in this *Gone with the Wind* fantasy at the beck and call of some rich fuck who sure as hell hasn't been shoveling any of his wealth toward Jokertown . . . any of the jokertowns. Yeah, so forgive me if I'm not all hail-fellow-well-met, Howard. I think we're done."

I reared and whirled. "You'll understand after you talk to Theodorus. You'll see," Troll called.

Since it was February and colder than a witch's tit up in New York, the balmy South Carolina air had me sweating in my sweater and suit jacket. I pulled off the jacket and tossed it over my equine back. I felt sweat forming on my palomino coat. While I might have the body of a horse, I still smell like a sweaty human when I get hot. Clara thinks if I'd go vegan that might change. I am not going to go vegan.

Bell slid me a sideways glance. "I'm surprised you'd be here as an emissary for the government. Particularly this government."

I got his drift even without him saying it. "The president is my wife's cousin. I might be the only joker they know."

We had reached the door of the giant greenhouse. Bell paused with his hand on the door handle. "But you were still willing."

"I'd also like to know just what the hell your boss is up to." I stepped inside.

I had been in the jungles of Vietnam. This was just like the damn jungles of Vietnam. Too hot, too humid, and stinking as various exotic plants, the wet loam underfoot, manure, and chemical fertilizer battled for primacy. I slapped aside the frond of a stunted palm that looked like a dinosaur should be sheltering beneath it.

It wasn't that I had anything against nature. I like nature just fine. I just didn't like nature that looked like it wanted to eat me. I stared at a trailing vine. *Or throttle me,* I added.

I heard music playing softly up ahead. Something classical. I followed the sound. You couldn't miss Theodorus. He was a giant snail-centaur. He was carefully potting a flowering plant. An iPod rested on a Bose speaker setup and was sheltered in a clear box.

There was a woman with him, a joker with no discernible neck and bright red skin. When she turned to face me I saw that her eyes were also a brilliant red. She was wearing an elegant power-woman suit and I could tell from the cut it didn't come off some rack in Dillard's. More likely Saks or Harrods or a runway in France. I know clothes. Since Dad was a famous Hollywood director I'd been on more than a few red carpets in my time.

The woman held out her hand. "Doctor Finn, I'm Mathilde Schwartz. And this is Theodorus."

The man merely nodded. On the other hand, he was wearing gardening gloves, which were covered with dirt. "You're bigger than when Tachyon examined you," I said.

"You know about that?"

"He was a doctor. He kept records."

Theodorus looked over at Mathilde. "See to it we get those records."

"You really are playing the reclusive billionaire thing, aren't you? And if you try to get those records I will sue you. I'll happily give you copies, but Tachyon's records are there to help us try to craft a cure for this hell-born disease." Theodorus was frowning at me. In for a penny, in for a pound. "Oh, and might I suggest a different playlist? In every movie it's always the bad guy who listens to classical music. Maybe Joker Plague or Lady Gaga. Or go country. That'll put everybody off-balance. . . . I'm talking a lot, aren't I?"

"Yes, you are." Theodorus sounded amused.

Mathilde broke in. She didn't look amused. "You asked for this meeting. So what do you want?"

"To find out what you're planning to do with these objects you're bringing in from the asteroid belt. The administration and the National Science Foundation are all a little nervous. You know, the dinos and all."

Theodorus snorted. "They have nothing to fear."

"So you say. I've seen a lot of disaster movies. What are you planning to do with these things?"

"Crash them into the Moon."

"What have you got against the Moon?"

He laughed. "Nothing. I have great plans for the place. But we should continue this discussion over dinner. I trust you didn't lie about your interstellar experiences."

"You didn't check out the claims? Sort of falling down on the reclusive billionaire thing."

"Ackroyd refused to talk to us," Mathilde said with a frown.

"And we were reluctant to approach your wife," Theodorus added. "A spouse would probably lie."

"If you knew anything about my wife you would know that would not be the case," I muttered.

Theodorus stripped off his gloves and began the laborious process of getting turned around. I felt pity for him. I knew how hard it was to manage my own bulk and my best guess was that this man was well over two thousand pounds and probably pushing three.

We left the greenhouse and crossed the manicured lawn toward the mansion. I studied the slime that was left by his body and wondered if he'd let me take a sample for Clara. My wife was brilliant, and since we no longer had Tachyon she offered the best hope for finding that elusive cure.

The house was what I expected, filled with expensive antiques, redolent with the smell of beeswax furniture polish and flowers. The doorways had been widened to accommodate Theodorus's massive form and there were no carpets on the polished wood floors. The dining room was arranged so Theodorus could just slide in to the head of the table and then back straight out. As expected, the table was huge—it could easily have seated twenty, which meant the three of us felt rather lonely huddled near one end. In the center was an enormous chased-silver epergne embossed with rearing horses and nymphs holding sheaves of wheat.

The joker serving staff was quiet, efficient, and discreet. They withdrew the minute the soup course had been removed and we had our mains. The crown roast of pork with mashed potatoes and cherry sauce was delicious, and the wine sure as hell wasn't Two-Buck Chuck from Trader Joe's.

I tried several times to bring up the reason for my visit, but Mathilde always smoothly directed the conversation into a discussion of my father's latest Academy Award–winning film or my mother's work with refugee relief. Throughout it all Theodorus said little. There was something almost alien in his silence and demeanor.

After dessert—an incredible bananas Foster—we were offered port, cheese, and nuts. Only then did Theodorus turn to the issue that had brought me there. "So, down to business," the big joker said.

"'Bout time," I muttered.

He studied me as if I were a curious new form of leaf mold on one of his plants. "Odd, I hadn't expected you to be . . ."

"What?" I asked.

". . . rude. Yes, that's the right word." It was said without heat and in a very clinical tone. I should have been offended, but I was trying to figure out how I'd diagnose him.

Mathilde leaned across the table. "But first you have to pay the piper."

"You promised me tales of your travels among the stars," Theodorus said.

I closed my eyes briefly and looked back across the years. "My wife's father was determined to separate me from his daughter. He made a deal with Jay Ackroyd . . . Jay can teleport people, and there's apparently no limit on his range. He had been to Takis, so when he honored the deal to send me away he really sent me away. Popped me to Takis, right into the fucking Ilkazam throne room. Thank God Tachyon was there to vouch for me or I'd probably be a stuffed trophy on some Takisian psi lord's wall. Anyway, after a couple of days to get my bearings and to look over some of the research that Tach and his team were working on—"

"What kind of research?" Mathilde interrupted.

"What else? A cure for the wild card. Until that happens I don't think Tachyon will ever get over his guilt for being involved in its creation."

"He did try to prevent its release," Theodorus said. "And he was kind when my parents brought him down to examine me."

"Yeah, he worked hard to expiate his sin, but Tachy loved . . . loves to wallow. Anyway, after a few days, he put me on one of the living ships with a Takisian crew. They were supposed to bring me home. Instead the ship got damaged in an ion storm. While the ship was repairing itself we got waylaid by pirates."

"Space pirates?" Mathilde's voice was filled with disdain.

"Yeah, I know, it sounds stupid. If it helps deal with the silly, they call themselves the Gatherers, but they're really just pirates."

Under their fascinated gazes I went on to talk about that two-year-long journey home—the planets I'd visited, the aliens I had met. There were things I wasn't going to share with Theodorus or Mathilde . . . or with my wife.

"I kept trying to find a way to send a message to Tachyon. Do you have any idea how hard it is to figure out alien technology that is centuries ahead of ours? People act like it would be simple, but try handing a smartphone to some dude from the seventeenth century and see how well he would figure it out."

Mathilde was staring at me. Then Theodorus asked, "Why did you ever leave?" There was a glow in his eyes, the dreams of adventure by a man who was trapped in a cocoon of horrifying flesh.

"Because I loved Clara and I wanted to get back home to her. And I'm a doctor and I wanted to get back to my patients. And I'm not a criminal. I did things in order to survive, but I'm not proud of them."

"Did you ever kill anyone?" Theodorus asked.

The question snapped me back to a time I would rather forget. A time when a worldwide conspiracy had attempted to kill every wild card on Earth. I had used guns for the first time in my life. I had killed people. Granted, they had been people who wanted to kill me, but it was a hard memory still.

Long ago I had memorized the updated Hippocratic oath written by Louis

Lasagna back in the nineteen sixties. Five sentences stood out. *I will remember that there is art to medicine as well as science, and that warmth, sympathy, and understanding may outweigh the surgeon's knife or the chemist's drug. Most especially must I tread with care in matters of life and death. If it is given me to save a life, all thanks. But it may also be within my power to take a life; this awesome responsibility must be faced with great humbleness and awareness of my own frailty. Above all, I must not play at God.*

I shook myself free of the heat, smells, and screams of an airfield in Vietnam a long time ago. I stared at Theodorus. "Never mind. I think you answered the question," he said softly.

"So how did you get back?" Mathilde asked.

"The Gatherer ship I was on ran out of luck and went up against a Network ship. We think we've got this all figured out—the Takisians, the Swarm. We don't know shit. There are vast civilizations out there that, so far and thank God, haven't decided to come calling. The Network is a trading empire involving over a hundred alien species in a loose conglomeration. I can't tell you all the races, but I personally dealt with Aevre, Embe, Kondikki, Ly'bahr, and Rhindarians. I was with them only a few months and they agreed to drop me off back on Earth. I'm still not sure if I sold my left nut or my firstborn when I signed that contract, but so far nobody's come to collect." I gave a hollow laugh.

They were staring at me incredulously. "And you never told anyone about this?" Theodorus asked.

"Of course not. I didn't want to be viewed as a liar . . . or worse, be believed and get locked up in some federal facility to be debriefed. I just wanted to go home, marry Clara, and go back to work at the clinic."

"How did they manage to bring you back undetected?" Mathilde asked.

"I think they had some kind of cloaking device on their shuttle. Landed me out in the wilds of New Jersey and I hitched a ride back to Manhattan in the bed of a pickup truck."

"Extraordinary," Theodorus said. We sat in silence for a few moments. I took a long pull on my port. "So what do you know about my activities?" he asked.

"I know you invented these spaceplanes and that you have a research base on the Moon. I know you're as rich as Midas. I now know that you sent a fleet of ships out into the asteroid belt and now they are heading back and the administration wants to know why."

"What do you know about terraforming?" Mathilde asked.

"Not much."

"It's the process by which a celestial body is altered so it can support terrestrial life," Theodorus said. "And I intend to do that to the Moon."

"Okay," I said slowly. "And what's that got to do with crap coming in from the asteroid belt?"

"My ships have been gathering up ice comets. Once they reach the inner solar system they'll be crashed into the Moon—"

"I ask again, what have you got against the Moon?"

His lips stretched into a barely discernible smile at my feeble sally. "This will begin the terraforming process. Once we have water we can begin to build a viable colony."

"A colony?"

"Yes, but more than that. I'm building a home world for our people."

Now he finally showed an observable emotion. I stared at the man, seeing the messianic fire in his eyes, his exalted expression. . . . I shivered as an icy spider seemed to walk down my spine. "Humans," I said.

"No, jokers. Only jokers."

It was the answer I feared. I went to pick up my port, realized my hand was shaking, and set it down again. "Well, forgive me, but I don't see a difference."

"Then you're a fool, Doctor," Theodorus said.

"How so? I have a physical deformity due to a genetic mutation, but I'm still human."

"Rejected by the rest of humanity. We have been despised, rejected, assaulted, and murdered by nats. And every time we've tried to create a place where we can live in peace, those moral, normal humans have come in and killed us. The Rox, Jerusalem, Vietnam, Egypt."

The icy demeanor was back. This wasn't genteel Southern courtesy, this was something worse. I now had my diagnosis. Alexithymia seemed the most likely suspect with its marked dysfunction in emotional awareness. This was a man cut off from all normal human emotions.

"I've got a news flash for you, Theo. Your joker paradise will be subject to the same greed and lust and hate and violence that plague every other human society. Because we're human!"

"No. Once I've put us beyond their reach, beyond their hate, we'll build a new paradigm. I've vowed to do this and I will, and nothing will stop me. Not this administration, not the UN, not the Committee."

I canted my human torso back and clapped sarcastically. "All hail the great Joker Moses leading us to the promised land . . . on the fucking Moon!" I leaned in. "I don't care how much ice you dump on that barren rock, it's still going to be one-sixth gravity. Great for you, I'm sure you'd love to shed a few pounds, but lousy for most jokers." He opened his mouth to object, but I barreled on. "I don't know much about this process, but I'm pretty damn sure it's not going to happen overnight, so you've got us, or at least the people stupid enough to buy into this crazy plan, squatting in holes in the ground for years . . . decades . . . probably centuries." I realized I was shouting and I clamped my teeth together.

"Get out." The tone was low, dangerous.

"Gladly." I backed up, whirled, and went clattering out of the dining room.

Now that it was all over, I had that greasy nauseated feeling in the pit of the gut that you get when you realize you have royally fucked up. So much for me being the joker emissary and diplomat.

I made my way to the front door and got outside. The fresh air helped cool my cheeks. As I stood there trying to figure out how to go back in, apologize, and get this back on track, Mathilde came hurrying down the front steps. "That could have gone better," she said.

I opened my mouth to argue, then nodded. "Yeah." We stood in silence, listening to the wind through the trees. "You're a joker. Are you on board with this?"

"It's his dream. I believe in his dreams."

"Those who dream by night in the dusty recesses of their minds, wake in the day to

find that it was vanity: but the dreamers of the day are dangerous men." I was amazed I remembered the T. E. Lawrence quote but was glad I did. "Look, Ms. Schwartz, I hate to be a big buzzkill, but has he thought through any of this? Will there be adequate medical care? Jokers have a lot of medical issues. You planning on building a state-of-the-art medical center up there?"

"If need be, yes. And you could help with that. Who better?"

I ignored that. There was no way I was signing up for this mad scheme. "What about population replacement? You have to know how difficult it is for two wild cards to produce a viable child. Ninety percent of all births will be stillborn or die within moments of exiting the womb. Within a few decades his joker paradise is going to look like Japan times a thousand with old, infirm people trying to live in an unrelentingly hostile environment." Mathilde was starting to look queasy as the words poured out of me. "And do you actually think the governments of the world are going to sit passively by while a bunch of jokers take over the Moon? I'm here because they're worried that one of Theodorus's little snowballs will miss and hit the Earth . . . which by the way would—"

"—be impossible! We have the best engineers in the business. Every calculation has been checked and rechecked."

"They said the same thing about the *Titanic*," I countered. "Okay, for the sake of argument let's assume this comes off without a single hitch. That still doesn't answer the issue. Theodorus and maybe you as well have a really jaundiced view of nats. I get that. And I'm not saying there haven't been tensions and problems, but hanging a deadly threat in the sky over their heads is not going to help improve the relationship."

"We would never do that."

"Great. Maybe you wouldn't, or Theodorus . . . though empathy doesn't seem to be his strong suit." I waved my hands. "Whatever, the point is someday neither you nor he will be around. What if some monster comes to power—and don't tell me you're naive enough to think every joker is a saint—and decides maybe sunning himself or herself on a beach in Tahiti beats the Moon, so they decide to arrange for a little nuclear winter back on Earth. Wait a few years for the air to clear and come back to empty real estate. Assuming any of your Moon goons could endure Earth's gravity by then."

"What did you mean about empathy and Theodorus?"

"Maybe you've been around him so much that you don't notice, or maybe he's always been this way. Tachyon didn't make a note of it in his files, but his emotional reactions are . . . off."

"No, he wasn't always like this. He was excited, enthusiastic. Now he's just driven."

She turned away, but not before I read her expression. "You're in love with him," I said.

She whirled to face me, anger and tears fighting for primacy. "And you think that's crazy, impossible, right?"

I couldn't help it. I laughed. "Oh hell no. I fell in love with the woman who developed the Black Trump, a virus that would have killed us all, every wild card." Mathilde stared at me in shock. "Believe me, I get crazy. The point is, she changed. People can do that. The heart wants what the heart wants, Mathilde, no one should apologize for that."

"I can't ask him to give up his dream," she whispered.

"I'm not asking you to; just convince him to make the dream a little bigger. Let this be the first human foothold on another celestial body. With Theo's fortune and brilliance this could be the first step. We could have colonies on Mars, out in the asteroids, on Jupiter's moons. Nats and jokers and aces all standing ready when the bastards come back."

"The Takisians?"

"Any of them. All of them." I waved my arm wildly at the sky. "We can face them together united as the human race." I realized I had gripped her shoulder. I mumbled an apology and stepped back. I wasn't sure, but I thought there was a hint of moisture in her eyes.

"Wait. Don't leave yet. Let me talk to him." She whirled, her skirt a swirl of color in the garden lights, and went back into the house.

I paced for what seemed like hours, though when I checked my watch she had only been gone for forty-eight minutes when she beckoned to me from the front door. I returned to the dining room to find Theodorus frowning at nothing. He gripped a brandy snifter tightly in his hand. "Mathilde is sentimental," he said. "I'm not."

"I get that. Then if you don't want to use your heart, use that great brain. We humans are dangerous when we're in packs and when we're afraid. You're about to create two truculent packs and make one of them really afraid. A pack, by the way, that significantly outnumbers us and outguns us, since they've got armies and shit."

"We'll have the Moon," Theodorus countered.

"And that, right there, is my point. You can turn the Earth into a frozen hellhole and they can turn the Moon into a ball of radioactive glass. So why don't we not do that and instead stand together against the threats that we know are out there?"

"You have faith in the goodness of humanity," Theodorus said.

"No, but I do believe in the goodness of individual people. We can find a compromise, Theodorus. And just think how much it will piss off the crazies on both sides."

"So what is it you want?"

"Talk to the president. She's a decent person who actually does want to make the world a better place."

It hung in the balance as he sat deep in thought for many agonizing seconds. He finally lifted his head and looked at me. "Very well. But I have conditions. . . ."

"Who does he think he is to order the president of the United States to come to him?" Campbell was apparently in the mood to fulminate.

I was trying really hard not to be impressed . . . but it was the Oval Office. I could tell from the expressions on the faces of the men around Pauline that they weren't happy about having a joker standing on the carpet with the seal of the United States with his four hooves.

Vice President Towers and his chief of staff were on the far side of the room. Towers had a horror of germs. My presence in the room had him ready to grab the hand sanitizer and maybe a surgical mask.

I answered Campbell. "He's a giant snail-centaur who weighs three thousand pounds and leaves a trail of slime wherever he goes." I gave the assembled men a smile. "You should be glad it's just my hooves on this nice carpet." I lifted a hind foot and watched as the Secretary of Homeland Security shrank back. "Look, I even wore my booties." I waggled my hoof. "Oh, and you'd have to knock out half of the wall for him to even get into the room."

Pauline sat behind the Resolute desk, hands clasped in front of her. The eagle carved on the front of the desk seemed to be snubbing the one on the carpet. Pauline was frowning at Campbell.

"Logistics—" the Secret Service agent began.

I cut him off. "Oh, come on! How hard can this be? The president goes to campaign events and museum openings, baseball games and Christ knows what else all the time." I turned to Pauline. "You don't have to publicize that you're going to meet Witherspoon. There's got to be some Toyota factory or high school you can go visit. Then we arrange for the meeting at the Witherspoon estate."

"You shouldn't be jumping on the say-so from some joker," said Towers. "You set that precedent and you're going to pay bigly for that."

I gave Towers a sweet smile. "Gosh, I seem to recall how the Justice Department brought suit against you and you had to pay a ton of money for discriminating against jokers in your rental properties. So maybe you don't have the best instincts on this matter." I gave a gimlet stare at the people in the room who might have a clue. "Look, let's get real here. I've told you what Witherspoon's planning. Let's not kid ourselves that this is going to be widely accepted. I remember my dad telling me about all the worries about how maybe Takisians would set up on the Moon, or there would be Commies there, or Democrats." Okay, yeah, it was a feeble joke and it lay like a dead fish in the center of the room. I cleared my throat. "How do you think bigots are going to react to jokers controlling the Moon? Hell, I'm not all that sanguine about it and I am a joker."

I could almost hear my two hearts beating as I waited for the response. The quiet felt like a stretched piano wire. Finally, Pauline raised her eyes and looked at me. "Tell them I'll come." She turned to Campbell. "Find us an excuse."

"Yes, Madam President."

Towers's thick lips were pursed in that pout that was so well known to all of us who lived in New York City. "I still think it's a really bad idea. Really, really bad."

"I don't recall asking for your opinion," Pauline snapped. If looks could have killed, Pauline would have been six feet under.

She waved us all toward the door. As we shuffled out, I noticed Towers's chief of staff busily texting. I figured he was contacting some source in the conservative media so they could run a story about how President van Rensselaer favored jokers over hardworking white Americans.

Just before I made my escape Campbell caught me. He whispered, "The president wants you there. You brokered this deal."

I heaved a sigh. I just wanted to get home to Clara and Caitlyn and the clinic. "Okay."

I was waiting at a lonely gas station some six miles from the estate. It was one of those places that couldn't decide whether it wanted to be a fancy gas station in Charleston or a charming country roadside stop that harkened back to the days of Burma-Shave signs and signs out west that warned travelers this was the last chance for water for two hundred miles.

I had arrived early, having driven my van down from New York so I wasn't beholden to either Theodorus or Pauline. I emerged from the inside of the station with a MoonPie, and a silly key chain for Clara. She liked to collect stupid things when we traveled, and when I'm nervous I always get hungry.

My cell phone rang. I fished it out. It was Mathilde. "So are we on schedule?"

"Far as I know. They had to slip the prez out the back of the hotel and into a nondescript car. They should be here in the next five to ten minutes."

"Good. Theodorus is . . . anxious. If they're late—"

"They won't be late. Pauline knows how much is riding on this for all of us."

"I hope . . . it better be worth it."

"Nothing in life is ever certain, but this is pretty damn close." I hoped I sounded more soothing than I felt.

"Okay." She hung up. I returned my phone to my pocket and finished my MoonPie. It felt like my jaws had been gummed together so I headed back into the station and got myself a coffee out of the machine. It was as awful as I expected, but it did wash away the cloying taste of sugar.

A car pulled up, a big silver Cadillac. Even on a clandestine mission it seemed the president needed to roll in an American-built car. I'd really hoped they'd have the sense to pick a nondescript Toyota, but I suppose they needed room for her security. There was a Secret Service agent driving, another riding shotgun, and a woman agent in the back seat. She and Campbell had the president wedged between them. I thought it seemed disrespectful to make the president sit on the hump.

The agent in the passenger seat was Colonel Centigrade. I wished it had been somebody with a bit more of a kickass power, someone like Lady Black, but people seem to have this idea that the mere presence of an ace will deter people from bad acts. On the other hand, not having a heavy hitter was probably smart. Otherwise Theodorus and his security might think this was just a way to get close and kill him.

I trotted over. Campbell stepped out of the car. "Okay, what now?"

"You follow me. They're expecting us at a gate in the back of the property."

Pauline scooted across the back seat, rolled down the window, and leaned out. "They should be aware that the top cabinet officers and the vice president have been informed of my whereabouts and if I don't check back in within two—"

A buzz like an angry wasp passed by my cheek and whatever she had wanted to say remained unspoken. Instead a hole appeared in her left temple and blood and skull fragments blew out the right side and onto the neck of the agent in the driver's seat. An instant later I heard the distant report of a large-caliber weapon.

"You bastard! You treasonous bastard!" Campbell roared. He lunged toward me only to have his head explode in a cloud of blood, brain, and skull fragments.

The assassin was good. His shot had killed Campbell instantly, but he had misjudged on Pauline. The angle of entry and the fact there was an exit wound meant there was a chance she could survive. *If we get her to a trauma unit quickly.* How much of the woman herself would remain was another question, but there was a chance . . .

I grabbed her and pulled her out of the car and onto the stained concrete. The agents boiled out of the car, waving guns and screaming at me. I screamed back. "*I'm a doctor.* Let me work!"

They were shouting into their shoulder mics. In the distance I heard the wail of a siren as their backup rode to a rescue that might come too late.

"Get me a drill! Ax, big knife, something . . . anything," I bellowed. Captain Centigrade stared at me blankly. "I've got to open her skull to relieve the pressure. There's still a chance."

Centigrade bolted for the building. Pauline was feebly pawing at my arm. "It's all right. It's all right," I said.

"Daddy. Don't . . . don't let Mommy . . . give away . . . my . . . puppy. . . ."

A high-pitched screaming passed overhead, and the gas pumps exploded in flames as a wire-guided missile hit. Somebody really, really wanted to be sure the president was dead. The heat washed across my face and engulfed the Caddy. I fell back, hooves struggling to find purchase on the concrete while still dragging Pauline with me.

One of the agents was waving his gun at me. Screaming at me to get on my knees, hands behind my head. I wondered if he had any idea how hard that was going to be for me. I shouted back at him, "I'm a doctor! *I'm a doctor!*"

Colonel Centigrade was on fire. His screams could be heard above the roar of the flames. "Use your power! Use your power!" I screamed at him. He finally did, coating himself in ice and smothering the flames. His face was a mass of burned skin and blisters and his hair had burned away. He collapsed.

The guy who had been threatening me was down. He had been slammed face-first into the concrete by the concussion and was bleeding from a cut on his forehead. The woman agent who had been in the car was dead. No one was bringing me a drill now.

I dropped onto the knees of my front legs. Awkward, uncomfortable, but I could at least hold Pauline as the inevitable happened. She died in my arms. Then it was time to turn to the living. Lurching to my feet, I grabbed the unconscious agent and dragged him away from the burning pumps and car.

My mind was stuttering. *No, no, no! This can't be Theodorus. Can it? Who talked? This can't be happening! Pauline is dead! No, no, no.*

There was no more gunfire. The assassin had done his work and left us in the ruins. The backup vehicles arrived. Agents were shouting, calling for ambulances, fire trucks, setting up roadblocks, talking about keeping a press blackout. I felt my phone vibrating in my pocket. I pulled it out only to have it snatched away by an agent.

"Who were you calling?"

"Nobody. Someone was calling me."

The agent answered. I heard Mathilde's voice. "Where are you?"

"Who is this!" the agent demanded. I could tell from his expression that Mathilde had hung up.

Shock was starting to set in. My face was stinging from the burns I'd suffered and I was suddenly deathly cold. I wrapped my jacket tightly around my human torso while my teeth chattered.

Eventually the fires were out, and the charred bodies from the car were loaded into body bags. Colonel Centigrade and the unconscious Secret Service agent were loaded into ambulances. At that point a couple of agents came over to me. One grabbed my arms and pulled them roughly behind my back. I wasn't surprised to feel the bite of handcuffs. The other agent stared at me with hate in his eyes.

"Bradley Latour Finn, you are under arrest for the murder of Pauline van Renssaeler, President of the United States, National Security Advisor Jackson Campbell, and Agent Dalia Sanchez. You have the right . . ."

I didn't need to hear the rest. I was the person who had convinced the president to slip away to a private meeting with a reclusive joker billionaire. Now she was dead and nobody in the world was going to believe this wasn't some kind of joker conspiracy. That there was a conspiracy was clear. What random Secret Service guy at the scene of a heinous crime would have known my rather obscure middle name? We had been betrayed by someone high in the government.

"Oh Clara, I'm sorry," I whispered. "I think it's going to be a while before I get to come home again."

Fatal Error

By Victor Milán and John Jos. Miller

"*FINN?*" SAID CHARLIE HERRIMAN, pushing himself up off the polished hardwood floor of his family's condo in a gentrified part of Jokertown with the short, green flippers that served him as arms. "That's impossible. That's insane. They're cousins."

"And relatives never kill one another, of course," said the face on the screen of the open laptop beside him through a neat white beard. "Much less in-laws."

Charlie slapped the tips of his flippers together. His older daughter, Leonore, squealed with glee from atop his back and clapped her own small hands together. She was five. Charlie, a classic late bloomer, was thirty-six. His three-year-old son, David, watched keenly from where he sat splay-legged next to the laptop. "Does he want you to represent him?" Charlie asked the screen.

"He does. He just doesn't know it yet. His father has hired a high-priced LA law firm to defend him. A new dream team. But we're going to poke our noses around anyway. Medical care in Jokertown is bad enough without losing Finn. Besides, he owes me money."

Never play poker with a man named Doc, Charlie remembered. Pretorius and Finn were both doctors, but . . . He had been invited to sit in at the weekly poker game of the Black Velvet Society once himself. Once had been enough.

"Where are you, Unca Henk?" sang out Leonore.

"Sri Lanka. Get your daddy to help you spell that for Google before he runs straight out the door."

"I can't run straight out the door," Charlie protested. "I have the kids."

"Your cousin's always free to watch your kids," Dr. P. said. "She's obsessed with the fact she can't have any of her own."

"How the hel—on Earth do you know that?"

"You always say Unca Henk knows everything," Leonore said.

Pretorius laughed. "Not to my face. I wish he and Sibyl would both stop thinking that way. The last thing the JADL needs is more yes-jokers." Dr. Henrik Pretorius had spent much of his eighty-two years as a lawyer crusading for wild card rights, much of the time on behalf of the Joker Anti-Defamation League. He knew everybody. He was also richer than God.

"What are you doing in Sri Lanka, running a hypermarathon?"

"Just a regular marathon. Old age is catching up to me. The hypermarathon's next week in Buenos Aires, but I believe I will have to miss it. I'm flying back on the red-eye, but don't wait on me. I want to stop in D.C. and speak to some of my people there."

The JADL had offices in Washington, and a full staff of lobbyists and attorneys, but Charlie knew those were not the people the boss was speaking of. There were jokers everywhere; in SCARE, in the FBI, in the Secret Service. If any of them knew anything, the Old Man would get it out of them. "What do you want us to do?"

"You start digging right there in New York. Charles Dutton is thick as thieves with Theodorus. We've argued about him at poker. See if you can find him. Talk to some of our friends on the *Cry* as well, see what's in their morgue. Dirt, gossip, anything. And head down to Fort Freak, see what they have in the files on Finn. I doubt it will be much. I'm sending Sibyl to Charleston to shake a few trees, poke around . . ."

"Isn't that like sending her into the dragon's den? Except maybe more directly into the dragon's mouth? Charleston's where Theodorus lives. It's his corporate headquarters. He owns that town! Do you actually think Theodorus had something to do with the assassination? He seems pretty sincere in his desire to make a better world for jokers. Literally."

"Sure. The critics who say he's just a huckster miss the mark by a long shot. But the greatest crimes are committed by the true believers. If you absolutely know what's best for the world, then anybody who disagrees has to be pretty much an actual devil, right? Invincible certainty breeds invincible self-righteousness."

He sounds unusually certain himself, thought Charlie. "So you think he's involved?"

"Did I say that?" The Old Man smiled. "The president was killed on her way to a meeting with him. Witherspoon has always been high-handed, imperious even. And these last few years he's been wandering deeper into a swamp of megalomania, messianism, and paranoia. Would he go so far as to remove someone he saw as threatening his dream? He might. I've never met Theodorus Witherspoon myself, but we move in similar orbits, you might say. We're a class that usually does not feel the same burden of constraints that the common folk do. And Theodorus has long been said to have a particular tendency to believe the end justifies the means. Do I think he was involved?" Pretorius snorted. "Of course not. Whether the Big Snail would go so far as to kill a president, I don't know . . . but I do know that he wouldn't do it so clumsily, and he'd never do it on his own doorstep. Whatever else he may be, no one ever accused Theodorus of being stupid. No, either there is a leak in his organization or someone wants to ruin him, or both. No one loves a billionaire, and a secretive joker billionaire is easy to hate. *Of course* he's up to no good."

The joker in the woodpile always gets the blame, thought Charlie. "I'll find out whatever I can."

"I know. It's what I pay you the big bucks for. Move!"

Jonathan Tipton-Clark slipped into Hot Mama's with his laptop under his arm and found a seat at an isolated table next to a wall, partially hidden between tall glass-sided display cases that contained clothing allegedly worn by members of

Joker Plague and the Jokertown Boys. Jonathan knew Drummer Boy, the one-time leader of Joker Plague, and he didn't think the torn and worn jeans in the Plague case would have actually fit him. DB was a pretty big dude, but . . . face it, all in all, it was hard to distinguish between old jeans. The costumes purport-edly worn by the Jokertown Boys were certainly more colorful and theatrical than those of the punk Joker Plague, but Jonathan really hadn't followed them during their mercifully brief heyday. After all, he'd never been an adolescent girl. Actually, he hadn't really been much of a fan of Joker Plague, either. He'd known Drummer Boy far too well and he couldn't bring himself to separate the musician from his music, as unfair as that was.

Hot Mama's was fairly crowded for a midweek afternoon. To Jonathan's jaun-diced eye it appeared to be the bastard child of Aces High, the legendary restau-rant atop the Empire State Building that had passed its peak of popularity soon after he'd been born, and the Famous Bowery Wild Card Dime Museum (admis-sion only $29.95, family discounts available).

Charleston wasn't exactly a buzzing hive of wild card activity, but a huge ma-jority of the Witherspoon Aerospace workforce were jokers who apparently found Hot Mama's a comfortable place to hang out. They provided the joint with steady custom, augmented by Charleston's teeming tourist crowd, many of whom dropped by to have a drink of Tachyon Tea or a Bloatburger and gaze at the uniform Slugs Miligne wore when he played that one game for the New York Yankees.

Jonathan popped open his laptop and surreptitiously surveyed the crowded room, mentally dividing the Witherspoon employees from the tourists. A waiter came by and he ordered an iced coffee. He waited for her to return with his drink and, after she'd delivered it, discreetly freed a few wasps from the flesh of his lower left leg. One by one they crawled out from under his pants cuff and quietly took off as Jonathan settled back, sipped his coffee, and concentrated on the threads of the various conversations overheard by his tiny aerial spies.

Most of the talk was mundane. Personal discussions, commentary on the foods and the exhibits, plans for the day. But, as might be expected, the assas-sination was also a common topic of conversation. Jonathan listened through his wasps and took notes on his laptop. It was all part of his job. He'd started out wanting to become a famous blogger, and ended up a reporter for *Aces!* with a steady salary, an expense account, a 401k, health insurance, and everything. Politics was something the magazine usually avoided, yet nonetheless here he was in Charleston, together with reporters from half the world's media, all chasing after an angle on the assassination.

"Try to get an interview with Theodorus," Digger Downs told him when he'd announced that he was sending Jonathan to Charleston.

"Everyone wants an interview with Theodorus," Jonathan had protested. "No one is getting one. Why would he make an exception for me?"

"Joker solidarity. Help a brother joker out."

Bugsy had stiffened. "I am not a joker," he said.

"I've seen wasps crawl up your nose. You're a joker. Get to Charleston."

Jonathan liked to go his own way, however. While hundreds of his fellow re-porter and TV crews were encamped outside the Witherspoon estate, hoping for a glimpse of the Big Snail, Bugsy preferred to let his wasps do the footwork while he sat comfortably at his table, sipping iced coffee and typing away. It was almost too easy. *This is the way to do investigative journalism. An hour, tops, and I'll have enough copy for a feature on the local reaction to the assassination.* Then he could clear the hell out of Hot Mama's and relax by the hotel swimming pool with an old-fashioned. And tomorrow he could check out that lead Digger had given him, some local nutcase with a story to sell. "Probably nothing," Downs had told him, "but you never know. Nose around, put a few bugs on her . . ."

"You shouldn't be here, Buck," a man said coldly, down at the end of the bar.

He wasn't talking to Bugsy, but the voice gave him the chills all the same. He gathered half a dozen scouts and sent them high above a couple of patrons huddled together alone at the end of the bar, to get a wasp's-eye view of the proceedings.

"Christ," an unfamiliar voice drawled in a countrified Southern accent, "you can't expect me to stay holed up with my brother in that damn motel room forever. Maybe he's happy eating Slim Jims and watching that damn pit bull show on the teevee, but I need more. I ain't never been to Charleston before."

"Charleston is crawling with police," replied the first voice, the familiar voice. "FBI, Secret Service, SCARE. If you don't want them crawling up your ass, take your brother and go somewhere far away. LA, London, Hong Kong, I don't care. We'll call you when you're needed again."

"Shit," the first replied in a disgusted voice.

What the hell? Bugsy thought. One of his wasps buzzed lower so he could get a good look at their faces. *SCARE, yes, he should know.* The man with the cold voice was a SCARE agent who went by the code name Justice: middle-aged, handsome, Hispanic, and tough as nails. The second speaker was white, older, lean, dressed in worn jeans and a short-sleeved T-shirt and wearing a baseball cap that had seen better days. *But what are they up to?* It made sense that Justice would be in Charleston. As he'd said, the feds were here in score, including a dozen or more SCARE aces. *But who is the chinless wonder, and how does he connect?*

"What the fuck?" the redneck said. He slapped at the wasp buzzing over his head, and connected. The wasp hit the top of the bar, bounced, and buzzed weakly, dazed. *Uh-oh,* Bugsy thought. His wasps were green . . . too green, too bright, too recognizable.

Through the eyes of a second scout Bugsy could see Justice's face turn suddenly hard. "Hive," he said. He looked wildly around. "He's here."

"The fuck!" Buck slapped his bottle of beer down upon the dazed wasp and Bugsy felt it blink out of existence as the redneck turned to scan the room.

Keep calm, Hive told himself as he shut his laptop and slowly got to his feet. The loss of one wasp didn't matter much to him—it was, after all, only a few grams of body mass. The fact that he'd been made was much more important. *Don't make any sudden moves. They'll never spot me in this crowd.*

"There he is," Justice said quietly, and pointed at him.

For a moment they stared at one another across the crowded bar. Bugsy didn't like what he saw in their eyes. He bolted like a panicked rabbit, just as Buck started through the crowd toward him. He was, Hive realized, a lot closer to the door to the parking lot than they were.

"Hey," someone protested as Bugsy banged into him as he was looking at the Joker Plague exhibit, spilling his drink. "Watch it, asshole."

Buck was closing, no more than a dozen feet away. Bugsy let his left arm dissolve (his right was clutching his computer). A stream of bright green wasps flew from the sleeve of his jacket as he ran, hundreds of them. They moved as one, descending on the redneck in a stinging, buzzing cloud. "Son of a bitch!" Buck exclaimed. He stopped and did a jittering dance, slapping at the air as the wasps engulfed his head and shoulders, stinging.

Bugsy reached the exit, dodging a couple of women as they tried to enter. He ran out into the parking lot followed by a trail of green wasps, fumbling his rental car keys from his pocket with his remaining arm. He reached the rental just as Justice made it out of the door, coming after him.

"Federal agent!" Justice shouted. "*Damnit!*" he added as a trio of wasps Bugsy had left behind on guard duty landed on him, stinging his neck and face.

Bugsy threw open the car door, tossed his laptop on the passenger seat, then slammed the door shut. He missed the ignition once, then with a supreme effort of will stilled his jittery hand, rammed the key home, and turned it. The engine caught and he risked a backward glance to see Justice staring at him as he whirled the rental out of the parking lot. Buck joined Justice and made a move to follow, but Justice grabbed his arm, restraining him as Bugsy roared away.

It was late morning, and the Waffle House was mostly empty.

"I'm sorry," the tall, lean brunette with the lethally long, sparkling purple nails said to Ice Blue Sibyl across her untouched plate of french fries. Her name was Siobhan. She was, not shockingly, a nail stylist. "Ginny cut herself off from all of us when she left Witherspoon."

"And Siobhan's her BFF," said the chunky blonde woman who sat beside her in the orange-upholstered booth. She was a bartender and psych student named Lynn. "I mean, she and I and Ginny grew up here in the same neighborhood in West Ashley. I'm pretty tight with her, too. Or was. But those two were like this." She held up her hand with two fingers with much shorter and less colorfully nailed fingers crossed.

Teena, the tall Black woman who sat beside Lynn, could not take her eyes off Sibyl's face. "How do you—" she blurted out, then shut her mouth as the details of Sibyl's expressionless face and unmoving lips fully struck her.

"Speak?" Sibyl asked. She couldn't smile—or frown, for that matter—but her voice remained pleasant. "In several ways," she said. "Can any of you read sign language?"

The three women shook their heads.

"Most people can't." She held up her wrist, showing the women a small electronic element strapped to it. "This is a Bluetooth vocoder. This"—she fingered the gorget that she wore around her slim neck—"is a speaker."

She skipped the technical details. While she didn't exactly have organs or blood circulation as humans understood them, Sibyl had something analogous to a natural neuromuscular system. The bioelectrical impulses that controlled it could be read by sensors, digitalized, and translated into speech by the vocoder and transmitted by the speaker.

"You do have a nice voice," Teena said.

"Thank you," Sibyl replied. "It's Peregrine's."

"Oh." The woman's face brightened. "I thought it sounded familiar." She gestured to the coffee cup on the table beside her. "Would you like some coffee? Tea?"

"No, thank you," Sibyl said. "I don't drink."

"Oh." Teena fell silent for a moment. "Of course."

"If we could get back to Virginia," Sibyl said. "How did you know her, Teena?"

"From work," Teena said. "I'm a materials scientist at Witherspoon Aerospace and she's a secretary, but we met in the cafeteria one day and kinda bonded because we started kidding around about how we lucked into drawing jokers a lot of guys think are hot." She giggled and touched one of the two short, curved horns sticking out of her carefully coifed hair. "I met Lynn and Siobhan through her, and we sort of hit it off, too."

Sibyl had spent the previous three days in the JADL's New York City offices combing various electronic databases for any clue, any slight anomaly, any strange circumstance or coincidence, that might help free Dr. Finn. She'd been on the computer for twenty hours a day, powering down for what passed for sleep for her only four hours out of every twenty-four when, against all odds, she'd found a slender lead. The private secretary to Witherspoon Aerospace's CFO had mysteriously gone missing the day before the assassination. With that slim lead in hand, Sibyl had hopped on the first available flight from Tomlin International to Charleston.

She'd taken a room in an appropriately anonymous motel on the city's edge, then gone out immediately and rented her vehicle of choice—a Triumph Thruxton 1200 café racer motorcycle—and gotten down to the almost impossible task of finding a single lost needle in the haystack that was Charleston. What made her job even more difficult was the probability that the needle wanted to be missing—and that was the best-case scenario.

The worst case was that she was dead.

"But none of you have heard from Virginia since she quit?" Sibyl asked.

Her lips a line, Siobhan shook her head. "I got a late-night text from her the night before she quit. Said something about not trying to find her because that was best for everybody."

"What do you think she meant?"

Siobhan shook her head.

"She always liked to drink," Lynn said. "But the month or so before she left Witherspoon—had to cut her off twice, myself. She yelled at me both times."

Sibyl was almost out of leads; none of Virginia's other coworkers she'd been able to identify wanted to talk about her at all. The ones she'd found who knew Virginia Matusczak seemed to believe she had been let go for neglecting her duties. Or that she had betrayed Witherspoon and her fellow jokers somehow by quitting. Facebook had coughed up these three as the missing woman's closest friends. On the flight down she had made contact with them and set up a meeting. If they didn't know . . .

The Waffle House had been Virginia's favorite restaurant, she had been told, a place where her friends would feel comfortable. After more than three decades of living among nats and ordinary humans, Sibyl knew that even by wild card standards her appearance could be disconcerting to someone who'd never seen her before. Ice Blue Sibyl was tall, five feet nine, and slim, with the general proportions of a Barbie doll. Also like a Barbie, she was smooth-skinned—although in her case it was a pleasing bluish-greenish shade—and totally lacked bodily orifices. Although she had full, attractively sculpted lips, her mouth was completely and permanently shut. Her finely chiseled, slender nose lacked nostrils. Her ears, set close to her hairless head, were without auditory canals. Her other abnormalities were hidden by the black leather motorcycle leathers she wore.

"Had Virginia been having trouble at work?" she asked.

"She did seem pretty uneasy and distracted," Teena said. "But when we were at work I only saw her when we ate lunch together once or twice a week."

"Is there anybody whom she might stay in touch with?" Sibyl asked. "Her family?"

Lynn looked up from her plate of strawberry and cream waffles. "Her drawing a joker freaked them out, and when she went to work for Theodorus—"

"—With a bunch of jokers like me," Teena said.

"Well, they didn't cope well. So she sees them for Thanksgiving and Christmas."

"There is someone—" Lynn began tentatively, then stopped.

"Tell her," Teena said.

"All right," Siobhan said, dropping her cool reserve. "It's her no-good ex. Cletus. Nobody knows his last name. Car mechanic, small-time MMA prizefighter on the side. Shaved head, tattoos, black Affliction T-shirts—you know the type."

"She dumped him," Lynn said. "He kept stepping out on her."

Sibyl was silent for a moment, thinking. The Waffle House air-conditioning was fighting the brutal summer steam cooker that was Charleston with equally brutal Arctic cold that felt pleasingly soothing on her shiny surface. "If they are estranged—"

"Well," Teena said, "it's not that simple."

"She still sees him sometimes," Siobhan said. "She wasn't above the occasional late-night booty call. She likes a lot of male attention. And she really liked his."

"Ginny liked to call him her stallion," Teena said.

"Self-destructive behavior is not an entirely unknown thing to Ginny," Lynn said.

"No kidding." Siobhan sighed. "If anybody knows where she is, it's him."

Charleston, Bugsy thought, was quaint as hell. Especially this part of it, a ritzy neighborhood not more than ten minutes from downtown. Small, but eminently exclusive, all the homes were fenced, sitting back from the street on manicured lawns and fronted by carefully maintained gardens, now a riot of summer blooms.

It was hot and humid on the sidewalk outside this particular estate, which was the residence of Malachi Schwartz, CFO of Witherspoon Aerospace. Bugsy had not been able to get near the House Secure, Theodorus Witherspoon's country estate, any more than any of the other journalists who had descended on Charleston from all over the country. Theodorus was not talking, and his grounds were protected by a small army of lawyers, a larger army of armed jokers and private security . . . and, if the tales were true, some kind of guard snails. Some of the other reporters had a good laugh at the idea of guard snails. Not Jonathan. A guy who turned into his weight in wasps was not one to laugh at killer snails.

His requests for an exclusive interview with Theodorus had gone unanswered as well. Bugsy figured they had ended up in the circular file with all the rest. But if he could not get to Witherspoon himself, there were other options. Like Malachi Schwartz, who spent more time at the House Secure than at home, but actually lived in the heart of Charleston, in a mansion that was no doubt modest compared to the House Secure, but still beat the hell out of Jonathan's studio apartment on the fringes of Jokertown.

The building was certainly antebellum. *Colonial style, maybe?* Bugsy wasn't really up on architectural styles. It was impressive, though. Two main stories, gray, with window and other trim mostly white. A two-story-tall porch wrapped around the front. The front door was off-center, with five gleaming white columns on the right side, three on the left. The top floor was similarly asymmetrical, with one large gabled window on the right side—no doubt, Bugsy thought, the master bedroom—and three smaller gables to the left denoting less lavish sleeping quarters. Between the single large and triple smaller dormers was a square tower that increased the height of that part of the manse to three stories.

Bugsy sweated bullets as he sat there on a small folding chair, an easel before him as he pretended to paint the mansion, a small but sensitive recorder in his shirt pocket that he murmured into as his troop of wasps picked up conversations scattered throughout the house. So far there hadn't been too much of import. He had tried making an appointment, of course, but a joker who looked just like Elvis Presley (if Elvis had been made of purple Jell-O) had turned him firmly away at Schwartz's front door. Hence the easel and the paint kit. The sidewalk was public property.

Schwartz was not presently at home, but when he returned, Bugsy would be ready for him. He had three wasps ensconced in Schwartz's study, hidden in strategic places, and more crawling on the ceiling in the library and hidden behind the drapes in the master bedroom.

He was getting hungry and thirsty and was starting to think that this was a bad idea and general waste of time when a black limo pulled up to the gate, pushed the call button, and was buzzed into the estate.

The vehicle pulled up to the front door and the chauffeur smartly hopped out and opened the rear passenger door. One of the wasps buzzed around his head and distracted him, to give Bugsy time for a good look at the men who emerged from the limo's rear seat. He knew the first man out: Troll, unfolding his towering nine-foot frame awkwardly from the car as he stepped onto the drive. Once he straightened, he offered a huge, gray hand to the second passenger, to help him to his feet. *Malachi Schwartz.*

Schwartz was an old man, somewhere in his seventies, but the nature of his joker made his true age hard to tell. His skin was light gray and smooth, with no sagging or wrinkles that would denote age, but the fringe of hair around the dome of his round skull was white. With his egg-shaped torso and hunched back he reminded Bugsy of depictions he'd seen of Humpty Dumpty in old children's books, but he was a pretty smart cookie. Witherspoon's right-hand man and financial wizard, he had a sharp brain and was rich as Midas. That made for a dangerous combination.

Who wears black in this weather? Bugsy thought. *Fuck. That's wool.*

A manservant of some sort was waiting at the front door to usher the master and his protector in. Bugsy squirmed in his folding chair, which was beginning to make his butt ache. *This might pay off after all,* he thought as they disappeared into the house.

Cletus the ex-boyfriend turned out to be surprisingly cooperative and touchingly concerned about Virginia. Sibyl sometimes had trouble reading human emotions, but he seemed authentically worried about her. He gave Sibyl the address of the seedy airport hotel where he'd visited her several nights ago after she'd called him furtively and seemingly desperately late one evening. She wouldn't tell him why she'd quit her job and why she was hiding out.

"I don't want you involved in that," she'd told him, but the last words he said to Sibyl were, "Please tell her I want to help."

"I'll let her know," Sibyl said.

"And—"

She paused.

"You look pretty sweet yourself," he added, taking a small notepad out of his shirt pocket. "Can I have your number?"

"Area code zero-zero-zero," she said in her melodious contralto. "Zero-zero-zero. Zero-zero-zero-zero."

He looked up from the pad on which he was writing to see her retreating form.

"Hey," he called out. "That's pretty cold."

She kept walking.

"Turns out Virginia's friends' suspicions were spot-on," she told Dr. Pretorius when she reached him at his Washington hotel. "She kept getting drunk and lonely and making booty calls to him. Also, not sleeping, which has him worried."

"That'll kill you," Pretorius said. "Or at least it would kill those of us more subject to human frailty than yourself." While Ice Blue Sibyl spent irregular periods dormant, she lacked the need for sleep as such.

"He says all she wants to do when he isn't around is eat microwave popcorn, drink, watch soaps, and read Shakespeare stuff she downloads off Gutenberg, of all things," Sibyl said. "She drives him crazy quoting it all the time."

"I take it he told you where to find her?"

"He did." She left out the part where Cletus hit on her. "Has Flipper turned up anything in New York?"

"Nothing of note," said Pretorius. "Dutton is out of town, we are told. Either that or laying low. Dr. Finn does not have so much as a parking ticket. I, however, am on the trail of something here in Washington. So you will forgive me if I cut this short. I have an appointment with a Chihuahua."

Bugsy studied the study through his wasps. It was the perfect man cave for the well-to-do intellectual. The furniture was large and chunky, from an earlier age, all soft, gleaming, dark woods. The carpets on the floor were from an even earlier age, if Bugsy was any judge. Antique, though still vividly colored and rich in design. The various tchotchkes on his desk, atop plinths scattered around the room and standing in nooks on bookcases fairly bursting with old and expensive-looking volumes, were objets d'art ranging from bronze statuettes to fragments of Greek or Roman statuary to Tiffany lamps and elegant glass and pottery vases that Bugsy couldn't identify if his life depended on it. It just oozed wealth, and, Bugsy had to admit, a wide-ranging good taste. Incongruously, however, one wall of the study was lined with computers, monitors, and television screens. Some of the equipment looked very cutting-edge; beyond Jonathan's means and knowledge, certainly.

Malachi wasted no time. He went straight to the study and grabbed for the phone, while Troll paused in the front hall to talk with Grape Jello Elvis. *Uh-oh,* Jonathan thought. *Am I being reported?* He had no time to ponder the question. On the phone, Malachi rang the kitchen to discuss what he was having for dinner (lobster thermidor and floating islands, whatever they were). Then he rang his valet to discuss how many new shirts he needed. After that came a series of calls about price overruns, balance sheets, and recruitment for some space project, most of it financial mumbo jumbo that sounded like Greek to Bugsy. *Maybe this isn't my path to a Pulitzer after all,* he thought.

Jonathan was so focused on Malachi in his study that he lost track of his immediate surroundings, which happened from time to time. Until a huge gray-green hand clapped him on the shoulder in a grip like iron, and a deep voice said, "Bugsy. I never knew you painted."

Jonathan started so badly he knocked over his easel. Troll was looming over him, all nine feet of him, scowling. "Uh," he said. "Hello, Howard. Fancy meeting you here." His left ear turned into half a dozen wasps and flew away. That sometimes happened when he got nervous. "Painting, yeah . . . ah . . . I needed a hobby. What do you think?"

"I think you should stick to blogging," said Troll. "Do you mind explaining why you are lurking across the street from Mr. Schwartz's house?"

"I . . . ah . . . I was hoping he could get me in to see Theodorus."

"He could, but he won't."

"Maybe . . . for a fellow joker . . ." Might as well use every card he had.

"There are twenty-seven joker journalists in that crowd outside the Witherspoon estate," said Troll. "You're not one of them. You were on *American Hero.* You were with the Committee. You write for *Aces!* magazine. You're an ace. Go away, Bugsy. If you need a story, write that Theodorus had nothing to do with the assassination."

When Troll let go of his shoulder, Bugsy got shakily to his feet. "Maybe, maybe not," he said, "but there's something dirty going on down here. I bumped into a couple of shady-looking characters at Hot Mama's the other day. And Digger got a call from a source, a Witherspoon insider with a story to sell."

"I know a guy saw Jetboy at the Piggly Wiggly last week," said Troll. "Maybe you should buy his story."

Jonathan drew himself up tall. "If there are dirty doings going on, I am going to find them." Wasps were buzzing around his head. "The public has a right to know what Theodorus Witherspoon and Malachi Schwartz are up to."

Troll sighed. "Go away, Bugsy. Oh, and if you got any little bits of yourself into the house, you had best pull them out, too, before I go looking for a can of Raid."

Jonathan turned and, as casually as possible, abandoned his easel, chair, and painting paraphernalia and sauntered slowly down the street toward where he had parked his new rental car, hidden a couple of blocks away. His wasps followed.

The pictures of Virginia Matusczak that Ice Blue Sibyl had downloaded off Facebook showed alert eyes and plump cheeks. With the points of her elf-ears sticking coyly out of her bobbed brown hair, Sibyl could understand why some men found her attractive.

But Virginia didn't look nearly so appealing when she opened the motel room door to Sibyl's knock. She was wearing a dingy bathrobe whose indifferent fastening suggested she wore nothing underneath. Her cheeks sagged and her hair stuck out in random zigs and zags like a nest assembled by drunk crows. If Sibyl was any judge, she looked past desperate, past caring and fear.

"Who the hell are you?" she asked.

"My name is Sibyl," her vocoder replied in Peregrine's dulcet tones. "I am an investigator for the Joker Anti-Defamation League. May I come in?"

Virginia's dark, bloodshot eyes flicked furtively around the motel parking lot, which was empty but for Sibyl's motorcycle parked before her door. "I'm gonna have to move again now," she said. "If you can find me, he can, too." She wheeled away and vanished into a room lit only by the muted TV conspicuously chained and padlocked to a wall bracket. Sibyl figured that was close enough to an invitation and followed her into gloom that smelled of unlaundered bedclothes and unshowered human.

The room was as seedy as Virginia's ex had said it was. Watermarked walls, threadbare carpet whose unpleasant shades of green and orange suggested the gallons of puke Sibyl was certain had soaked into it over the years, a bed that, were it not for the solid pedestal every hotel in America had installed beneath its box springs in the 1990s, looked as if it probably had a dead hooker hidden under it. Sibyl sat perched on the edge of a chair with her leathers touching as little of its surface as she could manage.

Without looking Virginia scraped her fingers at the bottom of the microwave popcorn bag that sat beside her chair on the room's little crooked desk and tossed some pieces into her mouth. "Are you sure you're not a reporter? Because I'm not talking to reporters. Not unless I am paid."

"Paid?" asked Sibyl. "Paid for what?"

"My story," Virginia said. "That's what you want, isn't it? The dirt. But I'm not giving it away. I'll tell all, but first I see the green."

Sibyl would have shrugged if she was given to human gestures. "I can talk to my boss about a payment. But unless I hear your story I won't know what it's worth. All we know is that you suddenly left your job as secretary to Theodorus Witherspoon's right-hand man, Malachi Schwartz, and dropped out of sight. As if, perhaps, you were afraid of something."

Virginia made a sound deep in her throat that might have been disgust or disbelief, or even just an attempt to clear it of phlegm. "Dammit! All kernels again." She heaved herself up from the orange upholstered chair with clear tape patching, made a token effort at pulling her robe discreetly closed, and shuffled to the chest of drawers under the TV, where several unopened popcorn boxes were stacked. "Yes, I'm afraid. I know too much."

"About the assassination?"

"Might be." Matusczak was fumbling open the top of her box of microwave popcorn. "Might be other stuff. Dirty stuff. Bribes. Money laundering. All sorts of crooked stuff." She opened the microwave door, slid a bag of popcorn inside the microwave, shut the door, and quickly punched in the heating time. "That's all you get until I see the green, though. I'm going to get an agent. The things I know are worth a million dollars, at least."

She hit the microwave's start button and there was a sudden crack like miniaturized lightning. A huge blue spark leapt from the microwave and enveloped Virginia's hand. She shuddered once with impossible violence, like a rat having its neck broken in the jaws of a terrier, then she slumped to the floor and onto her back as if her bones had dissolved within her.

Sibyl would have goggled with astonishment if she could. *You can't be—*

"Dead," Detective Redfern said. "Just like that, the CME says. Like flipping a switch." He shook his head. "Nobody has any idea what made the microwave zap her like that. Or how it did it. But there's no question that was the cause of death. The thing fried itself, too. Had to pass a really massive charge to do all that. Been working Violent Crimes for six and a half years now, and I've never seen anything like it. Thing is, you'd think the oven would be extra safe, on account of being a 'smart' microwave and all."

"The motel was a fleabag," Sibyl's tab said. It was a replacement, hastily purchased by an intern from the same JADL-affiliated local lawyer who'd helped spring her earlier that afternoon. Redfern hadn't lifted an eyebrow over its use. He was used to joker witnesses, and mostly just relieved at not having to hunt down a CPD sign interpreter. "What's it doing with a smart microwave? And an internet connection?"

"Even ratholes got free Wi-Fi these days," Redfern said. "How do you think the deceased downloaded all those Shakespeare plays? Plus we have learned they got these particular ranges on sale. My investigators did not fail to wonder about that detail, too, Miss Pretorius."

"Have your keen-eyed investigators uncovered any evidence at all of violence being involved?" asked William Joe Lousader, Sibyl's local attorney, in the rich baritone voice of a middle-aged Southern gentleman, which seemed totally discordant with his fresh, unlined, round dark face, black eyes, and straight dark brown hair. He looked all of twelve years old. Which would have worried Sibyl, if Dr. P. himself had not vouched for Lousader, when they'd called from the police station. "Or, indeed, of any crime being committed?"

"No to both," Redfern said. "Not by Miss Pretorius, anyway. Our investigators tell me it would require an advanced electronics whiz to pull off at all. Plus there's no physical sign the case was opened." He drummed his fingers on the desk in his cubicle. The rest of the evening shift tapped and murmured beyond the white walls. "It'll take a few days for the CME to type up her official report," he said, as if reluctantly. "But she tells me on the phone she's got to rule 'death by misadventure.'"

"So my client is free to go?"

Redfern sighed. "Yeah. But you know, jokers are not too popular in these parts just now, what with the president being killed and all. Miss Pretorius might want to enjoy the sights of Charleston at some later time."

Jonathan Tipton-Clark was lost in thought as he wheeled his rent-a-car though the quaint historic streets of old Charleston. He did not keep a car in Manhattan, and it had been a long while since he'd driven so much. As he turned a corner, his car fishtailed a bit, just missing a slim figure in black leather on a café racer motorcycle entering the parking lot. He roared off down the street, unfollowed.

He sighed. It felt like he had stumbled into something weird, but he'd no idea what, and he was disinclined to pursue it much further. The idea of enjoying a cool drink by poolside was still rather appealing. *Maybe a mint julep.* They made good mint juleps in the South, he'd heard. Perhaps he could sort things out given a few moments of calm contemplation.

He was on a main road on Charleston's outskirts, heading toward the airport and his nearby hotel. Traffic was moderate and he was moving along a little over the speed limit, his thoughts still centered on what had just happened, when suddenly a billowy white pillow exploded from the center of his steering wheel to fill his vision and punch him in the nose so hard that he blacked out for a moment, seeing only red stars dancing inside his skull. When his consciousness kicked in a heartbeat later his eyes were filled with white and his head was filled with pain. His ears rang.

Airbag! The fuck?

He couldn't steer because the bag was in his face. He tried to brake. The pedal sank straight to the floor without any resistance. Or any sign of slowing the rental car. The Lexus accelerated.

"Help!" he croaked helplessly. The pain was localizing to his nose, and he felt something hot running down his upper lip. He tasted salt. *Broke my damn nose.*

Cars were honking furiously all around him. Still too befuddled by the impact of the exploding airbag on his face to have a clue as to why his car had rebelled, Jonathan gripped the steering wheel with both hands and tried to at least hold it steady while peering around the airbag that blocked his vision.

"Aren't these things supposed to deflate right away?" he asked himself while silently praying that the road didn't curve. He tried to roll the driver's side window down, but the electronic switch wouldn't work. He tried the door. It was locked and stubbornly refused to open. He could turn into a cloud of wasps, but then he'd be a cloud of wasps still trapped in an accelerating car that would probably soon end in a fiery crash. Bugsy realized that he was running out of viable options as quickly as he was running out of clear road.

He caught a glimpse of a sudden flash of motion in the adjacent lane and rolled his eyes leftward to see a sleek motorcycle pull up beside him. Upon it was a woman clad in black leathers, wearing a black helmet and black leather gauntlets. She took her right hand off the handlebars and made a frantic gesture at him. After a moment he realized that she was urging him to roll down his window. He glanced at her helplessly and shook his head.

She seemed to understand. Her hand moved to a pouch at her waist, and, still showing amazing ability to guide her bike as she kept up beside him, pointed a small automatic at the window. Bugsy just stared at her for a long second in even greater shock, then suddenly realized what she was doing, and ducked.

A single shot smashed the window and Bugsy exploded outward in a swarm of wasps, tens of thousands of wasps pouring through the shattered glass as he left his human form and his clothes behind. He was mostly out when both car and motorcycle hit the beginnings of a sudden banked curve.

Bugsy watched through a myriad of wasp eyes as the cyclist swung the motorcycle so close to the car's gleaming gray flank it almost kissed her leather-clad knee. Reaching through the broken window, she grabbed the steering wheel and guided both hurtling vehicles across lanes of traffic. An exit was coming up, but steering the car on it would only be diverting the potentially deadly missile to a different target. With exquisite timing, the cyclist abruptly let go of the steering wheel and straightened up and with a loud, liquid bang the car rammed the water barrier beside the exit ramp. Its back end swung up in the air, its hood popped open, and it slammed back down on its suspension.

The bike wobbling beneath her, but still under control, she turned the machine right, laying the bike on its side so that only her booted foot was holding it up as she coiled herself to jump off her stricken ride. Instead it slammed into the safety rail and flipped her over it into space.

Bugsy coalesced into his human form halfway up the exit ramp. "My God!" he yelled as she dropped out of view. Heart still pumping with the terror induced by his wild ride, he lurched to the rail, grabbing it with shaking hands to stop from hurtling over after her.

To his horror he saw a busy side street below, cars and trucks honking furiously, screeching brakes, and veering to avoid the slim figure in black leather that was darting for the sidewalk. Once there his rescuer stopped, took off her helmet, and waved up at Bugsy.

He knew her. It was Ice Blue Sibyl, the ward of the joker lawyer Dr. Pretorius. Jonathan had never met her before face-to-face, but then, even in a world stricken by the wild card, she was a unique figure. "You all right?" he called out to her.

"I'm fine," she shouted back, her lips unmoving, but somehow producing a smooth contralto voice that was hauntingly familiar.

Bugsy felt his knees quiver in relief. "That was amazing."

She was making her way toward him. "Looks like you need some medical attention yourself." She paused. "Not to mention some clothes."

The cops that descended on them were rather dubious about Jonathan's claim that his car had just gone nuts and tried to kill him, but numerous motorists stopped to confirm his story, and Sibyl's. "The weirdest, craziest, bravest thing I ever saw," one witness said. He happened to be an off-duty policeman himself.

"Uh-huh," the sergeant in charge of the accident scene replied. "We usually don't see many blue folk around here," he added suspiciously, looking up from his notebook where he'd been scribbling furiously.

The cop who'd stopped to describe what he'd witnessed was Black. He frowned at the sergeant. "What does the color of her skin have to do with anything?" he asked.

"Um, nothing, sir."

"Right." The off-duty cop reached into his back pants pocket and took out his wallet. He removed a card and handed it to Sibyl. "You need me to confirm any part of your story, you just give me a call."

Sibyl glanced at the card. "Thank you, Detective Johnson. I'm sure we'll be fine."

"Now you sure you don't need any medical attention?"

"As long as I don't get burned, cut, or punctured, I'm really pretty durable."

He glanced at Bugsy. "How about you?"

Sibyl caught Hive's eye before he could speak and he understood the emotionless look she gave him. "I'm fine."

The cops took them down to the station house anyway, for further questioning, but the answers did not change, no matter how many times the same questions were asked. When they were finally told they were free to go, Bugsy told his rescuer, "I'd like to go to my hotel to freshen up and, uh, get some real clothes." He was wearing a spare set of scrubs borrowed from the EMTs who had already arrived on the scene. "The least I can do for your saving my life is buy you dinner."

"I don't eat. But we should talk."

"Ah . . . what brings you to Charleston?" Bugsy said awkwardly.

"Save it for the hotel room," Sibyl said, as she mounted her bike. Bugsy sat carefully on the seat behind her and gingerly put his arms around her as she pulled out into traffic. Under her leathers her flesh felt hard to his touch but pliant, and a perceptible coolness wafted off her. It was, Bugsy thought, like hugging an air conditioner set to low.

Holding her conjured images of past girlfriends. *At least,* he thought, *she is alive.*

Ice Blue Sibyl didn't have a trusting soul (if she had one at all), but her actions were largely guided by practical concerns. She tried to reserve her contemplation of such metaphysical concepts as trust and love and honor for nighttime, when people slept and she often powered down to rest mode. It passed the time and was certainly more entertaining than late-night television with its constant stream of useless infomercials.

Sibyl sat on a stained and rumpled bedspread. While she sustained herself on literal sunlight, by some process akin to photosynthesis, she ingested key additional nutrients by direct absorption through her blue-green skin. She had unsettled the Charleston police by spending some of the four hours she and Bugsy had been held at the station with one hand in a vat of Gatorade, helping her body repair the abrasion she'd suffered in her trip over the high side with her bike.

She stared at Bugsy, who was occupying her small motel room's only chair and sucking down a Slurpee they'd stopped to pick up at a 7–Eleven. That was all she could do when making eye-to-eye contact with someone. There was no way to soften her expression or soothe the blank mask of her features. Her lack of facial mobility disturbed most people, so, like everything else she had been dealt, she used it to her advantage when she could.

This Jonathan Tipton-Clark, whose file she'd conjured up from its place in her data bank of famous and infamous jokers and aces, did seem to have some useful traits. She wasn't sure if turning into a swarm of wasps could be considered an ace, but it was obviously of some utility. The wasps made good spies and trackers, and they could also sting . . . a minor kind of annoyance, but she understood that it discomfited some people. While Hive's physical courage seemed overmatched by his need for safety, that wasn't necessarily a bad thing. He clearly wasn't terribly bright, but he did seem to have a certain amount of cunning. She decided that she could work with him, and, to a degree, trust him. Sibyl pegged his mood as a mixture of melancholy and worry.

"What's the matter?" she asked him, Peregrine's voice sounded concerned, as he sucked up the last bit of Slurpee through his plastic straw.

"Oh, my laptop. It was destroyed in the crash."

"Surely you have backups stored in the cloud?"

"Yeah." Hive frowned at the empty plastic cup and lobbed it in the direction of the wastepaper basket adjacent to the desk. It clanked off the rim and rolled around on the linoleum floor, which at least was cleaner than a carpet of comparable age would've been. He sighed.

"What *did* happen with your car?" Sibyl asked.

"Weird stuff," said Bugsy. "It was like, like it suddenly had a mind of its own, and the main thing on it was to leave me dead on the highway."

"That's . . ." Even her lightning-fast brain had to pause momentarily. ". . . quite a coincidence. I was just interviewing a source who might have been able to shed some light on . . . whatever this is . . . but . . ." Sibyl looked at him emotionlessly, but there was a kind of odd tingling that ran through her neural network. ". . . she died in a freak microwave accident before she could tell me any details."

"A freak *microwave* accident?" Bugsy asked.

They looked at each other for a long moment.

"Two potentially fatal malfunctioning machines isn't a coincidence—" Bugsy said.

"—it's a pattern."

"There's more," said Bugsy. "The other day, I was checking out this local joker dive bar, and I spotted this SCARE agent. Justice, he goes by."

Sibyl had heard the name. "There are SCARE agents crawling all over Charleston. A dozen of them, at least. Jim Dandy, Phalanx, Tin Soldier . . . they even dragged old Nephi Callendar out of retirement, I understand. They are working with the FBI and the Secret Service to try and find leads on the assassins. The presence of a SCARE agent in Charleston is only to be expected."

"Maybe, but his presence in Hot Mama's was not," insisted Bugsy. "He wasn't investigating anything, that I saw. He was rousting some redneck and telling him to get the fuck out of town."

"A local?" Sibyl asked.

Bugsy shook his head. "I don't think so. He was a kind of scruffy guy. Justice called him Buck, and didn't seem too happy that Buck was out drinking. He told this Buck that he and his brother should go to Hong Kong or . . . I don't know, other places far away. Then Buck spotted my wasp and swatted it and I decided I had to get out of there. Buck came chasing after me, but I stung the shit out of him and drove off."

"You think this might connect with your car going crazy?"

"Maybe. Who the fuck knows? What if SCARE is involved in the assassination? You say there are a dozen agents in Charleston. Could be even more. SCARE has undercover operatives, too, I've always heard. Agents whose names never appear in the papers. Who knows what powers they might have?"

"The power to make machines go crazy, you're thinking?" Sibyl went to her saddlebags, pulled out her own laptop, took it to the desk, and opened it up.

Bugsy wandered over to where he could watch over her shoulder. "What are you doing?"

"Calling up the JADL's wild carder database. 'Buck' isn't all that common of a name. Let's see what comes up."

"You don't have all jokers and aces in that, do you?"

"No," Sibyl said. "Of course not. Socially prominent and important ones. Ones that the JADL has had business with. Ones in various accessible criminal databases."

Her voice ran down as she concentrated on her typing, and Bugsy leaned closer so he could see the screen better. "What's it say in there about me?"

Sibyl turned to look at him. Their faces were just inches apart. She just looked at him until he cleared his throat and flinched back.

"Or we can look later, when we have some spare time."

Sibyl returned her attention to the keyboard. "Here we go," she said after a few more moments. "Looks like . . . seven hits on the name 'Buck.' Hmmm. Buckaroo Bobby." She clicked on the name and the photo of an orange-skinned joker in a cowboy outfit appeared on the screen.

"Nope," Bugsy said.

"Buck-Toothed Jane. Probably a woman . . ."

"Better check, anyway."

Sibyl nodded. "Yeah. Joker hooker."

"Kind of cute—" Bugsy began, and fell silent when Sibyl glanced at him.

"Buckminster Fuller . . . no, he's dead."

"Buckminster Fuller was a joker?" Bugsy asked. "The geodesic dome guy?"

Sibyl nodded again. "Little-known fact. Eustace Buckington-Buckington . . . no. English con man . . . Buck McGee?"

Bugsy leaned in so close she could feel the warmth wafting off him. "Bingo. What's it say about him?"

"Nat handler of his brother, Blood, a canid-form joker of limited intelligence who has the ability to create interdimensional gates that can instantaneously transport people up to several thousand miles. Originally small-time criminals specializing in knocking over 7–Elevens and Piggly Wigglys throughout the South, they first gained notoriety while working for the Allumbrados. Since the sudden disappearance of the sect in the early 2000s, they have worked for several criminal organizations, most notably the Mafia, but can best be regarded as freelancers."

"The mob?" he said.

"There are reports of ties to the Gambiones in Cuba, the Grillet-Devereaux Gang in Marseilles, Ivan the Terrible in New York City, Julie the Weasel LaCanfora in Texas, the Praetorians in Rome . . . the McGee boys get around, it would seem."

"Shit," said Bugsy. "That's not good."

"Blood opens gates," said Sibyl. "What better way to get an assassin in and out without leaving a trace."

"Hot damn," said Bugsy. "We might just have found the assassin's wheelmen."

"We?" Sibyl asked.

"Sure, look, why don't we pool our resources? You want to see Finn freed. I want to break a story—"

"And see justice done?"

"Yes, of course," Bugsy assured her. "Justice. Absolutely."

Sibyl still didn't entirely trust him, but the more resources brought to the investigation, the better the chance of a good outcome. Even if one of the resources was a blogger who could turn into bugs. "All right," she said.

"Good," Bugsy said, rubbing his hands together with evident glee. "Great." He looked at the computer screen, then back to Sibyl. "I'm in. Absolutely. Teammates all the way. What's our next step, partner?"

Sibyl's cell phone suddenly trilled. She held up a hand to silence Bugsy and answered the call. "Yes?" She listened for a moment. "All right," she said briefly, clicked the phone off, and turned and looked at Bugsy, as deadpan as always. "We split up."

That took him aback. "What? Why?"

"Buck and Blood can go anywhere, it would seem, but they can't be two places at once," Sibyl pointed out. "And it would seem the other side has an ace who can make machines turn murderous as well. We are safer apart than together."

"Yeah," said Bugsy. Uncertainly. "So . . . where are we going?"

"Home," said Sibyl. "Separately."

"You Jonathan?" the burly young Black man behind the wheel of a six-year-old blue Yaris, rather shiny and well kept up, asked Bugsy.

Bugsy leaned down to peer at him as he opened the front passenger-side door.

And slid in the front seat. He smiled at the Uber driver engagingly. For some reason the young man didn't smile back. "You're Dwight, right?"

"Uh-huh." He stared at Bugsy for a long moment. "You the dude wants a ride to the Daughters of the Confederacy Civil War Museum?"

"Um, well, actually no."

That did not please Dwight. "The app said . . ."

"Well, I didn't want Uber to know where I am going. I'm on a, well, an important mission and I've got to go somewhere without anyone knowing I'm going there."

"You playing paintball with your old college buddies?" Dwight said. "I ain't got no time for crap like that. Get your stupid paint all over my car—"

"No, nothing like that." Bugsy shrugged. "I want to go to New York City."

The driver scowled. "New York City? By Uber? You fucking with me? You don't want to be fucking with me. You ever hear of airplanes?"

"I don't want to fly. I'm Jonathan Hive—"

Dwight frowned. "That dude who turns into moths?"

"Wasps. I turn into wasps."

"Oh, man, that's worse," Dwight said. "Get out of my ride before I get stung."

"I only turn into wasps when I have to," Bugsy said in exasperation. "You ever watch *American Hero*? I was a contestant. First season."

Dwight got a thoughtful frown on his face. "That was the year the brother won. Yeah, I remember you now. You were kind of lame. Were you one of the ones went to Egypt?"

"Yes," said Bugsy, warily.

"Okay," Dwight said. "I'm in."

"You are?"

"My mom a joker," he said.

"I'm—" Bugsy paused a moment. "—grateful for your help." He paused again. "I've got to tell you though, it could be very dangerous."

"You think being an Uber driver isn't dangerous?" Dwight turned the ignition key and the Yaris sped away from the curb.

Bugsy took his cell phone and regretfully tossed it out the window. He'd just paid eight hundred bucks for it. Or rather, *Aces!* had. Digger would bitch, but in the end he'd approve a new phone, so he could probably whistle up another one once he got back to the office. *If I get back to the office,* he told himself.

The brief phone call had been from Dr. Pretorius, simply telling her to return to New York as quickly as possible. "There's been a break in the case," he told her. "I prefer not to go into detail on the phone." Sibyl had known Dr. P. long enough to realize he had good reasons for being so abrupt. Most likely he was fearful that his communications were possibly being monitored. *You're not paranoid if they really are after you,* she thought.

Fortunately, flights between Charleston and New York City were rather frequent, and in little more than an hour she was winging her way back north.

The offices of the Joker Anti-Defamation League were located in an old gentrified three-story brownstone on the edge of Jokertown and Little Italy. Her adoptive father, Dr. Pretorius, owned the entire block. Not all of the businesses were owned by jokers—some were family firms that dated back well before 1946—but all catered to their customers.

As usual, parking was at a premium, so Sibyl had the cabbie who'd picked her up at Tomlin drop her off at the corner. It was a hot, humid day in New York, but not as hot and humid as it'd been in Charleston. Sibyl realized that she was glad at her return home and that made her feel even better. Human, somehow.

That feeling was heightened as she saw Pretorius exit the office building, limping on his cane, holding something in his left arm tight against his chest. He was staring straight ahead, looking for a cab, probably, not noticing her. Sibyl hurried down the moderately busy street toward him, dodging slow-moving pedestrians with the ease of the experienced urbanite.

As she approached she realized that Pretorius was holding, of all things, a tiny dog snuggled calmly against his chest. It had very short dark brown, almost black, fur with lighter tan highlights on its tiny muzzle and front legs down to its paws and inside its up-pointed little ears. It was so small that it looked as though it weighed no more than five pounds or so.

Pretorius stepped toward the street, raised one arm to call a passing cab, and one rolled to a stop, double-parked in the street, for him. He stooped to open the cab's passenger-side rear door and Sibyl called out to attract his attention. *"Dad!"*

He turned suddenly, and looked up the street at her, a smile on his face, as three close-spaced gunshots rang out. Pretorius dropped his cane and, huddled protectively around the tiny dog he carried, fell to the street as pedestrians around him started to react with various states of horror and panic. Some screamed, some stared, some ducked. A couple moved to Pretorius's side as the cab driver gunned the motor and took off down the street. Sibyl stared at him for the moment it took him to fly by her, burning his face and the cab's license plate and tag number into her memory.

Then Sibyl screamed, "Dad!" Peregrine's rich contralto twisted into a high-pitched wail. She ran to him, pushing her way through the crowd.

Dr. Pretorius's face was clenched in pain, but it softened when he recognized Sibyl. "You're just a little too late," he said, without reproach.

"Shhhh, quiet." She felt something she had never felt before and realized it was desperation.

Pretorius smiled. "It's all right, darling. I didn't have much left, anyway. But it's up to you now." He opened his arms a little. The tiny dog huddled against his chest was bloody.

"Is she all right?" he said, his voice starting to flutter.

The little dog was soaked in blood. Sibyl realized that she was pressed tightly against the bullet wounds in Pretorius's chest, trying to staunch the flow of blood with her tiny body. She looked up and Sibyl was shocked—another feeling that she was mostly unfamiliar with—to see intelligence and understanding in her eyes.

"Sibyl, keep her safe. At all costs, keep her safe. She's the key."

She wondered if Pretorius's mind was starting to wander, but then those few terrible seconds that encompassed the shooting played back in her mind, and she realized that it was probably the dog who'd been the target of the hit, and

Pretorius had gone down protecting her with his own body. It was a stunning realization.

The dog wiggled forward a bit and her tiny tongue came out and licked Pretorius's face. He reached out a bloody hand to grip Sibyl's. "I have to leave you now," he said. "It doesn't mean I love you any less."

"Oh, Dad." She put his bloody hand against the coolness of her cheek. She wished she could kiss it, she wished she could cry. Being human was a bitch. Being what she was, whatever she was, was harder. "I love you."

He nodded. He put his other hand out and Sibyl automatically took the dog and held it against her leather-covered chest. She held Pretorius's hand until it went limp and the dog let out a howl that seemed compounded of anguish and anger. Sibyl released his hand and closed her father's eyes with her cold fingers.

Then she waited for the cops to arrive, the dog nestled patiently in her arms. Anger, despair, and an overwhelming feeling of loneliness engulfed her. Henrik Pretorius had been the center of her life for a long, long time. She had been lost and frightened after the Professor had died, but Dr. Pretorius had found her, protected her, taught her so much . . . but now he was gone as well. *I will outlive them all,* Ice Blue Sibyl suddenly realized. *Everyone I know, everyone I love. They are only human, and I am . . . whatever I am.*

Fort Freak was the first precinct to respond: Beastie Bester, Rikki, Tinkerbill, and half a dozen other uniforms she did not know turned up one after another in a crush of squad cars. Sibyl didn't say much when questioned. She pleaded exhaustion from her recent flight and ignorance of current events.

She was only lying a little, keeping the license plate, taxi number, and description of the killer for her own use. She would hunt the gunman down herself. And then . . . and then, she didn't know. Rage at her father's killer consumed her, but her immobile features gave no hint of what she was feeling. Tinkerbill finally waved down a taxi for her, and directed the driver to take her to her apartment. As they pulled away from the curb, Sibyl unconsciously stroked the little dog and suddenly realized that the Chihuahua was staring right into her eyes.

It gave a little yip.

"You want to help?" she asked.

"What'd you say, lady?" the taxi driver asked, glancing into his mirror at her.

"I wasn't talking to you," Sibyl said.

The dog looked directly at her and nodded.

This, Sibyl thought, *is the first mystery that has to be solved.*

Sibyl lived in a high-rise condo a few minutes from the JADL office building. She paid the taxi driver and ducked into the vestibule, lurking behind a convenient column. She watched the street through the glass entrance doors. No one seemed to have followed the cab. She would almost have welcomed the presence of an emissary from their unseen enemy.

They went to the elevator and Sibyl punched the button for the top floor. As they went up she briefly considered attempting small talk, but that was not her strong suit at the best of times, and now she was definitely not in the mood. The little dog looked on with a degree of sympathy in its large, dark eyes, and Sibyl wondered what was going through its brain. Her, she corrected almost immediately, having realized that she was a female.

"Welcome to my apartment," Sibyl said. It was just down the hall from the elevator. She put the dog down so she could take out her key and unlock the front door, then she held it open as the Chihuahua trotted by her, her little legs flashing so quickly they were almost a blur.

Sibyl hit some toggles in the entranceway that opened into a spacious living room, and subdued light and sound came on, susurrating from hidden speakers all around the room, a recording of rain gently falling in a forest. Sibyl constantly played similar tracks of natural sounds to screen out the noise of traffic from below and the world outside.

She had large windows that let in plenty of light, but most of the living room's walls were covered by broad swatches of bright colors: red, green, orange, purple, yellow, and blue. They were juxtaposed according to an aesthetic that somehow employed discordant as well as harmonizing colors to form visually pleasing flows. Sibyl created these panels herself, changing them to suit her whim, using a combination of paints that allowed her to wipe the walls down to pure white when she wanted a change. She looked at the walls, wishing for such a change now. It was all too damned cheerful. She needed something dark and jagged and explosively discordant to match her current mood.

The room was sparsely furnished, yet entirely comfortable. There was a large white leather sofa, replete with a number of soft stuffed plush animals scattered upon it, fronted by a glass-topped coffee table supported by swoops of chrome piping. The table was empty, but for a closed laptop. Scattered around the couch were a number of smaller tables of various heights that held statuary, mostly abstract shapes in textures ranging from snaggletoothed lava chunks to bumpy coral branches to polished fragments of malachite and sprays of fragile, living blossoms, currently honeysuckle. Several bookshelves held a number of volumes, some of them Braille. Sibyl could read Braille as fast as a sighted person could read the printed page—faster than some. Oftentimes the simple feel of the raised bumps beneath her fingertips soothed her. Two upholstered chairs faced the sofa across the glass-topped coffee table.

Sibyl felt eyes on her, and looked down to see the Chihuahua standing by her side, gazing up at her. She realized that she'd been gazing for some time around the empty room. "I'm sorry," she apologized. "I'm being a very poor host. Can I get you anything? Something to eat—well, I actually don't have much on hand since I don't eat, but—"

She watched the little dog, now sitting at her feet, point to her mouth with a tiny paw and make panting motions.

"You're thirsty? Right. Make yourself comfortable. I'll be right back."

When Sibyl returned from the adjoining kitchen a moment later with a bowl of water, the dog had moved over to the sofa, and was sitting on her haunches on the glass table before it.

"Of course," Sibyl said, placing the bowl on the table beside the laptop. She sat down on the sofa and opened up the laptop as the dog drank daintily from the bowl. By the time she'd quenched her thirst, Sibyl had the laptop up and running and open to a word processing program, blank document ready.

The dog sat before the keyboard on her haunches, her remarkably tiny front paws no thicker than the average human forefinger. For a hunt-and-peck typist she was amazingly fast, and, for a dog, an incredibly good speller.

Sibyl sat on the sofa, peering at the screen as the electronic type crawled across it, sped by paws moving so quickly they were almost a blur.

I am scare agernt moon, she wrote, without bothering to use capital letters—except for those automatically inserted by the word processing program—or correct typos in her urgency to tell her story.

Of course, Sibyl thought. She'd never had direct dealings with Moon, but she knew of her; a joker in her human form, Moon was a shape-changer who could morph into any canid form, wild or domestic, living or extinct. And a SCARE agent. The JADL kept files on all known SCARE agents, active or retired. "I should have recognized you," Sibyl told the Chihuahua.

Is ok, Moon typed. Iam sorrty for what happened to Pretorius. He was agood man. Icame to him bercause I trusted him and I had tot ell someone what I know. I didn't know they were already oin my trail—

"Who?" Sibyl interrupted.

Jystice and the othr rogues. SCARE Agent Antonio Echeverrrria. He was the shooter. He killed presdent Van Rennssler.

"Why?" asked Sibyl.

To stop her gvng the moon to jokerfreaks, Moon typed. They knw better than to try and recruit me but i realized what was going on by overhearing bits opieces here and there. When they found me out and i was forced to run forit. I came to pretorius with my story—and you know what happened.

The sinking feeling turned into something else and Sibyl felt heat bubbling up and growing where her stomach would be if she were human.

But, listen, Moon continued. We should get out of hre, quick. They have a teleporter on the team—they can go anywhere.

"Buck," said Sibyl, with a sick, sinking feeling. "And his brother."

Moon nodded. They can find where you live.

"Let me grab a few things."

She didn't need clothes. They needed lawyers, guns, and money. And a computer. She could immediately put her hands on most of those things. She shut down the laptop, scooped it up from the table, shoved the sofa aside, and pulled up a piece of carpeting, exposing a good-sized floor safe. She opened it in a hurry and extracted an already packed bag, to which she added the laptop. Then she went to a closet off the living room and took out a leather coat. It was a little warm considering the weather, but it had deep pockets in which Moon would fit.

Sibyl put on the coat. "In you go," she said, and Moon leapt from the sofa and settled down into the pocket Sibyl held open for her.

They were not a moment too soon. There was an eerie sound and odd vibrations that neither Sibyl nor Moon, peering from her pocket, had ever felt before, and a dark semicircle appeared on a far wall of her living room.

Moon yipped excitedly. Sibyl did not waste words, but ran for the apartment door, slammed it shut behind her, and activated a special lock that could be opened only from the outside. "That'll hold them," she said, "for a few minutes, anyway. We better take the stairs."

She went down the steps quickly and was still breathing evenly when she reached the ground floor. The stairwell door opened out into an alley behind her apartment building. She peered out carefully. "Looks clear," she said in a quiet voice, and they went out into the alley, Sibyl walking at a fast clip. She hadn't taken five steps before three men stepped out from behind a pile of junk that lined the opposite alley wall. All three pointed guns at them.

"What do we have here?" one of the men asked facetiously in a heavy Russian accent.

"Pretty blue doll," another said.

"Where's the dog, Barbie?" added the third.

Moon peered out of her jacket pocket. Sibyl felt a flash of irritation. The only saving grace was that they were armed only with silenced pistols, not automatic rifles. She had a chance—

Moon bared her teeth and growled, long and loud. The men all laughed.

"Funny little dog," one said.

Moon leapt from Sibyl's pocket.

The men paused to laugh again, and sealed their fate.

By the time they dropped their pistols to cover Moon she was already at full speed, her tiny legs a blur as she dodged and jinked like a dark moth in flight. Each gunman fired a couple of shots, but their bullets whined off the pavement harmlessly, though one of the ricochets clipped Sibyl and glanced off without doing any damage. Their curses turned to laughter again as, still six feet away, Moon launched herself into the air right at them.

"Oh, no," one managed to say. The streetlights flickered for blocks around. In mid-leap Moon transformed and their laughter transformed into sudden screams.

Any canid species, Sibyl thought, *alive or extinct.*

Canis dirus. Weight, one hundred and sixty pounds. Height, two and a half feet at the shoulder. Length, six feet from nose to tail tip. Teeth, Sibyl thought, *a lot, and pretty fucking big and sharp. The dire wolf.*

There were some shrieks and a couple of wild shots and it was over. Sibyl watched Moon wipe the blood off her muzzle with one incredibly large paw and then lick it clean. It might have been better if she'd left one alive to interrogate, but then Buck and Blood could pop up behind them at any moment. "We'd better go," she said.

Moon shifted into a tiny Chihuahua again and leapt up into her arms. But before she did that she peed all over the bodies.

That'll give CSI some pause, Sibyl thought. Together they hurried away and turned out of the alley. As she walked rapidly to the busy street off the alley, she pulled one of the burner cell phones out of her bag, and hit one of the saved numbers.

"Go dark," she said, stopped for a moment, dropped the cell, crushed it under her foot, and picked up the pieces and put them in her other coat pocket.

Half a dozen despondent JADL high-level staffers and allies had gathered in the safe house, along with Sibyl and Moon, still a Chihuahua. Very few people had ever seen her in her actual human joker form, which was rumored to be so crippled that she could barely move about on her own and was actually less able to communicate than her canine forms.

Moon was sharing the sofa with Charlie Herriman and Vincent "Ratboy" Marinelli, who resembled a four-foot-tall rat with disconcertingly human-looking hands. The others, sitting silently in scattered chairs, were all jokers, all lawyers, investigators, or board members of the JADL.

Sibyl stood before them, half-hoping the proper words would come to her, half-fearing that they wouldn't. "You all know what happened earlier today," she began. "My father, our leader and guiding light for so many years, gave his life in service of that which he'd always believed in: justice. I miss him already; I'll miss him forever. But there's one thing I know." She paused a moment, gathering herself. "I will not let his death be in vain. I will strive with all my strength to see this case through, to prove Bradley Finn innocent and bring the conspirators to justice. Dr. Pretorius would expect no less."

Flipper looked up for the first time, meeting her gaze. "What do we do?"

"First, protect Moon at all costs. She is our key witness. Moon—" She shifted her gaze to the little dog. "You must put down whatever you know, all the details of the conspiracy, who's involved, times and dates, as complete a record of what you witnessed as you can. Your unsupported testimony alone doesn't constitute proof of the conspiracy, but documenting what we know about it is the first and proper step toward unraveling it. But we need more proof to back it up. And to that end—"

She turned her attention to the other occupant of the couch. "Ratboy?"

His whiskers twitched as he turned his disconcertingly pink eyes on her.

"You were able to get in touch with Jonathan Hive?"

"Sure. He's on his way in. He'll be in touch again when he gets into the city."

Sibyl nodded. "Have you gotten that special equipment I enquired about?"

"I got people working on it," Ratboy said. "It's not exactly shit you can pick up at the corner Radio Shack. I'll have it by the time Bugsy shows up."

"Right," Sibyl said. "We all have this other line of investigation to develop—the connection of the conspiracy to the Russian mob. I will deal with that."

Herriman frowned. "Sibyl—"

"Don't worry. I've already documented my investigation in detail. That will be available to you if, if I don't come back."

"Let me accompany—" Herriman pleaded.

She shook her head. "You're next in line if something happens to me, and you're our best lawyer, our client's best hope." She wished that she could smile. She checked her wristwatch. "It's just after midnight. I'd better get going."

Sibyl could smell the sea as she got off her café racer on a dark backstreet at two in the morning. There was no other traffic and not much in the way of lights burning over the Brighton Beach alley. She took off her helmet and stripped off her leathers, boots and all. She stood naked in the hot night air, feeling the cooling breezes wafting over her from the nearby sea. It was an almost sensual feeling that engulfed her entire body, the surface of which was one large sensory organ.

All she wore were her wrist vocoder, her gorget, a small tool pouch around her slender hips, and a coil of thin silken rope looped around over her right shoulder. All five feet and nine inches of her slender frame were hairless, blue-green, and nude. Not that there was much to see: she no more had nipples, genitalia, nor bodily orifices of any sort than the Barbie doll whose proportions hers resembled. The wild card had transformed her into something more mannequin than man, most people thought when they saw her. They were wrong. She was as the Professor had made her.

Naked and greenish-blue in the night air, Sibyl moved off into the warren of streets, the image of the map she'd memorized firmly in her mind. After a ten-minute walk through silent and sleeping streets she came to a tall brick wall, a little over two feet higher than her head and topped by shards of broken glass. Without hesitation she tossed the silken rope over the top of the wall. The rubber-tipped grappling hook caught silently against the other side and she swarmed up the wall like a blue lizard scuttling up a rock. She paused momentarily, holding herself up with one arm wrapped over the edge as she felt the shards of glass set into the wall. She cleared a space of a half foot or so, breaking them off with her bare hand. She didn't think that the shards would pierce her flesh if she stood on them, but she didn't want to take the chance.

Sibyl hauled herself up to the top of the wall, switched the grappling hook to the other side, and let herself down quickly and silently, feeling the rough surface of the stone wall rub pleasingly over the surface of her body. The rope came down with a simple flick of the wrist, and she coiled it up and left it at the base of the wall to use again when she exited.

She looked quickly around. She couldn't see in the dark, of course, but her other sensory apparatus, the fabric that wrapped around her entire body, was much more sensitive than any sense possessed by any human. She was inside the walled-in backyard of a large house at the far end of the swath of well-kept lawn. She could hear the guard dogs that roamed the backyard at night. If she was silent, she wouldn't draw their attention. Sibyl had no scent for them to pick up.

She moved quickly and quietly over the newly cut grass on naked feet, passing by a tennis court, a rather large swimming pool, and finally a meticulous garden, running mainly to roses and other flowering shrubs, sectioned off by looping dirt pathways. Statuary that looked to be of Greek or Roman origin stood and sat or reclined in various niches or atop marble plinths, all in surprisingly good taste. It was rather impressive, if one was impressed by that sort of thing. Stone images of ancient dead men actually meant little to her, but she could appreciate the—*What do the Chinese call it? The feng shui.*

She arrived at the back door of the imposing mansion, but moved over to the closed French windows beside it and took a glass cutter from her pouch. It was a moment's work to cut out an oval that allowed her entry. She paused for a moment before going in and stared hard, reaching into her mind to activate a deeper level of seeing than that she usually employed. In a moment she saw them, the crisscrossing laser scanner lines that indicated the motion detector that protected the interior of the house. Carefully she stepped inside and, with a contortionist's grace, moved silently over, under, and past them all.

As she advanced deeper into the dark house she could feel unseen waves of infrared radiation strike her as the second line of defense, passive infrared scanners keyed to human skin temperature, kicked in. She passed through them undetected like a ghost, fascinated by the riches each room held. Paintings, statuary, ancient rugs and tapestries and museum-level artifacts from many cultures and time periods—it could have been overwhelming even for her, if she wasn't completely focused on the task at hand.

She followed the floor plan that Ratboy had found on some clearly restricted website (whether governmental or illicit, she didn't know) to the proper staircase and silently went up it, down the heavily carpeted wall to the bedroom, three doors down and to the left. The door was closed but not locked.

The bedroom itself was crowded with amazing objets d'art, like the rest of the house. There was a cabinet against one wall that held a small collection of what had to be Fabergé eggs. The paintings on the wall were all jaw-clenched aristocrats that she didn't recognize but looked rather Russian to her. Czars, perhaps?

The bed lay against the far wall. The nightstand beside it held the last security device—an intercom unit—and a golden, intricately engraved tray that held a finely cut crystalline decanter filled with a brownish-gold liquid. No doubt some fabulously expensive liquor. She leaned over and did not turn off the intercom, but turned the volume knob so low that it would pick up only the loudest scream.

She turned to the massive four-poster bed, carved from dark wood—teak? Sibyl wondered—where slept Ivan Grekov, the head of the Russian Mafia in New York City.

Thankfully, he was alone. Sibyl had been worried about that.

She watched him sleep for a moment. He was an old man, thick through the shoulders and chest, but no taller than she was herself. Probably a little shorter. His lined face was slack in repose, his white hair was cut short. His equally white mustache was too big for his face.

He slept peacefully for a man whose nickname was Ivan the Terrible, a man who had committed every imaginable crime, either by his own hand or in his own name. *The man who had killed my father.* He snored, quietly. A little bit of drool ran from the corner of his half-open mouth, down his chin.

When she could no longer bear the sight of him she said, "Hello, Grekov," in a normal conversational tone.

Instantly the old man's eyes opened wide. The fear on his face turned almost into puzzlement. "What is this dream I am having, of naked beautiful blue angel?"

"It's not a dream. I'm not an angel."

Grekov squinted as if to see her better in the darkened room. He made no effort to move. "Who are you?" he asked. "What do you want?"

"The answers to a couple of questions." She moved closer, so that she loomed over the bed, touching the mattress with her knees.

Grekov stared at her with a certain wonder in his eyes. "You have my full attention."

"Why are you working with those bastards who killed the president?"

"Ah." Grekov shrugged. "Is just business. They needed some extra guns. They paid well. They suggested that a new administration might not be so . . . concerned . . . with our activities."

"Is that so?" Sibyl threw one leg upon the bed. The sheets were satin. She could feel them cool against her skin. Grekov stiffened for a moment, but he relaxed when he realized that she was simply straddling him. He looked at her, more curious than anything.

"What's the name of the man who shot my father?"

"Your . . . father?"

She nodded, leaning over him, putting her chest against his. "Dr. Pretorius."

"Ha. I—you must be the one they call Ice Blue Sibyl."

She nodded again, stooping, bringing her lips very close to his.

"Why should I tell you that, pretty lady?"

She looked down at him for what seemed like a very long time, her expression, as always, unmoving. Finally she said, "It does not matter. The gunman just pulled a trigger. You're the one who really killed him." She pressed her lips to Grekov's.

For a moment he kissed her, his lips moving against hers, his tongue probing her unopened mouth. He started to move against her, trying to push up, but she'd locked her legs around his hips, her arms around his neck.

"You . . . you have no mouth," Grekov stammered. "What are you?"

A good question, Sibyl thought. "Not a joker, if that's what you are thinking. I have no memory of a previous life before the virus. I think I'm—some kind of animated doll. A toy."

"But how—"

"I remember my creator. The Professor, he called himself. A fussy man, funny, secretive. He wore a sky-blue tuxedo to Hiram Worchester's Aces High parties, in the old days. I remember the smell of his pipe. And dolls and little robots on the shelves, with empty eyes. They creeped me out. Some of them . . . came alive. The Professor was a genius of sorts. Touched by the wild card. I was his crowning achievement, and he used his ace to give me life. Then—then I found him on the floor of his workshop, dead. It took me almost a week to realize that's why he didn't pay any more attention to me. I was that innocent, that ignorant. That's when I wandered out, on my own in Jokertown. The time between the Professor's death and when Dr. Pretorius found me . . . I never talk about that time. Pretorius saved me. Made me his ward, his assistant. The Professor was my creator, but Dr. Pretorius was my father. And you killed him. For money. But I am my father's daughter."

Grekov tried to turn his head away, he tried to buck her off, but she held on grimly.

"Your lips," he mumbled. "So cold. So . . . cold."

Ice Blue Sibyl leaned close and kissed him once again. This time she held the kiss, even as he squirmed and bucked beneath her. She sucked all the heat out of him and radiated it away, through her flesh, out into the room behind her. He fought her, once almost managing to roll off the bed, but she retained her relentless grip, continued her relentless draining of every degree of heat out of Ivan Grekov's body.

After five minutes he stopped moving, but she continued at it, draining the heat out of him and dispersing it all around them into the room. After ten minutes, she stopped and took her lips from him and pulled away, releasing him.

He was frozen solid, along with his silken pajamas and satin sheet, and probably a couple inches of the mattress on which he lay. On his face was a look of unbelieving terror.

"That's for killing my father," Ice Blue Sibyl said. That wasn't the only reason she did it. With Grekov dead that took the Russians out of the picture. His death would throw the Brighton Beach boys into chaos as they clawed one another for supremacy. She'd removed them from the equation. Now they could concentrate solely on Justice and the other core conspirators within SCARE.

She looked over at the nightstand and took the decanter by the neck and swiftly smashed it down on Grekov's head. Both the decanter and his head shattered into little pieces.

Let them figure that out when they find the body, Sibyl thought.

She left the mansion, wondering if she'd also left behind the veneer of humanity it had taken her thirty years to acquire.

Sibyl was back at the safe house by three thirty. All three bedrooms had been claimed by sleeping JADL staff members. The living room couch was occupied by Charlie Herriman and Vincent Marinelli, asleep. Marinelli slept in a compact ball, his naked pink tail, longer than his body, tightly wrapped around himself. Herriman slept upright on the sofa's far end. He snored loudly. Marinelli made little squeaking sounds in his sleep, as if he was on the trail of a really big piece of cheese.

When the doorbell rang at 4 a.m. Flipper snorted loudly, opened his eyes, and said, "Whaizzit?" Ratboy rolled to the floor, drawing a pistol he'd had in a shoulder holster.

Sibyl, who had been sitting silently on the La-Z-Boy, said, "Easy. I don't think the Russian mob rings doorbells when they come calling." She went to the door and peered through the peephole. Jonathan Hive stood on the doorstep, well lit by an overhead light, accompanied by a large, burly young Black man.

Sibyl opened the door. "Come in, Bugsy." And added to the young man who followed him inside, "And who are you?"

"I'm Dwight the Uber driver."

Sibyl looked at Bugsy. "You Ubered from Charleston to New York City?"

Bugsy shrugged. "It seemed like a good idea at the time. Um. Can you tell Mouseman to put the gun down?"

"I'm Ratboy," Marinelli snarled, but he lowered his weapon.

Bugsy nodded. "And, uh, can you pay my fare? I didn't want to use my credit card."

Sibyl nodded. "That's cheap of you. But ultimately very wise."

She went over to the bag that lay by her recliner and took out a stack of bills. She handed it to Dwight. "That should contain, give or take, ten thousand dollars."

Dwight's eyes grew wide. "Just what are you folks involved in?"

"Nothing bad," Sibyl said.

"Read all about it on the *Aces!* website in a couple of days," Bugsy told him.

Dwight reached into the front pocket of his shirt and handed Bugsy his card.

"Call me, anytime. You folks take care, now." And he went back out the door, shutting it behind himself.

Bugsy looked at Sibyl. "What now?"

She looked from Bugsy to Flipper to Ratboy, to the other staffers who'd come out of the bedrooms, roused by the noise, and were sleepily rubbing their eyes as they staggered into the living room. "Now," she said, "everyone goes back to sleep and gets some rest. Tomorrow, we plan. And then . . ."

"And then, what?" Bugsy prompted.

"And then," Sibyl said, "we smash this conspiracy to Hell."

Washington, D.C., in the summertime was as hot and humid as Charleston had been, with the added factor that Sibyl, Bugsy, and Ratboy were crammed into what was ostensibly a taco truck parked in the narrow concrete canyon of G Street, hemmed in by tall buildings that allowed not a hint of a fresh breeze to stir the stifling atmosphere.

Three JADL operatives were in the main body of the faux food truck, making and dispensing tacos, chimichangas, burritos, and chalupas. Bugsy, Ratboy, and Sibyl were in a small, self-contained, and closed-off chamber of the truck. Ratboy was working his tech, Bugsy was working his wasps, and Sibyl was the only one who wasn't soaked in sweat. She was as cool and untouched as usual, following the bank of monitors that took up an entire wall of the cloistered corner of the truck.

"So, what we got here," Ratboy explained with his whiskers twitching with excitement, "is an actual electronic observation deck used to monitor SEAL teams, or Rangers, or whatever you wanna call your black ops while they're off on their mission—"

"I call them wasps," Bugsy said.

"Whatever. Each monitor is tuned to a particular operative. You hear what they hear, you see what they see, and it's all transmitted back here"—he patted the control board with one of his disconcerting human-looking hands—"where it can be recorded or transmitted at will to any designated destination. The only wrinkle," he added with some pride, "is that I managed to wire the new microcameras and microphones—"

"Carried by my wasps," Bugsy said.

Ratboy fixed him with a pink-eyed glare. "Whatever. If it wasn't for my tech—"

"Shhh," Sibyl said. "The flight is entering the building now."

The building she was referring to was right across the street from them: the Eisenhower Executive Office Building, which contained the Vice President's Ceremonial Office.

Vice President Duncan Towers had been sworn in as president within hours of the assassination, but in the ensuing chaos most of his staff had not yet moved into the White House offices appropriate to their new higher standing. All of that particular mess was still being sorted out, so most were still ensconced in their old digs in the Eisenhower Executive Office Building, which was adjacent to the West Wing on the White House premises.

Bugsy's wasps, hardly encumbered at all by the microtech they wore, made their way, singly, unseen and silent, into the august halls of the Eisenhower Building, straight to the office of Reginald Fleming, the former vice president's chief of staff, where Fleming was entertaining a visitor. Antonio Echeverria of SCARE. Justice himself.

Fleming was not in the best mood. He leaned back in his overstuffed office chair to glare directly at Justice. "The Russians are out, then?"

Justice looked acutely uncomfortable. "They've gone to the mattresses. I don't know who is going to emerge on top. Grekov was killed in some horrible way, maybe by one of his own. No one knows. It looks like the work of an ace. If I didn't know better, I'd suspect the Colonel, but he's well alibied. Brighton Beach is blowing up. It's a war down there."

"Did Grekov talk before he died?"

"We don't know that, either. But he never knew enough to matter."

"What about the retard and his brother?"

"They're both retards," said Justice. "They're out of the way. Having fun down in Buenos Aires."

"They're liabilities," said Fleming. "I would sleep better at night if they were both out of the way permanently."

"I can take care of that," Justice promised, "but let's hold off a bit. We may have further need of their . . . special talents."

"Hold off, then," said Fleming, "but not too long. This needs to be cleaned up. Do what needs to be done. And keep me out of it. We need plausible deniability."

"You and the man," said Justice, "so if this falls apart, you don't know me. Is that what I'm hearing?"

"You were the shooter," Fleming said pointedly, "but don't get your panties in a twist. We're close. Our polling suggests that almost eighty percent of the public thinks the Big Snail took Pauline out. Once things settle down, we'll find some pretext to get rid of Lady Black, and you'll be the director of SCARE. And rich."

Justice seemed appeased. "Your boss knows I'm loyal."

"He knows you're loyal as money can buy," Fleming said.

"Hey, I'm Towers all the way—"

In the food truck, Sibyl and her companions looked at one another. She wished that she could smile. "Money shot," Sibyl announced. "Go live. It's time to share this with the world." She nodded at Bugsy. Bugsy nodded back, and Ratboy punched the buttons.

"Hello fans in cyberland," Jonathan Hive said into his microphone. "This is Jonathan Tipton-Clark reporting from the field—virtually live. We're working only with a slight tape delay to bring you undercover audio from the offices of the vice president in the Eisenhower Executive Office Building. The voices belong to SCARE agent Antonio Echeverria and Reginald Fleming, chief of staff to Vice President Duncan Towers. I'll just let them speak for themselves—"

Ratboy made the connection. "Transmitting to the *Aces!* website," he confirmed. The tape started from the beginning of the conversation, which continued into interesting details.

Fifteen minutes later the *Aces!* website crashed. Twenty minutes later a squad of grim-faced Capitol policemen were breaking down the door to Fleming's office.

Bugsy, no longer caring if the wasps were spotted or not, brought them down to get some great close-ups of Fleming's stunned face. They got it all. For good measure, he had one of them sting Justice on the nose.

Sibyl watched impassively as the cops marched the men out of the office. By then the FBI and SCARE had arrived to join the party. She didn't know if she wanted to laugh or cry, but she was capable of neither.

We got them, she thought to herself. *We got them all, Father.*

For Victor Milán. Ve con dios, hermano.

Within That
House Secure

X

Cahier No. 619
5 December 2017
The House Secure
Charleston, South Carolina

Pauline van Renssaeler was assassinated over six months ago, and despite what Jon-
athan Tipton-Clark and the JADL revealed about the conspiracy that killed her, de-
spite the arrests that have been made and the admittedly glacially slow work of the
Satterly Commission, half the world still thinks Theodorus was behind it.

Now, with the inbound ice bodies having been spotted and publicized by the global
astronomy community, more than half the world thinks we plan to bombard the planet
into a second ice age.

I wonder if they will kill us all.

Theodorus had been very worried about the billiards table. He was widely assumed to have been instrumental in a conspiracy that killed the leader of the
free world, and had been accused by her successor of initiating an effort to end
all life on Earth, and he was very worried about the billiards table.

The games room had been judged the best location in the House Secure for
the press conference, but it had required the removal of the table—not to mention the curio cabinets and shelves that displayed his large collection of antique
board games—and Theodorus had insisted on bringing in a team of experts from
Chicago to ensure that the table not be damaged when it was taken out of the
room. How one became an expert in billiards table removal, Mathilde didn't
know. What she did know was that she had been visiting the Witherspoon estate
regularly for nearly her entire life, and had never once seen Theodorus playing
billiards.

Four rows of chairs were lined up in front of a specially built dais. The dais
featured its own row of chairs and a podium, all in front of a backdrop decorated
with a repeated motif of the Witherspoon Aerospace logo. Mathilde squinted,
taking a closer look at the logo, then pulled out her worn old employee badge.
The logo on the backdrop was slightly different—the Os there looked like cratered
moons.

"When did they change the logo?" she asked Clifford Bell.

"Logo?" he replied.

"Look, see the moons there?" She showed him her badge.

He pulled out his own badge, glanced at it, and then showed it to her. It matched the backdrop.

"They're issuing new IDs?" she asked.

Cliff shrugged. "Not that I know of. This is the same one I've always had."

"Since when?"

He gave her a questioning look. "Since 2003, I guess. Maybe you just never noticed it until now?"

That was . . . well, that was entirely possible, actually. But it still made her uneasy for some reason. Cliff was looking at her oddly. Probably wondering why she was worried about logos when so much had happened, when so much was riding on the reaction to this press conference.

Vickie, the public relations professional who had been an employee at one or another of Theodorus's companies for even longer than Mathilde had been, walked over. She gave them both appraising looks, then said, "The makeup artists did a good job on you, Mathilde. Mr. Bell, we need to do something about your eyes."

Forestalling an argument, Mathilde asked, "Is everything set up? Are we ready to go live?"

Vickie shook her head. "Most of the networks are already live. Half of them are convinced that the authorities are going to descend and arrest Mr. Witherspoon at any minute and the other half think that, too, but that he won't go without a fight. They're expecting fireworks."

"Impacts," murmured Mathilde. "Not fireworks. They're expecting asteroid impacts. The end of the world."

"Thank you all for coming," Theodorus said. "I know that it has been some time since I made a public appearance or answered any questions from the press." The assembled reporters, producers, camera operators, and sound technicians all looked at one another. One of them, Mathilde couldn't see, actually laughed aloud. It had literally been years since Theodorus had appeared in public.

"To address the two questions that most of you no doubt wish to ask first," Theodorus said, "no, I had nothing to do with President van Renssaeler's death, and no, I am not planning to rain asteroids down upon the Earth."

The room erupted in a tumultuous scrum of shouted questions, imprecations, pleas, even threats. Mathilde looked over at Vickie. The woman looked shocked.

"If you didn't order President van Renssaeler's assassination, then who did?"

"Are you claiming that the astronomers are all wrong, that there aren't over fifty asteroids bound for Earth?"

"Why should we believe you?"

"Why should we believe you?"

"Why should we believe you?"

Theodorus nodded, but not at any of the reporters. In the back of the room, a technician activated the screen hanging from the ceiling in front of the backdrop. The image it showed was of a shapeless hunk of something gray and white floating in a void.

"This is, or rather, was, Asteroid 2013 GH22. It is an example of one of the newly discovered group of objects within the Koronis family consisting largely of water ice."

A woman's hand shot up, and she didn't wait for Theodorus to acknowledge her before asking, "Why did you say 'was'? Has something happened to it?"

Theodorus smiled broadly, and Mathilde winced. His smile didn't play well on camera. "Our friends at the International Astronomical Union are very particular about designations," he said. "2013 GH22 is no longer in the asteroid belt, so it is technically no longer an asteroid."

The object on the screen rotated to show what had been its aft side. A curved shape was appended to its surface, and fiery gases, immediately recognizable as the outflow from a rocket engine, jetted away from the unnatural feature.

"Technically, well, I suppose technically you could say that it's now a spaceship. It has an engine, as you can see. And in this case"—the picture zoomed in— "the engine is also the pilot."

More than one of the people gathered in the room, including Vickie up on the stage next to him, gasped. The closer view showed that the curved shape was a mottled nautilus snail shell nearly identical to Theodorus's own.

Theodorus spoke over a number of shouts. "Let me say a little more and save you all some questions. The ice bodies are bound in our direction, but toward the Moon, not toward the Earth. The first will impact the lunar surface in a little less than three years, on September 15, 2020."

"What's their purpose?"

"Is there any chance they could miss the Moon and hit the Earth?"

"Did President van Renssaeler approve of this?"

"Does President Towers approve of this?"

There were even more questions than those, but Theodorus just let them wash over him. Mathilde watched the faces of the reporters. She saw anger there, but more than that, fear.

"I've said all I plan to say about the president. As for your other questions, we'll be distributing a fact sheet and drives with more information and video for you in just a moment," said Theodorus. "But in brief, there are fifty-one ice bodies bound for the Moon, they are part of a terraforming project, and at least some elements in the United States government, as well as in the governments of most of the G20, have known about it for at least two years. Why they haven't shared their knowledge with the public, I do not know."

He didn't answer the question about whether one could hit us here, Mathilde thought. She wondered if that was on purpose. One of the few print reporters in the room, an aging nat man wearing an unfashionable khaki jacket, had been holding up his hand for the last few minutes. He hadn't stood. He hadn't shouted. "Simon," said Theodorus. "You have a question."

"Yes, Mr. Witherspoon," said the man. "Why?"

And Theodorus smiled again.

Cahier No. 620
6 December 2017
Charleston, South Carolina

Theodorus has been called to Washington to appear before the Satterly Commission, though he's adamant about not going. Neither, he says, will he answer any of the many other summons. He insists that he will not spend his valuable time testifying before four separate congressional subcommittees and two full Senate committees, and neither will he "trot off" to the Pentagon, Foggy Bottom, U.S. Space Command, the J. Edgar Hoover Building, nor, especially, not ever, the White House.

Malachi asked him if he's ever heard of such a thing as a subpoena.

Theodorus told him that it was his job to handle the paperwork.

"We need goodwill yet," said Malachi.

Malachi, who reads all those newspapers every day, must not have read any this morning. Goodwill is the last thing we're getting.

European papers are calling for the U.S. government to nationalize all of Theodorus's holdings immediately. Official news outlets in the Middle East and Central Asia have called for his arrest, and the subtext suggesting he simply be executed is not hard to pick up on. At least the string of nations around the equator where we've done so much for employment and infrastructure over the years are apparently reserving judgment, though even there, an opposition paper in Colombia this morning led with the headline "¿AYUDAMOS A CONSTRUIR UNA LUNA JOKER? DID WE HELP BUILD A JOKER MOON?"

Yes. Yes, you did, though of course we never told you.

It's only the fact that so many world governments knew about the inbound asteroids and concealed that fact for so long that's kept us from being the target of all the ire in the world, it seems. People are also very upset—marching in the streets upset, turning over police cars upset—with their leaders.

Clifford Bell raised the idea this morning that Theodorus "consider relocation," as he put it. By which he meant Theodorus should have Mollie Steunenberg open one of her portals and travel through it to one of our lunar bases immediately.

Theodorus said no.

When Cliff said he didn't know whether he could protect Theodorus here any longer, Theodorus said, "I did not name this place the House Secure lightly."

Governments, business leaders, religious leaders, the media—they're all calling for investigations at the least and outright seizure of everything we've done at most. Publicly. Cliff insists that the back-channel chatter he's hearing from his sources indicates that privately, the reactions are even more vehement.

Jokers interviewed around the world express everything from disbelief to enthusiasm to caution to rejection. A video clip being shown over and over again features a woman with a row of beautiful green eyes completely encircling her head saying, "It's insane, what did you expect me to say? You believe we all think the same?"

Dr. Bradley Finn, still technically a person of interest in the president's assassination but released on bail after the conspiracy was revealed, has gone on record calling the project insane.

Oliver is at the Marshall Islands base. I haven't been able to reach him.

The Sands of Mourning

PART 2

2017

"THEY'RE MASSIVE," ADESINA SAID, as they looked up at the monuments to the Living Gods. Her cobalt wings spread out, an iridescent sheen reflecting off them. "I mean, it's one thing to read about them, but in person they're, like, totes big."

The statues were carved of sandstone, rivaling those of Ancient Egypt. They lined the broad pathway leading to the temple. Figures of Sobek, Anubis, Bast, Tawaret, and Thoth mirrored one another. Past them were larger statues of Isis and Osiris. Dwarfing them all were Ra's twin effigies, bracketing the entrance to the temple. Ra was depicted wearing a falcon mask and traditional *shenti*. A golden ball of fire was suspended over his head. It was a neat feat of engineering.

A cool breeze whispered across the First Court inside the temple where they stood waiting to meet up with Bastet. *"Bubbles!"*

Michelle turned and saw Bastet walking briskly across the courtyard. She wore a *kalasiris,* but it was made from a stretchy, brightly colored, geometric print material, not the traditional linen. Her black muzzle had a few white hairs sprinkled in it now, Michelle noted. Bastet resembled Bast, but she was shorter and there was a roundness to her once-lithe body. Michelle found herself in an enthusiastic embrace. Bastet smelled of sandalwood and vanilla. Just the way Michelle remembered.

"How have you been?" Bastet asked, releasing Michelle, then turning to look at Adesina. "And you must be Adesina. You are your mother's daughter. Powerful and beautiful. I imagine you've had more than your own share of adventures."

"Oh, not so much," Adesina replied, smoothly avoiding her mother's gaze. It was a lie. Her daughter had been having far too many adventures as far as Michelle was concerned. Adesina had gone into a cocoon and had changed from a child to a teenager overnight.

According to Michelle, she was still just a child, but she didn't act like a child. And though Adesina still looked like a teenager, she wanted to be treated like an adult. Michelle didn't like that, either.

"I think your mother would disagree with you," Bastet said with a laugh. "How long has it been, Michelle?"

"Since the Caliphate War."

"It seems like longer," Bastet said. She patted Michelle's cheek. "And you're not playing fat today."

"You asked us to come for a visit," Michelle answered with a soft laugh. "I'm as incognito as I can be. And you know how it is—me being fat gets people nervous."

Bastet took Adesina by her right arm and Michelle by her left, then began escorting them across the courtyard. Before they got halfway, a man strode through the far entrance. He was dressed exactly like the statue of Ra: falcon mask, ceremonial robes, even a ball of fire floating above his head.

Under the mask was Drake Thomas, who had once been known as Little Fat Boy. Michelle knew who he was only because she'd been warned by Lohengrin. Klaus had told Michelle what had happened to Drake after she'd absorbed his nuclear blast and saved New Orleans. The ancient joker symbiote Sekhmet had left John Fortune to reside in Drake. Drake was so powerful that Sekhmet made him Ra: Protector of Old Egypt and First among the Living Gods. Without him, they would have been at the mercy of the Caliphate after the war. Only a handful of people knew that Ra was the boy who'd blown up Pyote, Texas.

"Bubbles." Drake's voice was deeper and darker than she remembered. When she'd known him before, his voice had just begun to crack.

"Drake," Michelle replied cooly, keeping her arm linked with Bastet's. She certainly wasn't going to hug him. And shaking his hand seemed weirdly impersonal given their history. How do you treat someone who put you into a coma for two years, even if it had been accidental? Michelle wasn't afraid of Drake. However, she didn't want to have anything to do with him, either.

"When Bastet told me you were coming I didn't believe her. It's been a long time. And who is this?" He gave Adesina a smile, but it was creepy and she didn't return it.

"My daughter," Michelle replied.

He nodded as if he had known the answer all along. "What a dork," she heard Adesina say under her breath.

"I guess I am a dork," Drake said. "Actually, I was once a fanboy of your mother's. But I put aside childish things when I came to Egypt. And now I must know . . . why did the Little Cat ask you to come?"

Bastet's body stiffened a little. "Because that's what people do, Drake," she said. That he had hurt her was obvious in the quaver in her voice. "They spend time together. Talk on the phone. Normal things."

"I thought it was because you have this ridiculous notion I need help. Assassins. Bombs. I have more enemies than you can count. None have succeeded in killing me yet. And I've told you to call me Ra when we're in public. It's confusing to the adherents if you don't. And I certainly don't need help. Not from you and not from her."

Michelle rolled her eyes. *Awesome,* she thought. *Drake isn't fucked up—he's turned into an asshole.*

"You know, I can work with that, Drake," Michelle said, giving him a broad, insincere smile. "Seriously, I'm here to catch up with Bastet and show Adesina some of Old Egypt. I don't know what this whole 'call me Ra' thing is about and

I'm pretty much cool with not finding out. Your ace parlor trick left me in a coma, kid. I'm not exactly your biggest fan."

Drake shrugged. "I'm not a kid anymore. And Ra . . . well, that's who I am now. It's incredibly disrespectful for you to call me anything else." He opened his hand and another fiery orb appeared. From the center of it, a jet of fire shot skyward. The heat that radiated off it was brutal.

Michelle guessed this was supposed to impress her. He gave her a smug look and the orb disappeared. *Oh, you wee thing*, she thought. *You couldn't destroy me when your powers were at their fullest. You're not going to scare me with Sekhmet controlling them. And I don't give a shit who worships you.*

Michelle pulled her hand from Bastet's arm and let a bubble form in it. It rose up in the air, hovering there. She let it grow. It was one of her favorite things to do. The bubble was beautiful, but it could be almost anything she wanted it to be. It all depended on the way things went.

"Anyone who insists on wearing a mask in public when it isn't Halloween or who doesn't have a joker so horrible they need to hide their face . . . well, that seems like pretentious bullshit to me. Or did your pimple problem never clear up?"

Ra pulled himself taller. He was still several inches shorter than Michelle, who stood almost six feet tall. "I'm a God," he said venomously. "People bow down to me."

"And they bow down to Sobek, too," she replied with a shrug. "I'm not sure this is a card you want to play."

His body language was all she needed to see to know how angry he was. She was enjoying it. After Talas, her control over her emotions had slipped considerably.

"Bubbles, stop it," Bastet said, grabbing Michelle's arm.

"Mom!"

"Oh, fine," Michelle replied, letting the bubble float away. "Honestly, Bastet, you never let me have any fun. And what did I say about calling me Bubbles?"

"That you wished you'd called yourself something like Effervescence and then everyone would have called you Effy and it would be less goofy than 'Bubbles.' There was also something else about it sounding like a fifties stripper name and how that was funny at the time, but now not so much and . . ."

"You know, I'm going to stop telling you things," Michelle said.

"Mom, you never told me you didn't like being called 'Bubbles.'" Adesina gave Michelle a speculative look.

"I think Bubbles is a perfectly acceptable name." A tall thin man wearing a gold death's-head mask walked slowly toward them, leaning ever so slightly on an ebony cane topped by a gold dragon's-head handle. Michelle recognized Charles Dutton. She had too many contacts in Jokertown not to.

"Mr. Dutton," she said, genuinely perplexed. "It's very . . . odd to see you here."

"I might say the same about you, Ms. Pond." It was difficult to tell if Dutton was being sincere because the mask muffled his voice. *Yet another mask,* she thought. *Really, what's up with that?*

"Mr. Dutton," Drake said, stepping forward while sparing Michelle one last *this isn't over with* look. "I wasn't expecting you until tomorrow."

"I thought I'd take an extra day. I move slower now than I used to. Do you suppose we can go inside? I don't do well standing for long periods."

"Of course," Drake said. Dutton walked past Michelle and she noticed that he was being very subtle about relying on his cane. She knew he'd funded various programs at Xavier Desmond High School that Adesina attended, which she found surprising given his history of being a slumlord.

"Aren't you going to join us?" asked Dutton. "I think you would be interested. Your daughter, too."

"Bastet," Drake said. "Come along." It was a command.

Oh, no, pardner, Michelle thought, *you did not just treat my friend like that.*

"I'm so sorry," Michelle said, not even trying to hide how annoyed she was. "Bastet promised lunch and catching up. I'm afraid you'll have to do without us. Mr. Dutton, it was an unexpected pleasure."

"The pleasure was all mine," Dutton replied. Michelle really wanted to know what was going on behind his mask.

"He's not well," Bastet said. Michelle, Adesina, and Bastet were in the cool, dark embrace of Sobek's Delight, a restaurant that Bastet claimed had the best food in Old Egypt. Adesina had excused herself to use the LGR, leaving them alone.

"I'm not seeing 'There's something wrong with Drake.' I'm seeing 'Drake's an asshole.' When I knew him, he was fucked up because he accidentally blew up his entire town, killing everyone he knew and loved." Michelle dipped her baladi bread into the generous bowl of besarah and was delighted to find it was better than Bastet had promised. The flavors of the besarah were complicated and the bread soft and still warm.

"This is really good," she said, her mouth full. "I think I can make a whole meal out of just this."

Bastet's copper-colored eyes narrowed. "You're not taking this seriously," she replied as she dipped her own bread into the besarah. "What you saw was Ra. That's not Drake. Well, he is Drake, but not really." She wiped her muzzle daintily.

"Just because a guy runs around in a falcon's-head mask and a fancy kilt doesn't mean there's something mentally wrong with him." Michelle took another bite of the besarah. She'd come thinking Bastet wanted a real visit, not one to get her involved with Drake. And she'd brought Adesina along only because she thought it was going to be a reunion. "Most likely it means that being treated like a God— not to mention having that kind of power—turns you dickish."

"Michelle, please," Bastet pleaded. She took Michelle's hand in hers. It was warm and soft. Michelle liked the way it felt. "Please just see Drake when he's alone. I can arrange it. When he's not with anyone else. Just us."

"What have the two of you been talking about?" Adesina asked as she pulled her chair up to the table.

"Nothing much," Michelle replied.

"Really? Because I'm pretty sure you're talking about the dork."

The waiter stopped at their table. Bastet snarled at him. He held up his hands as he backed away.

"That's no way to win friends and influence people," Michelle said.

Bastet growled softly. "All I'm asking for is an hour."

"I'm kinda wounded here," Michelle said sadly. "I thought you wanted me for myself." She gave a fake pout, but it wasn't altogether insincere. She was stinging from the notion that the only reason her friend wanted to see her was to help Drake. Michelle was not just here to see Bastet, she was also hoping to see how her Living God friends were doing. "You have any idea why Charles Dutton is here?"

Bastet shrugged. "According to Drake, he wants us to go to the Moon. All the Living Gods—and Drake."

"I thought Theodorus only wanted jokers." Michelle leaned back in her chair. "Drake is an ace."

"He has Sekhmet inside him."

Michelle nodded. "And as Ra he's ridiculously powerful. Who wouldn't want a weapon like that?"

"Yes." Bastet nodded somberly. "That, too."

"Seriously, you're trying to make me think that—" Michelle pointed. Drake was wearing his Ra mask and a linen robe. The ball of fire still floated over his head. "—that is just a misunderstood kid? He's an asshole!"

Bastet's fur bristled. "He's got problems!"

"Well, everyone does," Michelle snapped. *And some of us more so, thank you very much.*

"Stop talking about me like I'm not here," Drake said, his deep voice commanding their attention. He yanked off the falcon mask and shucked his robe. Underneath he wore a ratty RUSTBELT! T-shirt and tattered jeans. But he wasn't the kid she remembered. His mustache was wispy, but his acne had cleared up. His forehead bulged with the outline of a red scarab. Sekhmet. Michelle noted that there was a still softness to his body, a little gut. His arms had almost no muscle tone.

Drake's face crumpled and he began crying.

Bastet ran to his side and the ball of fire above his head vanished. She held Drake in her arms and he wept into her shoulder. "I hate him," Drake sobbed. His body shook. "I hate how he acts and I hate what he can do."

Oh, no, Michelle thought. *Extremely powerful ace. Mental issues. Tom Weathers situation much?* She immediately regretted bringing Adesina along.

"It's okay," Bastet said, patting his back. She looked at Michelle. *Help me,* she mouthed.

Michelle shook her head. *Not my circus. Not my monkey.*

Drake pulled back from Bastet and looked balefully at Michelle. He swiped his runny nose on the back of his hand, then wiped it on his jeans.

Oh, my God, Michelle thought. *Really? Really! Also, ew.*

"You came," he said dully. "Bastet said you would, but I didn't believe her. I mean, you haven't written or anything."

Michelle tilted her head to one side. Then she said, keeping her voice low, but filled with contempt, "Well, Drake, I'm pretty sure I mentioned earlier that I was in a coma for two years. You know, the one you put me in? And after that fun time, I've been all over the place with the Committee trying to keep the world from devouring itself. I've been kinda busy."

He hung his head and Michelle felt like she'd just hit a badly behaved puppy. "I know," he said softly. There was a click in his throat as if he was trying to stop crying. She hated seeing anyone cry, even Drake, but seeing him try not to was almost as bad. "I'm really sorry," he said, his voice wobbly. "We were sort of friends once, I think."

"We were friends for two seconds years ago," she said sourly. "Things change."

"I know," he replied. "They changed for me, too. Lohengrin brought me here after . . . after New Orleans. He said it was the only place for me now. Said that Sekhmet would help me control my powers."

Michelle looked around for somewhere to sit. The room was all granite, the benches and chairs made of the same substance. There were pillows tossed here and there. *Weird,* Michelle thought. Then it dawned on her. There's always the fire issue with Drake. Pillows are more easily replaced than furniture.

She sat down in one of the stone chairs. It was more throne-like and sitting in it she felt as if she was the ruler of damn near everything. Drake went to a chair on the other side of the room. Bastet turned into a black cat and jumped into Drake's lap. He started petting her and Michelle could hear her purring from across the room. Drake visibly relaxed.

Adesina looked around the room, then took one of the large throne-like chairs, mirroring her mother's pose as she tucked her large, cobalt-colored wings behind her.

"I really am sorry about New Orleans," he said. "I'm better about my powers now. Sekhmet is showing me how, but it's hard. Hey, you're Adesina," he said suddenly. He leaned forward and Bastet jumped off his lap, changing back into her joker form.

Adesina looked at him with dismay. She shifted as her wings started to unfurl. Then they slammed back against her body again. "Uh, yeah," she replied. "And you're Drake, but sometimes you're Ra? You should stop that because he's a douche."

"I'm not him! I mean, he does horrible things. That's not me—it's just a thing I have to do. But it's not me."

"Whatever," Adesina said dismissively.

"You play games, right?" he asked hopefully.

"You have a totes interesting conversation style. Like, I'm getting whiplash here." Adesina shook her head and her coppery dreads danced around. "And, yeah, I play games. Why are you asking?"

"I play, too," he said excitedly, pulling his phone out of his pocket. "Look, I've been following you on Twitch and in game."

Adesina recoiled. "You're game-stalking me?"

"No! Your videos are up there, you know."

"Mom!"

He looked imploringly at Michelle, as if he were a supplicant and she the deity. "I know she likes games and, well, she went through that whole transformation thing like I did."

"She can't boil the Nile dry. You can."

"I just thought she might want to play together online sometime. I know she likes the Ocelot games, and now that they've gone pretty hard-core with *Rampage: Ocelot 10*, well, it seemed like something we might do. . . ."

Adesina stood up and let her wings flare open into their full majesty. "Stop talking to my mother like I'm not here. What you're doing is hella creepy."

Drake flushed from his neck up to the top of his head. "I didn't mean anything like that by it," he said shakily. He tugged on his T-shirt and balled up the end of it in his fist. "I just don't have anyone here to play with."

He's a kid, Michelle realized, staring at him as if seeing him for the first time. *He's a goddamn kid. Whatever the story was with Ra and all that, Drake might as well still be a teenager. Shit. He's just a kid.* She looked around the room. It was cold and impersonal despite the myriad patterns of stone that had been used. It was a hard and mean room to live in.

"What's your friend situation here, Drake?" she asked. Out of the corner of her eye she saw Adesina flop back down in her chair. There was a dour expression on her face.

He shrugged. "Except Bastet? No one really. I mean, Sekhmet talks to me inside my head, but she's an old woman. Except for Bastet and couple of other people, no one knows I'm Ra. And I have to be Ra a lot."

There was a long pause as Michelle considered Bastet and Drake. She sighed. "Adesina, any chance you'd be willing to play games with this huge dork?"

"God, Mom," Adesina said, sounding horrified.

"It's your call, of course. I just know he's one pathetic excuse for a human being right now."

"Please," Drake said. The anguish in his voice was real. "I need a friend."

"Good grief!" Adesina exclaimed.

"Please," he said again. It wasn't pleading this time, it was filled with pain and loneliness.

"Fine," Adesina said, relenting. "But there are rules. No chatting, no in-game talking, none of that. Just send me a tell and I'll play for a while—if I can. I'm not your gaming buddy. Got it?"

Drake nodded enthusiastically and Michelle could swear she saw him tearing up again, but he rubbed his eyes on the back of his hand instead.

Fuck you, Bastet, she thought. *Fuck you for making me give a shit about this pathetic mess of a man-child. And fuck me for getting Adesina to play with him. And my daughter is far too good for any of us.*

"You're going to help him?" Bastet asked. "Yes?" Michelle was striding down the corridor and Bastet was having to trot to keep up with her. Adesina lingered back, texting on her phone, no doubt telling Ghost about what was happening.

"I'm not certain what you expect me to do," Michelle replied. "Adesina, don't tell Ghost everything that's going on here."

"God, Mom, she'd be pissed at me if she thought I'd agreed to start playing with some rando. She has very strict standards when it comes to who we play with. I'm not going to tell her exactly what the situation is, trust me."

"Michelle," Bastet interrupted. Adesina shrugged and went back to her phone.

"Look, Bastet, he's fucked up. Like a lot. He needs more help than I can give him."

"You see what's happening to him?"

"Yes, and it's not. My. Problem! Jesus, he's got a bifurcated personality."

"What?"

"He's split in two. Not really, but he thinks Ra is sorta apart from him."

Bastet grabbed Michelle's arm, and stopped her. "He's getting worse, Michelle, not better."

"Well, what the actual fuck do you want me to do? I got Adesina to start playing games with him."

"Nah, Mom, I did that myself," said Adesina. She slouched against the wall. "That's so not on you. I didn't have to, but, jeez, he's just so pathetic."

Bastet gazed up at Michelle with her penny-colored eyes. They were the same color as Adesina's. "Help me get him out of Old Egypt. Help me get him home to America. It's not only that he's ill, but so many people want him dead. Not just the Caliphate. There are factions here who want him gone forever. It's tearing us apart. And there are other countries who would want him to go away permanently, too. He's in so much danger."

"Are you kidding?" Michelle teetered between shock and full-blown amazement. "I can't get him into the country! He's wanted for being . . . for being him. Also, he blew up Pyote, Texas. Like, all of it. Not to mention New Orleans, almost. And how do you propose we get him into the country? And if as many people want him dead as you say, it's going to be a bitch to keep that on the DL."

A puff of air-conditioning ruffled Bastet's fur. She smoothed it down. "Old Egypt is a sovereign nation. We can issue official documents. We can turn Drake into anyone we want."

"Hasn't that been part of his problem?" Michelle walked to the door and shoved it open. It was remarkably balmy outside. "With this whole 'Ra' thing. It's bad enough he has Sekhmet in there whispering in his head, but now he's trying to pretend that his 'grown-up self' is separate somehow . . . Christ, what a mess."

"And that's why I want to get him out of the country! He has to stop all this Ra nonsense and get back to somewhere where he was just a normal person."

"Are you fucking kidding me?" Michelle felt as if the top of her head was about to explode. "He's, like, the most powerful ace in the world!"

"Mom! Language!"

"It's nothing you haven't heard, and worse, from Aunt Joey."

Bastet stepped in front of Michelle. "But you stopped him before."

"That was a special circumstance." Michelle remembered the blinding light. Drake in her arms as she fell to the ground, which collapsed around her. Then the darkness. Nothing but darkness for so long until Adesina found her. "I can control myself. He can't." It was a little lie. Michelle was finding it difficult to control herself these days.

"He has Sekhmet." Bastet grabbed Michelle by the arm. "And he has you."

"I have a teenage daughter to look after. I'm not going to babysit a full-grown man with mental issues. I don't care if you can get him into the country or not. Not to mention the whole 'everyone wants him dead' thing."

"I'm pretty sure I can take care of myself, Mom," Adesina interrupted. "And I'm not a teenager anymore."

Michelle rubbed her forehead. "You're not an adult just because you think you look like one. This isn't the place for that conversation—again."

Adesina rolled her eyes.

Bastet shook Michelle. "I really thought better of you. I thought you'd care."

"Don't try that manipulative bullshit on me, Bastet," she replied. "I'm no better than anyone else."

"But you try to be."

"Look where that's gotten me."

Sobek was waiting in the lobby when they got back to their hotel. He was ensconced in a comfortable-looking black leather armchair. He gestured for them to come over, then continued signing an autograph for a pair of tourists. As Michelle and Adesina came up, the man turned and breathlessly asked Michelle if she'd take a picture of the three of them. They even asked Adesina to step into the picture, too, because her joker looked so amazing, but she demurred.

"Sure," Michelle said as he handed his phone over. She snapped a couple of photos. One was of Sobek smiling broadly, showing his cigarette-stained teeth to great effect. She handed the phone back.

"You do know that you just asked the Amazing Bubbles to take your photo? Yes?" Sobek asked them.

"Oh, fer sure," the woman said. She wore a short-sleeved loud floral-print top and a rhinestone-encrusted baseball cap. "But you can see pictures of her anywhere."

With that, they wandered off exclaiming on their good luck at meeting a real Living God. "Such are the vagaries of fame," Sobek said. He lit one of his strong Turkish cigarettes and blew smoke out of his nose. It was very dragon-like.

Michelle laughed and sat down in the chair opposite him. "That was hi-larious. And to what do we owe this honor, Great Crocodile God?" Adesina perched on the edge of the couch and continued texting.

"That's not as amusing as you think it is."

"It kinda is."

"I'm here because you need to do something about Ra," he said. A haze of smoke was forming around him. It smelled pretty bad.

"You and Bastet. Are you in cahoots?"

"I don't know cahoots."

"Did you plan this together? 'Get Bubbles to Old Egypt and have her deal with our problem.'"

He took another pull on his cigarette. "No. She's none too happy with me. She's worried about Drake, but I'm concerned about Ra. Besides, even though you saved us all those years ago, I haven't been happy with your recent adventures."

Michelle ignored the shot. "Um . . . Ra and Drake . . . they're the same person. You do know that."

"Of course I do!" he snapped. It was impressive given the size of his jaw and the razor-sharp teeth nestled there. Adesina glanced up for a moment, then turned her attention back to her phone. "Ra is our only defense, and he's all too vulnerable. We need another solution."

"Like what? You're behind the curve here. You don't have a military. All you have is him."

"We might have another option."

"You mean going to the Moon? You do know that's nuts? I mean, that's the technical term."

"There's a meeting tonight. Charles Dutton is supposed to tell us about Theodorus's plans," he said. "Dutton is being very coy. You should come and hear what he has to say. I'd be interested in your opinion. Your daughter, too. She might be more interested than you are. After all, she's a joker."

"Joker-ace," Adesina said, not bothering to look up from her phone. "I'm not just a joker."

"Ah," Sobek said. "I see."

"Probably not," Adesina replied. "But whatever."

Michelle stretched her legs out and slumped back in her chair. "First, I haven't received an invitation. Second, I'm not a joker. Third, I most certainly wouldn't bring my daughter to this insane-clown meeting. Fourth, I don't wanna. I'm already vexed with Bastet for getting me here—and I wouldn't have brought Adesina along if Bastet had been up front with me about this whole situation."

Sobek ground his cigarette out, then lit another one. Michelle's phone pinged and she pulled it out of her pocket and found a text from Bastet inviting her and Adesina to Dutton's meeting. "I'm feeling very popular right now," Michelle said, wiggling her phone at Sobek. "Bastet wants us there, too. What is it with the two of you?"

Sobek shrugged. "Great minds think alike?"

"See, here I was thinking you are both working without tools."

"You're not as funny as you think you are, Bubbles," he said, his eyes slowly blinking. Again, it was pretty disconcerting.

"Yeah," Michelle replied. "I kinda am. Also, I'm not letting Adesina go to this ridiculous thing."

"Mom, you can't stop me, I'm not a child," Adesina said, looking at her mother intently.

"Chronologically you are."

"You know that's not how it works, right, Mom?"

Michelle knew she couldn't fight Adesina on this point. Adesina's wild card played with all sorts of things about her physical form, knowledge, and maturity. When she went into a cocoon state, who knew how she'd come out.

"I think your daughter can make decisions for herself," Sobek said, a big smile showing his cruddy teeth.

"You're not helping," Michelle replied. "Not helping at all."

◆

The Final Court in the temple was crowded with Living Gods and other jokers. There was a distinct lack of nats. Michelle wasn't bothered by the jokers or the lack of nats. She considered everyone infected by the virus pretty much in the same boat. Sure, aces had it a lot better, but people hated on them pretty much the same way they hated on jokers. That is, if her Twitter feed was any indication.

Hieroglyphs marched across the walls of the large room, portraits of the Living Gods inserted among them. Isis, Osiris, Anubis, and Sobek were prominent, but the carvings of Ra were double the size of the other gods. He was surrounded by radiating light beams. And the ball over his head was not in the style of the carvings, but in bas-relief and covered in gold leaf.

The room was crowded enough that Michelle, Bastet, and Adesina were forced to stand. They'd taken up a position on the west wall, leaning against it. Wearing his falcon mask and robes, Drake stood on the opposite side of the room.

Charles Dutton stood at a clear Lucite podium in front of the audience. A large flat-screen TV was to one side of him. On the screen, linked in from Las Vegas, were Isis and Osiris seated on their thrones. A large contingent of Living Gods had taken jobs at the Luxor years ago, and Isis and Osiris were their spokesmen. Both wore ceremonial garb and neither looked happy.

"I appreciate your attention," Dutton said. There was feedback from his mic and he jerked his head back and swayed. He looked frail as he gripped the podium to regain his balance. "I'd like to tell you in more detail what it is that Theodorus Witherspoon is offering you."

"We know what Theodorus wants." Sobek gave a rough hacking cough, then continued. "We're supposed to pack up everything we own and head to the Moon to colonize it. And we should just trust him for some unknown reason." He pointed at Dutton, then looked around the room. "We're in a perilous situation, friends. Remember, we know nothing of Dutton or his master."

"I know it sounds daunting." Dutton sounded as if he was struggling with making himself be heard despite the mic. "You'd be giving up so much, but what do you have to lose? The Caliphate couldn't touch you there. You wouldn't be aberrations on the Moon. You'd be the norm. I know what it is to be a joker." He removed his golden death's-head mask and a murmur ran through the crowd. Seeing him maskless was almost a letdown. Amber-colored skin was stretched tight against his skull. Long yellow teeth were pulled into a permanent rictus smile. His eyes were bloodshot, the irises a winter-dirt brown. His joker looked the same as his mask.

"To be clear," Dutton said, his teeth clacking together. "Despite having many ties to this world, I can no longer live in a place bent on the destruction of my kind."

"We aren't a kind," Bastet said loudly, startling Michelle. "We belong here on Earth as much as any other human."

"But we aren't human now, are we?" Anubis said, jumping to his feet. His fur bristled. "If we didn't have Ra, the Caliphate would invade and kill us in a heartbeat."

The low whisper of "Aten," "Aten," "Aten," slid through the room. Michelle noted that Anubis and several of the other Living Gods glared at Drake with a hostility Michelle found startling.

The Living Gods began to argue among themselves while the other jokers mostly sat silently, looking uncomfortable. It was beginning to look like a bad day in the British Parliament. Michelle expected it to turn into a full-blown brawl.

"I think it sounds pretty cool," Adesina said to Michelle. She wasn't slouching against the wall anymore and her wings were slightly open. An eager smile was on her face and her eyes shone. "It would be an adventure! How often do you get to go to another planet?"

"It's not a planet. It's just a satellite," Michelle snapped. A joker colony on the Moon might be all well and good for the Living Gods, or any other jokers fool enough to follow Dutton and Theodorus, but it wasn't a place for her daughter. "How are they going to get there?" Michelle asked. "How are they going to get back to Earth?"

"God, Mom, they must have that figured out."

"I've yet to see any evidence, except we're supposed to trust Theodorus—whoever he is."

Adesina leaned in close. "It would be awesome," she said softly, almost conspiratorially. "Go to another planet, satellite, you know, the Moon. Doesn't that sound like fun? It's better than running everywhere trying to keep people from killing each other the way you do."

Michelle's jade-green eyes narrowed. "You're not going to get me to go along with this. And you're not going to convince me that this is a good choice for you. What about school? What about your friends? Do you think Wally is going to let Ghost go? This is for jokers only. And you would be leaving me." A queasy feeling slid into Michelle's gut. This wouldn't be just one of Adesina's adventures. This could very well be permanent.

Adesina turned and started walking away.

"Where are you going?" Michelle asked with a note of panic in her voice. Suddenly, it felt as if her daughter was walking out of her life, leaving her alone.

"I'm going to text Ghost. There's no service in here."

Michelle watched as her daughter walked through the room, the arguing jokers parting as she passed by. There was a part of her that wanted to run after Adesina, and another that knew it would be a mistake. "This is all your fault," Michelle whispered. Bastet's ear flicked. "If my daughter ends up mixed up in this mishegoss, I'm blaming you."

"Brothers! Sisters! Stop!" Osiris's voice boomed from the speakers placed around the room. Silence fell. "This is not how we behave. We are the Living Gods. We don't squabble like children."

"You're safe in Las Vegas," came a voice from the back. Michelle glanced over and saw it was a young joker with ropey violet skin. Behind him she saw Adesina standing in the doorway. She was watching intently.

"You're celebrities at a casino," the lavender-colored joker continued. "You know nothing of the danger here!"

"Are you saying we don't have the ability to understand?" Isis asked. Michelle noticed there was a faint line of gray hair at her roots. Isis's face may have been unlined and still beautiful, but she was beginning to show her age. She had to be at least seventy, maybe eighty. How she and Osiris had kept their youthful appearance made Michelle curious. She wondered if they had an ace power. "We are Living Gods no matter where we reside. And yes, we are a sideshow here. Well-paid and coddled, but nonetheless, we are Other. We have as much invested in this plan of Theodorus's as any of you."

"Do you speak for all the Gods in Las Vegas?" Dutton asked.

Osiris nodded. "We do," he said in a grave voice. "We are choosing to stay. There aren't many of us left here and we don't wish to leave our home. We respect the wishes of any Living God who wants to leave for this new home in the sky. Those who want to remain on Earth will be welcome here if they don't wish to stay in Old Egypt. Contact us when you've decided what you will do." The link from the Luxor went dark.

Dutton turned back to the audience. They stared at him expectantly. "Those are but a handful of Gods," Dutton began, then coughed. Clearly, he wasn't well, and Michelle wondered just how old he was. Rumor had it his card had turned back in the '50s and he hadn't been young then. "Those of you who live here have committed to embracing who you are without making yourselves objects of pity and derision. On the Moon, you would be safe to continue your lives without constant threat."

"We have Ra. We don't worry about the Caliphate," Tawaret said in a mellow voice. She lumbered forward, her hippopotamus head held upright by a heavy metal cage resting on her shoulders. "Or do you wish to take him to the Moon and leave us defenseless, Mr. Dutton? We have followers here, jokers who do not look like gods, even some nats. Would Theodorus have us leave them at the mercy of the Caliphate? What is it that your master would have us do?"

A joker whose body was covered in multicolored scarabs stood so Tawaret could sit. She did so with a groan.

"There are arrangements we can make for the nats, but only jokers are allowed in the Moon colony," Dutton replied. He sounded excited, but it was difficult to tell given his rictus face. "Our goal is for all the jokers and Living Gods here to come with us."

"If we leave them behind they'll be slaughtered!" Sobek stood as he spoke, shaking his cigarette at Dutton. Ashes fell to the ground but he ignored them. "This whole 'worship us' thing was ridiculous, but we've encouraged it. We've made them believe in us. It's immoral to leave them here unprotected and alone. How will Theodorus protect them—and us?"

"The only way to be truly safe is with Ra here," Anubis said. His ears flicked forward. "If he leaves . . . well, this is why we can't stay even if we wanted to. We're at the whim of a symbiote and whoever is under that mask." He gestured at Ra, who stiffened. "There isn't any point in continuing this conversation until Sekhmet and Ra have made a decision as to whether or not they go." He snarled, showing his canines. "I don't need Ra or Sekhmet to decide for me. I'm tired of worrying about when the Caliphate might start another war. I'm tired of our safety being in the hands of this ace. Tell Theodorus I'm ready. Who is with me?"

Almost two-thirds of the room raised their hands. Half of the Living Gods among them.

Michelle glanced over to see Adesina's reaction, but she had vanished through the door.

♥

Drake stood rigid in the center of his room. His mask and robes lay on the floor. Bastet, in her cat form, was perched on one of the silk pillows atop one of the stone benches. She was watching him intently.

A bubble stood on the tip of Michelle's index finger. She was debating what to do with it. Her power was the one constant thing in her life since her parents had left. Except for Adesina. Since saving Adesina from the pit in the People's Paradise where she'd been tossed to die, she'd been the most important thing in Michelle's life. But over the last couple of days, Adesina suddenly didn't feel like a constant at all.

Michelle glanced over to see what Adesina was doing and saw that she was also staring at Drake intently. Michelle let the bubble drop and it went bouncing across the floor. A mass of other bouncy bubbles followed.

"What are you doing?" Bastet hissed as she turned into human form. "Drake and Sekhmet are talking!"

"Seriously?" Michelle replied, letting another barrage of bubbles go. These were like soap bubbles, but wouldn't break until she let them. They floated around the room. "We could have randy-panda sexual hijinks in here and he—they—wouldn't notice."

"Well, I'd notice!"

"Fine," Michelle replied sulkily. She let all the bubbles burst at once.

"I don't know if you've noticed, but this isn't going to do Drake any good. That's too much pressure for him in his current state."

"I'm sorry," Drake said. Michelle turned. He was already heading for one of the other benches.

"Sekhmet wants to go to the Moon," Drake said sadly as he sat. "And without her, I don't know how well I can control my power. But worse, if we go, we leave people unprotected. But I can't lose her! She's the only one who understands me!" He hadn't even changed out of the jeans and tee he was wearing the day before and his hair was greasy.

"It's okay, Drake," Adesina said kindly. "You've been here a long time. You can't live your whole life for other people." She glanced pointedly at Michelle, who let a barrage of soft bubbles rain down on Adesina's head. "Seriously, Mom? Is that really the best you can do in this situation?"

She's really good at the guilt, Michelle thought. *She doesn't get that from me.* With a sigh of exasperation, Michelle stood, putting her hands on her hips. "What do you want me to do? Wave a magic bubble and make everything all right?"

"You could do more to help him!" Adesina jumped to her feet and her wings opened wide. She let them flap once, and Michelle's hair floated on the breeze they produced. "Honestly. I think you don't even want to try."

There was the beginning of a headache right behind Michelle's left eye. She hated arguing with her daughter. "Could you really get documentation for him to leave the country?" Michelle asked Bastet with a defeated sigh.

"Of course!" Bastet replied. "Sobek and I have talked about it. But we can't just leave people here without protection. . . ."

"What about Sekhmet!" Drake cried. "She wants to go to the Moon. She doesn't want to stay on Earth."

Michelle wanted to strangle him. Much the same way she occasionally wanted to strangle Adesina, particularly now.

"I just want to do the right thing," Drake continued. "And I'm tired of everyone else telling me what to do. You know I can make my own decisions. I'm not a kid anymore."

"Then start acting like it," Michelle said, exasperated. "If we're going to get you out of here, Sekhmet or not, we need to make plans. And you." She pointed at her daughter. "No more talk about going to the Moon until . . . well, until I say so."

Adesina rolled her eyes. "Whatever," she said.

A table setting for five had been laid out in the dining room of Drake's suite. Gold silverware gleamed on a pristine damask tablecloth. A single lotus flower floated in a lapis-colored enameled bowl. "Thank you for agreeing to have dinner with us," Bastet said. "You know, not everyone gets to have dinner in the Temple."

Dutton nodded politely. He was wearing his gold mask again, but now that Michelle knew what was under it, she found the affectation a little weird. *Isn't that what happens when you have money?* she thought. *You're not weird anymore, you're eccentric. But, nope, this is still weird.*

"I confess," Dutton replied, tilting his head and considering Bastet. "I wondered what could have prompted the invitation. I'm acquainted with you three women. But this one." Dutton waved his hand dismissively at Drake. "I don't know who he is."

Bastet nodded and Drake took off his Houston Astros baseball cap. There was a wet line of sweat where the cap had been. Sekhmet's body seemed redder and more prominent. Drake hunkered down as if he expected to be hit at any moment.

"That's Ra," Michelle said.

Dutton laughed. "That's a boy. Ra is a man."

"Not so much," Michelle replied. "This is why we can't let you have Ra. Drake is in no emotional condition to keep on being the protector of anything, much less a base on the Moon. He can't be Ra anymore."

"But Ra is a Living God. He's possibly the most powerful ace on Earth—no offense, my dear."

"None taken," she replied. Out of the corner of her eye, she saw Drake cringe and sink lower in his chair.

"This is ridiculous!" Dutton exclaimed, reaching up and pulling off his mask, setting it down on the table. "Ra can't be this . . ." He pointed at Drake.

"And he's an American," Bastet said helpfully. "Not Egyptian at all. And wouldn't that be a scandal?"

"The Americans would never let an ace with this kind of power get away. How did he end up here?"

"Yeah, that's kinda complicated," Michelle said with a sigh. "Let's just say the symbiote—that's Sekhmet in his forehead—helps him control his powers, but he wasn't in control of them before and . . . shit happened. Really bad shit."

Dutton leaned back in his chair, looking drained. "This is a disaster. He's pathetic."

"Don't be mean." Adesina shifted in her chair and her wings started spreading out. "He can't help who he is. No joker can. Look around the table, Mr. Dutton, we're all wild carders here. Do you think any of us would have chosen this?"

Well, I might have, Michelle thought.

A silence fell. Dutton put his fingers to his temples and looked as if he were in pain. Bastet and Adesina exchanged glances and Michelle spared one for Drake. There was a flush across his cheeks and his eyes were downturned. She recognized the signs. He was about to cry. "Look, Dutton, you can't possibly want Drake under these circumstances," Michelle cajoled.

Dutton stopped massaging his temples. "I'm not so sure about that." There was a thread of steel in his voice. It was the tone of someone who was used to getting what they wanted no matter the cost.

"Well, *I'm* sure," Bastet interjected. "There have been multiple attempts on his life. As far as we can tell, from various actors. The only way for him to be safe is for him to stop being Ra and leave Old Egypt for good."

"Then the Moon is the perfect place for him," Dutton said.

"Do you really think the countries of Earth would let you keep an ace this powerful on the Moon?" Michelle asked. "Talk about something that would unify them."

"And where do you propose to hide him then, Miss Pond? Your face is impressively well known. He can't hide out with you."

"Perhaps we can come to an accommodation." Bastet reached over and touched Dutton's arm. He looked down at her hand with surprise. "Only a handful of people know that Drake is Ra. We could slip him out of the country. He could start a new life and no one need know he's an ace."

Dutton took her hand and gently laid it back on the table. She spidered it back into her lap. "Are you proposing that I aid in such an undertaking?"

"Jeez," Adesina said with a touch of asperity. "It's easy enough, Mr. Dutton. Drake gets a new identity and you stop bugging him to be Ra. Then Mom and Bastet will help you with the jokers."

"You're not one to mince words, are you, my dear." He looked at Drake. "You haven't said much while everyone here discusses your fate."

Drake shrugged. "I'm not going to the Moon with you."

"You would have been a god over all others."

"Done that."

Dinner came and Egyptian dishes were laid out on the table family style. Drake was served a cheeseburger and fries. "You're not having any of this, Drake?" Adesina asked. "It smells awesome."

Drake wrinkled his nose. "I'm not an adventurous eater. I just like what I like. And I like cheeseburgers."

Adesina shrugged. "Your loss. Pass me the duck."

"How do you intend to encourage the reluctant jokers to come with me?" Dutton asked Michelle. They were walking at Dutton's pace toward the entrance to the Final Court. The housing building, which included Drake's apartment suite, was connected to it through a small courtyard.

"By telling them that Ra is leaving Old Egypt. If they decide to stay and take their chances, so be it."

"That's a little draconian."

"So is expecting someone to give up their entire life and safety for others. My guess is this will clarify the situation for many of them."

Dutton stopped and leaned on his cane, catching his breath. Michelle moved to help him, but he waved her away. "And what do you get out of this, Miss Pond? You don't seem as if you're much of a fan of the boy."

"Ms. Pond . . . oh, never mind. Basically, I want the jokers safe. I'm not a fan of genocide—been there and done that here already. Personally, I hate the idea of Adesina going to the Moon, but I guess there has to be someplace safe for jokers in need of one. But if Adesina decides that's what she needs in the future, I want it to be there for her." She stopped and looked back down the corridor toward Drake's rooms.

"As for Drake, that's a favor for Bastet, but he's such a mess, I just, I guess I feel sorry for him and his situation. And Bastet is mad attached to him. And I'm her friend."

"Mom!" Dutton and Michelle turned to see Adesina half-running, half-flying down the hall toward them.

"There's something seriously wrong with Drake! C'mon!" Adesina grabbed Michelle's arm and began dragging her down the hall. "Mom, run! We've already called the doctor."

A stab of real fear shot through Michelle. There were people who wanted Ra dead. They didn't know he was little more than a fucked-up teenager. To them he was a massive threat.

She reached the doorway and an acrid smell hit her. Inside, she saw Drake lying on the floor next to a pool of vomit. Bastet was squatting beside him, trying to hold him, but he was thrashing about, holding his stomach and moaning. Then he rolled back onto his knees and began puking up black bile. There was a terrible gagging noise coming from him. Then he let loose a howl that made the hairs on her neck stand up.

"What can I do?" Michelle asked frantically.

"Nothing," Bastet said dully as she encircled Drake's convulsing body with her arms. "He's been poisoned. If the doctor doesn't get here in time, he'll be dead."

Bastet began crooning to Drake. It wasn't a melody Michelle recognized and it had a vaguely atonal, almost mewing, sound. Drake began convulsing again.

"Mom!" Adesina cried in a panicked voice. "Oh my God, Mom. What do we do?"

Michelle looked at Drake in despair. There had to be something she could do, but she was at a loss as to what.

As she watched helplessly, the red scarab under the skin of Drake's forehead began to move. Drake started shrieking as it burst out of his forehead, legs waving, onto his cheek. The scarab crawled unsteadily down to his chest. She was red, but turning black rapidly.

"Sekhmet!" Bastet cried. "I don't understand why she looks like that. She's always been red."

Drake shuddered and went limp as Bastet wiped the sweat and blood off his forehead. With a grunt, he pulled away from her and rolled onto his knees.

"Sekhmet." His voice was weak and papery. "Sekhmet. Why?" Tears were streaming down his cheeks now. No sobs or sloppy weeping. This was agony. Pain too deep for any normal response. He reached out and took Sekhmet in his hands, cradling her gently. "Oh, no," he moaned softly.

Michelle started to say something, but Bastet held her hand up and Michelle fell silent.

"She's dying," he said as he cradled Sekhmet's body to his chest. "What am I going to do without her? She took the poison away. Why did she save me? She should have let me die."

From the corner of the room, Adesina said, "She loved you. She loved you and made the choice for you to live."

Drake opened his hands. Nothing but ashes spilled out.

"Oh, God." He shuddered and the last bit of ash fell to the floor. Looking at his hands in horror, he rubbed them together, trying to cleanse them of the residue. But it wouldn't come off. Then he looked wildly around the room as if he was lost, then brought his hands to his face and rubbed them there, leaving black streaks on his cheeks and forehead.

"She told me I didn't need her anymore," he said woodenly. He let his hands hang limp at his sides.

Oh, shit, Michelle thought. It may have been the years spent in the field, or maybe just intuition, but she held her palms facing the ceiling and immediately encased Bastet and Adesina in bubbles.

"Why are you . . ." she heard Dutton say as she enveloped him, too.

"Shut your eyes," she said in a loud voice. "Now!" Then she willed the bubbles to fly out of the room. Exclamations of surprise and fear erupted from the occupants, but Michelle didn't have time to think of them now that they were out of immediate danger.

With a howl of rage and agony, Drake threw his arms wide, and heat and light poured out of him. It hit her and she expanded as she absorbed his power. It couldn't blind her. And he'd done far worse to her back in New Orleans.

She started bubbling and the first one was for him. A heavy, but still softish, one hit him full in the chest. It was designed to knock him off his feet, which it did. He sat down with an "oomph" that was very pleasing to hear.

"Jesus, Drake, calm the fuck down!" she yelled.

She let bubbles stream from her hands. It was going to be tough to keep the weight off if he was in full-blown meltdown mode and not controlling his power. Sure, he was hitting her hard as hell—maybe only Golden Boy could have taken it as well—but she was the Amazing Bubbles and this shit was cake.

Michelle lifted her arms over her head—a totally unnecessary act, but she was feeling dramatic—and let bubbles shower down on them both and they began filling the room. She allowed them to pop harmlessly. Drake clambered to his feet and shrieked at her, then hit her with another blast.

"I. Don't. Have. To. Calm. Down!" Each word was accented by a blast of heat and light. He started walking toward her, but she wasn't having any of that.

Michelle released a bubble. It was heavy and firm, not unlike the first she'd sent at him. This time she flung it at his chest, knocking him off his feet and making it grow heavy enough he couldn't get up.

"Stop it," she said wearily. There was no doubt that he was running on adrenaline now. It was the only way he could be functional after being poisoned—even if Sekhmet had taken the lion's share of it out before she died. The sound of him wheezing cheered her up. If she could keep him down without hurting him, maybe he would spend himself out. Bubbles rolled across the floor and rested on his arms and legs.

"You bitch," he grunted. "If you hadn't come none of this would have happened."

"Whoa, there," Michelle replied. Bubbles flew off her hands. She looked around the room for somewhere to sit, but all the cushions and pillows had been vaporized by his first blast. She sat cross-legged on the floor. "My being here has nothing to do with this, and you know it."

"People knew you were here. Wherever you go, things go bad."

That one hurt. "You think me being here is the reason you got poisoned? Are you really that delusional?" Drake rolled onto his stomach with a grunt. Michelle let two more bubbles land on him. He flailed about like a two-year-old having a tantrum, but finally gave up and lay still. "People have been trying to kill you for a long time, Drake. And you know it. Sekhmet died so you could get out of here and go to a better, a safer, place."

He managed to turn onto his side, and he blasted her again. Fat ballooned on her and she felt a delicious surge of power.

"Dammit, Drake, you know that doesn't do shit to me! I mean, it feels great, but seriously, what the hell."

He shoved the bubbles off, struggled to his feet, and staggered to the door, hitting her with another blast of flame. Bubbles poured off her free hand. Drake was almost to the door when her bubble caught him in the middle of his back. He flew forward and she heard him hit the opposite wall hard. He crumpled to the floor and lay still.

She spared a look to check on Adesina, Bastet, and Dutton. Then she let their bubbles evaporate.

"Mom?"

"It's okay, honey," she replied. "Everyone okay?"

Dutton groaned and, using his cane, slowly got to his feet. "I'm fine, though at my age my tumbling isn't what it once was."

"I'm fine," Bastet said dryly. "That wasn't how I expected to be saved, but it was an experience nonetheless."

Michelle waved her hand at Drake. "I don't think he's going to be in any condition for anything when he wakes up, Bastet. Between the poisoning, losing Sekhmet, and the light show he just put on, I doubt he'll have the energy for much."

Bastet looked down at Drake. "Are you sure? I'd hate to find out . . ."

"That he's going to go all 'Ra' again? I don't know . . . I've had his worst before, this was nothing like that."

"We could still use him," Dutton said.

"Did you see what just went on here, Dutton? Drake can't continue giving up his life for Old Egypt. Without him Old Egypt will cease to exist. It's time to do the right thing without haggling. I don't know how you planned on getting the Living Gods out of here and to the Moon, but it's time to stop screwing around and make it happen."

Dutton looked at Drake's still body, then back at Michelle.

"Very well."

"Thank you for meeting me," Michelle said as Sobek settled into the armchair in her suite. He stank of tobacco and now she was beginning to find it comforting. A sure sign she needed to go home. "I'll make this brief because we don't have a lot of time."

"Why is it you Americans are always in such a hurry?" he asked, his eyes slowly closing as he settled farther into his chair. They opened again, just as slowly.

"This has nothing to do with how American I am. There was an attempt on Ra's life yesterday."

Sobek bolted upright in his seat. "Is he alive?"

"He's fine now, but he's decided it is time for him to leave and find somewhere where he'll be safer."

"So he's going to the Moon." It wasn't a question.

"No. He has other plans."

"How do you hide an ace with that kind of power? Is he going to the Committee? Is that why you're really here? You don't need him! We need him!"

"Jesus, Sobek, settle down," she said. The drama from the day before had made her more tired than she realized. "We're making arrangements for him to have a private life where no one knows who he is. And no one is going to know where he is, either."

"Except for you," he snapped.

"Maybe. We haven't worked out those details yet. Suffice it to say that he just wants to fade into the night, never to be heard from again."

"Then who is going to protect us?"

"No one," she replied. This was the part she had dreaded. "You have three options, only one of which I would take myself. First, stay here. You'll likely be overrun by the Caliphate once they realize Ra's gone. Right now, we're having a large ceremony featuring Ra so no one thinks they've managed to kill him. We're hoping it'll buy us some time."

Sobek shook a cigarette out of a crumpled packet, then lit it. "And what are my other wonderful options?"

"You know what they are," she replied. "Go to the Moon or to Las Vegas. Or I suppose you could go to Jokertown, or any place where jokers are welcome. The point is, you get out of here while the getting is good."

Sobek scratched his snout while blowing smoke out of his mouth. "Once we start leaving, the Caliphate will pounce."

Michelle let a bubble capture the smoke from his cigarette. The bluish haze floated prettily in its iridescent shell. She went to the door and opened it, letting the bubble float into the hall. As she shut the door, she let it pop. "I've made arrangements for that, but you'll have to act fast. In two days Dutton will have arranged a way out of Old Egypt for the Living Gods and jokers that's fast and safe."

"And how is that?"

"I can't say." She continued catching his smoke with her bubbles. They hovered at the ceiling. "I trust Dutton. And I hope you can trust me. For old time's sake."

"And my job is to get the jokers to agree to leave."

"Simply put, yes."

"You do realize that if I don't get them to go, they'll likely die."

"Yes. Do you think I like this? You're not safe here anymore. You only had the illusion of safety while Ra was here. Anyone can die. It was foolish to think you could remain this way forever."

Sobek stubbed his cigarette out. There was a moment when Michelle thought he might actually bite her out of frustration, but instead he said, "Most people live their lives in a foolish way. I know Anubis is ready to leave, as are Nut and Geb. Tawaret might be difficult, but she's old and tired. Having the responsibility of leading us has weighed heavily on her shoulders. I doubt she'll be difficult to convince. Hathor and Horus I don't know about, they were quiet at the meeting. And what about the other jokers? How am I supposed to handle that?"

"You must have a way to contact them."

"Not all, but yes. We have private social media groups. I can put out a blast. This doesn't give people much time to settle their affairs."

"How about none, but we must do it fast. Once the Caliphate knows Ra is gone, none of you are safe."

It was breezy and cold in the First Court. The days may have been mild this time of year, but the nights were chilly. Adesina had wrapped her wings around herself. Dutton had a cashmere scarf tied around his neck and sported a heavy coat.

The First and Second Court were crowded with jokers of all sorts, among which the Living Gods were but a handful. Most were sitting on the ground with suitcases next to them and many had pets as well.

"What's taking so long?" Michelle asked Dutton.

"Patience is a virtue, Miss Pond," he replied.

"I'm all out of virtue at the moment."

Suddenly, a portal opened and a short, plump woman with curly red hair stepped through. She started walking toward them and when she got closer, Michelle could see the pinkish scars on her face. And Michelle really knew that face.

"Mollie?" She pointed at the woman and turned toward Dutton. "She's supposed to be in prison! How did you get her out? Really, you've broken I don't know how many laws here, Dutton. Also, she did some serious damage to my girlfriend when we were in Kazakhstan."

Mollie hung her head. "I'm so sorry, Michelle," she said softly. "I really am. Theodorus is helping me. He's helping me make things right."

"That's pretty much impossible, you know that, right? Things happened to all of us in Talas, but you just kept on going even after you were out of the zone. Not to mention what you did before . . . before you were ever in the zone."

"I feel as if we're missing something here," Bastet said. Drake nodded. Both looked deeply uncomfortable.

"That is Mollie Steunenberg," Michelle said, anger making her face ugly for the moment. "But you can call her Tesseract. She . . . ah . . . folds space. Super crazy. Meet Drake and Bastet."

Mollie looked as if she wanted nothing more than the floor to open and swallow her whole. Michelle thought that would be a perfectly delightful thing.

"You're being a tad harsh on the girl, aren't you?" Dutton asked. Michelle gave him the coldest smile she could, and he actually took a step back. "What matters here is she is the solution to our problem. She's been helping Theodorus, and he's agreed to let Mollie get the jokers out of Old Egypt."

"I see. So she's our transportation to the Moon, I guess."

"Not to the Moon just yet. We get the jokers and the Living Gods to one of Theodorus's islands. Then we prepare them for the Moon trip. After that, we'll sort out who wants to go where, but clearly, we need to go now."

Michelle heard a high-pitched whistling.

Before she could react, a bomb went off in the midst of the First Court. Screams and panicked cries went up from the jokers. Through the smoke, Michelle saw the broken bodies of Geb and Nut. The violet-skinned joker was missing his head.

"Oh, shit," she said. There had been no jet noise, and the area affected was small. *Drone?* she thought. "Mollie!" she shouted, running toward the blasted area. "Get that portal open. Now!"

Tesseract spread her hands and a portal shimmered open. Beyond the gate Michelle could see a well-manicured lawn leading to what appeared to be a hotel. Standing next to the portal was a row of jokers wearing khaki-colored uniforms.

"*Come on!* You don't have time to wait." Jokers started running for Mollie's portal. They got jammed up, and she widened it for them. Michelle let a barrage of bubbles spew upward, knowing that the drone could be anywhere, and unless it ran into one of her bubbles, it could continue to bomb them.

And then it didn't matter because Drake opened his arms and they were immediately covered by a heat shield. It spread out, protecting both the First and Second Courts. The stampede to the portal slowed. The jokers hustled through the portal silently, sparing only the briefest glances at Drake. He was wearing his Ra apparel and saving them for the last time, but he was also the reason they were fleeing. More than one of them gave him a murderous look.

The shield stayed up, a beacon in the darkness, until the last joker stepped through the portal.

"You ready?" Mollie asked. There were bruise-colored circles under her eyes and she looked like a junkie coming down hard off a binge.

The portal opened and Michelle saw her own living room. Adesina immediately stepped through, flopping down on the sofa with a happy sigh.

"You next," Michelle told Drake. He stepped through without sparing a glance backward. She suspected he wasn't going to miss Old Egypt at all.

"Are you sure this is what you want?" Bastet asked Michelle. "I may have disgusting habits."

"You're not going to live with me," Michelle replied. "This is a nice long visit while we get you settled somewhere. I'm just not sure what we're going to do with Drake."

"Jesus Christ, go!" Mollie snapped. Her eyes were suddenly wild and her body was shaking.

"Shit." Michelle pulled Bastet through the portal, which snapped shut immediately. She'd seen Mollie with that look in her eye before.

Bastet pulled an envelope out of her backpack and passed it to Drake. He opened it and read the contents.

"Hi there," he said happily as he held out his hand to Michelle. "I'm Aiden Moore. That's me."

Within That
House Secure

XI

MATHILDE HAD TO ADMIT, after three months on the run, that Theodorus made an excellent international fugitive. Theodorus fled in style.

When Malachi and Clifford Bell had finally convinced Theodorus that if he was not going to submit to subpoenas then the only alternatives were either going into open and armed rebellion against the government of the United States or fleeing the country, Theodorus had first made a comment about Charleston having a history of the former.

"Look how that worked out," Malachi had said.

The obvious place to go was the Moon, but Theodorus had other plans.

"Well, then, the bases. The launch facilities," insisted Cliff. "Keep moving from one to the other. Most of those properties are in nations without strong extradition treaties, and many of them are outright extraterritorial. SCARE won't send agents to an island where the only government is, well, you."

Again, Theodorus demurred. "Soon," he said, "we will be leaving for a new world. I think it's time I saw some of this one before that."

And so, with a small group of his closest associates, Theodorus embarked on what the unstable ace Mollie Steunenberg called his "Farewell Tour." Mathilde supposed that Mollie, with her power to open portals to, well, just about anywhere, was the pilot. The nine-foot-tall joker Troll was recruited to act as security. Malachi served, as he had for decades, as purser and general factotum.

Mathilde herself, to her annoyance, was the tour director.

"The Eiffel Tower looks exactly like a picture of the Eiffel Tower," Mathilde said. "You don't need to see it in person, it's too big a risk. Despite President Towers's comments in the press, France remains one of America's closest allies and my countrymen are not as progressive about jokers as they like to claim. Remember what we heard about their anti-terrorist squads attacking the joker community in the Catacombs? As soon as Mollie opens a gate and you glide out onto the Parc du Champ de Mars, security forces will swarm all over us."

Theodorus sipped his piña colada through a long straw. The floorboards creaked beneath his weight. The five of them were the only patrons of a bar built onto a reef in Parottee Bay, perhaps a kilometer off Jamaica's southern coast. Mollie had brought in the usual advance team that morning, and they had spread around the usual prodigious number of American dollars.

"Visiting our friends in the Catacombs is a good idea, too," Theodorus said. Then asked, "Why go to the Parc du Champ de Mars?"

Mathilde said, "Because that's where *le tour* is."

"I don't want to just *see* it, Mathilde. I want to stand on top of it. Mollie, could you open a gate onto the upper observation deck of the Eiffel Tower? And one in the Parisian Catacombs?"

Mollie Steunenberg was eating fresh grilled fish out of an aluminum foil wrapper with her bare hands. She acted like she hadn't heard Theodorus's question.

And maybe she hadn't, thought Mathilde. The woman was an enigma. She kept to herself, mostly, or at least as much as she could considering the little group's odd circumstances. She often muttered under her breath, and usually refused to be drawn into conversation. She answered as few questions as she could. She ventured no opinions unless badgered.

She was also the only one of them who had gone swimming off the reef. This despite the monitoring collar she wore around her ankle. Mathilde supposed that Mollie imagined the collar to be waterproof, which, technically, it was, as it was little more than a plastic box full of random wires and metallic bric-a-brac. Mathilde had built it herself at the little workbench she maintained in her office at Witherspoon Aerospace, built it to Malachi's specifications, which were purely visual.

The real collar, the one the federal authorities had designed to monitor and control Mollie's movements and use of her ace power, was now worn by the shape-shifting joker impersonator who had secretly taken her place at a hidden government facility in the American Southwest.

"Mollie," said Troll. He was stretched out on the plank floor, several empty beer cans beside him. His voice was a deep bass, and past experience showed that Mollie at least noticed when he spoke, even if she didn't pay attention.

Wonder of wonders, this time she did. "Good fish," she said.

"Mr. Witherspoon asked you a question," said Troll.

"Oh," said Mollie. "Oh, sure. Sure, whatever."

Malachi, who was wearing one of his best suits despite the surroundings, rolled his eyes.

"Did you hear what the question was, Mollie?" Mathilde asked.

Mollie shrugged. "Did it have something to do with opening a gate someplace?"

Mathilde nodded. "Yes, it did."

Mollie said, "Then sure. Sure, whatever."

So they went to Paris, and stood atop the Eiffel Tower, high above the City of Lights. Then they went into the Catacombs, deep below it.

And they went to Cambodia and saw Angkor Wat. They went to China, where they walked along an unobserved section of the Great Wall under a full moon. Mollie transported them to the Indian city of Agra to see the Taj Mahal, where Theodorus nearly caused a riot when he unexpectedly struck out on his own, saying later that he wanted to see if the sacred Yamuna River was as polluted as he had read. Troll took to keeping a closer eye on his employer from then on, and managed to prevent Theodorus from disappearing into the depths of Krubera Cave in the Western Caucasus Mountains.

New Zealand and Kenya and Chile and Mozambique and a dozen island chains spread across three great oceans. The Gobi Desert. The Canadian Rockies.

They followed Theodorus's curiosity. Were there really dozens of privately held libraries full of ancient manuscripts surviving in Timbuktu? Off to Mali (where nobody would talk to them about libraries or anything else). Was the Tsheringma herbal tea served in Thimphu as refreshing and reviving as he had read? Off to Bhutan (it was pretty good tea, Mathilde thought).

They moved so quickly, and so often, that the only indication they had that they were being pursued was via messages from Clifford Bell about U.S. government activities and world press reports. Well, that was almost the only indication they had. Malachi, as ever, had his own sources of information, which he, as ever, kept to himself. This was, ultimately, a good thing, because Theodorus would often overlook Cliff's warnings that there were SCARE agents closing in, but whenever Malachi cleared his throat in one particular way, and raised his eyebrow a particular height, Theodorus would decide it was time to move on.

Always with their secrets, Mathilde would think at those times. But she was always glad to move on. She didn't want to go to a prison in Duncan Towers's America any more than any other joker.

This was their life for months and months. Somehow, despite the hectic pace, it was a pretty calm life. Until they went to Kiev in the Ukraine. Until they met Marcus Morgan, the Infamous Black Tongue.

They went there because Theodorus wanted to see a bell tower.

"Seems like we go and see a lot of towers, boss," said Troll.

"Ah, but Howard," said Theodorus, using Troll's actual name, which even Malachi didn't do, "this tower was designed by Johann Gottfried Schädel nearly three hundred years ago and remains one of the most notable features of the Kiev skyline." He waved the tablet he was holding in emphasis.

"Yeah, I didn't remember who designed it, but I knew the bit about the skyline," said Troll.

Theodorus gave Troll a speculative look.

"Went to Kiev in 1996 on vacation," said Troll.

"I've seen it, too," said Malachi. "It's in that monastery. The one with the tunnels."

"The Kiev Pechersk Lavra," said Mathilde. "The Monastery of the Caves. Toured it during a trip you sent me on about twelve years ago."

Mollie was sitting on the floor of the great hall of the Lake Como villa they'd been staying at for just short of a week. She was flipping her way backward through the pages of an Italian language magazine. Without looking up, she said, "Gold dome."

Theodorus grumbled, "Fine, so you've all seen it. I haven't. And tell me more about these tunnels, those sound interesting."

"No more caves, boss," said Troll.

"I don't think you'd fit into them anyway," said Mathilde. She didn't care whether they went to Ukraine or not. By this point, one place seemed as good as any other. She was anxious to get back to work, anxious to hear from Oliver, whom she hadn't seen in over six weeks, anxious about how things were progressing on the Moon outside her direct supervision. At that exact moment, she was also mildly curious about whether Mollie Steunenberg read Italian, but that was a minor concern.

"How long do we have this place leased?" Theodorus asked.

Malachi blinked. "Are you asking me a question about money?"

Theodorus said, "I just don't want the owners to be inconvenienced if we leave it empty. Houses like this take a lot of upkeep, you know."

Malachi said, "Yes, I do know. As it happens, I own this villa myself. But don't worry, I gave you an excellent price, given the season and the short notice."

Mathilde tried to remember whether she'd known her father owned an Italian villa. She tried to remember if she'd ever told him about the time-share condo she and Oliver had together in Amalfi.

Theodorus just laughed. "Come on, then. Mollie, you've been there before so no need to call up a current view, correct? Let's go, let's go!"

Off again.

The Monastery of the Caves was a sprawling complex of religious buildings designed and constructed over the course of hundreds of years. At the moment Mathilde stepped through Mollie's gateway from Italy, it was also a battleground.

They appeared scant yards from a pair of men wearing nondescript suits, but one of them was brandishing what Mathilde thought was a distinctly dangerous-looking machine gun. The other had his hands held slightly apart, a sphere of crackling purple electricity dancing between them.

Both of them looked over at the arriving party in shock, then the man with the gun said, in New England–accented English, "Holy shit, it's Witherspoon! Forget the snake!"

Troll crossed the distance between the two groups with more speed than Mathilde would have given him credit for. He had just wrenched the machine gun from the grasp of the man who had spoken when the other threw his hands apart. The purple ball of lightning flew into Troll's chest, knocking the enormous joker flat. Aftershocks danced over Troll's skin, and his long limbs shook as if he were experiencing a seizure.

"Mollie!" Theodorus shouted.

A portal opened beneath the two men, and they screamed as they fell through what should have been solid ground.

"Bye bye," said Mollie.

Malachi and Mathilde hurried to Troll's side, but he was already sitting up, shaking his head. "Who the hell were those guys? What was that all about?"

Mathilde had a pretty good guess, but it wasn't her that answered. Just then, a Black man whose form transitioned from a muscular torso to the body of an impossibly gigantic coral snake slithered out of the shadows of a nearby chapel. "They were SCARE agents," he said. "And they were after us."

Who "us" was became apparent when a fine-featured woman stepped out of the church, holding the hand of a child. A joker child, with glowing eyes and four back-turned legs sprouting radially from her hips. Other figures milled behind the woman, beyond the high arched doors.

"You're Marcus Morgan," said Theodorus. "The man who smuggles jokers out of the former Soviet sphere."

"A man near the top of everyone's list of international fugitives," said Malachi.

Morgan, unexpectedly, smiled at that. "I used to be number one until your boss went on the run from Duncan Towers."

"We should get inside," the woman said, her accent indicating she was a local. "The monks have been kind, but they won't want us drawing attention."

As the group crowded into the church, Mathilde asked Mollie, "Where did you send them?"

Mollie looked genuinely mystified. "Who?" she asked.

There were perhaps thirty jokers in the church's sanctuary. Most of them appeared malnourished and exhausted. A trio of monks moved among them, offering food and, apparently, blessings. The refugees seemed grateful for both.

"I admire the work you are doing," Theodorus told Morgan. "We have a lot in common, I think."

Mathilde looked at the two men side by side. A snail-centaur and a snake-centaur. Both on the run from the law. Both doing whatever they could to help jokers around the world. She decided that Theodorus was right.

Marcus Morgan apparently didn't agree. He spat on the stone floor. There was a faint sizzling sound where his sputum struck, and the jokers nearest by stepped away.

"We have nothing in common. You think I don't know who you are? You think I don't know about your little vacation this past year? I've been underground for years, man. Do you know how many run-ins I've had with government aces since Towers became president? Do you know how many times I've been shot at, beaten up, electrified? One dude nearly froze me solid! Do you know how many of the people I've been trying to help have died in the fallout?"

The local woman, to all appearances a nat, stepped forward and stroked Morgan's cheek. "My love," she said. "I think we should talk to these people."

"Yes," said Theodorus. "We should talk. Because I think I can help you."

It took some convincing, of both Morgan and Malachi, but eventually Theodorus and the wary snake man began a long conversation.

That was how the refugees in the church wound up on the Moon. That was how the Infamous Black Tongue came into Theodorus's employ.

"It's a gambit," said Malachi. "The first move in some game that will see us all imprisoned or killed."

"I'm well aware of that," said Theodorus. "But a presidential pardon isn't something to be turned down lightly. And besides, aren't you tired of all this constant travel?"

Mathilde was sure Malachi was absolutely exhausted by the constant travel. The rest of them certainly were. But she wasn't so sure that Theodorus's eagerness to accept Duncan Towers's unexpected peace offering and return to the House Secure was particularly wise.

It was true that the Satterly Commission, still working, had released a preliminary report clearing Theodorus and his allies of any wrongdoing. Of course, this was the same body that had earlier released a report clearing Duncan Towers—if not his allies—of any wrongdoing.

"It doesn't cover Marcus and Olena," said Mathilde. She wasn't reading the pardon, but the summary of it and of the Commission's report that Clifford Bell had sent to them in Fiji. Oliver, who had joined them via a mundane commercial airline flight, was reading over her shoulder.

"So far as we are aware," said Theodorus, "the authorities don't know that they've joined us. Mollie can keep them moving until we've reestablished ourselves at home. Once that's done, they can join us there and no one will be the wiser."

"Balderdash," said Malachi. "Pardons only work backward, you know. Sheltering felons will put us right back in the fire."

"Malachi," said Theodorus, "the terms of the pardon require us to stop all work on the Joker Moon project, which is absolutely not going to happen. We'll be back in the fire eventually no matter what we do. As you said, it's a gambit. But I know a thing or two about games. I know how to play for time."

"And time is growing short," said Mathilde. "The ice bodies will impact the Moon on schedule, and there's nothing anyone can do to stop them at this point. And I'll need to be there—" She paused and took Oliver's hand. "—We'll need to be there once the volatiles have been released to begin the following phase." There would be so much work.

Oliver, curiously, did not squeeze her hand in return. He was still reading.

"Exactly," said Theodorus. "We need to return to the House Secure. We need to begin transporting people to the Moon in large numbers, and soon. We need to catch up with all the work we've gotten behind on."

Malachi still wasn't convinced, but he wasn't the one who needed convincing. He took his phone out of his pocket and began making calls. Mathilde took that as acquiescence, a sign that they would all be back in South Carolina soon.

She started to rise from the couch and noticed that Oliver had put the tablet down on the coffee table, still staring at it, but clearly not reading it. "What is it?" she asked him.

"The pardon," he said. "It doesn't cover me, either. It doesn't cover hardly any of us."

That "us," Mathilde realized, must be the vast number of Witherspoon employees on both the Moon and the Earth who were engaged in the project. But she was named in the pardon papers, she knew. So it was, heartbreakingly, an "us" that included Oliver, but didn't include her.

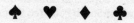

Diggers

PART TWO

THERE WERE NO WEEKENDS on the Moon. Every day for Tiago was just the same: smashing and clearing, shoring up, hauling equipment and materials. Church services were offered on Sunday mornings, but Tiago had never been very religious. "We're under a hard deadline here," Mike explained when Tiago asked whether they'd ever get a whole day off. "We need to have the habitat space ready for the scientists and engineers who will supervise the new ecology when the ice asteroids start landing, and they are already on their way." How much longer would this pace have to keep up? "Until the job is done."

The job, Tiago reflected, would not really be done until the Moon was completely habitable and every joker who wanted to had moved there . . . and that might be centuries. But Tiago's quarters lacked a window; apart from the gravity, he might as well have been working in a gold mine back in Brazil. So on Sunday mornings, despite his continued exhaustion, Tiago suited up for a recreational walk on the surface, just to remind himself where he was and how lucky he was to be there.

Signs in the air lock advised all personnel that EVAs should only be conducted with proper approval and accompanied by a buddy. But those signs were old and scarred, and the policies they described had not been enforced for years. The experienced vacuum hands—everyone knew who they were, and Tiago was definitely one of them—knew how to stay out of trouble.

He closed the outer air lock door behind himself—the creak of the hinges transmitted as a tingle through the door's regolene to his hands—and turned, fists on hips, to survey the lunar landscape. The sky above was clean and black, the nearby hills rugged and picturesque, a range of grays and browns limned by sharp-edged pitch-black shadows. All was silent and unmoving. He set out at a comfortable loping bound, skipping across the heavily tracked ground near the air lock and heading for a less-frequented area.

Being on the far side of the Moon was a weird and paradoxical situation. They were farther away from other people than anyone on Earth had ever been, even in the middle of a desert or at the South Pole. Yet, despite its isolation and its cavernous spaces, the Moon base was crowded—always noisy and often odorous—and getting more so every week as more and more jokers poured in. So Tiago often found himself desperately in need of fresh air . . . and, ironically enough, found it on the surface, where there was no air at all.

In recent weeks he'd been exploring a nameless plain on the far side of Dutton Ridge from the base. The ridge was steep and rocky, generally considered impassable, but with the sureness of his boots—as sensitive as bare feet—and the strength and dexterity of his plastic fingers, Tiago could scale slopes that were beyond the capabilities of machines and too dangerous for space-suited jokers. He found the plain peaceful and would often sit on a rock at its edge, looking out over its crater-pocked gray surface as though over a placid lake or idyllic meadow.

Occasionally in his wanderings he would find intriguing crystals or organic-looking twists of iron, just sitting on the surface waiting to be picked up. They could have lain there unchanging for days or millennia . . . but in a few decades they would all be washed away by the new lunar ecology. He kept the best of them in a box under his bed.

But on this particular Sunday morning he encountered something completely unexpected.

At first he was certain that what he was seeing was just something stuck in his eye. But then he reminded himself that his robot body lacked eyes as such; his power allowed him to see using the suit's entire face, giving him much better vision than any nat and even some very good cameras. He peered more intently and realized that the motion and color he had at first dismissed were real.

A human figure. An unsuited human. Dark face, black hair, a filmy garment of purple and gold. It stood still, as though stunned to have been noticed.

Tiago began walking toward the impossibility for a closer look.

Immediately the impossibility reacted, turning and running away. It whirled like a dancer, a swirl of purple and gold silk drifting on the air as it turned.

There was no air. This could only be an illusion, or a hallucination, or a projection of some sort. Yet gray dust puffed from beneath the running figure's feet, darkening the lower hems of its clothing. If it were an illusion it was, at least, a very comprehensive and detailed one.

"Hey!" Tiago called. But the figure didn't seem to have heard. Not surprising, given the lack of air. He put on more speed, changing his gait to a kilometer-eating low-gravity lope.

As Tiago closed the distance between them the running figure looked over its shoulder—no, her shoulder, he could see now—and ran harder. But each of Tiago's legs was as long as her entire body; he caught up with her in just a few long bounds, and soon cornered her in a V-shaped valley between steep basalt walls. Both of them slid to a halt in the powdery soil, the dust from Tiago's feet falling as fast as dropped gravel while the dust from the stranger's feet hung in the nonexistent air for a moment. Was she, in fact, somehow surrounded by an envelope of air like Bo's? Tiago doubted it; every stitch and sequin on her ornate sari was as crystal clear to his vision as the rocks behind her. But despite that clarity and detail, which argued that she was not just an illusion or projection, something about her felt . . . off. Not really there somehow.

Whatever she was, he had no desire to harm her, or even to frighten her. He held up his hands, fingers spread, and stood still, eight or ten meters away from her. She stared back at him from a defensive crouch, as though expecting a blow, panting heavily . . . but no sound came to his ears, and her face showed anger and determination rather than fear. It was a beautiful face, a face like a Bollywood star's, with fine dark features, intense brown eyes, and strong black brows.

"I mean you no harm," he said. She gave no indication of having heard—not really surprising—and as his suit had no face, she could not have seen his lips move. Tentatively he took a step closer, extending his open hands in what he hoped was a nonthreatening manner.

Immediately she ducked and ran, trying to escape around him to his left. But she underestimated his reach and speed; his hand darted out and caught her, gently but firmly, by the arm. It was the strangest sensation. The slim arm held in his plastic fingers felt exactly like a human arm, with smooth warm skin, muscle tensing beneath that, and the firmness of bone beneath that. But it lacked . . . presence.

Human flesh, like all organic materials, was subject to Tiago's power. No matter how he tried, he would never forget how he had reveled in the feeling of meat and guts and gore being incorporated into his bulk as he slaughtered and dismembered his way across the flesh-plains of Kazakhstan. But living flesh . . . he could sense it, in the same way he constantly sensed all organic materials around him, but when he tried to draw it toward himself, or add it to his body like a bit of wood or cardboard, it simply refused.

The beautiful stranger's arm was not like that. It had physicality—he could feel it as well as see it—but to his unique organic senses it was completely invisible. It might as well be a handful of moondust.

And, even as Tiago thought the word moondust, she gave him a withering look and faded away, skin and hair and sari dissolving into gray powder and blowing away in a nonexistent breeze.

He was left gazing in astonishment at his empty plastic hand. No, not quite empty . . . a few grains of dust remained in the joints. They itched as he slowly closed the hand into a fist.

What the hell?

All the way back to the base Tiago wondered what he had just seen and what he ought to do about it. He should probably report it to someone, but . . . who would believe him? Even in a world of jokers and aces, even in a secret base on the far side of the Moon, the idea of a Bollywood star wandering around on the lunar surface without a space suit was just too ludicrous to accept. And though the mysterious woman had looked completely real, the fact that she'd been imperceptible to his special senses seemed to argue that she had been nothing more than a figment of his imagination, and he'd found no other evidence of her existence—not even footprints.

He paused at the air lock door, looking back over his shoulder at Dutton Ridge, and decided not to tell anyone. *At least, not just yet.*

Weeks passed. He did his job, he ate and slept, and in his limited free time he explored the plain where he'd seen the inexplicable woman. He was far from the only person who chose to spend his Sunday mornings on EVA, but with his unique abilities he was the only one who could make it over the ridge and back on one tank of air. He showed the photos to a few people, but no one seemed to think there was anything particularly interesting or unusual about them. Looking at them dispassionately, he had to agree.

After a couple of months—months during which the mysterious woman failed to appear, and Tiago had almost completely convinced himself that she had been only a passing fancy—there was a sudden power failure, affecting the entire sector, and the diggers got to knock off a few hours early. Tiago wound up drinking in the commissary with Hardbody, Bo, and the crane woman, a Russian named Vasilisa.

"Does it seem to you that this is happening more often?" Tiago asked, sipping his beer. Even he, who had little experience with the stuff, could tell it was terrible.

"Maybe." Bo shrugged. "Before you guys got here"—he indicated Tiago and Hardbody with his bottle—"we were eating cold food by flashlight twice a week."

"Nuke plant stable for years," Vasilisa countered. "Now, is three times in last month." She held up her hand with thumb and two fingers spread. It was all the fingers she had. "Rumor says is sabotage."

"Sabotage?" Tiago gasped.

Vasilisa folded her spindly metal hands together and leaned forward over the table. "Cameras see people where no people should be. Strangers. Breaking things."

"Strangers?" Tiago blinked and leaned forward. Vasilisa's face smelled of iron and copper, but unlike with the mysterious Indian woman, Tiago could sense the human flesh beneath her metal carapace. "How could there be any strangers here? We are literally on the far side of the Moon."

"Jokers come in air lock without going out first," Vasilisa replied. "Jokers no one recognizes. So I hear."

"Ghost stories," Bo scoffed. "I've heard 'em, too. But the perimeter sensors haven't picked up a thing."

Vasilisa shrugged, her shoulders creaking. "Sensors or no, if nuke plant goes down and stays down, will get very cold in here." Tiago shivered. Having grown up in Brazil, he didn't deal well with low temperatures.

"Ha!" Hardbody guffawed theatrically, slapping the table with one enormous paw and making Tiago's beer slop out of its cup. "You all are so soft. Real jokers don't care about a little rough living!"

"To real jokers!" Bo proclaimed, and they all clacked their gray plastic cups together.

The shock of the impact on the regolene sent a painful jolt down Tiago's arm, and he gulped down the last of his beer to mute the pain.

There was one other *Carioca*—a native of Rio de Janeiro—at the Moon base, though her family had money and as such she might as well have come from a different planet than Tiago. Her name was Isabelle, she was lean and angular with too many joints, but her dark brown face was entirely human and wore a constant wry smile. Their meetings were only occasional, because she worked in the nuclear power plant at the very bottom of the base.

After that conversation with his digger companions, he made a coffee date with her. "*E aí,*" she said when she met Tiago in the commissary, clapping him on the shoulder and kissing both cheeks. "*Como vai?*"

"*Tudo bom,*" he replied automatically, though really all was not well.

Her face showed she'd noted the lie in his words. "*Oi?*"

He hesitated before replying. "I'm worried," he said, still in Brazilian Portuguese. "I hear rumors of sabotage at the nuke plant."

She looked both ways, then leaned in close. Speaking very low, also in Brazilian Portuguese—a language that few, if any, other jokers on the Moon shared—she said, "The rumors are true. People keep slipping in past security—we don't know who, we don't know how—and messing with the controls. They don't seem to know what they're doing, so the disruption has been minimal so far, but they keep pushing and whenever they find something that works they do the same thing again, and more."

"What do you mean you don't know who? Aren't there cameras?"

"Of course there are cameras!" She gestured to one of the ubiquitous lenses in the ceiling. "But the intruders are . . . well, they aren't any of us. Jokers, of course, or they'd stand out like a sore thumb, but no one anyone recognizes."

"Where are they coming from?"

"At first they were coming in the north lock. But there was no sign of them approaching from outside! It looks like they just appeared in the lock, came inside, and wandered around until they found something worth sabotaging. But since they found the plant they've been appearing closer and closer to the plant itself."

"Teleporting?"

"Maybe. Or maybe they are some kind of . . . construct? When we catch them they just vanish, leaving behind a little bit of moondust. We've tested it and it's just ordinary dust from this area."

Tiago sat back, considering this new intelligence. The north lock was the one closest to the plain where he'd encountered the mysterious woman. And vanishing in a puff of moondust sounded extremely familiar. "You should take this information to Schwartz."

"Oh, he knows about it! He's the one who told us to keep the sabotage a secret."

Tiago blinked. "Wouldn't it help to have everyone keeping an eye out for the saboteurs?"

"You'd think so. But he says it would be bad for morale. Schwartz won't let anything slow this project down, and everyone's scared to cross him."

"Maybe I can talk to him. He did say that if there was anything he can do for me I should ask."

That made her blink. "He said that to you?"

"He seemed to take a personal interest in me."

She shook her head; it might have been an expression of awe and wonder, or perhaps concern. "You are swimming in very deep waters, *companheiro*. Take care you don't get washed out to sea."

"Thank you for your concern. But if I don't do something . . . we might all get shipwrecked."

♥

Schwartz, Tiago learned, would be arriving on the Moon in just a few days, so he put in a request for a meeting. He was actually rather surprised when the request was granted, and indeed when he appeared at Schwartz's office suite—the space was larger than Tiago's quarters, and located deep underground, but everything was made of the same plain plastic and metal as the rest of the base—the secretary who met him looked him up and down suspiciously with her one large eye. "Tiago the digger?" she asked.

"I suppose so."

"What makes you so special? He hasn't even met with the environment team yet."

"I really don't know."

Schwartz, when he emerged from the inner office, was grinning broadly and bouncing like a flabby rubber ball. His coverall, Tiago noticed, was made of the same gray material as everyone else's, but was as impeccably tailored as the suits he'd worn on Earth. "So nice to see you again, Mr. Gonçalves!" he said. "Nearly as nice as being back in lunar gravity. I cannot wait until I can stop this endless shuttling back and forth and live here permanently."

Tiago waited until Schwartz had closed the door to his private office before raising his concerns. "I understand that no one likes to argue with the boss," he said after describing what he'd heard—but not identifying his sources, nor sharing his personal experiences. "But keeping this sabotage secret is counterproductive. We should have every eye on the situation."

"I thank you for bringing your concerns to my attention. It shows initiative. But there are aspects of the situation to which you are not privy."

This took Tiago aback. "What 'aspects' could be worse than sabotage at the nuke plant?"

"We are doing as much as we can to balance safety with productivity."

Tiago couldn't fail to notice that Schwartz hadn't answered his question. "You are certain this is the best course of action?"

"We are doing as much as we can," Schwartz repeated, tapping a finger on the table before him to emphasize each word. "And part of what we are doing is controlling the information available to the general population. To avoid issues of morale, you understand. I thank you again for bringing these issues to my attention, but I must ask that you not discuss them with anyone else."

Tiago felt his hands bunching into fists beneath the tabletop, and shook them out. He could tell from Schwartz's body language that there was something he wasn't saying . . . something significant. "Will you at least post guards at the plant?"

"This project is a machine with many moving parts, Mr. Gonçalves. Sometimes you cannot fix one thing without creating problems somewhere else. Rest assured that I and my staff are working with full information and with the project's overall best interests in mind."

This response didn't satisfy Tiago. "If the sabotage doesn't stop soon," he said, trying to hold his voice level, "I will put the word out myself."

Schwartz's black eyes contemplated Tiago for a disquietingly long moment before he replied. "My feelings toward you are avuncular," he said, "but my affections are not bottomless. I would encourage you not to test their limits." He leaned forward. "I will not allow anything, or anyone, to hinder the destiny of jokerkind. Not even you, my dear boy. Do we have an understanding in this?"

Tiago didn't look away. "I believe we do."

Just because Tiago understood Schwartz's position didn't mean he agreed with it. Sabotage was happening—Schwartz had as much as admitted it—but rather than pulling out all the stops to combat it, he was keeping everyone in the dark. To Tiago that made no sense, but he knew that if he told anyone else, Schwartz would find out about it and come down on him hard. Also, Tiago had information on the saboteurs—or at least he thought he did—which might be significant, but which he had not wanted to share with Schwartz for fear of seeming insane.

So he had no choice but to try to stop the sabotage himself.

Isabelle had told him that the saboteurs were entering the base through means unknown, making their way to the nuclear power plant, and doing as much damage as possible before being physically apprehended, at which point they simply vanished. The saboteurs struck only during the day—the base's day, that is, in the same time zone as the House Secure in South Carolina, rather than the two-week-long lunar day outside—and the attacks seemed to come in waves, daily for a few weeks followed by weeks of respite.

Working backward from the strikes, security camera records showed that the saboteurs were making good use of the base's crowded conditions—the same conditions Tiago and the other diggers were working hard to ameliorate—to hide themselves in the masses of jokers moving through the corridors between wherever it was they were gaining access to the base and the plant. The entry point, or points, must be in the cameras' many blind spots . . . but Tiago could see things the cameras could not.

With considerable difficulty, Tiago changed his work schedule to allow him to patrol the corridors during the vulnerable periods. Hundreds of jokers passed before his eyes as he pressed through the crowds, but it wasn't his eyes he was paying attention to . . . it was his other sense, his special sense, which would tell him who was made out of meat and who was just a ghost made of vacuum and moondust.

It was weird to focus on the slight, fluttery attraction of living flesh—a sensation he usually simply ignored, as it was drowned out by the much stronger tug of nonliving organic matter and the tingly discomfort of the regolene from which so much of the base was built—and even weirder to seek its absence. He wasn't even sure he would know it when he saw it . . . and he was even less sure that he would ever see it at all. All he had was a hunch, an educated guess, that the saboteurs were somehow connected to the mysterious Indian woman he had met on the surface so many months ago . . . if she even existed.

But still, he had to do something.

Already spread thin, Tiago now felt as though he had two jobs: building the base and stopping the saboteurs. The latter job had to be conducted in secret, and without any assistance from anyone other than Isabelle, who because of her position couldn't act overtly to help him. But she could provide information.

One thing Isabelle told Tiago was that the saboteurs were getting bolder . . . and more effective. Power outages were now occurring on a nearly daily basis during the weeks of attack, and she confessed that the saboteurs were coming perilously close to doing permanent damage. If the plant had to be shut down permanently, or even for an extended period, they would have no choice but to evacuate the base, which would set the project back by months or years.

So Tiago stepped up his patrols, forgoing sleep and all forms of recreation in favor of hours wandering the bustling corridors. As he didn't wear his space suit inside, he was constantly jostled, stepped on, and knocked into by larger jokers. It was mind-numbing, dispiriting work, constantly shouldering past grumpy and often smelly jokers who were just trying to make their way to the commissary or their quarters after another exhausting shift. Tiago, too, was exhausted—his own work in the tunnels had not slacked at all—but still he pressed on, keeping himself going with cup after cup of the base's harsh, acidic coffee.

And then came the day he had been waiting for, hoping for . . . and dreading.

He almost missed it. If a chance rebound off of another joker had not sent the stranger stumbling into him, he would never have noticed the absence. But once their shoulders touched, the strange sensation of not-being-there, which he had only experienced once before, was unmistakable.

Tiago's head whipped around to see a broad back, clad in gray regolene fabric like all the others, moving away from him through the crowd. The joker was tall, a hundred and eighty centimeters or more, and the back of the head was covered in red lumps. "*Oi!*" Tiago called, waving.

The joker turned, regarding Tiago suspiciously. The figure was distinctly female, but her face was as red and lumpy as the back of her head, looking nothing at all like the beautiful Bollywood goddess Tiago had met on the surface. For a moment Tiago was certain he was making a tremendous mistake. But then he noted that her jumpsuit lacked epaulets.

The epaulets had been introduced only a few weeks ago. It had been a remarkably large point of contention—derided by some as a useless frippery and hailed by others as a welcome injection of fashion into the otherwise completely utilitarian garment—but once the design change had been approved, all new outfits coming out of the fabricators had included them. And because all clothing was recycled and remanufactured rather than being washed or even stored, the change had rolled out across the entire population of the base in short order. There was almost no reason for anyone to be wearing a weeks-old garment.

Unless they were an intruder who had missed the debate.

"*Oi!*" Tiago repeated, approaching the stranger as though she were a long-lost friend. "*Como você está?*"

"Do I know you?" she replied in English. Her voice was remarkably high and soft for such a large person, and incongruously carried a lilting Indian accent.

"*Mi viejo compañero!*" Tiago insisted, and embraced the big joker woman about the waist in what seemed a friendly hug.

The close contact left no doubt whatsoever that this was no ordinary person, not even for a joker. For though the thick waist was firm enough, and the hands that pushed at Tiago even more so, there was no organic matter to her at all. Even her clothing, which seemed authentic enough to the eye, lacked the grating tickle of true regolene fabric.

But the strangely familiar sensation apparently went both ways, as their eyes met in a mutual wide-eyed stare of shocked recognition. "You!" the big joker said. "The white robot!"

"I didn't recognize you without your sari," Tiago replied, in English, acknowledging their previous meeting.

She pushed him away. "Do not try to stop me," she whispered. "You do not understand how important this is."

Tiago pressed forward, maneuvering the two of them out of the crowd and into a quiet side corridor. "Who are you?" he asked. "Why are you doing this?"

"Who I am does not matter. But the Moon . . . the Moon and I, we share a special connection. And I cannot allow anyone to pollute Her purity."

The vehemence in her voice took Tiago aback. "You sound like a nat," he said. "They're always going on about 'purity.' Are you one of those self-hating jokers? Or are you really a joker at all? Is this just some kind of disguise?" He poked her shoulder, lumpy beneath the gray fabric.

She brushed his hand away. "I am as much a joker as anyone here! But not even the jokers have any right to the Moon! The Moon belongs to Herself alone!"

"And you, apparently?"

A flash of something—annoyance, or perhaps recognition that he'd scored a point—crossed her face. "You do not understand," she repeated. "You have to leave the Moon. You all have to leave. I will make you leave if I must."

"Look, you . . . you don't know what you're doing. You could really mess up the nuke plant. You could cause a . . . a meltdown or something. People could die!" Her face showed he'd scored another point. "You don't want that."

She looked down. "I only want to be left alone." But when her gaze rose to meet Tiago's it was filled with determination. "And I will not be denied in this."

"We—we jokers, and you say you're one too—we only want to be left alone, too. And the Moon is our best chance." He reached to take her hand.

"Stop touching me!"

Immediately Tiago backed off, hands upraised. "I'm sorry, I won't do that again. I really don't want to hurt or offend you." He paused, considering. "Please, let's see if we can work out some kind of compromise. I can set up a meeting with Malachi Schwartz, the man in charge."

But at the sound of the name her lips drew back to show clenched teeth. "Schwartz? He is the worst of all of you!"

Again the stranger's vehemence took Tiago aback. "What?"

"He has secrets. I have seen things he keeps from the rest of you. He is an evil, evil man."

Tiago's hand approached the woman's shoulder as though of its own volition, but he held it back to respect her wishes. "He's been good to me, personally, but I'm sure we can talk to someone else if you—"

She waved the offer away. "You must all leave!" Then a new expression, sly and calculating, crossed her face. "And now I know just how to make it happen."

And then she vanished, leaving just a few motes of dust dancing in the harsh artificial light.

After that Tiago felt he had no choice but to go to Schwartz with what he knew, no matter how unbelievable the project manager might find it. But it took several days to arrange a meeting, during which time there were two more power failures, the second lasting over four hours. The temperature did indeed begin to drop, as Vasilisa had predicted, and Tiago's relief when the lights came back on was very great.

There were two burly jokers from the base's security detail standing in Schwartz's office suite when Tiago showed up for his appointment, and to his surprise they immediately began moving toward him. But even as Tiago was backing away, hands upraised, Schwartz appeared. "Leave him to me," Schwartz commanded, and the guards backed off, though they continued to regard Tiago with suspicion.

Schwartz ushered Tiago into his office, where he offered coffee. It was much better than the bitter stuff in the commissary. "I apologize for the guards' over-enthusiasm," he said. "The tensions have been appreciable."

Tiago told Schwartz the whole story, beginning with his meeting with the Indian woman on the lunar surface. After some hesitation, he even included the burly red joker's accusations against Schwartz.

"And you believe these two are the same person?"

"I can't be certain, but yes, I think so."

Schwartz stroked his almost nonexistent chin, his black eyes narrowing. "I'm sure you appreciate how implausible this story is."

"I do. Which is why I didn't tell you about it before."

"It is also extremely . . . convenient."

Tiago blinked. "What?"

Schwartz stepped to his desk, opened a laptop, and began tapping at it. "I must confess I have also not been completely forthcoming with you. One important datum I omitted was the primary reason for secrecy regarding the sabotage." He turned the laptop around so Tiago could see the screen. "Which was that we harbored suspicions that the sabotage was in fact an . . . internal matter, and we did not want the saboteurs to know what we knew."

The screen showed a black-and-white video, security camera footage from the nuclear plant. The image was still at first, save for a few blinking lights, but then a figure entered suddenly, immediately moved to a control console, and began bashing at it with a crowbar, sending sparks and fragments flying. The room lights began to flicker.

The footage was silent.

The figure was small and lithe, with parti-colored skin and hair.

It was Tiago.

"That isn't me!" Tiago protested.

"It certainly looks like you." On the screen, security guards entered and the figure faded away to nothing. The lights flickered once more, then died. "And you were in the vicinity of the power plant immediately before the incident."

Tiago looked at the time stamp frozen on the black screen. It was at the beginning of the four-hour power outage. "Of course I was! It was right in the middle of the vulnerable period. I was wandering the corridors near the plant, looking for the saboteurs."

"We also cannot verify your location afterward."

"Well, things got pretty crazy when the lights went out."

"How convenient."

"This . . . this makes no sense!" Tiago stammered. "If I could teleport and look like someone else, why would I do that"—he gestured at the black screen—"with my own face on?"

"You contend that the saboteurs are a single shape-shifter. Their behavior could also be explained as the actions of a coordinated group of base personnel. Which of these explanations passes Occam's razor?"

Tiago gaped in astonishment for a moment before formulating a reply. "But if I were a member of this . . . conspiracy, why would I risk myself like that?"

"Such a group's decisions as to which operative to employ in any given operation are not, at this time, open to us. But is it not rather suspicious that immediately after you were captured on video, you appear in my office with a rather implausible story about a mysterious shape-shifter who can teleport and breathe vacuum?"

"But I met the saboteur immediately before that! If she's a shape-shifter she could have, have, uh, imitated me! To cast suspicion on me."

"Is there any evidence for Mr. Gonçalves's meeting with the supposed red, burly joker?" Schwartz said to the air.

"No, sir," came a voice. "We've reviewed security footage for the time and area he mentioned and found no indication."

The whole conversation, Tiago realized, was being monitored and probably recorded.

Of course it was.

"We met in a, a side corridor," Tiago protested half-heartedly. "There might not have been a security camera there."

"How convenient for you."

Tiago's shoulders slumped. "Look, I didn't do it. That's all I can say."

Schwartz considered Tiago for a long time, his black eyes hard and cold. "Suppose I accept this story at face value."

"It's the truth!"

"'Though love repine, and reason chafe,'" Schwartz declaimed, "'There came a voice without reply, 'Tis man's perdition to be safe, When for the truth he ought to die!'"

"Que porra é essa?" To Schwartz's blank expression he translated, "What the fuck does that mean?"

"In this case it means that sometimes the 'truth' can be a matter of opinion." He held out his fat, flabby hands in a gesture of supplication. "This project has already come so far, Mr. Gonçalves, and has so much further to go. And you, too, have much farther to go. I put you where you are not only because it is a good match for your wild card abilities, but because I want you to literally have your hands on the foundations of this world." His expression now seemed genuinely pleading. "You have so much potential, my boy. Your abilities are . . . I believe you are capable of much more than you have as yet realized. I can see you growing up with this world . . . growing to take control of it. It would be a shame to waste so much potential over a . . . difference of opinion."

"So you don't really believe me."

"I am prepared for your sake to behave as though I do. But let us say this. If you do not persuade your supposed vacuum-breathing shape-shifting teleporting friend to immediately cease all efforts at sabotaging this project, I will not be so generous in the future. Not to you, and not to your coconspirators. And we will find them."

Tiago felt his heart pounding, slow and hard, as he considered Schwartz's words. "I don't have any influence over her. I don't even know if I will see her again!"

Schwartz shrugged, though the gesture was barely visible given his ball-like form. "At this point the choice is yours, Mr. Gonçalves. Return to your duties, and stop the sabotage—how you do so is not my concern—or be delivered at once into the gentle hands of base security."

It wasn't much of a choice . . . but if he retained his freedom, he would at least have a chance to prove himself innocent. "I will return to my duties."

Schwartz's hand was soft and flabby, but he seemed sincere as he shook Tiago's. "I want nothing but the best for you, my dear boy. Please do not disappoint me."

Tiago found himself smiling grimly. "I'll try not to."

Three days went by. Three days of vulnerability to sabotage. Tiago managed to change his work schedule to patrol the corridors during the day, but though he pushed through the crowds as fast as he could, rudely touching as many jokers as possible, he found no sign of the saboteur—or saboteurs, he had to admit. There were no further power failures, at least . . . until the end of the third day, when the lights went out right at the beginning of Tiago's dinner.

A collective groan arose from the jokers in the crowded commissary, for whom this was only a sadly-too-common annoyance and not a sign of ongoing sabotage. For this, at least, Tiago had to thank Schwartz's secrecy policy. But the groan and following grumbles began to take on a worried tinge as the darkness continued, with even the emergency lighting failing to come on. Phones and work lights flickered on here and there, giving Tiago enough illumination to set down his tray and begin making his way to the exit, heading toward the power plant in hopes of spotting the saboteur there. But as he was descending the stairs to the lower level the lights came back on, and when he reached the plant he found nothing but a phalanx of security personnel keeping everyone away.

He made his way back to the commissary, but the place had been thrown into chaos by the power failure, and he wasn't really hungry anyway. He returned to his quarters, where he turned out the light and lay on his bunk, his mind spinning.

He felt completely helpless. Was there anything else he could be doing to protect the base . . . and himself? Even if he did find the saboteur, what could he do to stop her when she could simply vanish from his grasp? And what would happen to him if he failed to do so?

Then his anguished ruminations were interrupted by a featherlight touch on his cheek, accompanied by a faint greenish light through his closed eyelids. Immediately his eyes snapped open.

Hovering above his face, wings lofting languidly in the low gravity, was an enormous moth.

Tiago's entire body jerked in astonishment, but he managed to keep himself from swatting the fragile creature away. It was beautiful and, apart from its unexpected appearance, seemed harmless enough.

The moth was the size of a dinner plate, mostly green but with pale blue and purple edges to its wings, and had a fuzzy body with long feathery antennae. Its wings glowed in the darkness, a pale green glow that was oddly soothing rather than menacing. The wings trailed off in long swallowtails that reached nearly to Tiago's waist.

This was no dream—Tiago's heart pounded and he knew himself to be completely awake. The slow motions of the moth's glowing wings sent a gentle breeze across his face, and his own exhalations stirred the fine hairs on its legs. But, on the other hand, Tiago didn't think that real moths glowed, or that they grew this large, and he couldn't imagine how one could have gotten into his room. And as he examined the creature closely he realized it didn't look exactly natural . . . it seemed more like a three-dimensional painting. The subtle green and purple patterns of its wings looked like brushstrokes, and moved slightly, flowing like ripples on the surface of a windblown pond.

And then the moth spoke, adding yet a greater degree of peculiarity to the situation. "I'm sorry."

"Wha?" Tiago managed.

"I'm sorry," the moth repeated. It had the same feminine voice and Indian accent as the red, knobby joker, and now Tiago realized that its body had the same lack of presence to his organic sense. "I . . . I thought I could rid myself of two problems at once. But I've only made the first problem worse, and put you in terrible danger you don't deserve. You seem a nice enough boy."

"Danger? What?" Tiago chided himself for his ineloquence, but felt completely out of his depth. "I don't understand."

"Hush! I have so little time to explain . . ." Suddenly the moth's glow began to dim. "Damn! Beware of—" Then the voice, the glow, the brush of air from the moth's wings, and the peculiar sense of absence all vanished completely.

When Tiago switched on the light he was not surprised to see nothing at all where the moth had been. But a few grains of grit dusted his face and chest.

He lay for a long time staring into the darkness, his already troubled mind now more anxious and confused.

He must have drifted off to sleep eventually, because the next thing he knew he was being awoken by an angry pounding on his door. It was Mike, the crab, accompanied by the rest of his digger crew. "You've slacked off enough," Mike said. "You'll be on shift this morning or there'll be hell to pay."

Groggy and incoherent, his protestations ignored, Tiago was dragged to the air lock. Eventually he gave in and suited up.

"What've you been doing with all your time off?" Hardbody asked as they set up at the rock face.

Tiago considered his answer carefully—as carefully as he could in his exhausted, distracted state, anyway—before replying. Hardbody was a coworker but not really a friend . . . in fact, he was kind of an asshole. Tiago didn't feel he could bring him into his confidence. "I've been dealing with a . . . personal problem."

"We've all got problems. I don't see why you're so special." Hardbody punched the rock wall then—it was not just a gesture, it was the beginning of his work for the day—and Tiago bent to clear the small amount of rubble that slipped past Hardbody's ace power and fell to the ground.

But as he stooped, he felt a tickle in his feet and looked up.

One of the robot forklifts was charging directly toward them—much faster than he'd ever seen one of them move. Faster than he'd thought they could move. It was now only a couple of meters away, and its headlights glared in Tiago's eyes. "Watch out!" he cried, and shoved Hardbody out of the forklift's path, incidentally pushing himself away in the opposite direction.

But, to Tiago's surprise, rather than slamming into the wall between Tiago and Hardbody, the runaway forklift immediately turned, spewing dust and chips from beneath its wheels as it slewed to a halt just short of the wall. This was more sophisticated behavior than Tiago had ever seen from a robot forklift before, and he suspected that someone must be remote-controlling it. This suspicion was reinforced as the forklift's wheels spun, making its whole body shudder and veer in the silence of vacuum as it built up speed . . . heading directly toward Tiago. Tiago leapt to one side, but the forklift immediately turned to follow.

The damn thing was fast. It nearly clipped him with its raised fork, then reversed itself in a couple of body lengths and charged him again like an enraged bull. The headlights splashed the walls as it turned, throwing crazy shadows in every direction.

But there was a reason jokers were better at this work than robots, even remote-controlled robots, and that was adaptability. The tunnel ceiling here was nearly six meters up, and in the lunar gravity Tiago could easily leap that high . . . where no wheeled forklift could follow. He sprang to the top of the wall and clung to a beam there. He could feel the beam's pain as his weight was added to the stresses upon it, but those stresses were far from its breaking point. He would be safe here until someone could come and disable the runaway forklift.

"Mike!" he called into his radio. "We need help here!"

But only silence came in response.

"Bo! Vasilisa!" No response. Letting go of the beam with one hand for a moment, he switched his radio to the emergency channel. "Mayday, mayday!" he called. "Equipment malfunction, tunnel sixteen, northwest work face! Immediate assistance requested!"

Silence.

"*Filha da puta!*" Tiago swore.

Looking down, he saw that the forklift, which was much faster and more maneuverable than Hardbody's bulky form, had him trapped in a corner. He was dodging it for now, but sooner or later it would pick him up and fling him against a wall, smashing his helmet. Tiago switched his radio back to the diggers' channel. "Hardbody, can you hear me?" he asked, not really expecting an answer.

"Yeah!" came Hardbody's panting voice. *Graças a Deus!*

"Climb the wall! It can't follow you!"

Hardbody replied with a grunt and immediately began climbing, his huge shovel-like hands digging into the solid rock. Most of the resulting rubble vanished due to Hardbody's ace power, but some fell onto the forklift, visibly denting its housing.

"Throw rocks!" Tiago shouted into his radio. "Kill the damn thing!"

Again Hardbody grunted—he was close enough now that, despite the harsh uncertain lighting, Tiago could see the wicked smile on his face—and he ripped a chunk of rock from the wall, flinging it down at the rogue machine. But the forklift dodged, bouncing on its wheels in the low gravity, and the rock shattered harmlessly and soundlessly on the rubble-strewn floor beside it.

With a roar, Hardbody reached and pulled an even bigger chunk from the wall. But in his haste and anger he also pulled down several of the supporting beams that braced up the fractured rock of the tunnel ceiling. Tiago, too, cried out, the broken beams' pain transferring through the structure to him, then again as he felt the damaged structure begin to collapse. Hardbody dropped the chunk of rock and clung tightly to a girder . . . an uncontrolled fall from this height could easily break his helmet, even in this low gravity, and even if the fall didn't kill him the forklift might.

Gritting his teeth against the pain, Tiago extended his awareness into the web of regolene beams that held the ceiling up. They were stiff and resistant to his power, but he flexed as hard as he could . . . and the half-broken structure stirred, like an injured spider, pressing back against the tons of rock above, which seemingly wanted nothing more than to crush this tunnel out of existence.

It might have worked. But the forklift, or whoever was controlling it, quickly realized what Tiago was doing . . . and began to ram repeatedly against one of the main supporting columns. The sharp edge of its fork broke big pieces off the column on every strike.

"*Ai!*" Tiago cried with each blow, tensing every muscle in his greatly extended plastic and regolene body, trying to hold it together by will alone. But will alone could not win out against thousands of tons of moon rock, a damaged system of beams and girders, and a murderous forklift.

With one final blow of the fork, the column shattered. Tiago screamed as he felt the regolene part, the stress transferring to other, already overstrained structural members, which snapped and buckled in turn. In the chaos Tiago was shaken from the beam to which he clung—the pain, at least, vanished immediately, but he found himself looking up at the cracking, collapsing ceiling as he fell helpless toward the floor below. He landed hard, feeling something break in his back, but of more immediate concern was the huge, sharp-edged fragment of rock that tumbled with the majestic slowness of one-sixth gravity directly toward him.

He couldn't move. He couldn't stop it. And he couldn't survive the impact.

And then a shadow blocked the light . . . and the falling fragment shattered into a million pieces, most of which immediately vanished. Only a peppering of small stones remained, striking painfully on his plastic skin but doing no serious damage. Tiago gasped and turned his head to the shadow, which turned out to be Hardbody, grinning with self-satisfaction and cracking his enormous knuckles. "Get up," he said, extending a hand.

He tried. "I can't!" Was his back broken? He'd heard something snap when he landed, and the pain was fierce.

But when Hardbody bent and tried to gently pick Tiago up, he didn't budge. "Shit," he said, then peered beneath Tiago's body. "There's some kind of black goo sticking you to the floor."

"It must be sealant." There was a container of sealant, in case of suit rupture, in Tiago's backpack unit. It must have broken open in the fall. Now that he knew what the problem was, Tiago pressed his arms and legs against the floor with all his might. It didn't help. "You'll have to pull me free," he gasped.

"I'm afraid I'll break your suit!"

But Tiago, glued to the floor and looking straight up at the ceiling, could see fragments continuing to break free and fall all around them. The whole thing would come crashing down at any minute. "Do it!"

With uncharacteristic hesitancy, Hardbody pried at one side of Tiago's backpack unit with his hooflike fingernails. With a cracking, tearing sound and a certain amount of pain, it began to pull free from the floor . . . and then a sharp hiss sounded and Tiago's ears popped.

"I'm leaking!" Tiago cried, and Hardbody stopped pulling. "No, no, keep going! Hurry!" If he wasn't up and moving before the ceiling collapsed they'd both be dead.

"All right . . ." And with a grunt Hardbody pulled Tiago off the floor.

Tiago rose, tumbling, thrashing, and helpless, into the airless space above, falling oh so slowly back down toward the floor. His arms and legs scrambled for purchase, but there was nothing nearby.

Black, gray, and white tumbled in alternation across Tiago's vision as he spun in midair, a crazy patchwork of illumination and shadow that reminded him, for one insane moment, of his own skin. Meanwhile the hissing sound increased in volume and Tiago felt the cold rush of escaping air across the skin of his lower back. And then, on one rotation, he noticed a person-sized roll of heavy plastic sheeting in its rack not far away. Could he use that to patch his suit? He reached out with his power to pull it to himself . . .

. . . but the roll and its metal rack were heavy, much heavier than he himself was, and his floating, tumbling body was pulled toward it instead. Stunned by the impact, Tiago nonetheless welcomed it, as it had gotten him back on the ground. Quickly he got his feet under himself and pulled the end of the roll, tearing off a strip of the stuff with the metal cutter provided. Then he tossed the strip of plastic into the air and exerted his power. Immediately it slapped onto his back, clinging to the outside of his suit and becoming a part of him. The hissing diminished slightly. "Help me with this!" he called to Hardbody.

Hardbody's clumsy fingers were little help, but together they got several square meters of plastic sheeting onto the outside of Tiago's suit. His power stuck it down, and the air leak slowed further. At the same time, though, Tiago kept one eye on the ceiling above. Before they were done patching his suit, the giant crack he'd been watching suddenly, silently, gaped wider, spreading like a jagged black lightning bolt. The ceiling was starting to come down. "Let's go! Now!"

Tiago pulled one more length of plastic from the roll as he scrambled out of the way of the falling rocks. As he ran he passed the forklift, which was already pinned under a pile of rubble. Its one functioning headlight seemed to glare balefully as he passed.

A moment later the forklift was obliterated by a huge falling rock, as the entire stretch of tunnel where they had been working collapsed.

Tiago shielded his plastic face with an arm as a hail of sharp fragments clattered against his suit, along with a blinding cloud of dust. But in the airless vacuum it all settled in less than a minute. He and Hardbody were left standing, panting and dust-covered, in the half-finished stretch of tunnel just inside the work area. There was no sign of the other diggers. "Mayday, mayday!" Tiago called again, but all channels were still silent.

"So now what?" Hardbody gasped.

Tiago slapped the last piece of plastic onto his suit—the leak had slowed to a trickle—then glanced at the readout on his left forearm. "I've got maybe two hours of air left."

"No new tank for you. Your backpack is all fucked up."

"Then we have to get inside before then."

"What you mean 'we,' white man?" Hardbody glanced at his wrist. "I've got ten hours, and there are spare tanks in every air lock. All I need to do is get to one."

"Let me remind you that someone is trying to kill us."

"Yeah, I kind of noticed that. Any idea why?"

"I have a guess, about who as well as why." Hardbody was in as much danger as Tiago now, he realized, and deserved to be informed. "You know all those power failures we've been having? It's because of sabotage at the nuke plant. I believe it's someone coming in from outside the base, and I've been trying to figure it out and stop it. But Schwartz thinks it's an inside job . . . and he thinks I'm involved. And now, after last night's blackout, I think he may be trying to kill me."

"So why's he trying to kill me?" Hardbody roared.

"You were in the wrong place at the wrong time," Tiago replied, realizing the answer even as he spoke. "If you'd died back there, you would have been collateral damage. Now you're a witness. Either way, I don't think an extra death or two at this point is going to bother him at all."

Hardbody raised one enormous fist. "If you're right, I can bring Schwartz your shiny plastic head and he'll let me go."

Tiago didn't even bother cowering. He was past that. "If you'd trust him to leave you alive as a potential witness—one who might be turned, or get caught in a lie, or whose very existence might interfere with whatever his story is for how this 'accident' happened—you're even stupider than you look." He gestured back toward the air lock. "Mind you, if you don't want to be associated with me, you're welcome to try and make your way back by yourself. But I think we're both more likely to survive if we stick together."

Hardbody growled, and the fist trembled, but it neither relaxed nor came down on Tiago's head.

And then Tiago noted the shadows shifting.

It took him almost too long to realize what he was seeing.

"Run!" he yelled, and did the same himself.

A moment later a rubble wagon, its bed filled with rocks, whipped around the corner of the tunnel between them and the air lock. Heavily loaded, its wheels had excellent traction on the tunnel floor, and it would hit hard if it did hit. It moved silently in the vacuum; it was only the wagon's headlights that had tipped Tiago off to its imminent arrival.

Tiago and Hardbody ran in opposite directions. Tiago was faster, and the smaller target, but the wagon immediately changed course to intercept him, rocks spitting from beneath its wheels as it turned. Plainly whoever was remotely controlling it had Tiago's death as their first priority.

There wasn't as much room here as there had been at the work face, and the floor was smoother, offering fewer obstacles to the wagon's rapid progress. Tiago dodged its thrusts several times, but though he nearly ran it into a wall once it didn't fall for the feint.

Hardbody, meanwhile, vanished around the corner toward the air lock. Tiago couldn't blame him.

Again and again the wagon slewed and skidded across the floor, narrowly missing Tiago each time. The battle was moving toward the air lock, which was good, but Tiago was tiring, slowing, making mistakes. It reminded him of his time dodging garbage trucks at the dump in Rio—but those had been slower, and hadn't been trying to run him over.

And then Tiago realized that the wagon was showing far too much intelligence and initiative—its behavior didn't line up with what Mike had said about the limitations of robots.

On the thing's next pass he dodged and, as it whipped past and turned for another run, he leapt up on top of where the cab would have been if the vehicle had had a driver. This was where its radio antenna was located.

With one triumphant twist of his giant plastic hand he snapped the antenna right off.

The wagon immediately reacted like a wounded animal, twisting and slewing in its path as though trying to throw him off. Its dump bed, full of rocks, slammed up and down, and he had to quickly shift his grip to avoid losing a hand. Then the electric motors growled—he could hear them as long as he clung to the vehicle's casing—and it raced at full speed toward a wall, obviously hoping to smash him between the wall and itself.

This wasn't at all what he had expected.

But he had an unexpected trick of his own—a new trick, which he had just learned in the past few minutes.

He reached out with his power and pulled the regolene beams above toward himself.

But they were firmly fixed in place, and the gravity was low, so instead of the ceiling coming down he rose up.

He hit the ceiling hard. But the wagon hit the wall harder—its whole forward end crumpling, rocks spilling from its bed and sparks spitting from beneath. The wheels ground to a halt and the thing didn't move again.

Tiago dropped lightly from the ceiling and headed back toward the air lock at a dead run. He knew it was just what Schwartz—or whoever was controlling the machines—would expect him to do, but he really didn't have a lot of alternatives.

Then he heard Hardbody's voice in his headset. "Damn it, Tiago," he panted, "I need help!"

"Where are you?"

"Cavern . . . four? No, three. Hurry!"

Tiago hurried. Soon he saw Hardbody, who was pinned against the wall by another loaded rubble wagon. It was a stalemate, for now—he was holding it at arm's length with sheer strength—but he was clearly weakening and in a minute he'd be crushed.

This cavern was nearly ready for occupancy, with proper lighting and insulated plastic paneling on its walls. Tiago reached and pulled, and the panels popped from their fastenings, flying through the vacuum and plastering themselves onto his body. Five, ten, twenty, fifty panels quickly added themselves to his bulk. Soon he was enormous, five meters tall, with strength to match.

He reached down and tipped the rubble wagon to one side, dumping out its load of rocks. That made it just light enough to lift. He picked it up—its wheels spinning in what seemed like frustration—and then slammed it down hard on the floor, breaking its axles and jarring the battery loose from its housing. The head lights immediately went out, and the wagon sat still.

"Damn thing was just sitting there," Hardbody gasped, "until I was almost past it."

Right when Tiago had killed the other one, perhaps? Could there be just a single operator, able to control only one machine at a time? But he didn't have time to worry about that now. "Come on," he said. "We have to get to the air lock before he finds another robot to send after us."

The air lock wasn't far. But when they got there the door was closed, and it wouldn't respond to a press on the DOOR OPEN button. "Of course," Tiago said. There was a manual override, but with the air lock full of air the door, which swung inward, physically wouldn't open.

"I'll smash it down!" Hardbody shouted, preparing to do just that.

"No!" Tiago said, blocking him with an arm across his chest. "We need to be able to close and seal it behind us, or we can't get in. Not without causing a blowout and killing a lot of innocent people."

"So?"

At that Tiago just glared, then turned his attention to the air lock's outer wall, thinking hard. "How small a hole can you dig through this rock?"

Hardbody's face registered confusion—not an uncommon expression for him. "How small?"

"Can you make it just big enough for yourself to pass through, but no bigger?"

Hardbody blinked. "Uh, I guess so. . . ."

Tiago relaxed his power, allowing the plastic panels to fall to the floor but keeping the plastic sheeting that held his air in. Now he was about the same size as Hardbody. "Do it now," he said, gathering up a half-dozen of the panels in his arms.

Still registering confusion, Hardbody drew back his fist, then punched the wall—hard, but not at his full strength. A small segment of the wall crumbled, his ace power making most of the fragments vanish even as the air within the air lock blew them out of the hole. The resulting hole was only a little wider than Hardbody's shoulders.

"Good job," Tiago said, ducking through the hole.

Though the air lock was a mess inside—not only because of the blowout Hardbody had just caused, but also because it looked like a large number of people had recently passed through without taking the time to properly rack their equipment—there were no bodies lying around. That was just good luck; with their communications cut off, he hadn't been able to give any warning that they were coming in.

"There should be some sealant in that cabinet," Tiago told Hardbody, and ducked back through the hole for another armload of plastic panels.

Soon they had patched the hole, a rough patch that might not hold for long. But it only had to last for one air lock cycle. Tiago pulled the EMERGENCY RECOMPRESS handle and was relieved at the rushing roar of air that followed. The emergency system was entirely mechanical, but there had been a chance that Schwartz would find some way to cut off its air supply.

Tiago paused with his hand on the inner door's manual override lever. "We're going to head for the Stormwing hangar," he told Hardbody. "I just hope we can convince one of the pilots to help us. I sure can't fly one myself. But we have to get to the hangar if we're going to get out of here. Smash walls if you want to, threaten people if you need to, but no unnecessary killing, all right? There's been too much death already."

"Spoilsport." But he plainly understood and agreed.

There were seven levels between here and the hangar. They'd have to fight their way up the stairs. Every joker they met, probably, would be trying to stop them . . . and maybe even every machine. Because if a rubble wagon could fight, there was no telling what a copy machine or a communications laser could do. And Schwartz, Tiago was sure, wouldn't hesitate to risk innocent lives for the sake of his damn project.

He held his breath. He pulled the lever.

The inner air lock door swung open.

Tiago found himself facing a wall of security personnel, guns drawn and leveled. Hundreds of jokers crammed the air lock antechamber behind them, making a confused ruckus. And in the middle of the line of security guards . . . one small, round, flabby figure.

Schwartz.

He looked terrible. He looked like he'd just fought and lost a battle to the death. Three battles to the death. But his coverall was still impeccable, and he still held his head high, to the extent that that was possible for him.

"Hands up!" called the brick-faced security commander, glowering menacingly over his pistol sight, and Tiago reluctantly complied. Hardbody did the same.

The guards moved forward to apprehend Tiago and Hardbody.

And then the crowd gasped.

Tiago didn't want to take his eyes off of the guards or Schwartz, but the stunned expressions and peculiar green glow on their faces convinced him to risk a look over his shoulder.

A gigantic moth—like the one that had appeared in Tiago's room last night, but even bigger, three meters across or more—hovered near the high ceiling of the air lock antechamber, its wings waving lazily in the lunar gravity.

"These jokers are innocent," the moth said, its voice the same Indian-accented, feminine tones as before, but now so loud that everyone in the antechamber and the corridors beyond could clearly hear her words. "It is Schwartz who should be arrested." And then it spread its wings still wider—each one stretched out into a broad rectangle two or three meters wide—and the patterns on each wing began to move and swirl into a new configuration.

A moving picture. Two moving pictures.

The left wing showed a view of Schwartz's office, taken from somewhere near the ceiling. The project manager and his subordinates, including the brick-faced security commander, were gathered around Schwartz's desk. The right wing showed security camera footage from the tunnels, where Tiago and Hardbody were just setting up at the rock face. The time stamp was less than an hour ago.

"I have reached the end of my patience with Mr. Gonçalves," the image of Schwartz declaimed, slamming his hands on the desk.

"Shall we detain him, sir?" said the commander.

"No. Leave him to me." He gestured the others to leave, then as soon as they had done so he settled into his chair, folded his hands on the desk, and closed his eyes.

Just a moment later, on the other wing, Tiago suddenly shoved Hardbody, and a moment later the murderous forklift charged into the frame, slewing silently to a stop between them.

"Kill that moth!" Schwartz commanded. The real Schwartz, in the antechamber. The Schwartz on the screen remained still and silent.

But although the security commander directed one of his guards—one armed with a much bigger gun than his own dart pistol, Tiago noted—to carry out Schwartz's order, the guard merely shook his head and lowered his weapon, his eyes still on the moth's moving images.

On the moth's right wing the battle with the forklift went on as Tiago remembered it, though everything happened much faster than it had seemed at the time. And when the ceiling fell in, obliterating the forklift—along with the security camera that was capturing the scene—on the other wing Schwartz jerked as though from a blow, his eyes snapping open with a gasp. But then he regained his composure, closed his eyes again . . . and on the other wing the view changed to a new camera, where a rubble wagon in an empty tunnel suddenly stirred itself and rushed out of frame.

"If you don't kill that moth I will do it myself!" Schwartz shouted, and reached to grab the gun from the guard next to him.

But the guard did not hand the weapon over, and it was not difficult for him to resist the rotund project manager's attempts to take it by force. Nor did any of the other security personnel move to assist Schwartz . . . not even the commander, who seemed to consider interfering in the situation, but carefully observed his staff and then stood still, watchful but unmoving.

The battle continued on the moth's wings, with Schwartz appearing to feel the destruction of the first rubble wagon as it occurred. And then, after the image of Tiago on the right wing smashed the second wagon—this time the Schwartz on the left wing collapsed to his desk, taking a long moment before bringing himself back to a sitting position with a groan—the moth closed and opened its wings like a book, introducing a new but similar pair of scenes.

This time Schwartz was alone in his office at the beginning, and the view from the tunnel showed a space-suited joker with enormous arms and pillar-like legs—she matched the description of the late Margot that Tiago had received from the other diggers. But the events played out similarly . . . except that Margot did not escape as Tiago and Hardbody had, but was crushed by falling rocks brought down by the forklift.

And then the moth closed and opened its wings again, and another scene played out. And again, and again. It wasn't always forklifts attacking, and it wasn't always diggers dying, but it was always Schwartz, alone and silent at his desk while some machine or device suddenly leapt into murderous action.

The crowd, and even many of the security personnel, grew increasingly outraged as the images piled up.

"You cannot accept these lies!" Schwartz shouted. "This is mere fabrication!"

"I'm sorry, sir," said the brick-faced security commander, nearly gently, "but I'm afraid this is only proof of something I've long suspected." He glanced around at his subordinates. "Something we've long suspected."

On the moth's wing, a spindly joker was being crushed between elevator doors while the image of Schwartz on the other wing smiled serenely, eyes closed. The dead person was apparently well known and liked, because the crowd shrieked and surged forward. The security guards repositioned themselves to protect Schwartz, tacitly leaving Tiago and Hardbody on their own recognizance.

"Hey, hey, people!" the security commander shouted, his voice booming over the crowd. "Let's not have a lynch mob here! Settle down!"

They didn't want to settle. But with the armed guards' encouragement, eventually they did so.

"I don't know what's really going on here," the commander said once the situation had calmed a bit. "But I'm taking you, and you, and you into protective custody"—he pointed to Tiago, Hardbody, and Schwartz—"until we get the whole thing sorted out."

As the guards courteously escorted Tiago away, the moth fluttered along above him. But when they reached the door of the high-ceilinged antechamber and moved into the lower corridor beyond, she faded out, leaving only a sprinkle of moondust where she had been.

Charles Dutton—the man after whom Dutton Ridge was named, and the new project manager—stared hard at Tiago across Schwartz's desk. Dutton's desk, now. "Are you certain this is what you want to do?"

"I am, sir," Tiago replied.

Three weeks had passed since Schwartz had tried to kill Tiago and Hardbody. Three weeks full of questions, investigations, and negotiations.

Schwartz's many murders and other perfidy had been proven without question, and he had been placed on "administrative leave" and unceremoniously shipped back to Earth. Tiago didn't know what Witherspoon would do with him and didn't really care.

The mysterious shape-shifting woman, whose name was Aarti, had left off her attempts at sabotage and begun negotiations with the jokers. Her desire that they leave the Moon was still adamant, but at least they were talking.

And Tiago had decided to return to Earth.

"You have been absolutely invaluable to this project," Dutton said, patting a thick personnel folder. "Mr. Schwartz had the very highest confidence in you, and, paradoxically enough, your role in exposing him only reinforces that. Your mind as well as your particular abilities make you the exact type of person we will need going forward."

"I understand, sir. But there's no place for me here." He gestured around, at the metal and stone and regolene that made up the project manager's office. "In the last few weeks I've realized that none of this stuff really even exists for me, or to the extent that it does it only causes me pain. I've never really been happy here. I belong back in Brazil, where the people need me and everything is made of . . . real stuff. Organic stuff. Where I can be myself and use my abilities for good."

"You'll be missed." Dutton extended his hand. "And if you ever want to return, you'll be welcome."

"Thank you, sir." Tiago took the hand and shook it. "But right now I just want to feel the Earth under my feet."

The Moon Maid

PART VII
November 2017

SHE'D STARTED WITH NARNIA. Fourteen years ago, in a cavern deep beneath the Moon's surface, far from any fear of discovery, Aarti began to paint. It was long, hard work. Painting came so much slower these days. But she had time. First a glowing ball of light, so she could see to work. *Fiat lux. Let there be light!* God's first words to the universe.

Aarti wasn't so arrogant as to consider herself the god or goddess of the Moon . . . but on the other hand, she had been granted the power to create and to destroy. How lonely He must have been those first six days, until the animals arrived. And then humans, at last, someone to talk to. Beautiful and strong, free from sin. *What a sad, misshapen lot we've become.* Twisted in body. Sometimes Aarti still woke from the Moon and turned her head in bed, startled by how large it was again. She'd reach a hand up, trace its bulbous, bald shape.

Then Aarti sighed, and let it go. The outsides mattered very little, after all. Her soul had gone black for a time, and now was, perhaps, lightening again? That was the question—could a person truly come back from what she had done? All her regrets were stones in her throat. Aarti had learned the names of the dead Russian cosmonauts. She whispered them to herself every night when she arrived on the Moon, surrounded by its stark beauty. *Never forget.* Her peace, her art, had been paid for in blood.

Deep underground, Aarti painted the lamppost first of all, its long black lines stark. She filled the lantern with light, which spilled out through the immense cavern, first of a chain of them, far beneath the surface and even farther from the joker encampment. There was no trace of her left on the surface. After the lamppost, the trees. Tall, clothed in dark green, but let them be Moon trees, too, not mere copies of Earth's wonders. Lewis had imagined a woodland not so different from the England he loved; Aarti created lunar trees that soared far higher, thinly branched and thinly leaved, providing a canopy of dappled light that filtered down to the dusty floor.

When she finished the last tree, Aarti paused a moment, contemplating her creation. She had painted hard, concentrating fiercely, going over the strokes over and over again. It had taken her months to build her forest, but she thought, perhaps, it would last. The light of the lamppost shone steadily, and in a wild spattering of whimsy, Aarti painted a host of snowflakes swirling around her. No wind, no cold that she could feel. But snow fell in the woods, and Aarti tipped back her head and stuck out her tongue, to catch a melting snowflake. She was a girl in Oxford again, seeing snow for the first time, when everything was fresh and new and possible.

The first signs of the stroke were almost imperceptible. Ten years ago, Aarti had gotten up to urinate, which her body compelled her to do at least six times a day now, often jerking her away from the Moon. They'd modernized the house decades ago, electricity and indoor plumbing, so it was only a few steps to the new bathroom adjoining her room. She might not even have noticed, but she decided to go down to the kitchen, help herself to a little mango ice cream. Saila's niece— what was her name? Yes, Niru, that's right—Niru was a dear girl, and always made sure to keep the freezer stocked with it. Aarti liked to open a cold bottle of fizzy Passiona and pour it over the top; she loved the tang.

Aarti was listing as she walked down the hall. That was what she noticed first. Her left arm kept reaching out to balance against the wall. Without it, she might have fallen over. Light-headed, and Aarti might have written it off to some aftereffect of being dragged from her beloved Moon, the sudden shift in perceived gravity. But it persisted, and when she tried to spoon the mango-passionfruit slurry up to her mouth, her hand trembled. Aarti spilled all down the front of her blouse, and the humiliation of that—*Like a child!*—sent quick tears pricking to her eyes.

Aarti made it back to bed, back to the Moon, but she was shaken. The next morning, Niru called the doctor, and they made the arduous trek to the hospital. Aarti's money was sufficient to ensure her a private room and a doctor who was studiously neutral, if clearly fascinated by her virus-shaped body. *It's definitely a stroke; that much is clear. If there are physical or cognitive impairments, they'll probably smooth out in a few weeks. We'll get you a physical therapist, if you like, to help with recovery. There's not much else to do for it but rest. You're seventy-nine, after all. At your age . . .*

The rest was implied. Aarti would probably be dead soon anyway. He'd clearly written her off, and was probably coveting her body, hoping she'd donate it to science and he'd get to do the autopsy. Hah! She *would* donate it to science; Aarti was still, after all these years, enough of a scientist for that. But *he* wouldn't get his grubby paws on it.

It took her a few days to return to painting after the diagnosis. Aarti watched the jokers instead. That had become one of her favorite activities. She still ghosted to them, sabotaged an item here or there, but honestly, it was more to keep them on their toes at this point than anything else. Their small challenges, failures, and triumphs were endlessly fascinating to her now, a better soap opera than any she might watch on television or the internet. In truth, Aarti was fighting a rearguard action now, against the onslaught, when she bothered to fight at all. The joker spaceplanes kept landing, with their quantities of supplies, heavy equipment, mining machinery. More jokers arrived afoot, through portals opened by the ace called Tesseract. Aarti played with the notion of killing her, to close off at least one way to her Moon, but the spaceships would still come, and she could not face the thought of more blood. A city was forming, in glorious diversity of color, form, and ability. She wanted to see what it would become.

The joker Tiago had gone back to Earth after she'd exposed Schwartz. His friend Hardbody had stayed. The jokers didn't seem to be going anywhere, and now that they knew who she was, Aarti couldn't hope to just scare them off with a little sabotage. It would take a catastrophic event to drive them away now.

In America, those affected by the wild card had become commonplace enough to be seen as entertainment. Aarti began watching reruns of the old show *American Hero*, grew addicted to it—a show where jokers and aces battled in simulated combat for the amusement of the world. It was fascinating—only in America! But elsewhere, the television told a darker tale.

In the Mideast, the Caliph ordered the Living Gods of Old Egypt and their joker followers to be exterminated. The gory bloodshed of that genocide, televised for all to see, was enough to terrify any joker. They called it "the Cleansing of the Nile."

How safe would Aarti be on the Moon, if such a thing came to India? If government goons broke into her home and killed her aging body? She had no Yajnadar to leap to her defense now—the servants would surely simply flee. How safe would little Anjali be against the mob? The child was nineteen now— how quickly the years flew by! Studying entomology in the States at Cornell; perhaps America would protect her, if a similar rabid fury came to India. Perhaps not.

So powerful on the Moon, so helpless on Earth. Aarti could do nothing to assist the poor Egyptian jokers; she simply watched, bore witness, tears streaming unheeded down her face. When it was finally over, Aarti turned off the news, had the TV and computer on her desk moved to a guest room. Was the world turning against jokers for good? Would more slaughter follow? Did they not understand, these humans, what the murder of innocents did to your soul?

Aarti was too old to endure such misery again.

And she had grown fond of these jokers who had trespassed on her Moon over the years. Anya Chakraborty had turned out to be a small slip of a girl—beautiful as any Bollywood star, if you saw her from the right side, but the skin on the left side of her body looked like melted wax. It ran and runnelled from forehead to shoulder to hand, and presumably under her clothes as well. She had looked so sad when she arrived. When Aarti ghosted close enough, she heard the girl talking to her friends, in a mix of Hindi and English.

"The boy wanted nothing more to do with me, of course. My professors started giving me worse grades, even though my work was just as good! And my father took back all my gold bangles; he said my sisters would get more use out of them, that no one would ever marry someone as ugly as me!" And then Anya was crying again, and the other young women patted her on the back helplessly.

Anya's family had cast her out, just like Aarti's had, so many decades before. The similarities couldn't be ignored, though their situations were very different— Anya's family had been much less wealthy, and Anya had been left with few options. She could've stayed in school, finished her engineering degree, but this Moon had seemed like salvation to her.

Aarti would have been tempted to play matchmaker, but that would have required her to leave her self-imposed isolation; after so many years, Aarti wasn't sure she could break her habit of silence even if she wanted to. She just watched. Eventually Anya caught the eye of one of the new engineers. Sunil was tall, dark, and handsome—if by tall, you meant close to ten feet! He and Anya were soon engaged, and within a few years, they married and Anya gave birth to a little boy who bore no mark of the wild card . . . though of course the virus was there in his genes. He might look like a nat, but sooner or later his card would turn. What would it be like for Sanjeevan to grow up surrounded by jokers? To him, they would be completely normal. Might he be the vanguard of a new society, one built on peace and understanding? Aarti could only hope.

Her painting continued. Narnia had grown beneath the Moon's surface and merged with Middle-earth. Cair Paravel stood atop its cliff face, with waves crashing beneath and Reepicheep's ship sailing away, in search of something he could not name. Aarti quite identified with the little mouse; in another universe, she thought they might have been friends. Not far away, a round green door sat in a hill—behind it a cozy home awaited, one full of cream teas and neatly pulled pints and the sautéed mushrooms rich with butter that she had loved as a student in England. Sometimes, all Aarti wanted was a little comfort.

One world flowed into the other, and if Rivendell's bridges were thinner and more fantastical than Tolkien had ever dreamed, Aarti had the Moon's gravity to thank for it. Here, you might jump high and hard enough to reach the top of—well, not the Misty Mountains themselves, but perhaps the Iron Hills? If you had strong joker thighs, and long joker legs, anything might be possible.

Her own creations joined the other worlds—palaces of crystal, silvered beaches where tropical sun lit palm tree huts, open to the breezes she conjured. No animals or creatures—Aarti couldn't bear the thought that after she passed, they might fade and die, too. The beauty of the buildings, the fantastical world, would have to be enough, lifeless though it was. Was this art? It was very far from anything she'd studied on Earth, but it might, she thought, have some true merit.

Aarti was building a fairyland beneath the surface of the Moon, and no one had any idea.

Hundreds more jokers arrived, set to work. They were building another vast underground complex, where they might live undisturbed. They hadn't discovered her wonderland yet, but now it was only a matter of time.

If Aarti acted very quickly, she could still, perhaps, kill them all, and thereby deter more from coming. But would the nations of Earth even allow such a threat to remain on the Moon? How many would she have to murder to protect herself?

An academic question at best. If there was ever a time when Aarti might have made the attempt, that time had long passed. Would refraining from killing be enough to win her a better fate in her next life, or would the murders that stained her soul condemn her to return as some wretched creature? She'd soon find out.

The doctors were a monthly necessity now. A second stroke, a small heart attack. No signs of cancer yet—Aarti might have been spared that, at least. That first smug doctor had been succeeded by a better one, a young joker woman with four serious eyes on eyestalks that extended when she was deep in concentration. *The better to take in every detail,* she liked to say. Aarti enjoyed her sense of humor. Maybe she'd let this one cut her old body open, when the time came.

"Sanjeevan! Sanjeevan, come here this instant!" Anya's sharp voice echoed through the cavern, catching Aarti's attention. She'd come to check on her little family, as she thought of them; she'd grown increasingly worried about them lately. Sunil had developed a strange hunch in the last few years; for a tall man, he seemed surprisingly short as he hurried through the passageways. "Sanjeevan, when I get my hands on you—"

"Don't tell her, please." The little voice piped up from near Aarti's translucent feet. Aarti looked down to see, around the corner of an outcropping of rock, little Sanjeevan. Her attention sharpened; he looked thin, undernourished. His breather—worn for emergencies, if the air failed—dangled from a scrawny neck. There should be enough rations for everyone, including the children. What was going on?

"You can see me?" Aarti whispered.

He shrugged. "You're not invisible. Just—sort of *watery*? I can see you if I'm paying attention. *Please* don't tell her where I'm hiding."

Children were observant, and this one, perhaps, had been forced to be more observant than most. Now that she was paying attention, Aarti could see telltale indicators—the way Sanjeevan flinched away when she moved, the focused alertness of his gaze. If she could smell, she would wager that fear rose off the child in a palpable stink. Why would a mother treat her child so? Was it the resentment of a once-beautiful girl against a child who still bore no visible trace of the virus?

Tempting as it was to assign some joker-specific motive here, there had been parents who abused their children throughout human history.

"Let me help you, little one. We can talk to the commander—" There was a new man in charge now, an elderly joker who looked like Death himself, and went everywhere masked and cloaked. Aarti shivered at the thought of speaking to him—it would be a risk, would likely send the jokers crashing into her beautiful refuge, once they were reminded of her existence. But she had to do *something*.

"No, no! Please," the child hissed in a frantic whisper. "She'll calm down in a few hours, when she's had a chance to sleep it off. Amma always does. I just need a good place to hide."

Aarti made a decision. In the end, it was easier than she would have expected—perhaps she really had been alone too long. And she couldn't deny that the artist in her had spent decades longing for an audience. "Can you be a little brave? It will take some time to walk down there, but I can show you an excellent hiding spot. No one has ever found it." He'd have to wear his breather, so Sanjeevan couldn't stay for long, but for a little while, her fairyland could be a sanctuary for him. Aarti would let him come back, as often as he wanted. After all these years, she could share her Moon, a little.

The child straightened up, meeting her eyes. "I can be *very* brave."

"I'm sure you can." Aarti extended her hand, and after a moment, Sanjeevan reached out and placed his small brown hand in her translucent gray one. "Follow me, little one—I am going to show you something wonderful."

Time passed. Aarti had started reading the news again, wondering what future would be offered to Sanjeevan and others like him. There were more riots in India, one after another, more dead. *Yajnadar, I remember you.* Horrific slaughter at one joker ashram, but elsewhere, things were even worse.

Maybe these jokers had been right, to come to the Moon. Maybe they needed Her refuge as much as Aarti ever had.

Thanks to the ace who could open portals in space—the universe was full of more wonders than Aarti had dreamt of, back in her student days at Oxford—tons of supplies, construction equipment, and workers passed through, and the jokers established another lunar colony. This one included an experimental agricultural station. They could grow food on the Moon, if all went well, make it truly self-sufficient. If Earth went up in flames, there would be a place where humanity—joker or otherwise—might survive.

Aarti learned about the ice asteroids in her home in Bombay, when astronomers started talking on private message boards and then, abruptly, stopped talking. She looked for herself—thirty-one giant ice asteroids headed their way from deep space. Headed to her Moon.

"I want to make a deal." Aarti stood in the commander's office in her natural form. A very old Indian woman, gray-skinned and moon-headed, in a re-creation of a silver sari that Yaj had picked out for her when they were both so much younger than she was now.

"I am eager to hear it, fair maiden." The new commander's name was Dutton, and he had risen when she materialized in a flurry of dust.

She snorted. "Fair maiden? Sorry, neither."

"I apologize," he said, looking faintly embarrassed. "A bad habit, I'm afraid—the records refer to you as the Moon Maid, and Michael Sampson's private journal waxed quite rhapsodic about your visit to him. For years, I've been thinking of you in my head as he did, wondering if we would see you again. It's Aarti, correct? I read the older records, too."

His eyes were wary—yes, if he'd read the cosmonauts' reports, so they should be. Dutton continued, "I take it the malfunctions we've been seeing in the agricultural station are your doing?"

"What?" Aarti said, genuinely startled. "No, no. I haven't interfered with your operations in years." She couldn't help chuckling, imagining how for the last years, every broken machine on the Moon had probably been attributed to her tampering. "I'm afraid that's just machines being their typical obstinate selves, breaking down when you least expect it."

"You have some experience with them, I see. Not just a ghost creature of the Moon?" Dutton's eyes were alive with curiosity.

"I used to be a scientist," Aarti said wistfully. "And I'm still an artist. That's what I came to talk to you about."

"We have no time for art right now, I'm afraid." Dutton frowned. "I suppose we could hang some pieces on the walls . . . if we do that, would you pledge to continue to keep from interfering?"

Aarti shook her head impatiently. "No, no. Look—you are bursting at the seams here, with far more people than you can reasonably accommodate, yes?"

"God, yes," Dutton said. His forehead was pinched, as if a headache had suddenly bloomed.

Aarti continued, "You're building as fast as you can. But what if you had a fourth settlement area, one that could easily hold hundreds of jokers, maybe thousands? It will need a little work, sealing it off and filling it with breathable air, but once that's done . . ."

Dutton was leaning forward now, eager. "What are you saying?"

"I want a promise that the Moon is a refuge for all." That was the nightmare that had started keeping her up at night. If things went dark on Earth—people could go dark so easily, their worst natures rising up to overwhelm them—what would happen to boys like Sanjeevan, who bore no visible mark of the virus? What if there was a joker girl on Earth, in danger, but in love with a nat? Would her Yaj have been able to join Aarti on the Moon? "I want to be sure that jokers will be welcome here, but humans, too. Anyone who comes in peace."

Dutton frowned. "I have no problem with that. But I won't be here forever. This is not my decision."

Aarti shrugged. She wasn't a goddess of the Moon, after all. There was so little that she could really do in the end. But she had to do as much as she could. "I know you can't do anything about the future, but a promise that at least under your watch—"

"Done." The commander's eyes were bright as stars now.

"Oh, Commander." Aarti smiled. "Let me take you to wonderland."

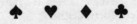

Within That
House Secure

XII

MATHILDE NOTICED A POOL of hydraulic fluid on the tile floor outside the entrance to the library and made a mental note to check the seals on the mechanical system that held the heavy oak door shut. All of the systems in this part of the house were mechanical, and she tended to them herself.

"Are you ready?" asked Theodorus, looming behind her. His voice, as it always did when they made these visits, sounded oddly timid.

"For this?" she replied. "Never." Then she inserted the appropriate key into the locking mechanism, turned it, and threw the lever that let the door swing open.

The morning light streaming through the windows showed motes of dust floating in the stale air of the library. Mathilde remembered how Alice Witherspoon had insisted that this room be kept spotless, though it had been her husband's domain. The thousands of books lining the walls had seemed mysterious, fantastical to her when she was a little girl. Now they just seemed . . . pointless.

The books were too outdated to be consulted for anything of importance to the project. And nobody at the House Secure had time to read for pleasure anymore.

Nobody but Malachi.

He sat on a low chaise longue, a leather-bound volume held open on what passed for his lap.

He looked up and said, "Ah. The Truth and Reconciliation Commission. I've just been preparing my latest defense. Listen to this . . .

> 'Earth rais'd up her head,
> From the darkness dread and drear.
> Her light fled:
> Stony dread!
> And her locks cover'd with grey despair.'"

Theodorus took his usual place beside his father's old desk. Mathilde went over to the fireplace, which hadn't been lit in decades.

"That's William Blake," said Malachi, "and what I mean—"

"We know the poet," Mathilde interrupted. "And we know what you mean to say. You mean to say nothing. You mean to *prevaricate*. As usual."

Malachi sighed. He placed a bit of black ribbon in the book, closed it, and set it to one side. "Ask your questions," he said. "The answers will remain the same."

"We know you killed at least fourteen people on the Moon," Theodorus said. It had taken weeks to convince Theodorus of the truth of Malachi's actions, more weeks to convince him to confront his old mentor and guardian. "We suspect you may have caused other deaths here on Earth, going back years. Including even your own secretary. You've done nothing to deny this, and you've done nothing to clarify why you did these . . . these monstrous things."

"And you've done nothing to show why we shouldn't do what Clifford Bell and Troll and the others want us to do, which is to turn you over to the authorities," said Mathilde. But she was looking at Theodorus. She was, again, laying her real accusation against him.

"I have done nothing, *nothing*," said Malachi, "for over thirty years, but work for the success of Joker Moon. I have done nothing that was not *necessary*."

It was what he always said. It was *all* he always said, as was shown now as he crossed his arms and stared off in the middle distance. Mathilde noticed that one side of Malachi's collar was bent out and up away from his tie. Nobody was pressing his shirts.

"And you would have gone on doing 'necessary' things for how long if that Indian woman hadn't exposed you?" asked Theodorus.

Mathilde raised her eyebrows. This was new. Usually, once Malachi shut up, Theodorus gave up.

Malachi surprised her as well, rising to the bait. "She is a menace, and you need to have someone eliminate the threat she poses. She's been responsible for acts of sabotage on our bases for years. She's been wreaking havoc up there for even longer than that. The Russian base—"

Mathilde interrupted him again. "She's expanded our living space by almost forty percent through her deal with Charles Dutton. And she's agreed to not interfere with our operations any longer."

"We don't know anything about her!" said Malachi.

"We know she's the Moon Maid," said Theodorus, somewhat wistfully. "She must be an ace of extraordinary powers to have made it to the Moon and lived there so long. Do you think she's responsible for the appearance of that structure on the lunar surface in 1958?"

They'd come in to talk about murders and now they were talking about flights of fancy from more than half a century before. Mathilde . . . she couldn't stand it. "The asteroids will be landing soon," she said, stalking over to the door. "We still don't know if Towers is going to try something, and we're spending our time talking to . . . spending our time *harboring* a mass murderer." A mass murderer who was her father. Mathilde left both men behind her. Neither of them tried to stop her from leaving.

♠

They were a long time coming. But in the end, they came.

That last morning, the Duesenberg dropped Mathilde off at the main gates. There was too much traffic on the grounds of the House Secure now—too much activity, *too many people*—for the ridiculous old car to wind its way all the way to the house.

After she checked in and the gate cranked open, she signed out one of the bicycles kept at the guard station to finish the trip. Mathilde had a great appreciation for bicycles. They were an example of a fundamentally brilliant engineering application that had, really, been only marginally improved upon in the many years since the initial design and development. Not that she wouldn't have appreciated a motorized ride through the busy grounds. *Even in a sidecar,* she thought.

There were, according to Clifford Bell's scrupulously kept logs, more than seven hundred people living on the former indigo plantation now, most of them jokers awaiting processing and transit to one of the lunar bases. She didn't know whose department it was to keep track of how many new buildings had been put up for their housing, feeding, and training. Hell, it was probably hers.

Come to think of it, she *had* been named in the suit brought by the county's development board regarding unpermitted construction on the "historically significant" property. One of the many tactics their many opponents had adopted—legal challenges to activities ancillary to the main project. These had proven just about as effective as all the other tactics—regulation, bribery, threats, violence originating from everyplace from local police forces to terrorist groups to supposed "lone wolves." Which was to say they had proven *somewhat* effective.

Measuring those kinds of metrics, tracking the extent of whether and how much their opponents were hindering them via such methods, well, that wasn't an engineering problem.

It was the kind of problem Malachi handled. It was the kind of problem he didn't talk about.

She stepped through the bike's down-swept frame, hitched herself up on the saddle, and pedaled away through the crowd.

Mathilde came out every day now, unless it was a weekend that Oliver happened to be in town. Today was a Saturday, but he was in South America chasing down a problem in a refueling system. She wasn't terribly worried about him. The launch facility down there was incredibly isolated and, after the last few years, very well defended. She doubted the local governments knew that the installation was guarded by mercenaries armed with equipment more sophisticated than anything their militaries carried. They probably didn't care, either.

"Isolation," Theodorus had said, "is the key."

And so they isolated themselves. The overseas facilities were already far removed from any population centers, but Theodorus had meant more than that. Witherspoon Aerospace had cancelled all contracts with other entities—corporate or governmental—over two years before, and it was far from the only one of Theodorus's holdings to turn inward. They only sold pharmaceuticals to themselves now. They only built things, made things, for themselves. They issued no press releases. The intent was to be forgotten about. "The Moon will grow green and blue," said Theodorus. "But it will do so slowly. They'll get used to it."

Mathilde doubted that. She didn't think anyone had forgotten and she didn't think anyone would ever get used to the idea of a joker-held moon.

Anyway, forgetting seemed to her to be antithetical to the whole project. Why else would Theodorus have hung all those newspapers in the old game room, if not to remember?

Mathilde ducked in there now. It was one of the few rooms in the main house that hadn't been given over to executive offices and conference rooms. The large, wood-paneled chamber was empty of any furnishings besides a few benches and the incongruous-seeming billiards table at the center. Framed, track-lit newspapers completely covered the walls.

The oldest one was a *New York Mirror* dated September 16th, 1946. The headline read, GAS ATTACK ON MANHATTAN.

She walked around the room, as she had so often, pausing every couple of steps. *The Los Angeles Clipper.* May 9th, 1953. NYC'S JOKER PLAGUE SPREADS WEST.

The International Herald. December 11th, 1967. JOKER ATROCITIES REPORTED IN LAOS.

Headlines in French and German and Spanish. Cyrillic letters, Arabic letters, writing she wouldn't even have recognized without the translating plaques in brass affixed below.

24 JOKERS KILLED IN SYRIAN CAPITAL. ANGRY MOB ATTACKS JOKER SLUM IN CALCUTTA. LATEST VICTIM IS 7TH JOKER CALL GIRL MURDERED, SAY POLICE.

Every part of the world was represented. Every year since 1946.

Seventy-four newspapers. Seventy-four years.

The last frame was different. It was a simple, open-topped plastic display and its contents were rotated every few days.

The Washington Gazette. July 6th, 2020. NO 'JOKER MOON' PRESIDENT PROMISES.

"Is that today's paper?" a woman's voice asked.

Mathilde started. She would have sworn she was alone.

Ah, she thought. It was Mollie Steunenberg, the fragile, powerful, *dangerous* woman who so much depended on now. The woman who could be wherever she wanted.

"Hot off the laser printer," Mathilde answered her.

Mollie walked over, reached into the frame, and pulled out the paper. She took a seat on one of the benches and began leafing through it.

"A lot on the schedule tonight," said Mathilde. "I'm surprised to see you up and about."

"Theodorus told me I'd probably have most of the night off," Mollie said. "Something about delays. Up there." She nodded upward, not taking her eyes from the newspaper.

Mathilde reflexively looked to the left and down just a bit, in the direction she knew the Moon to actually be at that moment. She saw that it had been a while since anyone had polished the tile floor. *Things are slipping,* she thought to herself.

"I've never understood how Dennis gets away with what he does," Mollie said. She was reading the comic strips. "My dad would have yanked a knot in that kid."

Mathilde never read the comics. She just shrugged.

"It says here the government wants to shut us down again," Mollie went on, even though the paper was still opened to the last pages.

Mathilde said, "Theodorus thinks the president is just saber-rattling. Trying to distract people from his problems with the Satterly Commission."

Mollie looked up, a confused expression on her face. "What?"

A loud trill sounded, emanating from both Mathilde's and Mollie's wrist phones. Theodorus's voice sounded, eerily doubled. "Please come to the control center immediately," he said.

Then a portal opened right beside Mathilde, and Mollie was grabbing her and pulling her along. Then they were elsewhere.

Clifford Bell and Troll must have been with Theodorus when he made the call, because there was no way anyone could have beaten them to the control center, even if they'd been right next door. The portal Mathilde and Mollie stepped through winked into nonexistence behind them, and Mathilde immediately went and took her place at a station flanking Theodorus's.

The room was located in a round bunker that, in turn, was dug into the floor of the largest greenhouse attached to the main house. Full of monitors, computer banks, and communications equipment, it was where Theodorus spent most of his time these days, only venturing out to tend his beloved plants.

Right now he was watching the main screen, which showed what appeared to be the side of someone's leg, decked out in fatigues of some kind. The knee was bent, so the person on-screen was seated, but the occasional jostling told Mathilde that whoever it was, they were riding in some kind of conveyance that was in motion.

The hatchway to the greenhouse opened and more people came in. Malachi and the joker snake man, Marcus Morgan. *IBT.* Theodorus had, over everyone else's objections, loosened Malachi's leash somewhat. The two people following them were a pair of Clifford Bell's guards. They wore the body armor and running shoes of his elite, having been trained to fight at the incredible speeds his power could grant them.

Theodorus had his hand held up, indicating that everyone should remain silent. There was sound accompanying the image on the screen, coming from speakers built into the walls. *Sounds like a diesel engine,* thought Mathilde. Then, over the engine noise, came a woman's voice.

"We're ten minutes out. Everyone knows what we're doing, right? Objectives clear? Mission parameters in mind?"

"Arrest the snail," said a man's voice. Mathilde wasn't sure whether it was just an illusion created by placement of the speakers, but it seemed to her that the speaker was the owner of the leg up on the screen. "Oh, and don't kill anybody if we can help it. We know the drill, lady."

The woman's voice replied, "Mr. Spencer, you are a civilian employee of the Department of Justice. Don't let your *nom de guerre* go to your head."

The sound cut out.

"Clifford?" Theodorus asked.

"I've got drones launched, but I haven't spotted them yet." He was typing rapidly. "Spencer is probably Alan Spencer, the ace Colonel Centigrade. He works for SCARE."

"I was on TV with him," Mollie said, her tone of voice making it sound like she was having a completely different conversation. "He's an asshole."

"What is all this?" asked Marcus Morgan.

"The transmission is from a body cam being worn by an ace who works for SCARE but who is sympathetic to us," said Theodorus.

A spy, thought Mathilde.

"Okay," Cliff barked, "I spot two, make that three armored personnel carriers heading down the state highway toward the main gate. There are two more on the county road that parallels the rear property line beyond the creek, and there's a fifth parked outside the Kincaid place already."

The Kincaids had owned the property next to the House Secure for as long as Theodorus's maternal ancestors had lived in the area. The two families had cordially loathed each other for nearly four hundred years.

"SCARE means aces," rumbled Troll. "But there are hundreds of people here, dozens of guards. What do they think they're going to accomplish with all this military-style bullshit if they're just here to arrest you?"

"My guess is that the woman we heard giving orders was Joann Jefferson, the current director of SCARE," said Theodorus.

"Lady Black," said Troll. "She was on the world tour with me. That was . . . shit, was it really thirty-five years ago?" He blinked. "She's all right."

"And is resisting retirement until the next administration is sworn in, according to my sources," said Theodorus. "She won't have signed off on this unless it's a by-the-book operation. But I wonder . . ."

Mathilde said, "This is it."

They all turned to look at her.

"They're taking their shot. I don't know what this Jefferson woman thinks is happening, but I'm willing to bet anything that at least one of the people with her has orders to take out Theodorus. And Mollie, too, if they've finally figured out she's here."

Theodorus looked at Mollie sharply, but the woman's scarred face was neutral.

"Mollie," he said. "You have to clear the House Secure."

Mollie shrugged, and a gateway shimmered into existence next to her. "I'll try. I'll send as many of the people on the grounds away as I can. Hopefully to the Moon." Then she was gone.

"Clifford, Howard, Marcus," Theodorus said, and the three men nodded in turn. "They're coming at us from three directions."

"And there's three of us, I get it," said Troll. He looked at the screens, one of which showed a schematic of the grounds. "I'll go see what's going on with your neighbors." He lumbered out.

On another screen, Mollie had appeared in a hall where a couple of dozen jokers were watching a lecture delivered remotely from one of the lunar bases.

There was no sound, but that hardly mattered as Mollie clearly wasn't explaining herself. She opened portals and shoved the surprised people through them.

"So now we're fighting federal agents again," said Marcus. "Olena is back in our rooms."

"I'll send someone to watch out for her," said Clifford. He nodded at one of his guards and the woman zoomed out.

"Can you make me go that fast?" asked Marcus.

Bell said, "Yes. You don't have a heart condition or anything, do you?"

"Just a need to get this over with," the snake man replied.

"Head for the rear of the property," said Theodorus. "Keep a channel open on the watch I gave you."

Then the Infamous Black Tongue was gone and Cliff said, "That leaves me and my folks for the main gates. Sir, you should bring Tesseract back here. You should go ahead and leave."

"Not yet," said Theodorus. He was punching buttons on his console. Screens showed greenhouse wall panels retracting into the ground all over the estate. They showed large shapes moving in the foliage. "I have to coordinate the defense."

Cliff seemed to be about to say something more, but then just turned and left with his last guard. "What do you want me to do?" Mathilde asked.

"For now," said Theodorus, "watch. Wait. Get ready."

Mathilde suddenly realized that Malachi hadn't said a word during the tense meeting. She looked over to where he'd taken a seat at another keyboard, and saw that he'd fished out a pair of earphones from somewhere. She'd never seen him wearing such before. And she never would have guessed he would be so deft in attaching them to a port in one of the computers arrayed before him.

"What are you doing?" she asked him.

He tapped a few keys on his terminal. He didn't look up from the screens, but he did answer her. "Everything I can," he said.

Mathilde had never particularly enjoyed watching television, and now she was trying to pay attention to what was being shown on at least a dozen monitors. It didn't help that Theodorus kept changing the feed on the big main screen, jumping views from spot to spot on the grounds, at the gates, even drawing on the cameras in Clifford Bell's high-flying security drones.

The feed from one of those was up on the big screen now. She watched as Troll reached the wall that separated the Witherspoon and Kincaid estates and easily clambered over it. An eight-foot wall wasn't much of a barrier for a nine-foot joker.

Suddenly, the screen went dazzling white, then faded to black. A message reading "No Signal" flashed up.

"Something took out the drone," said Theodorus. "They may have a flier."

Mathilde made a quick check of the other screens slaved to drones. "Maybe. Or it might have just been a coincidence. Look, there's a storm blowing in."

"It was an attack," said Malachi. His voice sounded strained. He was hunched over in his chair even more than usual.

All of the screens showing exterior views were darkening. Those that showed glimpses of the sky revealed roiling clouds, punctuated with lightning flashes.

"Forecast!" Theodorus said. One screen switched to weather data. Sunny and hot, it read, just as it had for weeks, now that Mathilde thought of it. The satellite photo of the area—time-stamped three minutes earlier—was clear of any cloud cover.

Theodorus keyed his microphone. "Friends, be advised that one of the government aces has some sort of weather control power."

One of the side screens showing a perimeter camera feed flashed white, then showed Troll climbing to his feet. He edged away from a smoking, scorched spot on the groomed lawn he was crossing. His voice came over the speakers. "No shit. I almost just got fried by lightning."

A computer at the station where Mathilde sat flashed urgently—a priority message from the larger lunar station. She read it and almost laughed aloud, forced that down, wondered if it meant she was panicked. She picked up a headset and spoke into it. "Mollie, can you hear me?"

There was a whistling noise Mathilde couldn't identify, then Mollie said, "Busy."

"You're porting people into the cisterns, Mollie. Some of them can't swim."

A crash, a shout, a scream. "Biggest place I can think of up there that has atmo. You have a better idea?"

Mathilde sighed. But then she said, "The Moon Maid's caverns. They'll hold a few hundred people at least."

"Then I'll send the next few hundred there. Hey! *Toward* the portal, moron! Go out that way and you'll get shot!"

And then Mathilde recognized that she *was* hearing gunshots. Cliff's people didn't carry sidearms—Theodorus despised them—so it had to be the SCARE team. But who were they shooting at?

Theodorus was muttering softly into a microphone, and she saw at least one source of the gunfire. Black-clad agents with submachine guns were walking in formation through the western gardens—the side they hadn't covered, the side where they hadn't identified a threat. They were laying down fire as they went, but what they shot at wasn't slowing down.

A trio of Theodorus's enormous war snails advanced toward the invading team, ripples showing in their flesh where they were taking fire. As Mathilde watched, one made contact with the SCARE point man and . . . engulfed him. It slowed, slightly, then moved its great head back and forth, seeking and finding another target.

"They're going to crash the gate." That was Cliff Bell, speaking to his security guards out front. "Let them through, then close on all three vehicles simultaneously. They'll try to disembark when they see us. Hit them hard as the hatches open."

"Are those tanks?" Mathilde asked as the lead vehicle smashed through, mangling wrought iron.

"Up-armored APCs," replied Theodorus, though he was paying scant attention to that part of the fight. "Military-grade hardware. You were right. They're not here to subpoena me."

Cliff's plan played out more or less as he'd directed for the first two vehicles. Ultrafast security guards swarmed the sides and rear as hatches opened, fists and feet flying. The people attempting to leap from the vehicles were as heavily armored as Cliff's guards, but didn't stand a chance against opponents moving five or six times faster than them.

The third APC was a different story. It skidded to a halt behind its two companions, but its hatches didn't open. The half-dozen Witherspoon Security officers buzzing around it slowed, then retreated. One of them slipped and fell on the driveway, and didn't rise.

A circle of ice was expanding from the third vehicle, whitening the asphalt, then actually *cracking* it.

"That must be Spencer, Centigrade," said Theodorus. "He's using his cold powers to keep Cliff's people away." As they watched, the APC maneuvered off the road and around the scrum going on at the first two vehicles.

"I still haven't spotted anything at the back," radioed Marcus Morgan. "Do the drones still show vehicles beyond the creek?"

"Check for him," Theodorus said. "I'm rousing more war snails from the pits."

Mathilde didn't even know what "pits" he was talking about, but rapidly brought the various camera feeds into active windows at her station. Only one drone was still in the air, and it wasn't covering the area near Morgan. She tasked it his direction and keyed her mike. "I don't have eyes beyond the back wall right now. I'll let you know when I do."

"These bastards are *shooting* at me!" shouted Troll. He sounded like his mouth was full of dirt, which was probably not far from the truth. The window showing the Kincaid grounds was confusing to look at, partially obscured, and Mathilde realized that a branch had fallen in front of the camera pointed that direction. The torrential rain falling in that area didn't help.

"That's all the big groups I can find," said Mollie. "Do you want me to go fuck up some government aces now?"

"Shit!" said Marcus Morgan. "Here they come! One of them just walked right through the fence. And I don't mean she ghosted through it, I mean she *busted* through it!"

"Theodorus!" said Mathilde. "What do we do?"

"The assault on the western gardens is contained," he replied calmly. "Who needs help?"

"They all do!"

Theodorus caused the main screen to flip through shots from a dozen cameras in rapid succession. Mathilde saw Marcus Morgan wrapping his coils around a helmeted woman while a half-dozen other agents clubbed him with rifle stocks. Troll was barely visible through the rain, but he was clearly wreaking havoc at the Kincaid house, bodies flying in every direction. Cliff Bell was surveying the scene at the front gates, pointing up the driveway at something she couldn't see.

The rest of the screens showed empty meeting rooms and abandoned dormitories. A few stray jokers were running in random directions, but in the main, the estate seemed like a ghost town compared to the crowded conditions she'd noted just a couple of hours before. Tesseract was nowhere to be seen.

"Did you hear me?" asked Mollie Steunenberg. "I asked if you want me to go fuck somebody up." She was standing right behind Mathilde.

"Jesus!" said Mathilde. "Don't do that!"

Mollie shrugged. "Okay. What *do* you want me to do then?"

When she said it, Mollie's breath steamed in the cold.

The cold? "Get Theodorus and Malachi out of here!" Mathilde shouted, shoving Mollie toward the center of the bunker.

"Got it," said Mollie.

Theodorus and Malachi suddenly dropped out of sight, furniture and all, as if trapdoors had opened beneath them and they'd fallen through. Which was probably pretty much exactly what had happened. Mathilde heard Malachi's startled, complaining shout, but it cut off almost instantly.

The closed and sealed doorway to the command center was rimed with ice, and the temperature was dropping fast.

"Where did you send them?" Mathilde asked, standing and turning to face the door.

"Front gate," said Mollie, arms crossed, briskly rubbing her upper arms. "I figure Cliff can watch them for a few minutes while we deal with the Colonel."

Mathilde reached over and brushed a finger against the back of Mollie's hand, raising her internal temperature a degree or two. "Why do they call him that? The Colonel part, not the Centigrade part."

Mollie said, "I'm not sure. I think maybe before his card turned he worked at a fast-food chicken place in Alaska."

The door shattered. The temperature dropped even further, and most of the view screens went dark. A man with terrible burn scars covering his face, wearing a white-and-blue parody of a military officer's uniform, was standing in the entryway. His white-gloved hands were held up before him, as if he'd been leaning on the door before it went. "He has an outfit?" asked Mathilde.

"I told you," said Mollie, "he's an asshole."

"Mollie Steunenberg! Mathilde Marechill!" He was obviously straining to speak in a deeper register than his natural voice. "You are under arrest!"

"Behind him," Mathilde said, and a portal opened next to her. She stepped through it, and out of its twin right behind Colonel Centigrade. She put her hand on his face, saw the startled expression there, and said, "Maréchal. Is it really that hard to pronounce?"

And then he reached up and took her by the hand.

Mathilde had never really been cold. And Mathilde had been to the Moon.

Oh, she registered temperature *differences,* of course. She knew, in a distant, intellectual way, that ice cream or a chilled glass of beer did different things to her palate than some sizzling peppers off a fajita platter at one of the goofy sort-of-Mexican restaurants Oliver so loved.

But she had been a joker for forty-two of her fifty-one years alive, and she only had faint memories to go by if she wanted to imagine what it felt like to be cold. December wind off the Atlantic on the waterfront of La Rochelle. Sticking her hand into an Alpine snowbank at a Swiss train station on a trip to Italy. But what she really remembered from those occasions was warmth. The warmth of her mother gathering her in her arms and snuggling her scarf tighter against the wind. The warmth of the steaming cup of tea that her mother pressed on her when she pulled her hands from the snow.

Her ace power made her body a furnace, if one she kept carefully damped and controlled. She could walk through a bonfire—secretly, she *had*—and even if her clothes burned to falling embers she would not be harmed. She could ignore heat, she could control it. She could manifest it and direct it.

But she had never really been cold.

Until now.

"You're an ace!" Centigrade said, his voice higher now. "They didn't say any—" He broke off, beads of sweat popping out on his forehead. He grunted, and Mathilde felt something happening. She looked down, and saw that their joined hands were now coated in at least two inches of ice.

She *pushed,* and the ice began sublimating, hissing straight to steam.

Suddenly, Mollie Steunenberg was there, a dangerous gleam in her eye. But instead of doing something spectacular and bloody, she said, "Cliff's calling. Everything's gone to shit at the gates."

Where Malachi was. Where Theodorus was. "Go! I've got this!" said Mathilde.

Mollie shrugged and disappeared.

The sharp, painful sensation that was engulfing her hand was now in both of her feet as well, but she didn't look down again. She locked her eyes on Centigrade's. He was whispering something, and though he was looking straight at her, he didn't seem to see her, seemed to be, instead, looking *through* her. The sensation crept up to her knees. She tried to step away, but couldn't move. *He's going to kill me,* she thought. *They're supposed to try to not do that.*

She thought of the gunshots and lightning bolts and the terrible blows she'd seen landing on the Infamous Black Tongue. *I wonder where Joann Jefferson is,* she thought. *I wonder if she knows what's really going on.* And then she pushed again, harder this time.

Centigrade opened his mouth, moved his lips like he was trying to speak, but Mathilde knew there was no moisture in his throat now. The painful sensation retreated from her knees. She could feel water streaming down her legs.

The two of them stood, nearly motionless, holding hands, staring at each other.

Then Centigrade held up his other hand. A dagger of ice extended from his fingers. He reached back, preparing to strike.

And Mathilde, terrified and saddened and awfully, awfully *thrilled,* pushed again.

Centigrade's features grayed. For the barest moment, he looked like a perfectly mimetic sculpture of himself done in volcanic rock. Then the pillar of ash that she had made of his body collapsed and the dagger of ice fell to the floor, shattering into a thousand shards.

Mathilde found the bicycle she'd ridden up from the main gate still in a rack next to the front door. Making her way through the greenhouse and the mansion had been a trial because the power was out and the sky was still dark and cloudy.

The storm had mostly passed, but fallen trees and the battered remnants of shrubs and bushes told the tale of how fierce it had been. In the distance, smoke was rising from a burning outbuilding. No one was in sight.

She tried her radio again. "This is Mathilde. Is anyone there? Theodorus? Cliff?"

No answer.

She mounted the bicycle and started coasting through puddles of standing water, steering around debris. It was a long way to the gate. She came upon the two armored personnel carriers Cliff's people had stopped. They were abandoned. There were a few bodies strewn on the ground around them. She was about to check them when she heard a grunting noise from the other side of one of the vehicles.

Malachi was sitting in a widening pool of his own blood, back to a running board. His eyes were glazed, but he clearly saw her, because he made the effort to wave his hand.

Mathilde rushed to his side, simultaneously shouting into her radio, "Mollie! Mollie, come to the front gate right now, we've got to get Malachi to a hospital!"

"No use," said Malachi, coughing. "Some kind of electronics dampening going on. Prevented . . ." He coughed up more blood. "Prevented me from doing much good."

"They *left* you here?" Mathilde demanded, aghast. She unbuttoned his coat jacket, his vest, his shirt, lifted his undershirt. God, why did the man wear so many clothes, where was all the blood coming from, how could she staunch it?

"Sent them away," said Malachi. "Tesseract's allegiance was always . . . to me. She sent the nearest government agents outside the grounds . . . took Theodorus and the others to the final redoubt."

The sounds of gunfire came from the direction of the Kincaid house. Mathilde ignored it.

"What's the final redoubt? The Moon?" Her probing fingers came across something sharp and Malachi gasped. It was, she realized, a jagged, protruding rib.

"Not yet. They're waiting . . . waiting for you." Malachi closed his eyes and took in a shallow, ragged breath.

"Malachi!" Mathilde shouted. Then, because it seemed right after all these years, "*Father!* Hang on! I'm going to find a car!"

"No," he said. "Wouldn't work . . . anyway. Electronics, remember?"

"Can't you do something about that?" she pleaded.

"No . . ." More coughing, more blood. "Whatever or whoever is dampening signals . . . shut me down . . . completely."

"There has to be something I can do."

He took her bloodstained hand in his own. "There is so much you can do," he said. "But not for me."

And then he died.

A portal opened a few minutes later and Troll stepped through. He had a large doglike creature tucked under one arm.

He dropped the dog and fell to his knees, taking in huge gulps of air. Blood trickled from wounds here and there on his torso and arms, and from one on his scalp.

Mathilde didn't say anything. She looked around for Mollie, but the woman was nowhere to be seen. "Mathilde," Troll said eventually. "Where is everyone? I was fighting all these bastards at the Kincaid place and suddenly they doubled in number, started popping in from nowhere." He stopped, saw that she wasn't looking at him. Saw what she was looking at. "Oh, Mathilde, oh, no. I'm so sorry. What happened? What was he doing out here?"

She took in a shuddering breath of her own. "He was trying to save the fucking Moon," she said. Then, standing, "Where's Mollie?"

Troll shook his head. "Haven't seen her."

"Then how?" Mathilde gestured toward where Troll had stepped out from the air a moment before.

"Oh! That was this guy!" He pointed at the not-quite-a-dog. "He's a teleporter, too. He was with the feds, but I think he wants to come with us."

Then Troll's head snapped back, the rear of his skull exploding outward in a cloud of blood and brain. He didn't shout or scream or react in any way, just fell to the ground.

"Right through the eye!" The drawl came from a grizzled man in hunting fatigues holding a smoking rifle, rounding the end of the APC. "That son of a bitch wasn't bulletproof after all!"

Mathilde held the back of her hand to her mouth, fighting the urge to vomit.

"And look here! Another one. Only this one's a lot nicer to look at."

The dog growled.

"Blood! There you are, brother! I was wondering what happened to you. The way you've been acting lately I thought you might have taken a mind to run off on your own. Can't have that, now, can we?"

The man leaned his rifle against the vehicle. He shrugged off his jacket. "Our new buddies in SCARE will be along in a few minutes, I'm guessing. But a few minutes should be enough." He put his hand on the APC, grinned a brown grin.

Mathilde put her hand on the APC, too.

"Ow!" the man said, jerking his hand back. "Why's this thing so fucking hot?" Then he saw that Mathilde was walking toward him and he grinned again. "Well, ain't this something? You ready for old Buck?"

And she said, "Yes," and she burned him to his bones.

The dog—she guessed she should think of him as a man—kept following her as she walked back toward the main house. She didn't know why. But then, she didn't know why she had an impulse to go back to the house, either. Everyone was gone. Or dead.

Then a shimmering gateway the size of a garage door opened, and an orange Duesenberg limousine rolled through. The passenger side door opened and Mollie Steunenberg called to her from the driver's seat. "Get in. We're all going to the Moon."

"I've always wanted to drive this car," said Mollie.

They were speeding along a lane at the rear of the estate. Mollie was a terrifying driver.

"Where did you get it? Wait, never mind. Where are we going?" Mathilde had briefly wondered as well how the Duesey was working before she realized that, of course, it had no electronic parts.

"The pits," said Mollie, amiably answering her question.

Mathilde remembered Theodorus referencing these earlier, during the attack. She wondered if they were the "final redoubt" Malachi had mentioned toward the end.

"You knew about those?"

"Not until a little while ago. I don't think any of the others knew about them, either. Except the boss, of course."

"Of course," said Mathilde. *Just Theodorus. Just him and Malachi.*

Mollie slammed on the brakes. The dog, Blood, slid off one of the rear seats onto the floor.

She turned off the ignition, and they all got out. There was nothing to see but a copse of poplars. Mollie jingled the car keys in her hands, then hurled them into the distance.

"Why did you do that?" Mathilde asked.

"Figure it'll at least cause a mild annoyance to whoever's coming to clean all this up," said Mollie. "Mild annoyance is about all I've got left in me. It's been a tough day."

"You teleported seven hundred people to the Moon," Mathilde said, just now realizing the scope of that. "In what, an hour?"

"Not to mention all the giant snails. I hope those things aren't poisonous. Theodorus made me use the cisterns for them."

"Is he up there now?"

"No, he's, well, he's down there." Mollie pointed. They'd come to a utility shed with its door open. The interior was lit with what must have been a battery-operated fixture mounted just inside. The only feature was a steep ramp descending into the darkness. "Careful here, whatever that stuff coating the ramp is, it's slick."

"Witherslime," said Mathilde. She shook her head, and started down to learn one more of Theodorus's secrets.

As secret underground facilities designed for the breeding and raising of giant snails went, the pits were actually quite nice. *He should call them something different,* thought Mathilde, walking into a well-appointed room decorated in French modern. Not that it would make any difference. They would never be used again.

Nothing at the House Secure would be, probably, at least not by them.

Theodorus was talking on his headset when she and Mollie joined him, Clifford Bell, and Marcus Morgan. The latter two both looked much the worse for wear. "Yes, well, we'll just have to divert water from the other bases for now,"

Theodorus was saying. He saw her then, and added, "Look, I'll be there in a few minutes. We'll discuss this then."

"So this is it?" Mathilde asked.

"My friend among the government aces has some more information for us. This wasn't the attack we've been fearing," said Theodorus.

Mathilde thought of the wreckage of the estate. She thought of a man turning to ash. "What are you talking about?" she asked.

"My source tells me that she's just learned this was a, how did she put it? A 'softening up.' There's an armored column of regular Army on its way here right now. A flight of helicopters. Special operations troops. The SCARE aces were just supposed to take out the more powerful among us."

"And it didn't work," said Marcus.

"It worked perfectly," said Mathilde. "Troll is dead. My father is dead. The House Secure has fallen. All we can do now is flee."

"And leave them . . . well, everything," said Theodorus.

Mathilde laughed without humor. "Did you hear what I just said? Malachi is dead and you're, what, worried about your plants? Besides, Theodorus, for all intents and purposes you own the Moon. They're hardly taking everything from you."

"My home," he insisted, rushing past any mention of Malachi. "And this is more troubling, all of the equipment we're being forced to abandon. All of our computers. All those records."

Mathilde thought about that. She thought of one man turning to ash. She thought of another burning to cinders. *Troubling*, yes.

"Are we sure that the estate is clear? We got everyone out?" Theodorus was asking Mollie, who was paying no attention. Clifford Bell nudged her.

"What? Oh! No, not at all. A bunch of 'em ran." She went back to considering her fingernails.

"We can't leave anyone behind," said Theodorus.

Mathilde remembered something that Malachi had said, back at the very beginning. She repeated him. "You'll never save them all," she said.

Theodorus heard something in her voice. He looked closely at her. He said, "I know what happened. You had to do it. You had to save yourself. And Malachi had to do what he did, too."

Mathilde shook her head. "I had to do it," she said. "I had to save *you*." Then she said, "Okay. Okay. Cliff, Mollie can port you back to Charleston, or to wherever you and your husband are going underground. But first, can you, you know, amp me up a little?"

Cliff said, "You've never asked me that before. Why now?"

"Because I'm in a hurry," she said.

"But we're leaving now," said Theodorus. "We're leaving for the Moon."

She smiled at him, full of sorrow.

He saw her. He knew. He said, "Oh."

All these years, she thought. *All that work. All those lies. And now I don't want to go. I can't go.*

"I'll arrange for Oliver to be safe," said Theodorus. "You'll be safe, too, when you find him."

Cliff nodded at her. Mollie waved impossible portals into existence, and then they were all gone. Mathilde ran through the night, moving from building to building, then from room to room of the main house, through the command centers and the greenhouses; she ran impossibly fast.

Behind her, the fires she left burned impossibly hot.

The Moon Maid

PART VIII

2020

AARTI STOOD ATOP MONS Piton, gazing down. She had reached the amazing age of ninety-two.

She was so tired. Tired of the body that had survived almost a century on the Earth; Aarti had hated that body, tolerated it, and even managed to love it for a little while. Now it was simply wearing out.

Let these jokers have the Moon—with her last breaths, she wanted something more. Her gaze lifted up, to where red Mars hung in the sky above.

What would happen, if Aarti were walking another world when her decrepit, decaying body finally gave up its struggle? Might she dream of continuing there, a ghost of a girl, discovering the secrets of an ancient world? What strange creatures might she paint there, well suited to the red sands of Mars? What fabulous abode might she build, if allowed to remain?

Aarti intended to find out.

Journey's End

by Walton Simons

IT MIGHT NOT HAVE been the first party on the Moon, but it was certainly the best, at least up to that point.

Dutton had designed his own living quarters, making them spacious, perhaps more than was needed. Still, at his age he could be forgiven for being a bit self-indulgent. There were so many people—people, not jokers anymore to his mind—that every room had multiple ongoing conversations. And laughter, more than he could remember hearing for quite some time. He'd made sure the liquor flowed freely, but not too freely. Dutton didn't want anyone passed out when the big moment came.

He wandered into the bedroom, leaning only slightly on his cane. Due to the lower gravity, it was more an affectation than a necessity at this point. He hadn't really finished decorating the place, or getting things put away, but it already felt like home.

IBT, the Infamous Black Tongue, had curled his serpentine body at the foot of the bed. A slim, young blonde woman perched comfortably in his lap. Dutton knew IBT well enough, but had only met Olena a couple of times. She didn't notice him looking about the room at the partyers. The pair were happily focused on each other. Dutton tried to remember when he'd felt about anyone the way they did about each other. If there had been a time, it was before he lost his face. His skull-like visage inspired only fear or revulsion. Up here maybe that could change. Dutton had a box of ornate masks stored away but was determined to keep it unopened.

Beastie Bester was steering his mother around the room, pointing out anything of even moderate interest. In spite of his efforts she seemed more inclined to revisit the bar.

A couple entered the room and seated themselves on the bed opposite Marcus and Olena. They appeared to know each other, but Dutton wasn't sure who the older couple was. That was true of many of the jokers at his party. He'd outlived almost all of his contemporaries.

Dutton let out a soft sigh and entered the game room. It was really more of a poker room. Dutton loved the game. He could even stand losing a bit if the company was good. An accepting attitude toward losing was a new development for him, but ninety-plus years would mellow almost anyone a bit. There was a big-screen TV dominating the wall opposite the poker table and a nearby bar. The TV displayed a view of the lunar surface with a countdown in the lower right corner. It wouldn't be long now.

Dutton had staked all the players to twenty-five grand in U.S. dollars, hoping everyone would come away feeling like a winner. Some more than others, of course. The game itself was a bit more raucous than what Dutton was used to. This was due largely to Drummer Boy, who was seated at the far end of the table. Dutton was surprised he'd decided to make the trip to the Moon, as he'd been quite popular with nats back home. He was undeniably an exuberant presence. He was down in his chips pretty dramatically, possibly because his five arms (the sixth was just a stump) made for more tells, or maybe because he just wasn't a serious poker player. The former SCARE agent Moon, appropriately enough, was seated at the opposite end of the table. Her pile of chips had grown more than a bit since the game began.

After watching a hand, Dutton moved back into the main room and settled into the chair that had been his favorite back in Jokertown. Dutton wasn't sure if it was empty out of deference to him, or if he was just lucky to find it unoccupied. He snagged one of the few remaining salmon hors d'oeuvres on a nearby tray and ate it slowly and with considerable satisfaction. He closed his eyes to savor the last morsel. When he opened them again, Mollie was there.

Mollie's gaze darted about the room. She looked as if this was the last place she wanted to be. In fairness, whenever Dutton had been around her Mollie seemed uncomfortable. A scar on her face was the only outward indication of all the terrible things she'd seen and done. In spite of the scar, Dutton envied the youth of Mollie's skin. "Nobody here really likes me, do they?" she asked quietly.

"I don't know," Dutton replied noncommittally.

She looked down at him. "You don't like me though, do you?"

Dutton sighed. This wasn't exactly party banter. "The short answer is no, I don't, but I hope you'll listen to the rest of what I have to say."

"Like what?"

"We've all done things we regret. Certainly I have. I don't pretend to know everything that's happened to you, but I know enough." He eyed another hors d'oeuvre, but decided this wasn't the moment. "There are more important things in life than being liked. This . . ." He spread his arms wide. ". . . would not exist without what you've done for us."

She shrugged. "There're lots of aces. Somebody probably could have done what I did."

Dutton pointed a bony finger at Mollie. "Perhaps, but they didn't. You did. A hundred years from now, when the young history of our world is written, you'll be remembered for only one thing. Bringing us, and much of the means of our survival, here to the Moon. Not a bad legacy."

Mollie tilted her head slightly. A moment of peace, perhaps even pride, flickered across her face. Then it was gone. "You need to get up to the observatory, Mr. Dutton," she said. She created a portal and he stepped through. Mollie remained behind. Dutton doubted she would linger long at the party.

For now, the observatory was the only colony structure rising above the Moon's surface. The dome was at least fifty yards across, large enough to accommodate a number of visitors. Theodorus towered silently in the dim light near the telescope, flanked by Anubis and his security chief, Throttle.

Sister Helena nodded to Dutton. She was the new spiritual leader of the Church of Jesus Christ, Joker. Helena was over seven feet tall with azure skin. Instead of hair, her head was covered with thick purple cilia. The same substance was on the bottoms of her shoeless feet, allowing her to glide across the floor when she so desired. She smiled at him, but said nothing.

Looking at her reminded Dutton painfully of Father Squid. He reflected on the many friends, acquaintances, and enemies who hadn't lived to see this moment: Gimli, Chrysalis, Troll, the Oddity, Xavier Desmond, Dr. Pretorius, so many others. Dutton had shared a time and place with them, some for decades. Together, they had built a community out of nothing but desperation, shared humiliation, and a desire to survive in something that resembled dignity. Charles Dutton wasn't a religious or spiritual man, but he felt their presence with him at that moment. Perhaps this was why he'd lived so long. To see this for them as much as for himself.

"About three minutes," the technician at the console said without looking up at the visitors.

Dutton moved slowly to the telescope and lowered his face to the eyepiece. The ice comet was plainly visible. It appeared to be suspended in space, rather than moving. The telescope had been programmed to track the comet on its final approach. This was the first of the comets in Theodorus's master plan. More would come soon enough. The first order of business in making the surface habitable. The comets were the first step.

"Are we broadcasting colony-wide?" Theodorus asked the control tech.

"Absolutely." A large-screen TV on the wall displayed a close view of the incoming comet. "We're on the air to everyone."

Dutton found a chair and relaxed into it. He felt something odd, unfamiliar, and realized it was adrenaline. In spite of his age, and his general boredom with existence, he was excited.

"Thirty seconds."

Dutton looked up at Theodorus and realized that everyone else was staring at him, too. This was Theodorus's moment, his triumph. His vision had brought them here.

Theodorus raised his arms and closed his hands into fists. *"Now I am become Life, maker of worlds."* His voice was deep and filled with jubilant conviction.

The view of the impact site filled the screen now. Dutton held his breath. There was a brief glimpse of something flashing into the surface and a massive cloud of dust. Dutton felt, or thought he felt, the slightest tremor.

A sound filtered into the closed room from below, faint but sustained. It was cheering.

Dutton smiled. If he had died at this instant, it would probably be the perfect time for it. He took a deep breath and let it out slowly, content to still be alive. Tears trickled down his misshapen face, but he wasn't ashamed. He would never be ashamed again. A new world was being born, their world. He couldn't wait to see what happened next.

THE BEGINNING